Candy K

Sunday Times bestselling author Freda Lightfoot was born in Lancashire. She always dreamed of becoming a writer but this was considered a rather exotic ambition. She has been a teacher, bookseller in the Lake District, then a smallholder and began her writing career by publishing over forty short stories and articles before finding her vocation as a novelist. She has since written over forty-eight novels, mostly sagas and historical fiction. She now spends warm winters living in Spain, and the rainy summers in Britain.

Also by Freda Lightfoot

Lakeland Sagas

A Champion Street Market Saga

A Salford Saga

The Poor House Lane Sagas

FREDA LIGHTFOOT

Candy Kisses

CANELO

First published in the United Kingdom in 2007 by Hodder & Stoughton

This edition published in the United Kingdom in 2022 by

Canelo
Unit 9, 5th Floor
Cargo Works, 1–2 Hatfields
London, SE1 9PG
United Kingdom

A CIP catalogue record for this book is available from the British Library.

Print ISBN 978 1 80032 804 4
Ebook ISBN 978 1 78863 671 1

Look for more great books at www.canelo.co

Printed and bound in Great Britain by Clays Ltd, Elcograf S.p.A.

1

Chapter One

1958

The rich scent of chocolate was strong in the air as Lizzie Pringle entered the tiny kitchen. She stopped in the doorway, smiling as she took in the sight of all those bright little faces, mouths rimmed with chocolate, small fingers sticky with the delicious velvety substance despite Aunty's strict rules that they must never be licked.

There was Joey, the tallest of them all, his spiky blond hair standing on end as if something had surprised him; eight-year-old Beth bossing her younger brother Alan around, telling him how it should be done as usual; and young Cissie who, at three, had to kneel on a stool to reach.

And there was Aunty Dot herself in her familiar flowered overall, supervising the entire operation: gently pouring the melted chocolate into a mould, tipping it from side to side so that it was evenly coated, and then pouring the excess back into the jug before placing the moulds, hollow-side down, on to waxed paper to set.

Occasionally she would reach across the big scrubbed table and gently guide a small hand struggling with a ribbon, or turn to jiggle the handle of the pram where a baby snoozed, oblivious to all the heat and bustle in the overcrowded kitchen; the happy noisy chatter.

Aunty looked up and smiled at Lizzie. 'We're making chocolate rabbits.'

I

'How exciting!' Lizzie took off her hat and shook out her dark auburn curls. She unbuttoned her coat and hung it behind the door. 'Can I help?'

'Not till you've put your feet up and had a cuppa. Put the kettle on, Beth, yer big sister's home from work.'

'It's okay, I can do it myself.'

'You will not. Sit down and read the paper for five minutes. I expect you've been rushed off your feet on that stall with Easter coming up. I hope so. Don't we need the money with all these greedy little tykes to feed?'

Aunty Dot beamed at all the rosy faces around her and they smiled happily back, knowing that stuffing them with good food was one of Aunty's greatest pleasures in life.

'Anyway, we need it for our day trip to the seaside, don't we, chucks?'

A loud cheer went up all round. Easter Sunday had been chosen for their day out, and all the children were excitedly looking forward to it. It would be a reward for all their hard work preparing chocolate eggs for Easter.

'Will we go on a train?' Joey wanted to know.

'We certainly will. And on the Big Dipper.'

Another cheer, louder this time, so that Aunty quickly brought them to order. 'Beth, don't forget that tea.'

The little girl scrambled down from her chair to do as she was bid, although reluctant to leave the chocolate rabbits and ordering her brother not to touch anything while she was gone. She ran to Lizzie and gave her a warm hug before pushing the kettle into place on the stove and lighting the gas jet under Aunty's watchful eye.

Lizzie likewise obediently did as she was told, settled herself comfortably in the chair by the fire and picked up the evening paper.

This was always a good moment in her day, when she returned home to the heart of her family. Not that it was a real family, not in the strict sense of the word. Beth wasn't her real sister. Five-year-old Alan might be the little girl's brother but none of the other children were related. Aunty Dot wasn't even their real aunt. But they felt as if they were a family, and that was what counted.

Aunty Dot was the children's foster mother. She was a small, plump woman who was always smiling, with a shiny nose, red as a cherry. Her round cheeks seemed to be permanently dusted with sugar or smeared with streaks of chocolate powder, and her eyes were like big brown sultanas.

'I'm like a Christmas pudding,' she would tell the children. 'Put custard on me and you could eat me right up.'

Aunty Dot had a heart as big as Manchester City football ground. Social workers, the NSPCC, or the 'cruelty people' as the children called them, knew they could bring a child or a baby to Dorothy Thompson's house at any time, day or night.

Clad in her blue-flowered overall with the two big pockets where she carried clean hankies, safety pins, and a few wrapped mints, she would gather them to her soft bosom for a cuddle. Then she would heat water and bathe them with Pear's soap till their skin was silky with cleanliness. She would shampoo their filthy hair and patiently comb out the head lice, teasing apart the dreadful tangles. She would tend the inevitable sores and bruises, the red patches of scabies and ringworm, then wrap the child in warm towels and give them hot cocoa and home-made biscuits for their supper before putting them to sleep in a clean bed, often for the first time in their lives.

For as long as they stayed at number thirty-seven Champion Street, Aunty Dot would do her utmost to put some flesh on their bony little bodies.

She'd done this for Beth and Alan, who'd been with Aunty for five months now. They'd come to her wild and unkempt with a background no one cared to explore too deeply; it hadn't been easy for her to tame and calm them into anything like normal behaviour.

She'd gently shaved every scrap of hair off Beth's scabby head, and carefully tended the raw skin till it healed and a fresh silky

3

crop of dark brown curls sprang into life. Aunty had weaned the small boy off his baby's bottle, the only food he'd known in his entire life, and given him the confidence to handle a knife and fork so that he could eat hot pot and creamy rice pudding like grown-up people.

Most children stayed only a short time with her and were then returned to their parents, who by then would hope-fully have resolved whatever problems had beset them. Others became regulars; the NSPCC using Aunty as a sort of respite home, a place where children could be properly fed and cleaned up.

So it was with Joey who'd first appeared at Aunty's door almost a year ago, one dark stormy night. He'd been locked in his own silent world and was only just starting to speak, thanks to Aunty's cuddles and endless patience. But his mother, who was struggling to cope on her own while hiding from a violent husband, wanted him to come home whenever it felt safe for him to do so. Too often she was wrong and the result of these visits would be Joey's abrupt retreat into that dark private world of silence once again, and when he returned to Champion Street he would sit in a corner and rock himself back and forth for hours on end.

Cissie had been here a week and was a sweet little girl, though she wet her bed every night. And the baby – there was always a baby – who'd arrived only yesterday morning, had rarely stopped crying. His poor mother had threatened to kill herself, or him, if they didn't take the little mite away.

For Lizzie, Aunty had done much more, something the young woman would never forget or be able to thank her for enough, if she lived to be a hundred. Aunty Dot had rescued her at the age of twelve from an industrial school run by the Sisters of Mercy. The pair of them had hit it off right away, and in this bustling household Lizzie had found the love and care she'd always longed for. Aunty Dot was the anchor of Lizzie's life, the centre of her heart and soul, and her loyalty and love for the older woman were unwavering.

Now Lizzie sat watching fondly as the children fetched trays and knives and forks, and napkins folded in their own individually painted wooden rings, while Aunty heated up the stew for supper. The chocolate rabbits were all made, and the family would eat the meal on their knees so as not to disturb the moulds on the table. The children weren't required to help. They could play with the toys that Aunty provided, or take a turn on the tricycle they all shared. But few of them could resist joining in with all the exciting culinary adventures that went on in Aunty's kitchen.

Lizzie felt exactly the same. There was nothing she liked more than to assist Aunty in making the chocolates and sweets for the Chocolate Cabin, the stall Lizzie ran on Champion Street Market. It wasn't possible to stock it entirely from this tiny kitchen, but Aunty did what she could because she enjoyed sweet-making and it helped keep costs down.

Today, after a busy day on the market, Lizzie was tired and glad of the opportunity for a rest. She enjoyed the stipulated five minutes, which actually lasted nearer half an hour, but when the food appeared she gladly set the paper aside. It had little in it of interest other than a story about Elvis Presley swapping his guitar for a gun, as he joined up to do his stint in the US Army.

There was never much conversation while they ate. To these children, who had known the reality of starvation, eating was a serious business.

Even so, Aunty couldn't relax. Every now and then she would get up to inspect how the process was coming along, and as the chocolate began to dry out would gently scrape away the excess from around the rim of each mould. Once it was completely set the chocolate shrank a little, and then Aunty gave each mould a gentle tap so that the half rabbit dropped easily out on to the paper.

'We've got a good crop,' she told her helpers, pressing one hand surreptitiously to her side as she returned to her seat and her plate of beef stew.

Lizzie considered her with a thoughtful frown, blue eyes clouding with worry, for there was a shadow over this happy household. Aunty was not her usual cheery self. 'What's wrong? Have you got that pain again?'

'It's only a stitch from leaning over the table too long. I should sit down. I keep telling myself, but do I listen?'

The children giggled. Aunty was famous for her talking aloud, issuing firm instructions to herself to hurry up or she'd miss the bus, or to keep her chin up and stop complaining. Not that she ever did anything but hurry, and never complained.

Following the death of her son in Tobruk in 1941, Lizzie knew that Aunty had buried the pain of her loss by caring for other people's children. First it was war orphans, now it was children who'd been neglected or abused. Aunty had suffered an abused childhood herself, her own father had terrified her. Consequently she wasn't one to tolerate bullies. Nor did she have much patience with the so-called authorities since she'd got little or no help from them at the time. But then Aunty Dot wasn't one to take any nonsense from anyone.

Lizzie was also aware that all that suffering had taken its toll. However chirpy Dot might appear in front of the children, more often than not she was dropping on her feet from exhaustion by the end of the day. Consequently, Lizzie did what she could to take as much weight from Aunty's shoulders as she possibly could. A task which was far from easy. But that pain in her side had started up recently, becoming a real worry. If only Lizzie could persuade her to see a doctor.

They were spooning up the last delicious scraps of rice pudding, when there was a loud hammering on the door. Aunty clicked her tongue in annoyance. 'Now who can that be at this time?'

'I'll go.'

'Right, kids, half an hour's play before bed, not a minute more.' The back door slammed shut on their disappearing figures before she'd finished speaking. Laughing, Aunty tickled the baby under his chin, then picked up the trays and began to clear away.

—

Lizzie opened the door to find Jack Cleaver standing on the doorstep. Jack was the commercial traveller for Finch's Sweets, Lizzie's main supplier. She wasn't surprised to see him here as he'd taken to popping round fairly frequently lately in a bid to persuade her to go out with him. Somehow though, with his forties-style, slicked back, brown hair and double-breasted suits, the prospect of a night on the town with Jack Cleaver did not appeal.

But because he seemed lonely and so obviously besotted, Lizzie always tried to be kind and let him down lightly. Not that he was good at taking no for an answer because he'd be back the next day, or the one after that. Now she braced herself for another polite refusal, but on this occasion he didn't have courting on his mind.

'Evening, Lizzie. Sorry to disturb you, but Mr Finch would like a word.'

'Mr Finch?' Now Lizzie was surprised. It was a rare occurrence for her to see Jack's boss, the proprietor of the sweet factory, and unheard of for him to call at her home.

'He's waiting in his car.' Jack nodded in the direction of a big black Humber parked at the kerb. It was clear that the large man seated inside, well muffled up in overcoat, scarf and Homburg hat against the cool March evening, had no intention of stepping out of it, so Lizzie walked over and tapped on the window.

'Good evening, Mr Finch. How are you?' She didn't know what else to say.

Cedric Finch wound down the window and considered her with eyes that looked cold and hard behind his spectacles. 'I've been hearing disturbing things about you, Lizzie Pringle.'

Surprised by this, Lizzie judged it wisest to maintain her silence until he'd explained further.

'I hear your Aunty has set herself up in competition.'

'What?'

'Don't deny it. I make it my business to keep my ear to the ground and be aware of what's going on. I have my spies, you understand, who keep me well informed. I believe the terms were set out clearly from the start when I agreed to do business with you. Finch's was to be your sole supplier.'

Lizzie was struggling to take in exactly what he was accusing her of. 'And so you are.'

'I think not. Jack informs me that your aunty also makes sweets and chocolates for the stall. Your chocolate Easter egg order is pathetic, almost non-existent. I have to say, Lizzie Pringle, I find that most unsatisfactory, most unsatisfactory indeed. It simply isn't good enough. Your orders are falling far below what I require from a customer. Unless you put a stop to the amateur efforts of that interfering Aunty of yours, and start putting *all* your business our way, then I shall have no alternative but to stop supplying you.'

Lizzie was incensed, not only by his nasty remarks about Aunty, but by his threatening manner. She had no intention of being pushed around by anyone, however posh they were. 'Finch's isn't the only factory that makes sweets in Manchester. I could find another supplier.'

Now he smiled at her, but the sight did nothing to warm her. 'I don't think so. I'd make sure no one else would look at you, love. Take my advice, have a word with dear old Aunty Dot. Tell her to stick to minding kids, and leave chocolate and sweet-making to the experts. Otherwise, it could be curtains for your little stall.'

Then he instructed Jack Cleaver to drive off, after an apologetic backward glance at Lizzie, leaving her standing on the pavement with her mouth hanging open.

Later, when the children were all tucked up in bed, Lizzie read them a story from the big book of *Grimm's Fairy Tales*. Aunty heated a baking sheet, then quickly touched the rim of each hollow rabbit against the hot metal so that when she placed the two halves together they melted slightly and stuck together to form a seal.

Usually, Lizzie would argue that this task could wait till morning, and Aunty would insist it must be done tonight and the chocolate rabbits properly stored away, so that the kitchen could be cleaned and tidied ready for breakfast. The children always ate their porridge sitting together at the big table.

But on this occasion Lizzie was thankful for the distraction of helping with these extra chores, telling Aunty it had only been Jack at the door, making a nuisance of himself as usual. She made no mention of his boss's threats.

Chapter Two

Dena Dobson wondered what it was that made her so strong. On this particular cold March day, one she'd looked forward to for almost twelve months, she felt strangely elated; blood pumped through her veins with a new vigour, a tingling excitement touched every nerve-ending. The past had finally been laid to rest.

She pushed back her chestnut brown hair and glanced about her at the crush of people still streaming from the courthouse, her eager gaze seeking out Carl, although she could see no sign of him yet. He would be somewhere close by, and she smiled to herself at this new burst of confidence and hope within her. Maybe now they could begin again, start afresh and put the unpleasantness of these last months behind them at last. They were still young, after all, with all their lives ahead of them.

Before the end of this month on 27 March, Dena would turn nineteen. It surprised her sometimes to think how very young she still was; when often recently she had felt world-weary, mature beyond her years. But then she always had been stubborn, never one to give up easily. How had that come about exactly?

Perhaps it was spending so much of her childhood with hunger sharp in her belly, largely because her selfish mother had been too busy fretting about her own concerns to remember to feed her. Or else later, when she was taken into care and had been forced to cope with the rigours of Ivy Bank Children's Home. But no matter how her character had been formed, she was undoubtedly a survivor. No one could say otherwise.

Despite an on-going sense of insecurity, the birth of an illegitimate daughter, and almost falling into the trap of marrying the man who'd caused the death of her young brother, Dena believed she'd dealt with the problems life had thrown at her remarkably well. She'd made a home for her child, built a successful business on Champion Street Market, and managed to hold her head high.

She loved her dressmaking work, and had made so many friends here on Champion Street Market: Patsy Bowman and Lizzie Pringle, Big Molly and Amy George, Betty Hemley, and best of all, Winnie. She had a lot to be thankful for.

Dena looked around again. In the crush of people leaving the court, the noise and mayhem of newspaper reporters pressing her for a comment on how she felt about the verdict, she'd completely lost sight of Carl. She'd been searching for him in the crowd ever since, longing for the man she loved to appear, sweep her up in his arms and carry her away to a new future.

But now she pictured the look on his face, the shock reflected there, when the verdict had been announced, revealing all too clearly his bitter disappointment that his younger brother, Kenny, hadn't been let off with a lesser plea of manslaughter; the heart-rending cry from Carl and Kenny's mother Belle had echoed dramatically around the courtroom when Kenny was sentenced.

It came to her then that that was where Carl would be: consoling his mother. Belle Garside had naturally hoped for a more merciful verdict for her younger son than being sent down for life for the murder of young Pete Dobson. Yet in Dena's opinion that verdict was entirely justified. In fact, Kenny was very fortunate that his neck wasn't going to be stretched.

'Are you all right, chuck?' Winnie asked, patting her arm.

Dena shook away the icy shiver that had rippled down her spine as she remembered the way her brother had died. 'Never better. The slate is wiped clean. Justice has been done and we can get on with our lives at last. A new beginning.'

In truth, she'd half expected the world to have changed in some way when she left the courtroom, for the sun to shine brighter, the flowers on Betty Hemley's stall to smell sweeter.

She'd even expected Champion Street itself to appear different, but it looked as it always did on any busy Friday. The stalls lining the pavement from Tonman Street to Deansgate, some little more than trestle tables piled high with goods, were being picked over by bargain hunters and browsers alike. There was the pot man juggling his plates, pretending to let one fall every now and then, just to get people's attention, before beating down his own prices and shifting dozens in a mock auction.

Molly Poulson was still squabbling with her daughter as they busily sold hot meat and potato pies. Jimmy Ramsay slapped his big fat, aproned belly as he called out in his great, booming voice: 'Best pork sausages in all of Manchester! No, love, they're not full of bread, they're full of meat. Try a couple, on the house – if you find a sandwich in there, let me know and I'll give you yer money back.'

That was Jimmy, always ready with the repartee. On any other day Dena would have laughed out loud, but today, after the strain of the trial, she could manage little more than a tired smile.

The last few weeks had been immensely stressful, leaving her tense and emotionally drained, yet now that it was over, Dena felt an airy lightness inside her she hadn't experienced in an age. Hope reborn, the feeling that she did have a future after all. She felt so overwhelmed by relief that the trial was at last over and done with, that she couldn't even bring herself to resent the fact that Carl was with his mother, and not rushing to her side with kisses and congratulations. How could he be expected to do that, when the man on his way to life imprisonment was his own brother?

But he would meet up with her later, she was sure of it.

Dena hugged Winnie, and kissed her paper-soft cheeks. 'Is our Trudy all right?'

'She's right as ninepence. Amy George is keeping an eye on her today, since Barry and I wanted to be there for the verdict. She'll be fine.'

'Good, I'm dying for a cup of tea.'

'Or something stronger? How about half a Guinness to celebrate?'

'A brandy and Babycham more like,' Dena said, and she did laugh this time, as if the bubbles were already fizzing inside her.

Linking her arm with Winnie's, she led her friend across to the Dog and Duck. Old men in flat caps and mufflers watched them go by as they stood smoking their pipes by the ancient horse trough, as they had been doing for as long as Dena could remember. No doubt they were eagerly discussing the odds on the three-thirty before handing over the shilling or two they could ill afford to Billy Quinn, the bookie, certain it would make them a fortune. Women in headscarves argued over the price of fish; harassed mothers kept a close eye on their children in case they should wander off and get lost in the crowds. The wind blew chip papers and cabbage leaves across the cobbles. A normal day on the market, just like any other.

But when had life ever been normal for Dena? It hadn't been when she was a mere slip of a girl working Saturdays in Belle's Café, earning the only money that came into the house, her mother Alice having taken to her bed in grief.

Dena's gaze turned inward at the thought, no longer seeing the market, but something entirely different, the scene playing in her mind like an old film. Their assailants had sprung out at them from the darkness – little more than shadows, jumping out upon them to attack with feet and fists, battering and thumping, punching and kicking.

She'd heard them running, fading away into the darkness, although not before they'd given her a good beating too, pummelling her in the stomach, kicking her in the back and legs when she fell so that she feared they might not stop till she too was a goner. Then with only the distant sounds of the city washing over her, and the wind whistling under the canal bridge Dena had risked moving a leg, terrified it might be broken because she had to get up. She had to save him.

But she hadn't saved him. Pete, her cheeky young brother, had drowned. Beaten up by Kenny Garside and his mates and tossed into the mucky canal like so much garbage.

Her young brother had died that day and Dena had carried the weight of his loss every day since. If only she could have saved him. If only she'd fought back more fiercely. But she'd been little more than a child herself and knocked near senseless by the faceless bullies. Even so, she'd jumped in anyway, and swum about in the filthy, tar-streaked water looking for him until she'd been in danger of drowning herself.

And now, at last, Kenny had stood trial for that crime. He'd been charged with murder and sent down on a life sentence. Justice had been done.

Dena became aware of Winnie's hand gently squeezing her arm. 'Keep that smile in place, love, this is a good day. Remember that.'

'Oh, yes, Winnie, I will!'

–

In the pub Winnie's new husband, Barry Holmes, waited with a bottle of champagne. Smiling friends gathered around to help Dena celebrate. She looked into their kindly, sympathetic faces and her heart filled with love for these people. Lynda Hemley, Marc Bertalone, Patsy Bowman, Alec Hall in his trademark pink bow tie, even Clara Higginson was here; anyone in fact who could manage to sneak away from their stall for five minutes to share in the celebration. They might have gossiped about her in the beginning, but when it came to the push, they'd stood by her in the end. How could she have got through it all without them?

Champagne corks popped, Barry was pushing a dripping glass into her hand and raising his in a toast to the sound of much laughter and clinking of glasses.

'To a new beginning for our Dena! A new future. She deserves it.'

'A new beginning!' cried Lizzie Pringle.

Dena could feel her cheeks grow pink as everyone kissed and congratulated her, wishing her the very best. 'Thanks Barry. Thanks to all of you.' But even as she sipped at the bubbles she found herself glancing around.

Two people were missing from this gathering: her mother Alice, which didn't surprise her since they were hardly on good terms. More significantly Carl, who still hadn't shown up. Dena began to feel a twinge of concern she could no longer ignore. Not surprisingly, given the circumstances, a gulf had widened between them in recent months. She was guiltily aware that deep down, in the place where she'd locked away all the pain and hurt, she couldn't feel real sympathy for anyone's problems but her own.

As the trial had drawn nearer she'd felt increasingly detached from this man she loved more than life itself, and from other people too, as if she were set apart from everyone, living in a different world. They fretted about trivial things like what to make for tea, what they should wear for a party, or the price of beef, while Dena felt as if she were hanging on to her sanity by her fingertips, waiting and longing to be set free from this nightmare.

There were other terrible events happening in the world: the Manchester United football team – the Busby Babes – had been killed in a terrible air crash only last month. Then there were the protests about nuclear disarmament with the CND planning Easter marches upon London. But Dena couldn't feel involved even in such vitally important matters.

Carl accused her of being selfishly wrapped up in own feelings. 'You don't need me any more,' he would complain. 'You don't talk, or share things with me like we used to. It's as if I'm superfluous to your life.'

Dena hadn't disagreed with that, because in a way it was true. She'd longed simply to turn back the clock and pretend that terrible day her brother had died had never happened. Since that was impossible, she wanted just to get the trial over and done with.

'We all feel for you,' Carl had told her when she'd tried to explain why she was like that. 'We understand how you must be feeling. But *you* have to understood how *we* have feelings too. Kenny is still my brother. Misguided, stupid, a violent bully, too ready to use his fists when things go wrong. I accept all of that, but I still can't look upon him as a murderer.'

'But he *is* a murderer,' she'd insisted. 'He murdered my brother! We can't ever get away from that fact.'

'In your opinion.'

'And in the judge's too, I hope,' she'd snapped, and they'd turned away from each other, on opposite sides of the chasm opening up between them.

But hopefully, now that the trial's looming presence was behind them, all this disagreement and misery would be set aside, and she and Carl could at last begin to plan their future. She could relax in the joy of bringing up Trudy, her precious child, and give proper attention to the development of her little fashion business. She might even dare to dream of a wedding... Dena sincerely hoped so because she loved Carl so very much.

'A toast to British justice,' Barry called out and, laughing, Dena kissed him. She really didn't know how she would have managed without Barry Holmes at her side over these last months. He'd been a tower of strength, like a father to her.

As more bottles were opened, someone struck up a tune on the piano and Dena settled in a corner with Winnie and Lizzie, the merriment around them increasing. Carl had clearly decided to stay with Belle, thinking it was not appropriate for him to join the celebration of his brother's conviction.

Dena was disappointed but in her heart she understood. They'd get together later, as Carl Garside was to be a major part of this new future she planned for herself.

Chapter Three

'Not another visitor. What a racket! Who would come calling at this time of the morning? It's getting as busy as London Road Station.'

Nobody rushed to answer the door. Lizzie was eating her porridge standing up while she fed the baby at the same time. Aunty Dot was helping Alan not to turn his spoon upside down before it reached his mouth, while stroking Joey's head and urging him to eat something at least, but the older boy only pushed the dish away.

'Don't like porridge.'

'Yes, you do. Put some syrup on it. You like syrup.'

'Don't like that school. And I don't care what anyone says, I'm not bloody going!'

Joey had been taken on a visit to the secondary modern school he'd be moving to in September, assuming he didn't pass for the grammar, which would be surprising considering the interruptions his education had suffered. Unfortunately he'd taken against it from the start.

Aunty was sorry he felt so bad but didn't scold him for swearing, because she knew that this was the kind of language he was most familiar with, and 'bloody' was a fairly mild expletive in his repertoire.

'I won't flaming be here by then!' he shouted, confirming Aunty Dot's view that he liked the school far better than he was admitting, but fear of an unknown future was overwhelming the boy yet again.

She kissed the top of his tousled head, told him everything was going to be fine, then went to answer the door, throwing a desperate comment back to Lizzie as she did so.

'I can't take another child, not today.'

But it wasn't the cruelty man, it was Winnie Holmes. She came bustling straight into the kitchen, beaming at all the porridge-smeared faces, the pom-pom on her woolly hat bouncing in a jolly fashion, which made the children giggle. 'It may not be any of my business, but I thought I'd let you know that you had a visitor yesterday, Dot.'

'You mean Jack Cleaver? Aye, he came pestering our Lizzie to go courting with him. So what? Half of Champion Street is in love with my girl.'

'I don't mean him.' Winnie jerked her chin meaningfully at the children. 'Someone else. Someone who is the bane of your life.'

Aunty frowned, then led Winnie out of the kitchen to a relatively quiet corner of the living room where they could talk in peace. 'Who?'

'It were that Miss Rogers what took our Dena off once, if you remember?'

Aunty patiently nodded, waiting for Winnie to get to the point. 'I do.'

'You need to watch her. She's a right nasty piece of work, a real hard-faced madam.'

'I can handle Miss Rogers. She's a regular at this house, as you know, so what was it about her that bothered you particularly on this occasion, Winnie?' Aunty quietly asked, privately thinking this was probably all an excuse on her neighbour's part to dig out a bit of gossip, or to pass some on.

Winnie lowered her voice to a dramatic whisper. 'It's not for me to say, but she was in a real lather, banging on your door loud enough to wake the dead. Barry went over in the end and told her you were out, probably taken the babby to the clinic and wouldn't be back for an hour or two. He offered to take a message but she tartly told him to mind his own business, said that she'd call again later.' Winnie sniffed. 'Something's up, so I thought it best to warn you. I wouldn't trust that woman as far as I could throw her!'

Aunty nodded, saying nothing, and half glanced over her shoulder at Joey who was scooping his porridge down at record pace now. 'Well, thank you for telling me.'

'I don't know how you cope, I don't really. How many have you got staying with you this week?'

Aunty had Winnie by the arm and was edging her towards the door, anxious to be rid of her nosy visitor. She was a good woman, at heart, but Dot really didn't have time to chat right now, not when she was rushing to get the children off to school, and the baby was already starting to grizzle though he'd only been awake five minutes. Winnie, however, was determined to milk her fabricated moment of drama for all it was worth and she hung back, glancing towards the kitchen.

'Poor little beggars. No one else but you would give them house room, Dot. Soft as butter you are. It must break your heart every time you have to give one of them up. Still got that Joey, I see. Oh, aye, that reminds me. Our Barry wants to know if the lad's coming to the boxing club tonight. He missed on Tuesday, and Barry has hopes for him in the under-twelves trophy, if he sticks to the training. He's very particular that his lads keep up their training.'

Aunty turned to Joey and relayed the question to him. When the boy didn't immediately answer, she gently asked him again: 'Joey, I'm speaking to you. Will you be at the boxing club tonight?'

Joey vehemently shook his head. 'No!' he said, with surprising firmness for a boy who only spoke when it was absolutely essential.

Aunty smiled apologetically at Winnie. 'He's not too happy this morning. He doesn't like the look of the new school he'll be going to. I'll speak to him later about the club. Tell Barry he'll be there, not to worry. As for that other little matter, I'm sure it was nothing important. Probably just someone wanting me to take another child, only I'm full right now.'

Or to take one away, Dot thought, finally managing to manhandle Winnie out on to the doorstep. She always hated it when children left, but some were more precious to her than others. And some she really had no wish to lose at all. Dot just hoped it wasn't Joey, Miss Rogers was after. Or Beth and Alan, for that matter. That was the only downside to this job she loved. She really would have preferred to keep all the children, given the choice. Instead she had to live with endless goodbyes, and not show her true feelings.

'Oh dear, try not to think about it,' she muttered to herself, as she closed the door on Winnie, then watched through the window, frowning, as her neighbour walked away, spine rigid with self-righteous indignation that her dramatic announcement hadn't received the attention she felt it deserved.

But why would she go to such trouble to come and tell Dot about a visitor who called at this house at least twice a month, if not every week? Most odd. Then the baby started to cry and Aunty returned to the business of getting her brood off to school, putting Winnie and her nosiness right out of her mind.

–

Jack Cleaver called twice at the stall to see Lizzie after Mr Finch had issued his warning, partly by way of apology and partly to warn her.

'You'll have to do as he says. He won't give up. Once my boss has issued a threat he generally carries it out. You must talk to Mrs Thompson, insist she stops making all those sweets and chocolates.'

Lizzie paused in her task of filling up the jar of sherbet lemons, looking at him with eyebrows raised in polite surprise. Yet, deep inside, the wrath she felt was so great it was as if a fire burned in her soul, a red-hot sea of anger she had to fight to contain. If there was one thing Lizzie had learned throughout the turbulent years of her youth, it was how to keep her thoughts private, for none of this emotion showed in her serenely lovely face. 'I suppose he told you to say that, did he?'

Jack's tone remained conciliatory. 'He didn't, as a matter of fact, but it's true, Lizzie. You must listen to what he says. If Finch's stop supplying you, where will you be then?'

'Looking for another supplier,' Lizzie calmly retorted. 'He isn't the only sweet maker in Manchester.'

'No, but he's the best. Top dog.' Jack Cleaver spoke as one might to a small child, painstakingly emphasising each word. 'He'd tell everyone you were a debt risk, or some such. Make sure nobody else would do business with you. He's used to having his own way.'

Lizzie's blue gaze was unwavering. 'He doesn't scare me. Tell Mr Cedric Finch, I'll not be bullied. I do what's right for my family, as well as good for my stall.'

Jack groaned and his tone became wheedling. 'Nay, Lizzie lass, you know I care for you. I'd cut off me right arm if you asked me to, but don't ask me to stand up to Finch. I want to wake up in a morning all in one piece, not with me head bitten off. He's a difficult man to cross. Rules that family of his with an iron fist.'

But Lizzie only smiled at this confusing declaration of allegiance, toughening herself, at least outwardly, and damping down the flutter of nerves within. She'd come across hard men before in her life, her own father included, not to mention a whole stream of 'uncles'. She'd thought they were bad enough until she'd spent time in the industrial school, where she'd learned that women, or those nuns at least, were far more heartless than any man when it came to inflicting pain.

Thanks to Aunty Dot her time in that school had been blessedly short, but after all she'd endured she wasn't going to run scared from one measly confectionery supplier.

Lizzie stiffened her spine and looked Cleaver straight in the eye. It was easy to do since she was easily as tall as him, maybe even an inch taller. 'Aunty has made some toffee apples for the children's trip to Blackpool on Easter Sunday. I'm going to ask her to make a few more. I reckon they'd sell well on the stall. I warrant I could shift dozens this summer.'

Jack scowled at her, his fleshy cheeks and chin quivering as he struggled to keep his smile in place. He'd been chasing Lizzie Pringle for months, eager to get his hands on her little business empire, which he hoped would provide him with the respectability he craved. So far he was getting absolutely nowhere. Now impatience got the better of him. 'You're a stubborn woman, Lizzie Pringle!'

She burst out laughing. 'Thank you, sir, for the kind compliment, and you've got another button coming off your jacket. How do you manage to lose so many? Pop round one evening and I'll sew it on for you.'

Lizzie made her offer with a beaming smile, meaning to reassure him that even though they'd disagreed over this matter she was still willing to be his friend. For all the good wages he must earn working for Finch's, Jack Cleaver rarely spent much on himself. He was known for being careful with money. The cuffs of his old double-breasted demob suit were frayed, and his highly polished brogues had cracks in the leather. Maybe if he smartened himself up a bit, she might look upon his approaches more kindly. Lizzie considered those wide, flared nostrils, like twin hairy caverns, brown eyes that always managed to look slightly furtive, and a thin mouth diminished even further by fleshy cheeks and jowls. No, that *would* be stretching their friendship too far.

Encouraged by her kind offer, Jack stepped closer, a flash of hope rekindled in his fervent expression. Lizzie willed herself not to take a step back, or to recoil from his bad breath and the overpowering smell of tobacco that emanated from him. Jack Cleaver was a pipe man, no doubt with slippers to match.

He wagged a gently admonishing finger in her face to drive home his point. 'Think on. If Finch sends his lads round, they won't be nearly so polite or considerate as me, Lizzie love. Nay, let me look after you, you know I'd give my right arm to do that.'

'I know you would, Jack, and I'm grateful.'

Jack Cleaver was forever at pains to prove how much he cared for her, how, given half a chance, he would devote his entire life to looking after her. This was the last thing Lizzie wanted, but she could almost smell the loneliness in him, and pity overwhelmed her.

She knew very little about his background, or his childhood, except that he claimed it had been equally as miserable as her own. He'd spoken of being found on a doorstep in his home area of Islington, and of spending time in a Dr Barnardo's home, although he'd once also mentioned an Aunt Doris, which didn't seem to fit with his story. What had happened to his parents she'd no idea, nor did Lizzie enquire! In her view people had a right to their privacy, and to devise a tale to disguise the horror of their past if they so wished. Jack Cleaver was a bit of a mystery man, but largely to be pitied.

Smiling with genuine sympathy, Lizzie leaned over and gave him a quick peck on the cheek. 'You're a good man, good to me, and to the children. I appreciate your thoughtfulness and concern, but you've no need to worry. I can stand up for myself. I've no intention of letting myself be bullied by anyone. It only brings out the stubbornness in me and makes me more perverse than ever. Tell your boss that.'

'He won't like it.'

'Nor do I like being told what to do by him. But I don't have a glint of red in my hair for nothing, Jack Cleaver. It matches the fire in my belly. Tell you what, I'll go and see him myself. "Beard the lion in his den". I'll get this matter settled once and for all. You can tell him that too.'

24

Chapter Four

Disappointingly, the elation, like the champagne, hadn't lasted long. The bubbles had soon popped, leaving Dena feeling flat and distressed and with a slight hangover the next day. Old wounds had been opened, memories laid bare, and the pain had risen again in her as hot and raw as ever, like a band of scalding iron compressing her heart.

Carl never had emerged from his mother's café to join the celebration, and finally Dena had gone home early to bed, although not to sleep. He hadn't come near her all weekend either, except to push a note through her letterbox on Friday night to say that as Belle needed him badly right now, he'd come round to see her just as soon as he could.

He'd signed the note: Love, Carl, and added three kisses, but it wasn't the same as having them delivered in person.

Now, on what should have been a bright Monday morning, Dena treadled away on her Singer sewing machine nursing a confusion of emotions, but pleased at least that business in the rag trade was booming. She was churning out dresses, capri pants and blouses, and her famous skirts decorated with an appliqué daisy, just as fast as she and her stalwart crew of machinists could make them.

Trudy, her beloved daughter, was beside her, sitting on the floor playing with the button bag, sorting the pretty colours and designs, or pretending they were cakes in a baker's shop; happily chattering away to herself in her make-believe world.

'Can I go and play with Gabby?' the little girl asked, pushing the buttons into a heap.

Gabriella was the youngest of the Bertalone girls. The Bertalone's were an Italian family who ràn the ice cream parlour, and Trudy idolised Gabby because of her dark Latin beauty and the fact that, at eight, she could do clever things like roller skate and ride her bicycle standing up. Trudy would dearly have loved to have a go on the roller skates, but wasn't allowed because she was still too young. Gabby and her sisters would try to squeeze her into their doll's pram instead, saying she was only a baby. Trudy hated being called a baby but she adored Gabby.

Dena smiled, content to see her daughter so well and happy, privately wishing she could stay a baby forever. She felt so grateful that she even had her, could so easily have lost her if Miss Rogers, the social worker, hadn't helped her to find accommodation and a job. Caring for a child alone hadn't been easy and the stigma of illegitimacy still hung over Trudy, but she was bouncing with health, full of mischief and would be three years old in September. How time did fly.

'In a little while, darling. Mummy just has to finish this skirt then we'll go and have an ice cream. How about that?'

Trudy let out an excited cry. 'Ooh, yes, please!' and went back to playing with her buttons, turning them into soldiers this time and making them march in line.

She was such a joy, Dena thought, as she manoeuvred the fabric skilfully beneath the flying needle. Not a scrap of trouble, and so bright and bubbly with her soft brown curls, amber eyes and cheeky little smile. How fortunate she was to have such a beautiful child.

She really should be the happiest woman on earth. She and Carl so desperately in love, he as eager to marry her as he had been a year ago when he'd first asked her. Now the trial was over and the right verdict given, so far as Dena was concerned. Everything about her life should feel perfect.

But somehow that burst of optimism outside the court, that moment of pure happiness, had dissipated. Where was he? Where was Carl?

She unclipped the foot of the machine, turned the fabric and clipped it down again, anxiety darkening her brown eyes, clouding the bright flecks in them to a dull gold as she treadled and stitched.

Why hadn't he come to see her?

Winnie, her dearest friend, had allowed her to continue to live in her old house, charging Dena only a nominal rent when she'd moved in with Barry Holmes after their wedding a few months back. At first Dena had found the prospect of having the house to herself exciting. She'd looked forward to cosy evenings spent by the fire with Carl, with Winnie nearby should she ever need help in caring for Trudy. Barry too was always willing to babysit. But nothing had turned out as she'd hoped.

Perhaps it was because the house had felt empty without her friend's reassuring presence. Both she and Trudy had missed the older woman's lively chatter. Nobody knew more about the goings-on of Champion Street Market than Winnie Holmes. But besides that things hadn't been as they should be between herself and Carl. The strain of the trial had undoubtedly taken its toll on their relationship.

Dena broke off from sewing cotton and shook out yet another completed skirt. 'There you are, Joan, that just about completes the Harvey's order, I think.'

Joan Chapman, who had been with Dena almost from when the business first started, smiled and ordered her to take a break. 'You look proper worn out, love. Go and get yourself a bite of lunch, and that child her ice cream, while you've got the chance. I'll pack up this order and get it dispatched.'

'Bless you, Joan, what would I do without you?'

'I hope you won't ever think of trying,' the older woman responded, her plain, homely face wreathed in smiles.

Dena glanced down again at her daughter's bright, expectant face. Ironically she was Kenny's child, but an absolute sweetie despite that disadvantage, and the centre of Dena's universe. Having been seduced by Kenny before ever she realised he'd killed Pete, even now that she knew the truth, how could she wish her own darling child unborn?

'Right, ice cream it is then.'

'Goody, goody,' Trudy yelled, and flung herself excitedly into her mother's arms.

–

Once outside in the fresh air, the smell of Betty Hemley's carnations competing with the fish market and Jimmy Ramsay's herb and garlic sausages made Dena feel nauseous. She knew that she hadn't really wanted a lunch break, didn't feel hungry. Not even the delicious aroma of Big Molly's famous meat and potato pies could tempt her to eat.

She bought Trudy an ice cream cornet from the Bertalones' stall, but felt far too tense and unhappy for food herself. Although maybe a cup of tea would help to take away this sick feeling in the pit of her stomach, that still hadn't gone despite the trial being over.

It was with a feeling of guilty relief that Dena saw Bellè wasn't at work this morning, fortunately postponing the moment she would have to face her. No doubt she was still haranguing the solicitor for not getting her beloved Kenny off.

Dena sipped gratefully on the hot tea. The noises of the market, of the stallholders calling out their wares, children crying, music playing, all seemed strangely muted, adding to her sense of unreality. Garishly coloured strings of beads dazzled her; a row of false legs clad in fishnet stockings might normally have brought a smile to her face, but her mind failed to see the humour in them this morning. Even her response to her daughter's happy chatter was no more than automatic.

If only Carl had come and joined them at the celebrations, when she'd been feeling so buoyant and full of hope, she'd have felt as if the problems they'd been experiencing could finally be resolved. So many times she'd postponed their wedding, insisting they should wait until after the trial. Surely it would all be different now that they were free at last to make proper plans?

But if that were so, then why did she feel so flat, so deeply depressed, as if nothing had changed?

Trudy tapped her on the arm, attempting to gain her attention. 'Mummy, can we go to the park?'

'I'm not sure I have the energy.'

'Aw, but we always go to the park in the afternoon. Can I play with Gabby then?'

'She's at school.'

'I want to go to school. Why can't I go to school?'

'Because you aren't old enough?'

'Why aren't I?'

Questions, questions, questions. She never seemed to stop. The child's bright mind was brimful of curiosity. How wonderful to be so young and excited about the world, instead of feeling this awful sense of dread for no reason whatsoever.

The tea didn't seem to be having any calming effect at all. But then she'd never really thought that it would since her sickness was caused entirely by worry, not some debilitating illness.

Dena remembered Carl's last words to her before the start of the trial. 'When it's over, I'll ask you one last time.' And wasn't that what she wanted: to marry the man she loved? But for all the love in his eyes, those words had sounded more like a threat than a promise. He was telling her the time had come for her to make up her mind, once and for all. And in her heart of hearts, Dena knew what her answer must be.

–

Miss Rogers sat on the faded old sofa, cup and saucer in hand, her tall angular figure seeming to tower over Aunty, sitting beside her. They'd been discussing the fate of the baby, who was to be fostered with a view to adoption by a couple who couldn't have children. Cissie was sitting on Aunty's knee, thumb in her mouth, and the little girl's frightened eyes were fixed on the other woman.

'I hope you can see how well little Cissie is doing. You like it here, don't you, chuck?'

The child nodded, then buried her face in Aunty's soft bosom. Dot ruffled her brown curls and whispered something in her ear. Cissie gave an excited giggle before scrambling off Aunty's knee and dashing off upstairs.

'She's going to show you a picture she's done of her mam and dad, so be ready to praise it. They look like two stick insects with giant heads but it's a start, isn't it? Do you know anything of her history?'

'We never divulge the family history of a child, as you well know, Mrs Thompson.'

'I just wondered. There are times when a bit of information might help, but she never mentions them. She's a shy little thing and needs her confidence boosting, so just say how wonderful it is.'

The social worker, with whiskers bristling disapprovingly over thin lips, didn't look as if she'd ever praised anybody in her life, certainly not a small child. But when Cissie returned with the picture, all done in black and purple, was hardly encouraging. Miss Rogers did manage to smile and say something pleasant. Cissie went off to happily play with her doll.

'Was there anything else?' Aunty asked, setting down her mug and rubbing her hands on her knees, indicating she had more important things to do than sit here chatting.

'Joey has been seen wandering about the streets of an evening, unsupervised. It won't do, Mrs Thompson. It won't do at all.'

Aunty's jaw dropped open. 'Wandering about the streets? I don't think I rightly know what you're implying, Miss Rogers. Joey plays out with the other lads, like normal. They take their trolley-cart and race it down the hill. So what? Didn't you have a trolley-cart when you were a nipper?'

Miss Rogers wouldn't have been seen dead on such a dangerous vehicle, even as a child. 'Word has it that he's out and about late.'

'Well, word – whatever *her* name might be – would be wrong. He's always in bed by nine, nine-thirty at the latest.'

Miss Roger's dark bushy eyebrows, liberally speckled with grey, came together in a disbelieving scowl. Her brown hair with its heavy fringe, looked as if someone had put a basin over her head and cut round the rim of it. Dot wondered if she ever had been attractive, or even young. She never revealed a glimmer of compassion for all the supposedly caring nature of her work.

'Is he still attending his boxing club?'

Dot frowned, recalling Winnie's comments. 'He's missed once or twice lately, but usually, yes, he is.'

'A boy should be involved in something worthwhile, vent his aggression in a healthy sport.'

'I agree, although our Joey isn't really the aggressive type. I'll see he doesn't miss again. Right then.' Dot was on her feet. She'd had enough of having her life picked over by this interfering old bat. 'I'll have the baby ready first thing in the morning, as requested. You'll be collecting him yourself, will you? I hope he goes to a good home.'

'He certainly will. The couple have been carefully checked out, as always.' At the door the social worker hesitated before asking an unexpected question. 'Do you ever see much of Winnie Holmes?'

'Who doesn't? She pops in and out of folk's houses round here more often than the little figures in my weather house.' Dot pointed to a miniature wooden Swiss chalet on the wall of her living room where a little carved lady carrying an umbrella stood at the ready.

Miss Rogers reached for her black umbrella, which she'd left propped by the front door, and frowned at the lowering sky. 'And is Dena Dobson still living at her old place?'

'So far as I know, why?'

'No reason, I just like to keep an eye on girls I've helped in the past, to make sure they're all right.'

'Oh, aye! Dena's doing all right for herself, no mistake as she's a clever lass. Well, thanks for calling, Miss Rogers. See you again soon, I expect.' And with a polite smile, Aunty Dot saw the woman out and closed the door with a relieved sigh. She was only taking the baby. What a relief!

-

'I'm sorry, I just can't bring myself to do it.'

'I don't understand. What are you saying?' Carl was staring at Dena with a mixture of fury and exasperation on his face, and she really couldn't blame him.

He was so good-looking with his olive skin and untidy black curls, disturbingly so. Almost foreign looking, as if he were a handsome Italian instead of a lad from Manchester, but then there were all sorts of folk living here, giving the city its vibrant quality. Even as she begged for more time, Dena longed to rumple those dark curls with teasing fingers, to kiss that exciting mouth and have him make love to her as only he could. In Carl's arms she could escape the troubles and fears that clouded her mind. Yet even as the thought of his kisses tantalised her, the gentle mouth she knew with such intimacy twisted into a snarl, the wide nostrils flared and dark blue eyes glared at her with glacial coldness.

'So you still prefer our Kenny, is that the way of it, despite all he's done?'

'Don't be ridiculous! That's not what I meant at all, and you know it. I hope they lock him up forever and throw away the key.'

'I believe that's exactly what they've done, although Mam intends to bring an appeal.'

'An appeal on what grounds?' Dena was horrified. 'There's no question that he did it, so what new defence could possibly be found? He's lucky he isn't going to be hanged!'

Carl rubbed the palms of both hands over his face in a gesture of exhaustion. He looked bone-weary, and there was a greyness beneath the olive skin, indicating a lack of sleep. He shook his head in despair.

'The solicitor is still talking about manslaughter. He insists there's no positive proof that Kenny was aware Pete was unconscious when he threw him into the canal, nor that he knew the boy couldn't swim. The offence wasn't premeditated and the lawyer is convinced the judge failed to make it clear that Kenny could have been found guilty of the lesser charge of manslaughter, which would bring a lighter sentence. Ten or fifteen years instead of a probable twenty-five.'

'And you think I should be pleased about that?'

'What difference does it make? Anyway, the appeal might not succeed. If they think Kenny intended to cause Pete grievous bodily harm, even if he didn't intend to kill him, he could still get life.'

Dena's eyes filled with a wash of tears. 'And so he should! I have to serve a life sentence, why not Kenny?'

Carl stretched out both hands towards her, palms uppermost, in a gesture of helplessness. 'It's you who's important to me, not Kenny, so explain to me *why* you keep on pushing me away. I love you, Dena. I thought you loved me. I asked you to marry me a year ago, and you said *yes*. Why have you changed your mind? What's gone wrong?'

Dena couldn't bear to meet his gaze. She sat huddled on the stool, arms wrapped about herself. She looked at the floor, at the toes of her shoes, at Trudy's doll as she sat patiently on her small chair waiting for a morning when her owner would attempt to wash her face and clean her teeth. She looked at the Bush television set in the corner, the shining brasses in her clean tiled hearth, the second-hand gate-legged table that she'd polished to perfection, and the clippy rug beneath her feet that she'd stitched herself under Winnie's supervision. All evidence of the cosy home she'd created for herself and her daughter.

None of it had been easy. Dealing with Kenny when he'd turned nasty and stalked and bullied her hadn't been easy. Nor had facing the cruel gossip when she bore his child, frozen out by people she'd known all her life because that child was illegitimate. Then she'd started her own little business from scratch in order to put bread on the table. This security had been hard won.

Dena thought of her daughter asleep upstairs, cuddling Looby Loo, the home-made knitted doll she always took to bed with her, and her heart melted with fresh love for her. Trudy was her life, her future, her reason for living. Yet Carl was good with her, so these doubts she had, this fear, were nothing to do with Trudy.

Dena struggled to answer his question. 'I don't know what's gone wrong. I just know that every time I'm with you, I think of Kenny and what he did. It feels like there's a great wedge between us.'

'You mean, you can't bring yourself to marry into the family of a murderer?' Carl's tone was harsh and Dena inwardly winced.

'Put so bluntly it sounds awful, but yes, I suppose that is exactly how I feel. *Your* brother killed *mine*. He lied and led me on and got me pregnant, so how are we ever going to get round that sufficiently to have a happy, normal life together? It doesn't seem possible.'

'We surely could if we loved each other enough.'

'Life isn't that simple. It won't ever go away, what Kenny did. The memory of the violence that robbed my brother of his life will stay with me forever. How could it not? Even if your Kenny never really intended Pete to die when he picked that fight, he meant to hurt him, badly. Kenny threw a young boy into a filthy canal without caring that he'd beaten him senseless. Pete

34

couldn't hope to protect himself, even if he *could* swim.' There were tears in her eyes now, standing proud on the lower lids as, unblinking, she refused to let them fall. 'How can *we* – you and I – learn to live with the memory of your brother's malice?'

'Because it is *his* malice, *his* guilt, not *mine*. Nor *yours*, for that matter. You did what you could, Dena, and it wasn't enough. And I did what *I* could to help Mam tame Kenny into some sort of decent behaviour.'

Dena rubbed an ache on her temple. 'Did you? Do enough I mean? It seems to me Kenny was allowed to do exactly as he pleased. I blame myself for not saving Pete, how can you not take responsibility for Kenny?'

Carl looked at her with sadness in his eyes. 'We've been through this a dozen – a hundred times. Let's stop it now, shall we? Do we have to deny ourselves any chance of happiness because Kenny is as he is?'

'You always make excuses for him, put him first. Where were you after the trial? Why didn't you come to me?'

'Mam was upset. She needed me most. You must see that?'

'I see that this trial has brought back all the pain of Pete's loss for me. Now I'd like a little more time to think things through.'

'Think about what – whether you still love me?'

Dena didn't soften at the plea in his words. It was beyond her to do so. 'About all the implications of marriage for us when we've been quarrelling so much lately. There's no rush, I'm not nineteen till the end of the month, and if your mam really is set on an appeal… maybe we shouldn't see each for a while. I need a bit of breathing space, some time on my own.'

One tear fell, rolling unchecked down her cheek. Carl stroked it gently away, cupping the perfect oval of her face and kissing the small, straight nose.

'I love you, Dena. I love Trudy. I want us to be a family, but I won't be messed about. If you truly loved me, then nothing our Kenny has done would stand between us.'

Dena blinked as she stared up at him, desperate to make him understand how she felt. 'He *murdered* my *brother*!'

Carl's face tightened with fresh anger. 'Don't keep saying that. Don't use that word. Kenny is stupid but he's *not* a murderer. It was just a daft prank that went wrong.'

She raised her hands in despair. 'No, it wasn't. The judge and jury didn't think so.'

'Well, I *do*.'

'And I *don't*! Look at us, quarrelling all over again. How can we *ever* hope to get over this? *I* can't pretend it never happened. I thought I would be able to once the trial was over, but I feel as if my bones have been laid bare and my heart torn out. Can't you understand that?'

'No, I can't! I think you're telling me that you can't be sure you still love me.'

All the energy drained out of her, leaving Dena as weak and exhausted as if she'd run a marathon. 'Let's take a short break from each other, then maybe I'll be able to clear my head and start to think and feel again.'

There was a silence as Carl digested her words. At length he said, 'You need to know that if I go, Dena, I leave Champion Street, possibly forever. I can't see you every day around the market and not be allowed to love you.'

When she didn't answer he asked, 'Is that your last word on the subject?'

Choked with emotion and unable to speak, Dena stared at her tightly clasped hands and did not respond. After a moment Carl got up and walked away, out of her house and out of her life.

Chapter Five

Finch's Sweets was situated close to the docks, not far from Catlow's distribution depot, which was handy. It was often necessary to send orders further afield from Manchester, perhaps to Liverpool, Birmingham or Wolverhampton, so the ready availability of transport was essential. London Road Railway Station wasn't far away but the Ship Canal was cheaper, if considerably slower.

Lizzie knew Cedric Finch was an important man with a rapidly expanding business, but she was determined not to let her sense of trepidation show as she rang the bell.

But it wasn't Finch who opened the door, it was a young man, and for a long telling moment Lizzie could do nothing but gaze into his eyes. They were a clear pale grey, set wide apart in a boyish face under tousled blond hair that made him look the spitting image of Tommy Steele. And he had the cheekiest smile.

Neither of them seemed able to speak for some moments. Lizzie distinctly felt desire unfurl within her, as if something long dormant had been awakened. He took a step back to usher her inside with a slightly theatrical bow. 'Sorry, I'm forgetting my manners. I wasn't expecting to find an angel standing on the step when I opened the door. And, to be honest, I wish I hadn't.'

'Oh! And why would that be?' Lizzie didn't know how to respond to this contradictory remark, but did her best to sound cool and composed, far from the way she was feeling.

'Because you've spoiled me for any other girl who might stand on that step in the future.'

Lizzie flushed bright pink, then glancing down at the step in question, sharply remarked, 'I'd say it needs a good scrub myself.'

He laughed and stuck out a hand, only to drop it quickly and wipe it on the seat of his grey flannels. 'Charlie's the name.' They were smart flannels, spoiled slightly by being worn with a belt with a snake clasp that he must surely have owned since he was ten years old. His shirt was blue, the sleeves rolled up over muscular forearms since he wore neither jacket nor tie. 'Have you an appointment?' he asked.

Lizzie shook her head, her own smile quickly fading at this reminder of her errand. 'I – I just came on spec, but I need to see Mr Finch. It's urgent.' She suddenly felt overwhelmed by an unaccustomed shyness, though why that should be Lizzie couldn't imagine. She was behaving like a tongue-tied school-girl who'd never set eyes on a good-looking lad before.

'I'll see if he can fit you in. Take a seat, please.'

The young man left her sitting on a bentwood chair while he disappeared through a doorway. Lizzie could hear the murmur of voices coming from the room beyond but she tried not to listen, keeping her attention fixed instead on a series of posters stuck around the room advertising Finch's products.

Mints have refreshing healing powers, said one. Another displayed a mouth-watering selection of chocolates. Then there were posters showing pear drops, coltsfoot rock, Pontefract cakes and various other sweets. Lizzie hadn't worked her way around them all before the young man re-emerged, the grin on his face wider than ever.

'Sorry, I forgot to ask *your* name. Not that I was bowled over by your charms, or anything daft like that.'

''Course you weren't.' She grinned too, warming to his gaucheness. 'My name is Lizzie. Lizzie Pringle.'

She saw the fine blond brows draw together in a slight frown, and the bright eyes cloud a little. 'Pringle? Not *the* Pringle from

Champion Street Market?' His smile was definitely more forced now.

'The very same.'

'R-right, back in a jiffy.' He sounded less certain as he once again disappeared into the back room and the voices inside rose slightly in pitch, so that she was able to hear her own name mentioned, more than once. Then the door was flung open and there stood Cedric Finch, large and menacing even without the benefit of his usual black overcoat, his round belly almost bursting the buttons of his waistcoat. And the look on his face was like thunder. He might have been the devil incarnate.

Lizzie swallowed hard and managed a polite smile. 'Good morning, Mr Finch, I wonder if I could have a word?'

Silently he held the door open for her to pass through into what must surely be the jaws of hell.

–

Dena was doing her utmost to carry on with life as normal. She bought a pair of blue-checked tea towels from Leo's Bargains and a cream-filled Easter egg for Trudy from Lizzie's sweet stall, chatting idly with her for a moment about the weather and how cold it was. It was one of those chill March mornings when the rain drizzled down and you were reminded that winter still lingered. People were rushing about the market with their noses tucked inside their collars, not sparing much time for gossip and chit-chat.

The hot chestnut man was doing a roaring trade, despite its being early in the day, and most of the stallholders were well clad in scarves, woolly hats and boots, yet still looked half frozen. Working on a market was no joy in this weather.

'I hope trade picks up before Easter,' Dena said to him, content to linger to avoid crossing the market and running into Carl.

'It's allus quiet at this time,' the man cheerily remarked.

The trouble was that although she'd been the one to end the relationship, Dena couldn't help but look for him everywhere she went. Wherever she walked she expected to come face to face with him at any moment. Admittedly for several days after their quarrel she'd avoided going round the back of the market hall where he ran his household goods' stall. But a part of her had half expected him to call on her, and insist they talk some more. He hadn't been near.

Before heading for her workshop and the next batch of skirts she had to stitch that day, Dena called at Barry Holmes's stall for half a cabbage and some potatoes for tea. She meant to make a bit of bubble and squeak for her and Trudy. The first thing he asked was where Carl was.

'Why would I know?' she snapped, mentally steeling herself against discussing the matter as she went on to order a pound of onions. Her reaction swiftly changed to one of concern when Barry explained that he'd seen no sign of Carl or his stall in days.

Dena stared at Barry in silence for a long moment as she paid for the vegetables and a few shiny red apples for Trudy, then despite her better judgement she decided she had to see for herself. She half walked, half ran to where Carl's stall would normally be, only to find the pitch empty, the trestles and planks stacked away.

She asked around, spoke to Jimmy Ramsay whose own butcher's stall overlooked this section of the market, but Barry was right. No one had seen Carl in over a week.

Where had he gone? There seemed only one way to find out and that was to ask his mother, Belle Garside.

Dena contemplated the pros and cons of doing this. Although she'd once got on reasonably well with Carl's mother, Belle wasn't easy to deal with now as she still bore Dena a grudge for dumping Kenny in favour of his elder brother. As if anyone in their right mind would have done anything different!

If Carl had gone off some place to lick his wounds, then that was for the best. And Dena really had no wish to see him in any case, did she? It was over between them. Finished. His choice, not hers.

Yet she had to be sure that he was all right! Dena needed to convince herself too that he would be back, once his pride had recovered and the wound had healed.

An ache seemed to have lodged itself somewhere beneath her heart and Dena couldn't help wondering if her own wound ever would heal. She might well have caused it herself, but it was no less difficult to deal with. But was it all her own fault, or simply the result of circumstance? Worries over the trial had overwhelmed her until she'd felt driven to beg him for a breathing space. Why hadn't Carl appreciated that? Why hadn't *she* appreciated that he needed her assurance she still loved him, and stop blaming him for what his brother had done. Oh, it was all such a mess.

She'd let him go because they couldn't seem to stop quarrelling, but Dena realised now that she'd acted without pausing to consider if she had any real chance of happiness without him.

–

Lizzie stood in his office and told Cedric Finch, in no uncertain terms, that she had not asked Aunty to stop making her *very special* sweets and chocolates, nor had she any intention of doing so. She went on to explain that Aunty's products were most popular on the stall, particularly with children.

'I'm sorry if you're not happy with my Easter egg order, Mr Finch, but such is life. The Chocolate Cabin is small but I know my customers personally, and always aim to provide them with the kind of sweets and chocolates they like best. Aunty Dot enjoys making specialist items, such as Easter eggs, toffee apples and chocolate truffles. It's a limited range and I see nothing wrong in that. I'm sure that I do sufficient business with Finch's over the year to make supplying me worth your while. Now I hope this will be an end of the matter.' Having said her piece,

Lizzie inclined her head with a brief smile and turning on her heel, prepared to leave.

'Hold on a minute, girl. I've not done yet. I'll tell you when you can go.'

Lizzie considered him with haughty disdain. 'I wasn't aware I needed permission. I've said what I came to say, that's all there is to it.'

'Well, that's where you're wrong, miss. I don't care to be told what's what by some whipper-snapper only just out of the classroom. If I say something must be done, then I mean *something must be done*.' Finch took a step towards her, and Lizzie quailed a little before him. He was an ugly man with bulbous cheeks, a down-turned mouth and baggy folds of flesh beneath his eyes. His hair looked as black as his temper, nothing like the tousled blond mop of the boy fidgeting uncomfortably beside him.

'Can I just say something?' the young man put in.

'No, you can't.' Without even glancing at him, Finch bestowed a wintry smile upon Lizzie, showing teeth gone yellow with age, or from eating too much treacle toffee.

'May I remind you,' Lizzie bravely interrupted, before he could say anything more, 'that I am the customer here. If I'm not satisfied with your service then I'm free to go elsewhere. The customer is always right, as the saying goes.'

He laughed as if she'd made some sort of joke. 'I'm feeling generous today, lass, since you obviously have a hearing problem, or a brain defect, you only being female and very young. The fact of the matter is I'll give you a month to put a stop to your aunt's meddling. If I don't see an improvement in your orders by the end of May you'd best start preparing yourself for bankruptcy.'

Lizzie was stunned. She'd been convinced he couldn't possibly be serious about cutting off her supplies, nor had she entirely believed the threat he'd made to blacken her name to other suppliers. She'd hoped it was all bluster and bluff. Why would he do such a thing? What could it possibly matter to Finch if Aunty produced a few items for the stall?

She cleared her throat. 'It's only a few sweets and chocolates Aunty enjoys making, and our customers love to eat them. I really can't see what all the fuss is about.'

'Oh, you can't, can't you? Well, that's because you're only an ignorant young lass and I'm a clever businessman. I haven't got where I am today by letting interfering old bags sell their amateur products alongside my more professional offerings. Cheap, badly made sweets sold next to mine on a stall give Finch's a bad name.'

Lizzie took instant exception to this criticism. 'I could understand your argument if that were true, but Aunty's sweets aren't badly made. They are delicious, and as professionally produced as she can make them.'

'In her kitchen?'

'Indeed.'

'My point exactly! Amateur.'

'You can't possibly expect to have a monopoly.'

'Who says I can't? I can have whatever I want. You'll sell Finch's sweets and only Finch's sweets, or you'll sell nothing at all. I could set up in competition, right alongside your poxy stall, and put you out of business.'

Lizzie was shocked. 'You wouldn't dare!'

He stuck his face so close to hers, she could smell mints mingled with whisky on his breath. 'Make no bones about it, girl, I could and I would, if you annoy me too much.' Then rocking back on his heels he slid his thumbs into the pockets of his waistcoat. '*Now* you can take your leave. I reckon you've got the picture clear by this time, eh? And I have more important business to attend to. I wish you good day.'

Perversely, Lizzie now considered staying and battling it out with him, but had the sense to recognise that she would get absolutely nowhere by doing so. He was the rudest man she'd ever met, and she could feel herself shaking inside from a strange

43

mixture of fear and fury. She turned to leave, coming face to face again with the young man, which somehow made her humiliation complete.

'Charlie, show the young lady out, if you please. Then come back here sharpish, son. We have work to do.'

'Son? You're his son?' Lizzie spun about to face the young man the moment they were alone in the outer office.

Charlie nodded bleakly. 'Afraid so.' But his grin looked unconvincing now as he winced apologetically.

'Then you have my deepest sympathy.' Lizzie stalked away, furious at her own failure, and anxious to get back to the Chocolate Cabin, Lynda Hemley was minding for her. Charlie rushed to block the door before she could dash through it.

'Can I take you out some time? To the flicks maybe, or just a drink, whatever you fancy.'

It was plain that he was desperate not to lose her, or let her walk out of his life when she'd only just walked into it. Lizzie considered him with her cool blue gaze. 'I don't think it would be wise, do you?'

'You mean, considering who my father is? Hey, I didn't get to choose him, my mother did. Not one of her better decisions, I will admit, but there's nothing I can do about it now.'

Lizzie made a sound in her throat that could have meant anything. As she walked away, her head held high, Charlie called after her: 'Six o'clock in the Dog and Duck on Champion Street. I'll be there waiting for you tonight and every night, till you come. Please don't let me down.'

–

Later in the morning, with a stack of skirts at least partially finished, Dena headed over to Winnie's stall to pick up Trudy, give her some dinner, then take her to an afternoon nursery class. As Winnie's haberdashery stall was situated next to her own, her friend often kept an eye on both while Dena was over-seeing the machinists in the workshop. And sometimes minded

Trudy as well, as she had today. Both stalls, unfortunately, were situated close to Belle's café, which meant that Dena's arrival was noticed. Even as Trudy flung herself at her mother and fastened her arms tight about her knees with a squeal of delight, Dena heard the click–clack of Belle's high heels behind her.

'What have you been saying to our Carl, then?'

Dena lifted Trudy up in her arms to give her a cuddle, then turned slowly about to face the older woman. 'Hello, Belle, how are you? Better than the weather, I trust?'

'Cut the cackle and answer the question. As if it isn't bad enough to lose one of my sons because of you, now the other has vanished off the face of the earth.'

Dena sighed, biting her lip against the urge to defend herself. It didn't seem to matter how many times she protested that Kenny had been the master of his own misfortune, her words washed right over his mother. Her boys were like plaster saints in Belle's opinion. No one was allowed to criticise them or find fault with their behaviour, but Belle herself.

But while Dena hesitated over how best to reply, Winnie butted in without pause for thought, all guns firing. 'It's nothing to do with Dena what that jury decided. Your Kenny got himself into this trouble, not the other way around.'

'It's all right, Winnie, I can fight my own battles.'

'Then why don't you?' Belle poked a sharply pointed, scarlet, fingernail into Dena's chest. 'Speak up! Admit it. You've chucked him, haven't you? You've done to our Carl the same as you did to our Kenny. You've led him up the garden path then slammed the door in his face. If that's not the way of it then explain to me why I got a note this morning telling me he'd gone, and wouldn't be coming back?'

Belle waved a piece of paper in Dena's face and a chill settled around her heart. Not coming back? She hadn't believed him when he'd said he couldn't bear to stay around the market if he wasn't allowed to love her. Now a chasm opened inside and Dena felt sick. In that moment she saw that she couldn't even begin to contemplate a future without him. What had possessed her to sacrifice any hope of happiness just because the trial had upset her?

Her voice shook with emotion. 'I swear I don't know where he's gone! I wanted to ask you the very same question. It's true we haven't been getting on too well lately, what with the strain of the trial, and we did have a bit of a row. Carl told me you were intending to appeal the sentence, which I found difficult to deal with on top of everything else. I felt I needed a breathing space and suggested we shouldn't see each other for a while, to give me time to come to terms with things. Carl wasn't happy about that. He wanted me to agree, there and then, to marry him, but I couldn't.'

''Course she couldn't,' Winnie chipped in, until Dena silenced her with a look.

Belle's painted lips curled. 'I think you should be grateful my son was prepared to marry you at all, not to mention taking on his brother's child as his own. I'm surprised you'd even consider refusing. I reckon you must enjoy the notoriety of being an unmarried mother.'

Dena felt the blood drain from her face and instinctively put out a protective hand to Trudy. 'This isn't the time or place for such a discussion.' She turned to go but Belle grabbed her wrist, making the little girl rock in her mother's arms and start to whimper.

'Mam!'

Winnie stepped forward, the light of battle in her eye. 'Here, don't you harm that child or you'll have me to answer to.' She was pushing up her cardigan sleeves as if preparing for a fist fight.

Dena put a gentle hand on her friend's shoulder. 'It's all right, Winnie. Don't cry, Trudy, Mummy's fine. Belle, please stop shouting and threatening us, you're frightening her. This isn't the way. Can't you see you're upsetting Trudy with your drama-queen tantrums?'

'Tantrums? Is that what you call a mother's right to defend her son? I haven't even started yet. There's going to be an appeal, and we're going to win it. I'll show you what sort of drama queen I can be! A real Boadicea. And you'd do well to remember that I've as much right to that child as you have, more even since I'm her grandma and have far more sense than a slip of a girl like you. More than nosy Winnie Holmes here.'

A beat of fear started up in Dena's chest. Belle liked to push her nose in where it wasn't wanted, but never so bluntly. 'I'm not sure what it is you're trying to say, Belle, but although you can obviously do as you choose for your own son, you have absolutely no rights over my child. None at all. Trudy is mine.'

'Just tell me where Carl is or you'll find out how much trouble I can cause. He must've said something about where he was going.'

'I've told you, I've no idea, and whatever took place between us, is our business, not yours. Now, I'm taking *my* child home, thanks very much.'

'Your *bastard*, you mean!'

Whereupon Winnie did pop her one, right on the nose. And as Belle went flying and blood spurted, Dena fled.

Chapter Six

Belle Garside did not take kindly to being crossed. She was a woman who liked to have her own way in most things. As she nursed her sore nose she went over her encounter with Dena, cold fury in her heart. Anybody with any sense knew that Dena Dobson's brother had been a bit of a tearaway, always up to mischief. Was it any wonder he'd got himself into the kind of bother that led to tragedy?

Belle was certain the lad had been the one who'd started it all, had merely got what was coming to him; sad though it undoubtedly was that a young life should be lost in such a tragic way.

But why should Kenny be made to suffer? It wasn't his fault entirely. Belle was convinced it must have been an accident, a boyish joke gone wrong, and her son did not deserve a life sentence. She wanted him out of that horrible jail as soon as possible.

Carl was innocent in all of this, having done nothing worse than fall in love with his brother's former girlfriend.

Belle told herself she'd always nursed doubts about that girl who ran for cover the minute there was any talk of long-term commitment. Oh, but didn't *she* know just what made that little madam tick? Dena Dobson obviously enjoyed having a handsome man at her beck and call. Well, who didn't? Belle had enjoyed the company of many men in her life, besides the two who'd fathered her sons, and could appreciate how easily a girl's head was turned. There were many on this market who'd been ready to call Belle a brazen hussy in her day, but then she'd always been stunning. Still was, in fact, while Dena was no more than pretty at best.

Yet the lass was far too full of herself, no better than she should be, that much was all too evident, and ruthless with it. She'd dumped Kenny and got her claws into Carl, dangling him like a fish on a hook for over a year.

Shameless and selfish, that was Dena Dobson. And if someone else, even the child's own grandmother, showed the slightest interest in that precious Trudy of hers, she turned difficult.

There might be another reason for her erratic behaviour, though. Belle had observed it often enough in the past with girls who came into the vicinity of her younger son. Dena Dobson was scared stiff. The lass was furious that they'd lodged an appeal, terrified that if it was successful and the charge was reduced to manslaughter, Kenny would be out in ten years or so and coming back home to Champion Street to haunt her.

And no wonder. He wouldn't take kindly to her having had him arrested, just so she could get her hands on his brother. Serve the little madam right if he did give her what for! Neither of her boys were wimps, but Kenny was definitely the one to be most wary of.

Unfortunately, soft Carl had fallen for the girl hard and taken her rejection too much to heart. Where could the daft sod be hiding? Belle guessed she'd have her work cut out to find him and help him get over this mess.

But that little madam shouldn't be allowed to chuck both her precious boys and get away with it. It wasn't right, not in Belle's opinion. It was long past time the stupid girl paid for all this bother she'd caused. And come to think of it, hadn't she already set up the means to her own downfall? A smile came into Belle's violet eyes and curled her scarlet lips as she considered how best to use it to her own advantage.

–

With Easter almost upon them, Lizzie had started work early this morning, and trade had been brisk. So busy that she anxiously counted her remaining stock of Easter eggs. Not being able to repeat the order with Finch's was going to lose her valuable trade. She'd hardly slept a wink these last few nights going over that interview time and again in her mind. Had she handled it badly? Was there something she could have done differently?

Lizzie hadn't gone to meet one fair haired, grey-eyed charmer in the Dog and Duck that evening, nor any evening since, although the thought of him waiting in vain for her had kept her awake too.

How was she going to survive? She'd already rung a few alternative supplies and so far had got nowhere. Everyone was too busy, saying they'd talk to her after Easter. In the meantime, she was running short of stock and there was a limit to what she could expect Aunty to do.

Later in the morning, Lynda Hemley wandered over for a chat about her latest boyfriend. On the spur of the moment, Lizzie asked her to mind the stall for half an hour while she popped back to check on Aunty.

'Would you mind, Lynda?'

'Not at all. I hope she's not sickening for something.'

'So do I, particularly since we're so busy, but I'm that worried about her. She's not herself. Keeps clutching her side but refuses to see a doctor.'

Lynda looked concerned. 'I could ask Mam to have a word with her, if you like? Few people can argue with our Betty.'

Lizzie laughed. 'Would you? I'd appreciate it. I'll not be long. Help yourself to one of those strawberry creams, they're delicious.'

Lizzie found Aunty Dot boiling sugar in a copper pan and stood silently by in respectful silence, sipping the coffee she'd quickly made. It wasn't unusual for her to pop over for one if Lynda was around to give her a break. Now she was here, though, Lizzie didn't know how to begin, how to explain that their livelihood was in danger despite Aunty continually working her socks off.

'Have you made an appointment yet to see that doctor?' she began.

'I'm going tomorrow.'

'To see him?'

'No, to make an appointment. As you can see, I'm a bit busy today. My word, but you've a long face on you this morning. What's up?' Aunty asked, neatly changing the subject as she cut two large coconuts into slices and proceeded to grate them.

'Nothing I can't deal with.' Maybe it would be best not to mention the problems she was having over lack of stock, Lizzie reasoned. Aunty had enough on her plate already and she'd no wish to worry her over things she could do nothing about. As Lizzie sipped her coffee she tried to think of other solutions to her dilemma, yet was having trouble keeping her straying thoughts away from one eager young man. She smiled up at Aunty. 'What are you making, coconut ice?'

'The kids love it.'

'So do I.' Lizzie got up and went to stand beside the older woman. Cissie was playing with the latest baby on the rug. The other children were at school and the house seemed strangely silent without them.

'Has your glum mood something to do with all them visits we've been getting lately, from Jack Cleaver?'

'Nothing much escapes you, does it?'

'Not when it concerns my best girl. I saw Finch's car parked outside when Jack called the other week, so I guessed it was something more than the love bug that was biting him. Is this what the mighty Finch is objecting to?' Dot indicated the frothing mixture in the pan. 'Does he see me as competition? If so then I'm flattered.'

Lizzie chuckled. 'Anyone would think twice before taking you on, Aunty. I doubt he'll carry out his threats.'

'And what might these threats be?'

Lizzie let out a sigh. 'He's just throwing his weight around, that's all. I'm sure it'll all blow over if we ignore him.'

'Tell me exactly what he said.' Dot checked the temperature of the boil, and, satisfied with the result, began to add the grated coconut to the pan as Lizzie told her the full story.

When she was done, Aunty Dot snorted her derision. 'If it came to a war between him and us, you don't need to be a genius to work out who'd win. Cedric Finch is not well liked, hereabouts. Too full of himself with his big house and grand ideas, *and* he treats his workers like dirt. But everybody loves you, our Lizzie, everybody who knows you, and your customers would stand by you.'

'It's the ordinary customer who doesn't really know me, we should be worrying about. We can't afford to lose any trade, and Finch's claim that he has the power to stop anyone else supplying me is a bit worrying.'

'It won't happen,' Aunty said, sliding the big pan off the heat and graining the sugar by rubbing small portions of it against the pan with a wooden spatula. 'It wouldn't be worth his while. As you say, he's making a lot of noise about nothing and will soon see sense. So stop your fretting and get back to that stall. I want to have this batch finished before the kids come charging in for their dinners.'

So saying, Aunty began to pour the coconut mixture into the prepared tins. ''Course, there is one solution we should consider. I could just do as he says and stop making sweets.'

Lizzie looked at this woman she adored, as soft as a caramel cream when it came to children, but with iron in her soul and fierce brown eyes. She recalled the numerous occasions when social workers and cruelty men had attempted to bully Dot into submission, and lived to rue the day. 'I can't believe you're saying this. You're not usually one to run for cover.'

Aunty chuckled. 'Nor am I now. I was just thinking about you. Taking on Finch won't be easy.'

There was a slight pause in which Lizzie considered the truth of this simple statement. Finch was perfectly capable of making her life extremely uncomfortable. The only thing was, Lizzie was perverse enough to hate being told what to do. And she would forever regret it if she gave in to his demands.

'We need more toffee apples. Do you reckon you might have time to make some of those tomorrow?'

Dot's round face creased into laughter and her currant bun eyes twinkled. 'Just try and stop me.'

Lizzie smiled. 'Would I ever?'

—

'Why don't we go out to the flicks and cheer ourselves up?' Winnie suggested. 'You've been down-in-the-mouth for days now. Our Barry would babysit, wouldn't you chuck?'

'Aye, course I would.' Her husband began to tickle Trudy, making the little girl wriggle and gasp with helpless laughter. 'We could have a grand time, eh, you and me?'

Dena shook her head, dragging the child away from Barry and lifting her protectively in her arms once more. 'No thanks, I'm not in the mood. Another time perhaps. I just fancy a quiet evening alone, thanks all the same.'

'Well, if you change your mind, you know where to find me,' Barry offered, looking disappointed as always whenever she refused his offers to babysit. Dena was aware that Barry loved children, and Trudy in particular, but didn't like to take advantage of his good nature. And she felt the need at the moment to be on her own, to lick her wounds and think things through.

Life seemed to be spinning out of control. She hadn't intended Carl to vanish off the face of the earth just because she'd asked him for some breathing space before committing herself. Nor had she expected Winnie to get into a fist fight with Belle Garside, though she'd often been tempted to do the same herself.

Winnie walked with her along Champion Street to the door of her old house where Dena now lived, Trudy between them, holding each woman by the hand.

'Eeh, this is a right kettle of fish and no mistake, though a bust nose is the least of Belle's problems. I can't say I've much sympathy for the woman. She brought it on herself. She should've kept them lads of hers on a tighter leash, instead of believing the sun shone out of their backsides.'

'I'd rather you didn't lump Carl along with Kenny. They're as different as chalk and cheese. It's no fault of Carl's what his brother did, or that I've called things off between us. It's all down to me. The fault is mine entirely. I just needed time to think, time to get over the trial. I wanted to be sure that marrying Carl was the right thing to do, in the circumstances.'

''Course you did. Nothing wrong with giving yourself a bit of breathing space. Chin up, chuck,' Winnie said, addressing the remark to Dena while tickling Trudy under the chin. The little girl was looking from one to the other of them, clearly worried by their tone of voice.

'What's a bastid?' she suddenly asked, making heads turn as her clear young voice rang out, surprisingly loud in the quiet street. Dena and Winnie looked at each other, startled, and then fell to giggling.

'We shouldn't laugh, it's a serious matter,' Dena whispered, and attempted to explain to her daughter that it was a rude word people should never use.

'That lady said it.'

'I know she did, and it wasn't nice.'

'She looked like the mad Queen in my *Alice In Wonderland* book.'

'Aye,' Winnie said, chortling with glee. 'She did an' all. Child's got it in one. That's what Belle is, a madwoman, though more like the Wicked Witch of the North than the Queen of Hearts.'

'Stop it,' Dena scolded, struggling not to laugh. 'You'll be giving Trudy nightmares. Take no notice of Winnie, love, she's just telling one of her fairy stories.'

'I want one. Tell me a fairy story, Aunt Win.'

So Winnie had to come into the house and read Trudy a story to distract her. When she'd gone, and Dena and Trudy were finally alone, Dena ran a bath and put in some bubbles. Then giggling like a two-year-old herself, she lifted Trudy into the water with her and the pair of them had a fine old time splashing each other. Trudy piled bubbles on her mother's head, and caused tremendous storms in the bath water in an attempt to upset the little blue yacht, which bobbed about between them.

By the time Dena was wrapping her child in a big warm towel and drying her off with Johnson's baby talc, the unpleasant exchange with Belle had gone out of her mind. Winnie was right, there was nothing at all wrong with asking for breathing space. Carl should have understood and been prepared to give her time. He surely would be prepared to do that, once he'd cooled down and thought things through. Maybe he too needed a bit of time on his own, wherever it was he was hiding. He did love her, Dena was sure of it, but he was also fiercely loyal to his brother.

In the meantime, she had her own family to think of. Dena kissed Trudy's soft round cheek, scented with baby powder, and thought how lucky she was to have such a lovely child. Who could ask for more?

–

Lizzie had a busy afternoon on the stall, selling lots of Easter eggs and baskets of yellow marzipan chicks in bright sugar waistcoats. But she couldn't get the image of that cheeky young man out of her mind, wondering if he had indeed waited for her night after night in the Dog and Duck. If he went on waiting, as he'd promised, what did she care? She'd no intention of going to meet him, not this evening, nor any other.

Getting involved with Finch's son would bring nothing but trouble into her life, and she really couldn't be doing with any more. Finch was a bully, so wouldn't his son be tarred with the same brush? Lizzie told herself this very firmly, as she helped Aunty put the younger children to bed at six o'clock that night.

So how was it that an hour later she found herself going through the swing doors of the Dog and Duck, wearing her favourite plaid skirt, matching tam o'shanter, and new blue jersey? She really couldn't understand it herself.

He was sitting in a quiet corner and leapt to his feet as soon as he saw her, his grey eyes shining with such delight Lizzie's heart shifted inside her, or so it seemed.

She stood before him, not sure where to put her hands and carefully avoided meeting his gaze. 'I only came to tell you to stop waiting for me because I'm not going out with you.'

He looked at her, an irrepressible smile lifting one corner of his mouth. 'That's why you're here now, is it, to tell me you're not coming?'

'That's right,' Lizzie agreed. 'I should have come and said it that first night but I had other things on my mind, as you will appreciate. Anyway, I thought I'd come over and make the situation clear, just in case you were waiting.'

'Well, thank goodness for that. I'd hate to have sat here for the rest of my life, and all for nothing.'

'That's what I thought.'

A slight pause while he considered this. 'I might not be waiting for you at all, but just sitting here having a quiet pint.'

Lizzie flushed. 'I realise that, but I wanted to say that if you *were* waiting for me, then don't. I never asked you to.'

'I never wanted to clap eyes on you in the first place. *You* were the one who came to the factory. I never asked you to show up in my life, so it's your fault if I'm stuck with thinking about you all the time. Hardly fair, is it?'

Lizzie cast a startled glance at him through her lashes, curious to understand exactly what he was saying, whether he was being argumentative or simply teasing her. Something in his falsely aggrieved expression made her want to laugh out loud, and her lips twitched. 'You don't have to think about me at all. I didn't ask you to do that either.'

'I never intended to, that's for sure. It's most annoying. Well, do you want a Coca-Cola at least, then I haven't come all this way entirely for nothing?'

Minutes later Lizzie was sipping Coke through a long straw, spluttering with laughter as Charlie continued to complain about her sudden appearance in his life.

'You realise I was about to join the Navy and sail the seven seas? I had every intention of enjoying exciting adventures, fighting pirates and doing a bit of swash and buckle like chaps do. How can I enjoy any of that now?'

'I'm not stopping you.'

'I can hardly just walk away from the loveliest girl I've ever set eyes on in my whole life, now can I? Be fair! But if I've made this huge sacrifice and agreed to remain a landlubber, couldn't you at least make a smaller one and come out with me? I doubt I'll bother asking you again. I can't waste too much of my valuable time chasing after you, pining away like some lovesick fool. I'd never do that. It's not in my nature, you understand.'

'Oh, yes, I understand completely,' Lizzie said, pressing her lips firmly together to stop herself from laughing out loud.

His face was alight with mischief. 'Good, I'm glad we've got that sorted out. Tomorrow at six?'

'Certainly not! It's Easter weekend and I've better things to do.'

'Next week then?'

'I'm busy.'

'Or next month?'

'I'll think about it. Will that do?'

'Okay, but don't expect me to hang around forever. I've wasted more than enough evenings waiting for you already.'

'I'm not asking you to wait. That's why I came along tonight, to tell you not to hang around.'

He looked suddenly morose. 'So you said. Are you always this cruel?'

'Oh, no! Only with people I really dislike.'

'That's all right then.' And he gave her his irrepressible grin.

Lizzie had never believed in love at first sight, but in her heart she knew she'd fallen for Charlie Finch, hook, line and sinker. There was absolutely no getting away from it.

—

Dena vomited into the bathroom sink and knew, without a doubt, that she was pregnant. She was only a couple of weeks late but the signs were already unmistakable. Too late now to wish she hadn't rashly rejected Carl. Not a day had passed since he'd vanished when she didn't long to see him striding across the market towards her, his loving smile directed only at her.

How had she even contemplated facing life without him when she loved him so much? Where was he, she worried, and would he ever return? Not for one moment had she expected him actually to *leave*, yet was it entirely fair of her to expect him to hang around when she'd point-blank refused to marry him?

They'd been through so much together. He was a good man, a kind man, and he loved her. He'd accepted Trudy as if she were his own daughter. Even put up with Dena's dreadful mother. And she'd get no help in that direction.

Dena had thought she'd seen the back of Alice, yet somehow she hadn't been surprised when she'd turned up at the door one day like a bad penny, claiming to be homeless and begging to be taken in. Wasn't that typical of the selfish woman she was, with the hide of a rhinoceros?

But although Alice Dobson was a whining, difficult, over-critical, snobby pain in the backside, how could Dena leave her own mother without a roof over her head? She hadn't been able to find it in herself to refuse, although she'd been sorely tempted as it hadn't worked out. In no time at all they'd been at each other's throats, just like the old days only worse, with complaints and criticism, morning, noon and night. It hadn't been long before Alice had gone off again in one of her sulks.

Dena told herself she was not responsible for her mother; that she no longer needed to run around fetching and carrying for her, running all the errands, making the meals and doing all the work around the house to the tune of her constant disparagement. She was no longer that half-starved, neglected child, scorned and intimidated by a feckless, selfish mother. She was a young woman, and a mother herself who'd been through the mill one way or another.

Was that part of her problem? Rarely would you find Dena's dark curling lashes wet with tears these days. She was all too aware that she was very much in control, rarely showing any sign of emotion.

But then she'd learned, at Ivy Bank where the social had sent her without a word of protest from her mother, that any sign of emotion was seen as weakness. And if you were to survive, it was a dangerous indulgence you simply couldn't afford. Strength at any price was essential. Pride, hurt feelings, regret, guilt, all of that stuff must be set aside in order to pit yourself against the harsh challenge of surviving another day.

The day her childish need to rebel had led her to lie with Kenny Garside was the day she'd relinquished all her self-respect, one she'd later come to regret with all her heart. But Dena now possessed a precious child, and would put her own life on the line to keep her safe.

And despite the problems between them, it was hardly fair to blame Carl for the sins of his brother.

Maybe she wouldn't have acted so hastily if she hadn't been desperately upset by the trial, where she'd been required to give evidence. That hadn't been easy, and now it looked as if she would have to go through it all over again at the appeal. Would she be showing by then? Would the judge and jury look down their collective noses, thinking here is a harlot, a whore, a silly young girl who has borne the illegitimate child of one brother and now carries the child of the other?

Shame scoured her raw insides as Dena's already empty stomach convulsed yet again. What a fool she'd been! What she wouldn't give to have her lovely Carl back, to hold him close to her heart and admit she'd been wrong, that she'd panicked, when really she was dying for love of him.

But he was gone. She'd lost him.

Footsteps pounded up the stairs and Dena quickly wiped her mouth on the towel, desperately trying to summon up a smile as she reached for her toothbrush.

'Mummy, Mummy, Aunty Win says breakfast is ready, and it's gone eight o'clock.'

Winnie had developed the habit of popping round to cook breakfast, or just to help her 'get the child ready'. Dena had tried times without number to persuade her out of it, so far to no avail. Winnie undoubtedly missed having them around now that she was married to Barry and living in his house further down the street.

'Aunty Win says she's fried you two sausages, so will you be quick and come and eat them all up?'

'Oh, God!' Dena put her head in the sink and longed simply to die.

Chapter Seven

The need for revenge against Dena continued to fester inside Belle Garside, convinced she'd treated both her sons badly. Later in the week, when Miss Rogers called in for a cup of frothy coffee, she took the social worker aside for a quiet word.

Belle placed a shortbread biscuit before her, smiling when the older woman protested that she hadn't ordered one. 'You were looking a bit down in the dumps on this wet morning. I thought it might cheer you up.'

Miss Rogers pursed her thin lips, unused to such acts of kindness. 'Thank you. I must say few people appreciate the pressure I'm under, and even fewer would think to be so generous.'

'Don't mention it.' Glancing about her, Belle quickly checked that all her customers had been attended to, then sat down opposite. Miss Rogers looked surprised at her presumption, as well she might. Undeterred, Belle asked, 'Do you still keep an eye on Dena?'

'I keep a close eye on all my gels, as I like to call them. Those who have been under my care at one time or another.'

Belle scratched idly at a ketchup mark on the blue-checked tablecloth with one crimson fingernail. 'I expect you were thinking she'd be getting married soon, and then your task would be complete?'

'I believe she is to marry your elder son, Mrs Garside?' Miss Rogers never had approved of the Garside family, although Carl was infinitely better than his brother, no question about that. Dena claimed he was gentle and kind with a strong sense of family. Even so, she really thought the girl could do better. But then anything would be better, in Miss Rogers' opinion, than having Belle Garside as a mother-in-law.

'She was. It's all off now.'

'I'm sorry to hear that.'

'I thought you should know.'

'I'm most obliged.' A pause while Miss Rogers considered the implications of this revelation. She didn't take kindly to sudden changes of mind where her 'gels' were concerned. Generally speaking they needed stability in their lives, not constant change. Suddenly, Carl Garside seemed like the perfect answer to all Dena's prayers, particularly since he was so family-minded.

'I really feel it's time better arrangements were made for the child, don't you?' Belle said, interrupting the other woman's thoughts. 'It means, you see, that poor little Trudy is still without a father, while her mother is nothing more than a foolish butterfly flitting from man to man.'

A description Miss Rogers thought she might apply to Belle Garside rather than Dena, the girl's faults being largely the result of a difficult childhood and youthful rebellion. 'Are you suggesting you may apply for custody yourself, Mrs Garside?' Miss Rogers sharply enquired, privately deciding that hell would need to freeze over before she agreed to such an arrangement.

Belle began titivating her hennaed curls as she noticed Alec Hall approaching. 'I have far greater experience of motherhood than that little madam. I would be delighted to oblige, as always.'

Watching her pout her scarlet lips and smile at the new arrival, Miss Rogers managed to avoid the obvious response. 'It's a pity about her and Carl breaking up. Dena must be upset.'

Belle stood up, smoothing down her flirty little apron over the tight, black skirt that strained over voluptuous hips. 'It was she who dumped him, not the reverse. Bad reaction to the trial, apparently, and worries over a possible appeal. Carl suffered the consequences, poor lad. He was so cut up about it he's run off, God knows where. To join the Foreign Legion, I shouldn't wonder. He's potty about that girl, and she's a heartless little madam.'

'I can sympathise with the emotional upset caused by the trial, but to react so hastily was very foolish of Dena, very foolish indeed. This is most regrettable, most regrettable indeed.' Miss Rogers sucked in her breath. 'Do you think Carl might come back soon?'

But Belle was too busy making sheep's eyes at Alec Hall to discuss the matter further. In any case, she'd planted the seeds of doubt in Miss Roger's mind, made her own generous offer, and really had no more to say. 'Sorry, love, I'll have to go. Customers to feed, you know how it is.' And off she sashayed to cook Alec his regular full English, which he enjoyed every morning.

Miss Rogers proceeded to eat her free shortbread, a frown of deep concern on her face. This did not bode well for Dena's future, not well at all.

–

Alan revved up his engines to a high-pitched whine before shouting, 'Chocks Away!' and starting to taxi along the cobbles. Champion Street Market wasn't the easiest runway to take off from, he decided, as he negotiated his way between the late afternoon crowds busily checking out the rows of stalls with their striped awnings and racks of merchandise.

He spotted Joey and called out to him, 'Where you off to, Joe?'

'None of your flamin' business.'

Alan throttled back so that he could hear better over the sound of the engines. 'Going boxing, are you?'

'Aye, it's an exhibition match tonight.'

Alan forgot for a moment that he was in the cock-pit of his Spitfire and jumped up and down on the spot. 'Ooh, can I come?'

'Don't be daft. Boxing is for big lads like me, not tiddlers like you.'

Alan looked crestfallen. 'Will *you* teach me then, Joe? On the quiet like.'

Joey thrust his hands in his pockets and walked on. 'No, I won't. You don't want to get into no bloody fighting or somebody might knock your daft noddle off.'

There was a time when Joey had enjoyed showing off his prowess in the ring. He could jab and cross better than most lads his age, which was why Barry Holmes was always putting him in for competitions, but he'd never had any great enthusiasm for fighting. He didn't want to end up like his da, believing he could win any argument by belting the life out of someone.

His father was far too keen on using fisticuffs, claiming it was the best way to keep his wife in line, his son too if he got half a chance. Joey had learned never to retaliate. If he couldn't escape his father's drunken temper then he would hunker down and hope the beating didn't last too long. He didn't even do anything to protect his mam, not these days.

Once or twice, when he was younger, he'd flown at his da, screaming for him to leave her alone. But his small fists and feet had made little impression and Big Joe had simply swatted him aside as if he were nothing more than an annoying insect, casually splitting his lip or cracking his head against the wall; using him like a punch bag till Joey was whimpering and begging him to stop.

There were times, when his da was off the booze, when he could be sweet as pie, although that didn't happen anywhere near often enough. Joey privately saw himself as a coward because whenever he saw the rage building up in his da, he scarpered. He'd run out of the house leaving his mam screaming and begging for mercy from her brutal husband. And Joey did nothing to help her, too busy vomiting his guts out into the gutter.

Even to this day he always felt sick if he saw anyone getting hurt, even a cat. But then his da had been fond of kicking the

64

shit out of those poor animals as well. Joey's last one had ended up tied to a tree by its neck, being used for batting practise.

He wished he could explain all of this to Aunty Dot, but how could he when she never asked any questions? She just went on and on about how he needed to be healthy and keep fit, and how boxing helped to give him a full body workout, whatever that might be. She'd probably read it in some magazine or other, or else she was just glad to have him off the streets and out of her hair for an hour or two.

The only thing Aunty Dot had said that made any sense was when she'd looked him straight in the eye and declared, 'You need to know how to defend yourself, Joey, me lad.'

That had been like a revelation to him. It was for this reason, and this reason alone, that he'd agreed to join the club. After all, he'd only got away from his old life after his da had put him in hospital by cracking a couple of his ribs.

After that incident Mam claimed to have dumped her husband and to be trying to make a go of it on her own with Joey's three brothers. Joey loved his mam and liked to go home now and then to see her. He'd go home more if he could be sure that his da wouldn't turn up. But more often than not Big Joe would come round at some point, even though he'd been told to stay away. He'd be out of his skull on the booze and beat the living daylights out of them all.

Then his mam would be in pieces and Joey would be sent back to Aunty's, thankful the cruelty people hadn't sent him to a stranger. Joey had endured more foster homes in his time than most people had hot dinners, and he was tired of it. He didn't trust any of them. Sanctimonious do-gooders, most of them. You only had to spit or have an accident on their precious flaming sheets and you were back in that so-called orphanage faster than you could say 'Jack Robinson'.

So Joey had devised a plan. He liked living with Aunty Dot. Her house was safe and peaceful, good food appeared on the table at regular intervals, and they all had a bit of a laugh.

Most of all, Joey was tired of being beaten by his old man, so his dream was that, much as he might hate the boxing, if he kept up the training then one day he might find the skill, small as he was, to turn the tables on the brute and knock him out cold. He'd like to see his da, instead of his mam, sprawled senseless on the floor with blood spurting from his fat nose.

Joey lived for that day.

–

Tonight Joey was swapping a few punches with Spider, who could be real mean when he put his mind to it, and was a few years older than him. Undeterred by the other boy's greater skill Joey was giving his all, not that Barry was ever satisfied.

'Get some power behind that right hook, lad. Follow through, like I showed you. Go on, keep moving, and watch your timing. Look out – duck – oops! Pick him up, someone, dust him off.'

Joey's head rang as someone splashed a cold sponge in his face, Barry still barking instructions in his ear, reminding him how much he had to learn. 'You don't have the killer instinct yet, lad, but we'll put it there, don't you fret. One way or another, we'll put it there.'

Joey hoped Barry was right. He needed to acquire it before his da did for him, or his mam, first.

Barry was pleased with the boy's progress, proud of him as he was of all the boys. As a treat this evening he'd invited someone special along to meet them.

Smiley O'Donnell was one of boxing's great legends, a celebrated Irish bare-knuckle fighter. A star from the thirties, the old fighter had agreed to stay on afterwards and go a trial round or two with any budding new talent.

He was getting on a bit now, but never had hung up his gloves and could still be seen in the Arena on Rochdale Road. He may appear to be a grey-haired, old has-been to some, but to his local fans he was still a big favourite. He was a great big laughing, cheerful bloke who wanted to be everybody's friend. Hence the nickname.

'Watch and learn,' Barry told his lads as he ushered them into their seats for the exhibition match. The small room he used as a gym was packed to the doors with boys and their parents, standing room only, everyone eager to witness the old warrior in action.

'Smiley's finest fight was beating local welterweight champion Flinty Connors. They slugged it out for five rounds before Connors finally threw in the towel. Ain't that right, Smiley?'

'I'd've got him in four if his mother hadn't been in the hall. Didn't want to show him up too soon.' And he winked, making everyone laugh.

Billy Quinn had set up the match tonight, since he acted as agent for several professional boxers as well as for a few old-timers like Smiley. Barry didn't much care for Quinn, a nasty piece of work who'd sell his own grandmother, if he had one, to earn a bob or two. But Quinn could always be counted on when a game needed promoting, or a match fixing for that matter.

Barry's club wasn't licensed to run proper boxing tournaments, but a demonstration by a seasoned pro was allowed, since it gave young hopefuls the opportunity to watch in the flesh a boxing legend who'd once earned a small fortune fighting the young bloods of Manchester in the Junction Stadium and Belle Vue.

Smiley had earned top whack then, getting as much as eight quid for a fifteen-rounder, and bookies such as Billy Quinn had always been in attendance whenever a match of his was promoted. They preferred the six-rounder where young lads would be out to impress, boxing their hearts out to get noticed and picked for the big time. The stakes were always raised if a few side bets were laid on the game, the desire to win, often causing youngsters to lose control and make rash mistakes. Barry strongly disapproved, as he intended to keep a close eye on events this evening, to make sure his lads weren't taken advantage of.

Smiley entered the ring with all the swagger of a Roman gladiator while Barry's young hopefuls watched in wide-eyed admiration as he skilfully dispatched his opponent.

It was to thunderous applause following the exhibition match that Quinn stepped forward to address the spectators gathered about the ring.

'Aren't we all aware that this fine fighter here started his career working the boxing booths? And to show how generous he is, Smiley has agreed to give some of you young bloods the chance to show off your skills in the grand tradition of those days. If you "catch the gloves",' Billy Quinn told them with a wink, 'you get to fight this great champion. In the old-time booths you'd've had to go three rounds, but I know that Barry here would say that's too much for you young 'uns.' Quinn grinned across at him and winked.

Barry wanted to object, to say that his lads were nowhere near ready to take on the likes of Smiley O'Donnell, but how could he without demolishing their confidence? He'd keep a close eye, though, make sure no harm came to them.

Quinn said, 'And since Smiley is on his own tonight, sure we don't want to tire him out, now do we? So we'll say that if you're still standing at the end of one round, you win half the bets placed. Can't say fairer than that now, can I?'

A great cheer went up. Then Quinn was at Barry's side, challenging him to place the first bet. 'Come on, Barry, me lad. Sure, and isn't it in a good cause, giving your boys a leg up the ladder to success?'

Barry gritted his teeth and dug deep in his pocket. He already owed Quinn a fair sum and really had no wish to get mired any deeper, but felt powerless to protest.

The first few 'volunteers' didn't last longer than thirty seconds, a minute at most, but all left the ring beaming, content to have had this opportunity to exchange a few punches with a boxing legend. And the cash was mounting as proud parents were all anxious to place a bet on their lad.

And then the gloves fell on Joey's lap. He was far too young at eleven, and didn't look half so thrilled to be chosen as his predecessors, yet valiantly he stepped forward, ready to play the game.

–

Smiley could have given him a pasting but he was gentle with the boy, acknowledging his youth and something vulnerable in him. Joey put up his fists, struggling to think clearly, to guess ahead what his opponent's likely move might be while striving to react quickly enough to the jabs that were raining down on him with alarming regularity. It might not have been the longest round in the world, lasting less than a minute, but the lad didn't disgrace himself. Then an unlucky punch of Smiley's sent him sprawling and Barry called a halt.

Joey looked dazed and tottered slightly as he climbed out of the ring to great applause, the next boy already eager to take his place.

'You put up a good show, boy,' Barry told him, 'though you look like you've walked into a door with that split lip. Old Smiley never meant to hurt you, I reckon you caught his glove at the wrong angle. Aunty Dot'll kill me though if you go home looking like that. Come on.' He marched the boy off to the cloakroom to mop him up. He believed in taking care of his lads.

Barry cleaned him up carefully, making the boy wince as he dabbed at the lip with witch hazel.

'That's better, now get into the shower and keep warm.'

Joey had just stripped off when the door opened and in walked Quinn.

'Now what would you be doing with that young lad, Barry Holmes?' he asked in his treacherously soft Irish brogue.

'It wouldn't be the first time though, would it?' Quinn and Barry were standing in his office, Joey having gone home after his shower, ignorant, or so Barry hoped, of the implied meaning behind Quinn's nasty remark. 'Yer not trying to tell me that you've always been as pure as the proverbial driven snow? Sure, and I'd not believe a word of it, not with all these pretty young lads around. You must be aware of the rumours, which have circulated around the market for years.'

Barry was white to the lips. 'I *am* aware of the gossip, yes, just because I've been single a long time, but that doesn't make it true. Any such rumours are entirely unfounded. Whatever people might say, I look after my boys. I'd give my own life for them.'

Quinn lit one cigarette off the butt of another, a smile twisting one corner of his wide mouth. 'If you say so, Barry, old chum.'

Barry walked to the door. 'I'd like you to leave now, if you please.'

'I don't think I'm done yet. Surely there was something else I wanted to say, if I could but recall what it was? Ah, yes, I remember, so I do.' Sauntering over to him, Quinn stuck his face so close, Barry could smell the rank odour of whisky and stale cigarettes on his breath. 'I was thinking that *meb-be* you and me could be useful to each other. Scratch each other's back, as it were.'

Barry's lip curled. 'I wouldn't exchange the time of day with you, Quinn, if I didn't have to. I'm grateful to you for setting up matches like this one tonight, but that doesn't mean that you and me are buddies. We have a working relationship, nothing more.'

Quinn patted him gently on the cheek. The gesture was meant to be patronising and insulting. Barry jerked away. Quinn made a little tutting sound.

'Aren't I happy to be of service? And it could be so much more, could it not? I do ye a favour, like tonight, and in return you do one for me.'

Barry frowned. 'I haven't the first idea what you're talking about.'

Quinn turned away from him, dropped into Barry's chair and swung his booted feet up on to the desk, making himself at home. 'I was thinking, since you're so *handy* with kids, you could find one for me too. You must know who'd be willing to turn a few tricks to earn a bob or two.'

The shock on Barry's face said everything. 'If you mean what I think you mean, then I'm calling the police right this minute. Get out of my club.'

'I'd hold your horses, if I were you, Barry old fruit. What would the *polis* have to say about what I witnessed just now?'

'You witnessed *nothing*! I was mopping the boy's cut lip then sent him for a shower. All perfectly innocent.'

'So you say.' Quinn gave a philosophical shrug as he drew on his cigarette. 'But how long had that lad been standing there in his altogether, absolutely starkers? Long enough for all sorts of mischief to have gone on. And to be sure it's only your word against mine, is it not?'

Silence hung between them for several long minutes as Barry struggled with his temper, clenching and unclenching his fists. He was beginning to sweat a little, could feel it running down the back of his collar. He didn't trust Quinn an inch but beating him up, as he itched to do, would get him nowhere. Not worth the risk. The man had too many minders, some of them standing right outside this very door. You had to be canny, use your wits not your fists where Billy Quinn was concerned. The trouble was that Quinn was no dummy himself. Evil to the core he may be, yet he had brains in that Irish skull of his.

'The boy would speak up for me. And why would the police believe you, the notorious Billy Quinn? They've been wanting to get you inside for the last twenty years to the best of my knowledge.'

71

Quinn gave a weary sigh as he got swiftly to his feet, as if he were suddenly tired of all this prancing around and was ready to come in with the killer punch. At the door he turned to regard Barry through narrowed eyes, a wisp of blue smoke from the cigarette that hung from his lower lip curling about his careworn, but still remarkably handsome face.

'It's not for myself, you understand, my tastes are more – conventional, as you might say. But I have a friend, a business colleague who would be interested in whatever you could procure for him. And were you to be generous in this regard, it might help me forget what I saw just now. Age and sex immaterial, but find a kid quick, Barry lad, if you want to save your reputation, not to mention your marriage to that new wife of yours.'

Chapter Eight

Easter Sunday was here at last and Lizzie was determined to put her worries aside and enjoy it. All the Easter eggs and rabbits had been sold, plus lots of other sweets besides, and a fair profit made. This money, together with the sixpences and threepenny bits that Aunty Dot had saved in an old teapot on the mantle, was sufficient for everyone's train fare, and an ice cream cornet and a donkey ride each on the sands.

Lizzie was buttering mounds of bread, happily making sandwiches for the trip while attempting to supervise Cissie as she struggled to tie her shoe laces. Beth was engaged in bossing Alan, making him change the old school socks he'd put on for a clean pair.

'You look like you were dragged up,' the little girl said to her brother, using one of Aunty's pet phrases.

His grey trousers came down to his knees, to allow room for growth, hanging loosely from a pair of braces over his check shirt. Lizzie smiled encouragingly at him.

'You'll be able to take your socks off when you go paddling.'

'Will I?' He gazed up at her wide-eyed for a second, blinking behind his National Health spectacles, then his sister gave him a nudge and told him to polish his shoes. Poor Alan. Hen-pecked already.

Aunty had the baby on her lap. This one was a girl and Dot changed her nappy with care because of the bad nappy rash the poor mite was suffering from. When the baby had arrived three days ago she was in such a mess, and stank so strongly of ammonia, that Aunty doubted she'd had her nappy changed more than a half dozen times in her entire young life.

Now, watching Aunty apply cream, balancing the baby expertly on her spread knees, Lizzie thought she looked even more tired than usual. A day in the fresh sea air would do her a world of good.

Despite the weather being dreadful all week, Easter Day had turned out surprisingly fair and warm, a relief for them all. Aunty had spent the previous day, all of Easter Saturday, cleaning the house from top to bottom. She'd scrubbed floors, beaten carpets, changed beds, and done the day's usual washing and ironing. It was a never-ending task with so many children to care for, doing everything she could to leave the house tidy and clean, as if they would be away for a week and not simply a day.

This morning they'd all enjoyed a special breakfast of boiled eggs and toast soldiers; each egg with a face painted on it in cochineal. And now, with the baby ready and in her pram, Aunty was lining the children up for inspection, looking down upon them with pride as they stood before her in their best clothes.

'By heck, don't you all look like toffs? Proper bobby-dazzlers you are.'

Alan flung himself at her, as was his wont, to cling to Aunty's leg and grin up at her.

'Aye, you an' all in that fancy bow tie. I swear I never saw the like in all my life. Where did you get it?' The question was accompanied by a slight frown, since Alan wasn't above helping himself to things off the stalls on the market. Dot was still trying to teach the little boy the difference between what belonged to him, and what didn't.

'Mr Holmes give it to me. It were one of his old ones that he don't need no more.'

Aunty smiled her relief, tugging it straight. 'That's all right, then. Well, I hope you thanked him nicely. Is the picnic all ready, Lizzie?'

'It is,' Lizzie agreed. 'Egg sandwiches, jam tarts, orange pop. Oh, and a few special Easter eggs I happened to have left over.'

A loud cheer went up and the children jumped up and down with excitement. Aunty quelled them with one of her looks. She didn't tolerate bad behaviour, particularly in public.

'First things first,' she said, taking the big brown jar of malt and cod liver oil down from the kitchen cupboard and issuing the usual spoonful to each open mouth. Even something as exciting as a day trip to Blackpool wasn't allowed to stand in the way of promoting good health. Cheeky Alan ran around licking everyone's spoon, despite the risk of catching their germs, because he loved it so much.

'Right then, our Joey, you're in charge of the tickets for the circus. I don't know of anyone here who wouldn't lose them in a second, including me. You're the best man for the job.' This was a special treat for the children, to see Blackpool Tower Circus. What a thrill!

Joey preened himself with pride as he took the brown envelope containing the tickets and tucked it carefully into his jacket pocket. Lizzie smiled. She knew he would guard them with his life, if necessary. Aunty had a wonderful way of making all her children feel special by giving them important jobs to do.

'Lizzie is in charge of the picnic. I have Cissie and the new baby. Beth, you keep a tight hold of Alan's hand. Right then, you lot forward march to Blackpool, and here we come!'

All of Champion Street came to their doors to watch the little procession pass by. Aunty Dot was well-respected tin the neighbourhood and they remarked how well turned out all the children were, and cooed at the baby, as they would at the one who came each week. Baby's all looked cute, so what did it matter what they were called?

Lizzie walked at the back, proudly chivvying the children along. The market was always closed on a Sunday, and she was more than ready for a day out herself. She'd been run off her feet these last few weeks with business being so brisk. Now the sun was shining and she felt as excited as the children at the prospect of a day by the sea.

—

They all had a wonderful time. Aunty kept them entertained on the long train journey by singing them songs, inserting each of their names instead of the usual one, so that 'Daisy, Daisy' became 'Joey, Joey', making the young boy blush bright red. 'Black-eyed Susie' became 'Brown-eyed Cissie', and for Beth and Alan she sang 'Hoots Mon', which had them both in fits of giggles. She liked a good laugh did Aunty Dot.

They managed to find space on the crowded sands where they set up a deckchair for Aunty, and spread out the rug they'd brought with them so that Lizzie could do a bit of sun-bathing. But first everyone scrambled into their bathing suits and dashed into the sea for a paddle, except for Aunty, who said she'd keep watch over their clothes and the picnic basket, then promptly closed her eyes for a bit of a snooze in the sun. Fortunately, the baby was asleep too.

Cissie cried a bit when a bigger than normal wave splashed her in the face, but Lizzie was there to hold her hand and reassure her. 'The sea must like you, Cissie. It's giving you a kiss.' And soon the little girl was laughing again.

They built a whole battery of sand castles: Alan and Joey competing to claim they'd made the biggest, and Beth digging a long trench leading from the sea so that water would run in and fill the moats. After that they ate their picnic then it was time for a donkey ride. Joey refused at first, saying that such soppy treats were only for babies, but he changed his mind at the last minute when the man offered him an especially large donkey, strong enough to carry big lads.

'Can I make it gallop?'

'No!' said the man, keeping a firm hold of the donkey's bridle, but he did allow it to trot a little making Joey feel very important.

Money was always tight, Aunty not being paid much at all for her fostering. But there was enough in her savings for a stick of pink candy floss, as well as an ice-cream cornet. Poor Cissie got it all caught up in her hair and had to be taken by Lizzie to the ladies lavatory to get it washed out.

And there was still the excitement of the circus to come. It took place in the Tower, Blackpool's answer to the Eiffel Tower in Paris, and more than lived up to expectation with its bright lights, pretty girls swinging high on the trapeze, ponies running round the ring, and the clowns charging up and down between the rows. The most famous clown of all, Charlie Cairoli, tipped a bucket of water at Beth and the little girl screamed, thinking she was going to get wet, but only flowers came out and she laughed in delight.

It was a very tired little party who finally trooped back along Champion Street: Lizzie carrying Beth, and Joey giving Cissie a piggy-back. Alan sat on the front of the pram, his little head nodding with tiredness. He would have crawled in with the baby had he not felt it to be beneath his dignity.

'We'll have a lie-in tomorrow, since it's Easter Monday,' Aunty told them as she tucked them up in their beds, Cissie already fast asleep. Alan would have been too, were it not for Beth who kept nudging him awake again to listen to Aunty. Minutes later, peace descended on the little house and Lizzie went to put on the kettle for a welcome cuppa.

--

It was as they topped up their mugs a second time that Aunty gave Lizzie the opening she'd been looking for. 'You'd make a grand little mother,' she said. 'You're so good with them kids.'

Lizzie laughed. 'I've not got it in my diary to embark on child-rearing any time soon, so you can hold your horses on that one. Nor will Jack Cleaver be the proud father. Makes me shudder just to think of it. Nice man, but...'

Aunty Dot chuckled. 'Poor Jack, one of life's losers, but a real wide boy. I can just see him trying to sell nylons during the war – I bet he didn't even manage to do that very well. I'd like to see you settled, though, before I shuffle off this mortal coil.'

Lizzie looked at her keenly. 'What a thing to say! You're not even sixty yet.'

'I'm not immortal either.'

There was a short silence in which Lizzie's mouth felt so dry and her mind so dazed by fear she couldn't seem to get any words out. It was hard to imagine a world without Aunty Dot. She'd looked after Lizzie ever since she was twelve years old, when she'd rescued her from the Sisters of Mercy. Since then she'd been more of a mother to her than Lizzie's own, not that it was difficult. Lizzie's mother would have sold her for the proverbial thirty pieces of silver, given half a chance, to any of the so-called 'uncles' who used her house as a home-from-home. Lizzie shut her mind to these thoughts. Her childhood was a closed book, not something she cared to think about.

'If anything happened to me,' Aunty was saying, 'you'd see them babbies were looked after all right and proper, wouldn't you, lass? See they went to somebody kind.'

'Nothing's going to happen to you,' Lizzie fiercely responded, setting down her mug with a clatter and going to put her arms about the older woman. 'You're overtired, that's all. And is it any wonder, with all you do? You should ease off a bit. Not work so hard. You don't have to make them sweets and chocolates for a start. You can stop any time you choose. You've enough on your plate with the children.'

'But I like making them. I wouldn't do it if I didn't enjoy it, and how would we manage now if I did give up? You'd not want to go cap in hand back to Finch would you, saying you'd changed your mind and given me the push? I can't see you doing that, not if you're the lass I think you are.'

Lizzie sighed. 'I know things are difficult. I'll find an answer, I swear it.'

She unpinned Aunty's bun she wore close to the nape of her neck, and reaching for her brush off the mantelshelf, began gently to brush her hair to soothe her. It was long and wavy, Aunty's one vanity, and since she hated the thought of it going grey, she dyed it.

More often than not she bought whatever bottle first came to hand. Unfortunately, she rarely left the dye on long enough, or else left it on too long because she'd forgotten about it as she dashed to do some other job at the same time, so it was never the same colour from one month to the next. She'd long ago forgotten what her natural colour was, but today it was a soft golden brown with a hint of Titian.

'This colour suits you. Makes you look dashing,' Lizzie teased.

'Did you hear Alan coughing? You don't think the little lad is sickening for something, do you?'

'No, I don't. The train was smoky and smutty, that's all.' Determined not to let this chance slip, Lizzie continued, 'It's a pity you don't take as much care of your own health as you do of the children's. Put your feet up more. And have you made that appointment with the doctor yet?'

'Doctors! What do they know?'

'*I* know you're getting that pain in your side more than you should. More than you used to. You should get it seen to.'

Dot shook off Lizzie's ministrations and got to her feet, gathering up both empty mugs as she did so. 'If you're set on spoiling a grand day out, I'm off to me bed. No doubt I'll be woken at the crack by the babby, but I shall stop in bed for as long as I can for once. Will that suit you? And see you do the same.' So saying, she deposited the mugs in the sink and shuffled off up the stairs in her carpet slippers. 'Good night, lass.'

'Good night, Aunty.'

Lizzie knew when she was beaten. Aunty Dot didn't hold with doctors or illness. But maybe this had been the wrong moment to tackle her. She'd try again another time.

Oh, but what a perfect day! Nothing must be allowed to damage her lovely little family, certainly not Cedric Finch. Once the Easter holidays were over, she'd really put her mind to finding an alternative supplier. Lizzie had no intention of toadying to Finch's stupid rules and threats. He could take a running jump!

Chapter Nine

Dena was hurrying across the market, since she was late for work and had a full order book, when she spotted Barry Holmes talking to Billy Quinn. She thought Barry looked unusually agitated, waving his arms about and gesticulating. It was clear, even from this distance that the two men were arguing.

It wasn't the first time she'd seen Barry talking to Quinn and had once or twice remonstrated with him over this. 'Why do you bother with that man? Why do you even speak to him?'

Barry's answer had been unequivocal. 'Nobody with any sense refuses to speak to Quinn. Not if you want to wake up and see the sun shining tomorrow morning.'

Quinn was a bookie with a dubious reputation who'd recently moved into number seventeen, Champion Street. Dena had disliked him on sight, as he seemed to spend a inordinate amount of time studying people with his piercing blue eyes, particularly women. There were plenty who couldn't resist the man's Irish charm, or his lean good looks and high cheekbones, long straight nose and wide, seductive mouth. But he made Dena feel deeply uncomfortable and she went out of her way to avoid him.

This morning, however, evasion proved impossible. Trudy pulled herself free from Dena's hand and bounded up to Barry, who had turned away from Quinn to stack apples on his fruit and vegetable stall. Barry swung the little girl up in his arms for a hug before handing her a pear.

'There you are, petal, but only eat it when your Mummy says you can.'

'Can I eat it now?' the child instantly demanded.

'No,' Dena said firmly, taking the fruit from her and dropping it into her basket. 'You've only just had your breakfast.'

'Top of the morning to you, Dena.' Quinn eyed her with a lascivious grin, running a swift appraising gaze up and down the length of her, making Dena feel as if he were stripping away every scrap of clothing she had on. Disgusting behaviour for a man in his fifties, however well preserved he might be, and however much he might spend on his smart outfits. Right dandy he was. No one could ever accuse Quinn of being scruffy with his fine tweed overcoats with their velvet collars, expensive lounge suits, and his impeccable taste in silk ties. Although the mind inside that handsome head of his was entirely the opposite, being utterly filthy and evil. Dena knew that for a fact. She'd seen the young girls who were frequent visitors to his house, and it wasn't hard to guess the reason for this.

The man had the nerve now to tickle Trudy under her chin, making the little girl giggle. 'Going to be a real looker, this one, just like her mam.'

Reaching over, Dena almost snatched Trudy from Barry's arms. She had no wish for Billy Quinn to touch her beloved child. She kissed Barry on the cheek and told him she couldn't stop to chat as she was running late this morning. But as Dena turned away, anxious to open up her workshop and get the sewing machines whirring, Quinn called after her.

'If you ever get fed up of the rag trade I could find another job that might suit you better. It'd certainly pay more.'

Dena cast him a scathing look. 'I would never be that desperate.'

Quinn gave his lop-sided smile, his trademark cigarette hanging from one corner of his mouth. 'You never know. The day might come when you'll be glad to earn a bit extra. A pretty lass like you would never be short of customers, and you'd get to lie down on the job, don't forget, while the pounds came rolling in. Can't complain about that now, can you?'

Dena walked briskly away, not giving him the satisfaction of a reply. With Trudy clasped tightly in her arms, she was anxious to escape the sound of his guffawing laughter.

On the way back to her own stall she passed the Chocolate Cabin and paused to ask Lizzie if she'd seen anything of Carl recently. Her friend sorrowfully shook her head.

'I'm sure he'll be back soon,' Lizzie consoled her, without much conviction.

Jack Cleaver was hovering nearby, as was ever the case, and he too said he'd seen no sign of Carl. 'My word, isn't young Trudy growing up fast?' he said ingratiatingly. 'Now I expect I've something in my bag here for such a pretty little lady.' And rummaging in it, he brought out a pink lollipop. 'Can she have this, Mummy? Finch's make the very best lollipops.'

'Ooh, can I, Mummy? Can I, please?'

Dena couldn't help but laugh. 'My word, you are popular this morning. Maybe I should take you shopping with me more often. I might get some free groceries thrown in.'

'She's doing better than me, I can't get so much as a mint humbug out of Finch's representative this morning,' Lizzie remarked, and cast Jack Cleaver a scathing glance that should have shrivelled him on the spot.

'Say thank you for the lollipop,' Dena instructed her child and Trudy politely did so, dimpling prettily. 'Now I've got to dash. I'm late for work already. Bye, Lizzie. Bye Mr Cleaver. You'll let me know, Lizzie, if you hear anything about Carl?'

'I will. I promise.'

-

It was Betty Hemley seated at her flower stall and observing all that went on in the market, who spotted the unusual activity at the back of it. She mentioned this to Dena as she was dashing past on her way to work the very next day.

'Hey up, there's someone moving into Carl Garside's pitch. Now who might that be, do you reckon?'

Dena's heart plummeted. This was the worst possible news. If the pitch was taken, how could Carl ever come back? She didn't have time to go and investigate right then because she was rushed off her feet all morning. Later, when she went out to get herself a sandwich for dinner, Lizzie asked if she'd noticed what was going on.

Dena said, 'I'm afraid it looks like you're about to get some competition. The stall that's replaced Carl's has been filled with rows of boxes which appear to contain Finch's sweets. The only consolation I can offer is that the girl in charge doesn't seem to be *mown out* with customers.'

Even though she'd been half expecting it, Lizzie was stunned, and as distressed by this news as Dena, if for different reasons. It was still April, only a few weeks since Finch had issued the threat, so he hadn't even given her until the end of May, as he'd promised. The man was even meaner than she'd first thought.

Lizzie had already made several enquiries about an alternative supplier, but so far with little luck. The fact that Finch's stall was not having many customers on their first day brought little consolation. This was a disaster, no doubt about it.

'It's all very well for me to talk bravely about standing up to him, but Cedric Finch is a rich factory owner. How on earth can an old woman and a girl hope to compete with him?' Lizzie complained to Dena. She might tell herself that she'd faced worse problems in the past, but this was one battle which could be beyond her. 'We might lose,' she mourned. 'And if we do, what will happen to the children? They could all be sent back into care, the thing they dread most.'

'I'm sure you're a match for Finch any day,' Dena reassured her, suppressing a shudder. The two girls had grown close over the years, partly because of a similarity in their backgrounds. In their youth both had spent time in care, and this had formed a special bond between them.

Seeing the troubled expression on her friend's face, Dena's heart was filled with pity. Yet as her gaze lifted again to the new stall, her thoughts returned to her own problems. For once she wasn't thinking about children's homes, or the fact that she would once again have to raise yet another illegitimate child alone, as she'd done before she and Carl got together. Dena thought only of the man she loved, and the deep regret she felt at losing him.

Dena loved Carl Garside. She missed him, and saw the new stallholder as an intruder on the space she'd hoped would be kept open for him. The loss of Carl's pitch seemed to reinforce her fear that he'd gone from her life for good, and might never return.

–

'You need an evening off, that's your trouble,' Winnie told Dena, when she saw her glum face. 'You've not been out of this house in weeks. It may not be any of my business but I reckon a night out would do you a power of good.'

Dena knew it was true that she hadn't stepped outside the front door, except to go to work and buy a few essentials like food, in all the weeks since Carl had left. If it weren't for her friends on the market she'd have gone mad, but there was always someone to talk to, a cheery smile for her or a wave as she went about her business. Now she admitted that she did feel a bit jaded, so maybe Winnie was right. 'What were you thinking of?'

'We could go and see Yul Brynner and Charlton Heston in that new picture *The Ten Commandments* at the Plaza. It's supposed to be fantastic. Or we could just have a glass of milk stout in the Dog and Duck, if you prefer.'

A night out at the pictures suddenly appealed, might indeed do her good, Dena decided. She gave Winnie a hug. 'Why not? Would Barry babysit?'

'Like a shot.'

'We could ask Lizzie if she wants to come with us. She needs cheering up too.'

'Do that. We'll make a party of it. I'll ring up in case we need to book. It's bound to be popular. I mean, Charlton Heston himself made a personal appearance when it first opened at the Plaza.'

Arrangements were soon made. Lizzie was delighted to have a night out with her friend. Despite falling for Charlie Finch, she was undecided about the wisdom of going out with him and had still not accepted his offer of a date. A drink in the pub was as far as she was prepared to go, for now.

Dena asked her about this as they waited for the bus to take them to Oxford Road. 'The lad looks decent enough, and he seems smitten. I've seen him hanging about your stall looking like a helpless puppy, bless him. I know you're having problems with his dad, but that's not his fault, is it?'

Lizzie frowned, feeling her cheeks grow pink as she recalled the eagerness of Charlie's attention. She did like him, it was true, had felt an immediate affinity with him, but Lizzie had been more shocked than she cared to admit that Cedric Finch had actually carried out his threat by opening up in opposition to her. It would make their survival problematic, so how could she trust his son?

The bus arrived and they climbed on board, going up to the top deck to sit at the front from where they could look down on the shops, on men scurrying homeward in their raincoats and trilby hats, and women queuing for the last bargains of the day. The bus was crawling along, caught up in a traffic jam behind a Morris Traveller and two more corporation buses, so she had plenty of time to think.

The bus conductor come running up the stairs, his pouch chinking with money. 'Right, you lot, warm up your pennies. I'll take a note off you with pleasure, but if I get me hands on it, you won't get no change out of me.' Laughing at his own feeble joke, the conductor began to make his way along the bus.

'What if he's only hanging around just to spy on me?' Lizzie whispered to Dena as they all searched their pockets for the correct change. 'Maybe Charlie Finch only wants him to go out with me so that he can tell his dad what I'm up to. Sweets are selling the most – I'm doing so well.'

Dena laughed out loud. 'You mean he'd be a spy for his dad? That doesn't sound very likely, does it? For goodness' sake, Lizzie, don't let your imagination run away with you.'

Lizzie looked sheepish. 'I do get a bit carried away at times, I suppose, worrying about it all, and about Aunty Dot. I can't help it. I may not make a lot out of that stall but Aunty depends upon me. The last thing I want is to be a burden to her, or to risk losing any of the children.'

'I know.'

'Aunty doesn't get much money for fostering, and if we couldn't manage properly, you know very well Miss Rogers would put them all back into care in an instant, in some children's home or other. And I don't have to tell you, Dena, what that would mean.'

Dena shuddered. 'I hated the years I was in Ivy Bank after our Pete drowned and my mother couldn't cope. I still have nightmares about that place. It's certainly not somewhere I'd want any child of mine to go.'

Lizzie agreed. 'I was lucky. I was only with the Sisters of Mercy for a couple of years before Aunty took me in. It could have been much worse.'

'You never said why you were in there. What happened to your mam?' Dena waited a moment for Lizzie to explain, or give some details. When she said nothing more but kept her eyes cast down, her cheeks stained with a flush of pink, Dena took her friend's hand and gave it a little squeeze.

'Forget I asked.' Dena knew well enough that some things were just too painful to talk about. 'Anyway, you aren't the only one with a problem, I don't mind telling you, I've got a big one.' She glanced across at Winnie and then quickly shook her head. 'Not here, I'll tell you another time. I think I'm putting weight on, this new cross-your-heart bra is killing me. Anyway,

'I'm sure you're getting it all wrong where Charlie Finch is concerned. Spy indeed! Whatever next? Life isn't a Hollywood movie, you know. Much as I like Hitchcock's scary films, this is Champion Street Market.'

'Eeh, I like Alfred Hitchcock films an' all,' Winnie said, coming in at the tail end of the conversation after paying their fares to the conductor, and getting it all wrong. 'Did you see *Strangers on a Train*? Ooh, and *Rear Window*. That were right scary.'

The two girls exchanged a quick glance, then burst into fits of giggles and happily discussed the merits of various films for the rest of the bus journey.

–

Barry was in his element. There was nothing he liked better than to have little Trudy all to himself. What a joy she was! So bubbly and full of fun and affection, always ready to give him a kiss or a cuddle. And she was such a pretty little thing with her soft brown curls, amber eyes and cheeky little smile. Barry had helped her to colour a picture of her Magic Painting book by splashing water over the page to bring up the colour, as if by magic. She'd undressed her dollies and put them to bed, apart from Looby Loo the rag doll who always went to bed with her. Barry had helped, amid great hilarity, by putting one doll's hair in curling pins, explaining to Trudy that by morning she would have curly ringlets. Now they were happily playing snap while Trudy ate a biscuit and drank her milk.

In a moment, Barry would take her upstairs and tell her a story. Trudy loved traditional fairy stories. *Goldilocks and the Three Bears* or *Cinderella* were two of her favourites. As she sipped on her milk he started to tell her the story of *Little Red Riding Hood*. He got carried away and began to embroider the tale a bit, describing how the Wolf would chase Little Red Riding Hood through the woods whenever she ventured out to visit her grandmother.

'Then he'd tickle her, like this,' Barry said, making Trudy squeal and spill her milk as he tickled her bare feet.

They got even sillier as the story progressed then Barry remembered that Dena did not approve of getting Trudy excited just before going to bed. She would often reprimand him for doing that, so he tried to calm the little girl down. But Trudy had drunk up all her milk by this time and was running about the living room, squealing with delight and pretend fear, taunting Barry to chase after her and catch her if he could.

'What time is it, Mr Wolf?' she chanted.

'Time for my supper,' replied Barry, pouncing after her.

With a shout of joy Trudy ran round and round the sofa then suddenly dashed out into the lobby. The front door was never locked. Barry hadn't even realised that Trudy had grown tall enough to reach the handle. In a trice she'd flung it open and, with a scream of triumph, ran out into the street in her pyjamas and bare feet.

He saw the car coming far too late, even though he was only a few feet behind her. '*No!*' Barry shouted, and flung himself in its path in a desperate bid to reach the child.

Chapter Ten

As luck would have it Jack Cleaver happened to be passing by at precisely that moment. He carried a bunch of flowers that he'd bought from Betty Hemley's stall with the intention of persuading Lizzie to come out with him this evening. Unfortunately she wasn't in, or so Aunty Dot had told him, as kindly as she could.

He'd been deeply disappointed and completely at a loss to know how to win Lizzie round, having tried every tactic he could think of. He wasn't good with girls, never had been. He'd never had a proper girlfriend, not since the start of the war when a girl called Mavis had laughed at him for failing to live up to what she believed sailors were famous for: making love to every girl they clapped eyes on. He'd tried to please her but just wasn't up to the job; no wonder since she'd been lippy and sarcastic throughout. She'd given him a right earful for his perceived shortcomings and then gone off with his best mate. Jack had generally found women to be unreliable, stupid creatures, not to be trusted. Not even his mother.

He'd thought Lizzie was different, so gentle and kind, almost childlike in her vulnerability for all her show of fierce independence. Unfortunately, despite the thick skin he'd needed to acquire as a commercial traveller her continued rejection had hurt him badly. He could sense she was doing her best to avoid him now.

Having failed to impress her with his manly charms he'd tried to play on her sympathy. The part about him spending time in a Dr Barnardo's home was true enough, like plenty of other kids caught in the poverty trap. In his case it had been only for a few weeks when his Aunt Doris had been taken ill. She'd suffered a mild stroke from which she'd fortunately recovered, for all she'd never been the same after that. The other tale he'd told Lizzie of being found on a doorstep was entirely make-believe, a lame effort to sway her heart in his favour, as well as to disguise the truth.

Jack's background had in fact been respectable middle class. The family home was a large detached house with a Wolseley car parked in the drive. His father had been a head teacher at the local school and his mother a devoted housewife. At least, that was the impression they'd presented to the world.

In truth, his father's expensive tastes had been funded by his defrauding of the local cricket club, and other charities where he was a treasurer. He was dipping his fingers into their bank accounts until he was inevitably discovered, charged, and sentenced to serve three years for fraud. Jack's mother, a pathetic creature unable to cope with this shame and the subsequent bankruptcy, had run off with their neighbour, abandoning her young son to her spinster sister.

At least Aunt Doris had done her best by him until her health had broken down, then young Jack had needed to look after her. His resentment over the disgrace, and mess in his life had been festered throughout his boyhood. Jack hated his father, a man so selfish and greedy, so full of his own importance that he'd destroyed his own family. The young Jack had secretly hoped and prayed that the war would finish him off, so that he'd never have to clap eyes on him again. Unfortunately, his father had survived, as the wicked so often do while the good are taken.

The last time Jack had seen him was back in 1945 when he'd come on a visit after the war. There'd been no cheerful 'hello', or 'pleased to see you, son', not even any apology. He'd merely demanded the answer to one question: 'Why the hell didn't you join up instead of skulking behind women's skirts?'

Jack had resented this deeply. As if his problems were of his own making! It was true that he'd turned eighteen in 1941 and in theory should have joined up then, but even when he'd explained all about his asthma and weak chest, and how he'd consequently been excused service, his father had just laughed sarcastically. Clearly he thought it all a cowardly dodge.

But washing his family's dirty linen in public wasn't Jack's style. Far better, he'd decided, to come up with something much more moving and melodramatic such as being found as an abandoned baby, which he knew would appeal to Lizzie's sensitive nature. And it was true in a way that he had been abandoned.

Lizzie had taken it all in, tenderly kissing his cheek when he'd first told her the fabricated tale and assuring him that if he didn't have a family, he at least had friends.

But Jack Cleaver meant to have much more than that, if only he could persuade her to go out with him. He tossed the flowers into a nearby rubbish bin, but was suddenly startled out of his self-obsessed reverie as the accident unfolded before his eyes.

The child seemed to come out of nowhere, screaming and running out into the road with Barry Holmes right behind her. As if in slow motion, the oncoming car braked and slid inexorably towards her.

—

Jack was really proud of how proficiently he dealt with everything, particularly the driver, successfully managing to calm the poor man down.

'I never saw her! She was just suddenly there, right in front of me. Dear God, is she dead?'

Jack made him sit on the kerb with his head on his arms, in case he should pass out, while he examined the injured. The child seemed to have been thrown clear, whether by the car or Barry Holmes he couldn't be sure. Barry was clearly in a mess but managed to lift his head.

'Never mind about me, take care of her,' he said, when Jack went over to examine him. 'Trudy, are you all right, love? Be a brave girl. I'll help you in a minute, soon as I can get my legs to work.'

After that, everything seemed to happen very quickly. Other folk came rushing out of their houses, fetching blankets to cover Barry, offering to make tea or give him whisky.

'Should we help him up?'

'No, best not to move him,' Jack instructed, remembering the first aid he'd learned during his training in the Home Guard. 'Looks like he's broken his leg or something.' Then seeing that the child was stirring, he gathered her up in his arms.

'Will somebody stay with him while I see to the little lass? She's going to be fine but she's gashed her knee badly. I've got a phone in my house so I can ring for an ambulance.'

'Mummy,' Trudy whimpered, and Barry called out to her again.

'Don't worry, chuck. Try to be a brave girl and do as the man says. He'll take care of you.'

'Aye, ring for the ambulance, Jack. Quick! I don't have a phone.' Molly Poulson had rushed over, offering to help, but then Barry groaned and in the general confusion that everyone was at least alive and well, Cleaver slipped quietly away, the child still in his arms.

–

Jack laid Trudy on the sofa while he made the call, giving the necessary details to the ambulance centre, then carefully washed the child's knee, which wasn't as bad as it had first appeared. Her pyjama trousers were all torn at the knees and soaked through with urine. She'd obviously wet herself so he took these off and stuck a big pink Elastoplast on her knee. She was starting to come round from the shock and beginning to cry, tears running down her dusty face. Jack pulled her onto his knee and began to rock her in his arms.

'There, there, you're all right, love. Don't cry.'

She was so small, so helpless, her soft pink flesh all dirty from falling in the road. He slid one hand up and down her plump little legs, rubbing them gently to warm her as he kissed her damp cheek. Then, unable to resist her childish vulnerability, very slowly he slid one finger into her, and then another, gently moving them back and forth. 'Is that nice, love? Does that make you feel better?'

Trudy stared at him, amber eyes still wide with shock, her small mouth pursed as she struggled not to cry. 'I want to wee-wee!'

'In a minute, love, in a minute.' Jack could hardly breathe, and there was a tight constriction in his chest, an ache starting up deep in his loins. He'd never known such excitement, such a thrill pulsating through every vein.

Why was he doing this? Was it wicked? No, he told himself. Wouldn't the child stop him if she didn't like it, if she wasn't in need of this little show of affection? He knew about children. Jack understood how they needed love, as he had done as a child and never received it. This wasn't the first time he'd given pleasure and love to a child, after all, and he'd never yet found one who'd protested.

'You like it, don't you? I can tell.'

He was fumbling with the buttons on his trousers, hastily trying to get them undone as he lifted her to a more favourable position. Trudy still had her mouth screwed up tight and was staring in horror at the huge snake that was now pushing against her plump thighs.

'Open your legs a bit more, love. Don't worry, no one will know. This will be our little secret. You mustn't say a word and I won't tell that you've been naughty. We don't want them to blame your mummy for leaving you, now, do we? Or else they might take you away from her. I'll say you've been a good girl, just like Uncle Barry asked. You'll feel much better in a minute.'

But Trudy didn't feel any better at all. She felt a thousand times worse. The little girl began to sob and cry for her mummy, but it was Molly Poulson who eventually came rushing to her aid.

'The ambulance is here now. How is the little mite?'

The minute he'd heard the front door open, Jack Cleaver quickly adjusted his clothing, and pulled the little girl's pyjama trousers back on again, damp though they still were. They'd been in the house no more than ten minutes, now he handed the child over to Big Molly.

By the time the ambulance men had taken her off to hospital – just to be on the safe side – she was wrapped warmly in a tartan rug and wasn't crying any more. Trudy was utterly silent, and very still.

–

It was three hours later before Dena arrived at the hospital fearing she would find her child dead or dying, or at least with several broken limbs. She cried with relief when she saw Trudy sitting up in bed eating a chocolate biscuit, a nurse beside her. Dena gathered Trudy in her arms and smothered her in kisses.

'What happened?' she asked the nurse over the child's sleepy head. 'What was she doing out in the street in her pyjamas?'

'That's what we'd all like to know, Mummy. But don't worry. We're a bit bruised and sore here and there, but we're going to be fine, aren't we, love? However, the doctor would like a little word, if you don't mind.'

Dena sat and listened to what he had to say in horrified disbelief. 'What are you talking about? What on earth do you mean… interfered with? How *could* she have been interfered with?'

'We wonder if that is the reason she ran out into the road. Who did you leave her with, Mrs Dobson? Who was babysitting?'

Dena heard his use of the word 'Mrs' but didn't trouble to correct it, she was too appalled by what she was hearing. 'Barry? You think Barry would do such a thing? Never!'

'Please try to remain calm, Mrs Dobson. At first we thought Trudy's injuries were no more than superficial, but the moment I touched her pyjama trousers the little girl screamed the place down. My suspicions were instantly aroused, and her behaviour thereafter convinced us that further investigations needed to be made.'

The doctor, a young man with red-brown hair, a sprinkling of freckles across his nose and the kindest expression in his grey-green eyes, was obviously not enjoying telling her all of this.

'It couldn't have been Barry. He adores Trudy… has helped me with her since she was born. He's been like a grandfather to her.'

The doctor looked unconvinced. 'Even close relatives are known to carry out such acts of gross indecency. In fact, it's usually the case that the perpetrator is a relative or close friend, I'm afraid, in cases of child abuse.'

The words rang in Dena's head like a death knoll. *Child abuse!* Someone had hurt her lovely Trudy? 'I can't believe it. I won't believe it!'

'Nevertheless, I fear I've had to report my findings to the police.'

'I should hope so. We need to catch the bastard, whoever it is.' What was she saying? Who else could it have been but Barry? But why would he do such a thing to Trudy? He absolutely adored her, had always been keen to babysit. Surely that didn't mean that he…

The young doctor was still speaking, but Dena was having trouble taking in what he was saying to her. It was as if his voice was coming from some far distant place, the sound muffled and confused.

'…they'll no doubt conduct their enquiries with discretion, but you must watch her carefully over the next day or two, Mrs Dobson. She may be subdued, or show signs of abnormal behaviour. Most importantly, you must watch out for any sign of infection.'

'Infection? What sort of infection?'

'Possibly urinary! At worst, there's no easy way of saying this. She may have contracted a sexually transmitted disease.'

'Oh, my God!'

'I hasten to say that I think it unlikely. The little girl hasn't been penetrated, you understand, but there's evidence that indicates efforts were made to do so. Possibly he was interrupted, or that was when the child broke free and ran out into the road.'

Dena felt nauseous, wished she didn't have to listen to any more of this filth. She tried to shut out the doctor's voice but it was relentless, explaining, describing, telling her things she'd much rather not hear. Why had she gone out? What had possessed her to leave her child unprotected? But she hadn't been unprotected. She'd been with Barry. *Barry!* Dear God, what had he done to her? It really didn't bear thinking of.

Chapter Eleven

'Tell me exactly what happened! Every last detail.' It was the following morning and Dena was in the men's ward asking this question of Barry himself. She was almost shouting, her voice loud enough to turn heads and cause considerable curiosity among the other patients in the ward. Winnie, seated beside her, flapped a hand, clearly embarrassed as she attempted to shush her. Dena ignored her.

Barry had sustained nothing worse than a broken ankle in plaster, otherwise had sustained no serious injuries. He'd been kept in overnight for observation. Now he was already dressed and seated in the statutory wheelchair, waiting for the ambulance to take him home.

Trudy was still in bed in the children's ward, being watched over by the eagle-eyed nurse. The little girl was to be allowed home later that day, once they were happy there would be no long-term effects, such as concussion. But it was the other harm she had suffered, most concerning for Dena.

'Well, are you going to tell me? Why did she run out into the street?'

'We were having a bit of fun,' Barry began, wishing he could turn back the clock and do things differently.

'Fun? What sort of fun?'

Dena wondered how long she could control the rage that was boiling up inside her. The police had come to her first thing this morning and explained that they'd spoken to Jack Cleaver, who'd rung for the ambulance and administered first aid to the child. He'd confirmed that he'd seen Trudy run out into the street, clearly distressed. He thought she'd been screaming or shouting something. She'd run right into the path of the car and Barry Holmes had been chasing her. Cleaver had witnessed the entire incident.

They'd questioned him, naturally, but as the child had only been in his house for a few minutes; just long enough for him to make that call and put a plaster on her knee. Molly Poulson confirmed he'd been cleared of any suspicion. Besides, he was a well-respected man who worked for Cedric Finch. Barry Holmes, on the other hand, had been the subject of gossip about his friendships with boys for years. The police were convinced they had their culprit.

'I'm waiting,' Dena said now, needing to hear the explanation from his own lips. 'What made Trudy run out into the street in her pyjamas and bare feet? What sort of *game* were you playing?'

Barry told her all about *Little Red Riding Hood*. Never had he felt such shame in all his life, felt such a complete and utter failure. 'I've let you down, Dena, love, I know that. I can't tell you how sorry I am. I know you said that I mustn't get her excited before bedtime but we were having such a good time and she did get a bit giddy. We were playing "What Time Is It, Mr Wolf?" and she was running round and round the sofa. I was trying to stop her by that time, remembering what you'd said. I did recognise that it'd got a bit out of hand—'

'Oh, you did, did you?' Dena's voice was cool.

'And then, before I guessed what she was about to do, she just took off up the lobby. She was out in the street before I could reach her. Oh, but I did try, Dena love. I did. As you can see.'

Dena looked dispassionately at his foot in plaster, and at Winnie, seated solemn-faced beside him. 'You deserve that. In fact you deserve more than that. I'd like to break the other for you myself. I know why she ran out into the street. The doctor has explained to me exactly what dirty business you were up to, that frightened my child. Frightened her so much that she upped and ran blindly out into the path of that car. I believe you'll find the police will be wanting a word with you later, but if you ever come near my Trudy again, Barry Holmes, I swear I'll kill you with my own bare hands.'

–

Trudy would say nothing. In fact, she didn't speak a word all day. Acting on the doctor's advice, Dena didn't ask her any questions. She cuddled her for a while, then tucked her under a soft warm blanket in a corner of the sofa with Looby Loo and a new picture book. At tea-time Dena managed to persuade her to eat some scrambled egg and toast soldiers, but the little girl still hadn't spoken, nor even glanced at the book. By the time Dena brought her cocoa, she drank in complete silence.

Trudy refused to put her dollies to bed, as she normally did every night. She simply ignored them, picked up Looby Loo and walked away. Seeing the two neglected dolls, Dena gave one a cuddle, hoping it might inspire Trudy to do the same. 'Did you put these curlers in, love? My word, she will have beautifully curly hair in the morning.'

Trudy snatched the doll off her, and ripped out the curlers with such force that clumps of the doll's blonde hair came with them. Appalled, Dena tried to stop her but then again remembered the doctor's advice and held back. Maybe the child needed to get this anger out of her system.

Trudy hated the sight of the doll because it had been put safely to bed in curlers. She hated Uncle Barry because he hadn't done the same for her and saved her from that nasty man.

Most of all she hated herself, because if she hadn't been naughty and ran out of the house then the bad thing wouldn't have happened. She couldn't tell anyone what that bad thing was because the man had said if she did, they'd blame Mummy for going out and leaving her, then they'd take her away. Trudy was very frightened that she might never see Mummy again.

She didn't want to think about the bad thing, or last night ever again. Never to speak about it.

Trudy began to tear up the Magic Painting book.

'Don't do that, sweetheart. You haven't finished all the pictures yet. Come on, I'll read you a story. What would you like, *Cinderella*? That's your favourite, isn't it?'

Dena had carefully not mentioned *Little Red Riding Hood*, but suddenly Trudy started screaming and stamping her feet. She threw herself into such a tantrum, lying on the floor and drumming her heels, then crouching in a corner with her head buried in her arms, that by the time she'd calmed the child down and finally got her into bed, Dena was in tears too.

When Trudy was at last sleeping soundly, no doubt completely exhausted after her tears and tantrum, Dena made herself a soothing cup of tea. She wondered if Winnie would call in later and hoped that she wouldn't. It was this thought that set her off crying again, and Dena realised that everything had changed. Friendship, trust, any sense of normality had vanished in the face of this evil. Winnie had said little on the matter thus far, except to remark tartly that Barry would never do such a thing. Her faith in her husband was unshaken.

'He lost his own daughter, don't forget, in an air raid during the war,' she'd reminded Dena. 'His wife too, in the same raid! He'd cut off that broken foot of his before he'd hurt our Trudy.'

But all the evidence stated otherwise.

What was happening to Barry now? Had the police finished questioning him down at the station? Was he in a cell, or would they allow him to come home until they had conducted their enquiries? Dena knew in her heart that she didn't want him to come home. She felt sick at the thought of ever seeing him again. And how could Trudy face him, play the same innocent games with him, let alone see him as a grandfather figure? They had all lost so much that night.

'Oh, Carl, I do wish you were here. I need you now more than I've ever needed anyone.'

And Dena wept some more as longing for the man she loved threatened to overwhelm her. At length, emotionally exhausted, she dabbed at her swollen eyes with cold water. What good did crying do? It had never helped in the past. She made herself a fresh pot of tea and sat at the kitchen table to drink it, trying to think things through calmly and rationally.

—

If Dena slept that night, she wasn't aware of it. The hours seemed endless as she tossed and turned, horrifying images playing over and over in her mind. Try as she might she could not shut them out. Who would do such a thing to an innocent child? Not Barry surely. But if not him, then who?

The following morning she learned that Barry had indeed been charged. Winnie came round first thing to inform her. She was inconsolable, sobbing that her lovely husband had been maligned, it was all speculation built on nasty gossip and circumstantial evidence, and really he was completely innocent.

Now it was Dena's turn to say nothing. What was there to say when she too believed him guilty?

She didn't go to her workshop. Joan and the rest of her workers would just have to manage on their own for once. Dena needed to stay at home and look after her child, who today seemed remarkably composed, almost unnaturally so.

Trudy ate a whole Shredded Wheat for her breakfast then played with her dollies as if nothing untoward had ever taken place. Dena wondered if she was whispering secrets in their ears, and wished one of them could speak and tell her what the child was saying.

Jack Cleaver came knocking on her door later that day and Dena stood on her front doorstep and thanked him for his 'Good Samaritan' act. 'It was so lucky that you had a telephone and didn't have to go to the call box at the end of the street. You were able to take proper care of my child and I do appreciate your help.' Even as she spoke Dena looked at him and wondered. Could it have been Jack Cleaver and not Barry?

No, how could it have been? Nobody could be absolutely sure on timing in all the confusion, but it had apparently been little more than ten minutes before Molly Poulson had dashed in to take Trudy to the hospital. In that time Jack Cleaver himself had called the ambulance, *and* tended to Trudy's injuries. Constable Nuttall had assured Dena that his sergeant was perfectly satisfied, and the police had quickly dismissed him from their enquiries. Cleaver was not responsible. Dena still didn't particularly like this man with his slicked-down hair, old-fashioned suits and smarmy manner, but he was outwardly respectable and there was no reason to suspect that he was the culprit.

Was this how it was going to be from now on? Would she never be able to trust anybody again?

'I did very little,' Cleaver was saying, 'only washed the little girl's knee and put a plaster on. She was very distressed. I do wish I could've done more. I heard Barry Holmes had been held in a police cell overnight. Is something wrong?'

Dena looked up into his kindly, enquiring gaze and managed a glimmer of a smile, albeit a strained one. 'I'd rather not talk about it right now, if you don't mind. I'm sure it'll all come out eventually, but I'm a bit fraught this morning.'

''Course you are. Well, you know where I am if you need me. I'd be happy to look after the little lass at any time. Any time at all.'

'Thank you. That's very kind of you. Thank you for everything.'

—

The following morning before it was barely light, before Dena had even got out of bed to make her first cup of tea of the day, she was woken by a loud hammering on the door. She reached for her dressing gown. Now what? Had Winnie come round with more bad news about Barry? Dena wasn't sure she was ready to face her yet, not till she'd come to terms in her own mind with everything that had happened.

She paused at Trudy's door to look in upon her child, still fast asleep, thank goodness, her beloved Looby Loo cradled against one pink flushed cheek. Dena had bought her the doll because she was such a fan of *Andy Pandy*, and she'd never gone to bed without it since. The hammering came again.

'I'm coming, I'm coming. Keep your hair on.' Dena ran down the stairs, struggling to tie the cord of her dressing gown as she unlocked the front door.

It wasn't Winnie standing on the doorstep but Miss Rogers. The tall, overbearing woman didn't even pause to say good morning as Dena gaped at her. She just stepped over the threshold bringing two men with her, one of them Constable Nuttall, then headed straight for the stairs.

Dena watched in bemusement, still rubbing the sleep from her eyes. 'What's going on?'

Constable Nuttall said, 'I'm sorry, Dena. We're just doing our duty, doing what needs to be done. Don't make a fuss.'

'Fuss? Duty? What are you talking about?' And then she heard Trudy cry out her name. The sound of her child's cry sliced through her like a knife. 'Dear Lord, what is that woman doing?'

She didn't even manage to reach the bottom of the stairs before Constable Nuttall had hold of her, taking her arms in a fierce grip. The other man was waving a sheaf of papers under her nose, saying something about a place of safety, and Dena not being a fit mother.

Then Miss Rogers was standing before her, a wriggling Trudy held firm in her arms, and the expression on the social worker's face was cold as ice. 'I'm disappointed in you, Dena Dobson. Deeply disappointed. You've let me down, let us all down, most of all little Trudy here. We have to take her. You must understand that. First you send Carl away, thereby spoiling your one chance of a secure future. Now this! Leaving her in the care of – well, I won't put a name to him, not in front of the child. It's clear you're no longer a fit and proper person to care for this child. She must be taken to a place of safety as the NSPCC inspector here has explained to you. I'm sorry, but that's the law.'

And long before Dena's scream of protest had died away, Miss Rogers in her black coat and sensible tie shoes had taken Trudy away.

your time chatting. Forget it, Betty, you've got to lie in the bed you've made. You'll only upset things if you make a fuss. That's law with his bullying ways, and she's not prepared to put up with it. She must be trying to pick up a customer that Nancy imagines they are as popular as ever. I wonder, just the same.'

And Lizzie took a long drink of her own cider, glad, like as not, she'd not taken on those two when Body...

Chapter Twelve

Charlie appeared just as Lizzie was pulling down the shutters on Pringle's Chocolate Cabin, hands thrust deep in his pockets and a great big grin on his face.

'I've come to take you for a pick-me-up before you go home. How does a glass of cider sound?'

It sounded wonderful and, despite her resolve to cold shoulder Finch's son, Lizzie found herself grinning back at him. She came to her senses once they were seated in the pub, however, and turned to him with an accusing light in her eye.

'Have you seen what your dad has done? He's opened up a sweet stall in direct competition with me. Why Belle Garside has allowed it I really can't imagine, but there isn't the business on this market to sustain both of us.'

Charlie frowned into his cider. 'I'm aware of what he's done, Lizzie, and I'm sorry about it.' Then he lifted his clear grey gaze to hers. 'I hope you won't let this stand in the way of our friendship. I've been patient for a long time now. I'd hoped you'd succumb to my charms long before this.'

'It's been difficult, what with little Trudy's accident and everything.'

'I know. I was sorry to hear about that. She's on the mend though, I understand.'

'Yes, but things aren't what they should be. She's been taken into care and Dena's naturally devastated. Winnie too, as you might imagine.'

They both looked across at the older woman sitting in one corner of the bar, quietly sipping on her Guinness instead of buzzing about poking her nose into other folk's business, as she usually did. It was awful to see the usually interfering busybody sitting so quiet and morose, all on her own.

Lizzie had spent hours with Dena, consoling her, offering all kinds of support and suggestions, most having fallen on deaf ears. But then, what comfort was there to offer?

'Anyway,' Charlie was saying, 'I was hoping to receive a favourable answer to my question tonight. You know I want to get to know you better – really well in fact – so I hope you appreciate, Lizzie, that I've no control over my father's actions. None whatsoever. He's a law unto himself.'

His voice was gentle and concerned. As he talked, he casually slid one arm along the back of her seat. Lizzie felt the warmth of it close to her shoulders. If she leaned back only a fraction of an inch it would touch her neck. Fortunately, she managed to remain straight-backed and summon the requisite coolness to her tone. 'Clearly he is.'

'And you don't blame me? You'll still come out with me on a date? How about Friday?'

Oh, she wanted very much *not* to blame him. But how could she ever trust him? This could all be part of Finch's grand plan, sending his son to sweet-talk her so that Charlie could spy on her and tell his father what she was up to. He was persistent, and had called at her stall almost as often lately as Jack Cleaver.

In fact, Cleaver had stopped off at her stall earlier that very day, and once again had asked her out. He seemed to have a new aura of confidence about him. People were viewing him as some sort of local hero for administering first aid to Trudy, and calling the ambulance so quickly.

It made Lizzie feel a bit guilty for the way she'd ignored him in the past, constantly refusing his offers to take her out. She'd always felt sorry for the man previously as he'd obviously had a difficult childhood, being found abandoned as a baby and brought up in a Dr Barnardo's home. Was that the reason she'd weakened this morning and finally succumbed, out of a sense of guilt or shame?

She'd been appalled to hear the words of acceptance coming from her mouth. Almost the instant she'd said them, Lizzie had regretted the decision. Simply witnessing the delight on his face, his stuttering excitement and immediate plan to book them a table on Friday at the Midland Hotel so that he could take her out for 'a slap-up meal worthy of her beauty', had left her flushed with embarrassment. She really had no wish to give him false hopes. Just because she felt sorry for him didn't mean she wanted to get to know him any better. Yet there seemed no way out of it now that she'd accepted.

Lizzie thought that she could at least use this foolishness to her own advantage. She was about to make it clear to Charlie that she had no wish at all for them to be 'better friends', that she had a date already, 'thank you very much', when suddenly he moved the arm from her shoulder and tucked a lock of her hair behind her ear. The gesture was so startlingly intimate, so gentle yet sensuous, that it sent a quiver of longing rippling through her over-sensitised skin and utterly robbed her of speech.

'You must know that I'm badly smitten,' he said. 'I think you're gorgeous but I'm having problems getting past your prickles. You're a bit like a hedgehog who rolls itself into a tight little ball whenever anyone touches it.'

Feeling anything but tightly coiled and prickly, more of a softening and unfurling inside, like the birth of something amazing and wonderful, Lizzie had to struggle to keep her mind properly focused. It was as if a whole new part of her had suddenly been discovered. With her gaze firmly fixed on the glass of cider before her, she resolutely continued with her argument. 'If your father insists on trading against me, how will I manage to stay in business? I can't even find anyone else to supply me. No one will come near, exactly as he predicted. Funny that, don't you think?' And she glared at Charlie, her blue eyes fiercely accusing.

But instead of being angry and defending his father, Charlie gazed right back at her for a long moment and then he did an incredible thing. He kissed her.

The kiss startled Lizzie so much that she actually jumped, shoved him away and slapped his face good and hard. 'What the hell do you think you're doing?' Lizzie regretted the slap the instant she'd done it. Not that it seemed to trouble Charlie, his reaction being as obstinately perverse as ever. His eyes shone with mischief and what she could only describe as desire, his soft mouth remaining temptingly close.

He must have noticed her moment of weakness as he gave her an utterly disarming grin. 'I'm not going to apologise for kissing you, so don't think I am. Why should I, when the fault lies with you, not me? You're so lovely I simply couldn't resist tasting the sweetness of you.' As if that wasn't bad enough, he blithely continued, 'so far as your problems with my father go, there is one possible course of action. You could always ask your aunt to make more sweets, enough to supply you completely.'

Lizzie gasped, as this was the exact opposite of what his father had intended, and then laughed aloud at the very idea. 'That's the craziest notion I've ever heard in my life. Aunty Dot has enough to do looking after the children. She couldn't possibly make enough sweets to stock my stall.'

'I'm serious. I think it could be the answer. Why don't you come out with me and we can talk about this some more? I'd like to help. I *want* to help. How about Friday? I'll pick you up at seven. Or we could meet here, if you prefer?'

'So that's why you made this crazy suggestion, just to persuade me to go out with you.' Lizzie sighed. 'Men! Throw out any old line to get their wicked way.'

He looked hurt by her reaction, his face solemn and those grey eyes of his deeply troubled. 'I'm sorry, that was clumsy of me. I never meant it that way. I really like you, Lizzie, won't you put those prickles away?'

She looked into his steady gaze that seemed so utterly sincere, at his face — so boyishly good-looking, at his tousled blond hair and temptingly soft mouth. He had hold of her hand and his touch was gentle yet compelling. Strong, capable hands, the sort you could rely on. Lizzie wanted to accept. She longed simply to say yes, but where was the point in falling for Charlie Finch when it couldn't possibly go anywhere? And in her heart Lizzie knew that there were other matters, besides his father, that stood between them. Issues she preferred not to think about, hidden deep inside her like a dark secret, must never be allowed to see the light of day.

Whenever she'd been foolish enough to risk revealing any of this to young men in the past, they'd generally dropped her like a hot cake. She had no wish to experience that sort of treatment from Charlie too. Why torture herself with hopeless dreams, far safer not to get involved in the first place?

'I already have a date for Friday, thanks all the same.'

'Cancel it. You know you'd much rather come out with me instead.'

Lizzie abruptly stood up and told him that she'd sooner have a date with Billy Quinn himself, the bookie everyone on the market loathed, than socialise with the son of the man who clearly intended to bankrupt her.

'Don't you trust me?' There was surprise in Charlie's tone, and what she could only describe as a note of pain.

'No, frankly, I don't,' she told him, and walked away.

With what she was already recognising as his typical blind stubbornness, Charlie called after her. 'I'll wait for you anyway, at this very table. Don't forget, Friday evening, seven o'clock precisely.'

–

Jack Cleaver couldn't believe his luck. His persistence had finally paid off. He wasn't interested in Lizzie's reason for accepting, didn't care if it was only because he'd played on her pity. He'd do whatever it took to win her round. All that mattered was that she'd actually agreed to go out with him.

He meant to have Lizzie as his wife and helpmate, all wrapped up together with her nice little business, which would be his means of escape from the tyranny of working for Cedric Finch. He was very fond of her, no question, although he had no real sexual desire for her. She wasn't particularly his type, not so far as physical intimacy was concerned, but in every other respect marriage to Lizzie Pringle would be perfect. It would solve all his problems in one.

Admittedly his own bland appearance and lack of emotion counted against him, but he could surely fake a little love and passion, at least long enough to win the fair lady.

Lizzie being a woman, was much more emotional and he'd noticed that she did tend to rail against things in her fiery way at times. But he didn't mind that. She'd calm down and mellow in time, once they were married, Jack was sure of it. It was merely the recklessness of youth and lack of direction from a good husband.

All he had to do was to continue to play the courting game as women did. It was really only another way of telling lies, at which he was adept. Hadn't he fabricated his entire life history? And wasn't he an expert at keeping secrets? He'd made definite progress today.

Jack Cleaver was sure that once she got to know him a little better, getting Lizzie to the altar would be no problem at all.

-

Trudy felt as if she were sleep-walking. One minute she'd been in her bed cuddling Looby Loo, the next a big, tall lady with a moustache had swept into the bedroom and carried her away. Why had Mummy let her to do that? It had all happened so very quickly and she'd been so frightened that she'd dropped Looby Loo. But the tall lady hadn't even allowed her to pick her up. Trudy wondered if Mummy would look after her. Poor Looby Loo would be scared on her own without Trudy to cuddle her.

Trudy had a sudden image of her mother. She was being held by two men and she was screaming and crying. Trudy thought she too might have been crying but then the lady had jumped into a car with her still in her arms, followed by the two men, and the last she'd seen of Mummy was through the back window of the car as it drove off down the street. Mummy was running behind, but she hadn't been able to catch it, even though Trudy had screamed for her to run faster, as loud as she could.

Now Trudy found herself in the biggest bedroom she'd ever seen. It was filled with row upon row of iron beds, and girls of all ages. They were all staring at her but no one spoke. No one had spoken to her since the lady had brought her in.

Trudy could remember little of the journey. She'd no idea how far they'd come or where she was now, except that it was a big building surrounded by fields and gardens. The heels of her shoes had echoed loudly as the tall lady had led her down a long corridor. At the end had been a beautiful arched window but she couldn't see out of it, couldn't see any of the trees or grass or nearby houses, because it was too high up.

The tall lady had handed her over to another who wore a long black dress and had rough hands that had hurt her. She'd taken all Trudy's clothes away, even her knickers, and Trudy had screamed and cried and stamped her feet, furious anyone would do such a thing to her. Next, the woman had taken a big pair of scissors and cut off all her hair. Trudy had watched in horror as soft brown curls had fallen to the floor all about her. Did this lady not like little girls and want her to look like a boy?

But she hadn't said anything. The angry look on the woman's face had frightened her too much.

After that she'd been given a grey skirt that was far too big for her, and a jumper that scratched her skin. Her own shiny new brown shoes, which Mummy had bought for her on the market at Easter, were taken away and she was given a pair of ugly black ones instead that pinched her toes. She'd even been given someone else's knickers that shocked Trudy greatly.

'Them aren't mine,' she'd protested, wriggling furiously as the woman in black had tried to put them on her. 'I want me own knickers.'

'Don't be silly. Yours are wet and filthy.'

Trudy sulked. She'd forgotten about wetting herself in the car. She felt ashamed about that. She wasn't a baby who wet her bed. She was a big girl now who could go to the lavatory on her own. But then she'd been upset, and the tall lady wouldn't let her do a wee-wee before they'd rushed off.

Why had her mummy sent her away with no clean knickers?

This continued to trouble her throughout that first long day. Trudy spoke to no one, and did nothing. She just stood and watched, trying to understand what was happening to her. Food was put in front of her but she couldn't eat it. She was taken to a playroom full of toys, but didn't feel in the mood for playing. Trudy wanted to ask when she could go home but since nobody spoke to her, she wasn't sure who to ask.

Then she was given a wash bag with a flannel and a tooth-brush that wasn't hers either. They weren't new, young as she was Trudy could tell that was awful. Her mummy was very particular about buying her a new toothbrush every few weeks, sometimes pink or blue.

It was a bigger shock to Trudy when it dawned on her that she was going have to sleep in this big, cold bedroom, and that her mummy wouldn't be there to tuck her in and read her a story. She had to queue to use the lavatory and nearly piddled in her pants again she was so frightened, but just managed to hold on.

Now, as she lay in the cold, strange bed between scratchy darned sheets, listening to strange night noises and other girls quietly sobbing, she struggled to understand it all. But it was the loss of her own knickers that troubled Trudy the most.

It was some time around dawn during that long sleepless, frightening first night that Trudy finally worked it all out in her confused mind. This terrible thing that had happened to her was all her fault. Mummy would have remembered about the knickers, wouldn't have allowed the nasty tall lady to take her away at all, if she'd been a good girl. But she'd done a bad thing. Two bad things, in fact.

First she'd run out of the house and Uncle Barry had been knocked down by that car. That was all her fault. If she'd gone to bed like Rosemary, her best doll in the curlers, it would never have happened and they'd all be safe.

Then Uncle Barry had said she must be brave and go with the man who'd picked her up out of the road and put the Elastoplast on her knee. 'Do as he tells you,' Uncle Barry had said.

And she had. She'd tried to be a good girl, hadn't cried too much at all. But the man had told her that she would like the bad thing he did that had hurt her so much, that it was all her fault for letting him. He kept on calling her a naughty girl. He'd said that he wouldn't tell, that it would be their little secret, but he must have lied. He must've told someone, and that's why she'd been locked up here in this nasty place. She'd been very, very bad and her mummy didn't love her any more.

Chapter Thirteen

Dena was distraught. She couldn't believe this was happening to her. She could hardly breathe, her heart and lungs pounded, an iron band of pain gripping her chest. She vomited throughout the day now, not just in the mornings, couldn't keep a thing down.

On the morning they'd taken Trudy away she'd stood in the street watching the car disappear in a cloud of dust and felt utterly helpless, paralysed by fear, unable to move.

It had been too early for the market to be open, although some stallholders were already there, too busy chatting with each other and setting out their stalls to see what had taken place, or notice her distress. Dena had stood in the middle of Champion Street for what seemed like hours, her legs like lead, feeling utterly lost and disorientated, not knowing what to do or where to go for help.

Dena could recall seeing Betty Hemley filling her flower buckets with water, Jimmy Ramsay washing down the new glass roof over his butcher's stall with a long brush. Pigeons were scavenging among the debris by the rubbish bins, and there was the sound of milk churns clinking, the smell of fresh bread being delivered. Yet all of these sounds and images, taken for granted on any other morning, seemed to exist in a separate world from the one in which she had been locked, trapped in a bubble of fear.

Her precious child had been taken into care and she didn't know where to turn for help.

Normally when she was in difficulty Dena would go to Barry. He'd been a friend to her brother Pete when the boy had helped on Barry's fruit and veg stall, and had stood by Dena from the moment she'd brought Trudy home from hospital as a baby. But how could she go to him now when he was the cause of her problems. Whatever had possessed him to do such a dreadful thing? How would she ever be able to face him again? And worst of all, who could she trust now?

Eventually she'd felt a trembling in her legs as sensation gradually returned. She'd begun to walk, then broken into a run. The stallholders had watched in open astonishment as Dena raced between the stalls, brushing past them without so much as a glance to right or left. She hadn't stopped running until she'd reached the hospital.

Dena wanted to see the young doctor she'd spoken to before but was told that he was busy with his other patients. But on hearing how upset she was, screaming and crying in reception, he had agreed to see her, showing compassion and sympathy. He remembered Trudy's case well. He sat Dena down in his office and offered her a glass of water.

'I don't want water, I want my child back! They've taken her away. They blame me for what's happened, can you believe it?'

'I'm sorry to hear that, Mrs Dobson.'

Something inside Dena snapped then. 'I'm *not* Mrs Dobson, I'm not married, and my name is Dena.'

There was a small silence while the doctor had assimilated this crucial piece of information. 'I see. Well, I'm afraid there's nothing I can do, Mrs – er – Dena. The police obviously feel they have a case, and the authorities must always act in the best interests of the child.'

'And it's best she be taken from the mother who loves her, is that it?' Dena's chestnut brown eyes were wild and raw with pain. 'I can't believe this is happening. I've done nothing to her, *nothing*! Why would Barry do such a thing? He loves Trudy too. Why would anyone do such a terrible thing?'

The doctor had cleared his throat, on surer ground now with a straightforward medical opinion. 'The perpetrator of such crimes often does pay a great deal of attention to the child in question beforehand, is seen to be acting generously and affectionately towards them, even claiming to love them. The only way I can explain it is as a sort of sickness. He may have been abused or neglected himself as a child, perhaps has difficulty with sexual relations and feels more comfortable with the young. He'll make excuses, say the child instigated the fondling, that she was to blame, that he was only showing her affection and she enjoyed it. It's a kind of mental disorder and I wish to God we knew how to treat it.'

This had shocked Dena. 'Trudy would never encourage anything of that sort, not willingly. She isn't even three years old. *And now they've taken her from me!* How do I get her back? Tell me that, doctor. How do I get her back?'

The doctor looked sorrowful. She remembered him shaking his head in despair, his expression kind and concerned. 'As I said, Dena, I'm afraid there's nothing more I can do to help.'

Later that day, Constable Nuttall had said very much the same when she'd gone to have it out with him too. 'These things must go through the due process of law, Dena love. I'm sure the little lass will indeed be returned to you, once they're satisfied she's no longer in any danger.'

'But she wasn't in any danger, not from *me* anyway. Are you saying that it's my fault Barry did this thing to her? That I was the one responsible just because I chose to go to the pictures and left her with him? That's not fair. I want to speak to him. I want to ask him *why*!'

'Nay, that won't do no good.' Constable Nuttall had striven to calm her, insisting it wouldn't be wise and that she should talk to Miss Rogers. But there was no help from the social worker either.

'I'm sure the authorities will allow you to visit the child, once she's settled in,' Miss Rogers had tartly informed her.

Dena's chest had gone tight with fear. 'Settled? Settled where? Where have they taken her, do you know? She's not in Ivy Bank, is she? Dear Lord, I spent years in that dreadful place. Don't tell me that's where they've taken her?'

'I'm not at liberty to say, as you well know, Dena. If you aren't satisfied, I'd advise you to find yourself a solicitor, someone to ask these questions officially on your behalf. A solicitor is by far the best person to put your case in the proper fashion. I can do no more.'

Now Dena sat at her kitchen table, the sink full of unwashed pots and yet another cup of tea gone cold before her, choking back the tears. No one could help her. She hadn't a soul in the world to turn to. But did they really expect her to sit back and do nothing, to allow her child to be removed from her care without so much as a protest? Their advice might be well-meant, but was utterly useless. Could she even afford a solicitor? Whatever the cost she must find the money somehow, if she was ever to get Trudy back.

—

Lizzie was still dithering over whether or not she should have agreed to go out with Charlie, and what had possessed to say she'd go out with Jack Cleaver, when Friday came around, all too quickly. Aunty Dot was busily making chocolate caramels. Since this involved boiling sugar and milk, the children had been banished from the kitchen. Alan and Beth were taking turns with a pair of roller skates in the street, Cissie was playing skipping games with her friends, Joey was doing his homework, and the baby was asleep in its pram in the backyard. Lizzie, however, was hovering in the kitchen, a fretful look on her face, not doing anything useful at all.

'So do you think I should go out with Charlie tonight or not? And if I do, what should I do about Jack Cleaver?'

Aunty Dot carefully added a teaspoon of cream of tartar to the boiling mixture. 'Don't involve me in your convoluted love life. It's your decision, not mine, love.'

'But you must have an opinion.'

'I've never met this Charlie, so how can I have?'

'All right, I'll bring him home, shall I, then you can tell me what you think?'

'What I think is that I'll never get these sweets done if you don't shift yourself. If you will insist on getting under my feet then chop up that butter for me. It's already weighed out.'

Lizzie picked up the knife and began slowly to chop the butter into cubes, her mind racing. 'You know *why* I'm hesitating, don't you? It's not that I don't like Charlie, I do. Very much, in point of fact. But his father has done exactly as he said he would. Finch has opened a stall in direct competition to us, without even allowing me the time he'd promised to find an alternative supplier.'

'So you said,' Aunty continued, in her calm, unflustered way. 'Right, you can start adding the butter now, and stir well as we don't want the milk to burn.'

'I have tried,' Lizzie continued, desperation in her voice. 'But I suspect Finch has done as he threatened. All the companies I've contacted so far have some excuse or other why they can't supply us. Mostly they say they don't deliver in our area, which has to be rubbish. We're in the centre of Manchester for goodness' sake, not the back of beyond.'

It was hot working in the tiny kitchen, but the smoothness of the caramel paste as she stirred the butter into it, soothed Lizzie. She'd always found the making of sweets and chocolates a satisfying occupation, and the smell as Aunty added a vanilla pod or two was utterly mouth-watering.

'Will we coat these with chocolate once they've been chopped into squares and cooled?'

'We certainly will.'

'I do love chocolate caramels. You don't suppose we *could* make enough sweets and chocolates for the stall *without* the need for a supplier, do you?'

Lizzie tried not to let the suggestion sound too pressing but her churning thoughts had kept her awake half the night. This idea, put forward by Charlie himself, confusingly enough, was beginning to seem less and less of a crazy notion the more she thought about it. Although it wasn't the only reason for her sleepless nights recently. Just remembering Charlie's kiss brought a hot flush to her cheeks and made Lizzie tremble.

Here she was, an hour from her deadline and still in a terrible dilemma. She had dates with two men on the same evening and couldn't make up her mind whether she wished to go out with either of them.

Aunty was checking the caramel mixture with her thermometer to see if it had reached crack temperature, and gave Lizzie the opportunity to turn her mind to other things. Fortunately the heat in the kitchen would excuse the colour in her cheeks.

'What do *you* think, Aunty?'

'I reckon another few minutes. Keep stirring.'

'I mean about producing our own sweets.'

'I know what you mean.'

'So could it be done?'

Aunty looked at her. 'You're serious about this, aren't you?'

'It's surely worth considering.'

Aunty Dot let out a heavy sigh as she wiped down the Formica work surfaces. 'I'm happy to help, but to be honest I reckon we'd be pushing it, Lizzie love. I have my hands full enough already with them childer. It would be a major task to stock the stall entirely.' She put a hand almost protectively to her side and guilt washed over Lizzie.

What was she thinking of, even asking? How could she have forgotten that Aunty hadn't been well lately? Lizzie still hadn't persuaded her to see a doctor. Dot never took a minute to rest or put her feet up. Even now, as well as supervising the caramel mixture the older woman was also mixing a bottle for the latest baby. Aunty Dot had an amazing facility for doing two things at the same time, but sadly even she had her limits. Expecting her to turn herself into a small sweet factory on top of being a foster mother probably was asking too much.

'Well, what about this other matter then?'

'What other matter?'

Lizzie stifled a sigh. Her concentration had a habit of slipping, always having too many things on her mind. She was probably mentally compiling her next shopping list, or working out what they would have for tea tomorrow.

'As I explained, I could go out with Charlie Finch tonight, simply to talk over this idea of producing our own sweets, you understand. But the problem is he's the son of our sworn enemy so maybe that's not such a good idea.' Lizzie's lovely face tightened in anguish.

Aunty looked at her and waited, knowing there was more to come.

'And that's not the only problem, as you and I are only too aware. He might start asking questions about my family. I don't mean you, Aunty, I mean my mother… Oh, you know what I mean. That would be worse, wouldn't it? That would be dreadful!'

Aunty gave her a measuring look. 'Weren't you planning on telling him then, this lad of yours?'

'No, well possibly, or eventually! I suppose I might have to one day.'

'Might have to?'

'I never really thought about it.' And then, as Aunty Dot looked at her askance, Lizzie gave a low groan. 'All right, I don't like to think about it. I don't *want* to think about it – about her.'

Aunty checked the thermometer again. 'I saw her the other day, by the way. She asked after you.'

A hunted expression came over Lizzie's face, the tension in her such that she clenched her fists into tight balls. 'It's hopeless, isn't it? I can't see him, I can't ever. Every time I've been open about it to boys in the past, it's all gone horribly wrong, you know it has.'

'Maybe that's because you haven't met the right chap yet.'

'It's because of her, my flaming mother! Oh, why can't life be simple? Maybe I should just play safe and go out with good old Jack Cleaver instead. He never asks me any questions and is no trouble whatsoever. Oh, Aunty, what *do* you think I should I do?'

'I think you should lift up that pan and pour the mixture out on to this oiled board. It's ready for rolling.'

–

Aunty was sitting darning Alan's socks when the lights flickered. 'Penny in the slot,' she called. She kept a small pile of coins by the electricity meter, even though neighbours warned her that this was a foolish thing to do as it was simply asking to be robbed by any burglar who chanced to pass by and glance into her hall.

Joey called out to her, 'I'll do it, Aunty.'

They also warned her not to trust the children, constantly implying that the temptation would be too much for them and one would be sure to steal from her eventually, if she didn't watch out. Aunty Dot would smile and nod and go on trusting them, stacking up the pennies and the shillings by the meter, just as she always had.

Lizzie had gone off on her date; which one she'd decided, she hadn't mentioned. The younger children were already in bed, the chocolate caramels all made, and she and Joey were lingering by the dying embers of the fire, enjoying a mug of cocoa together before going off to their own beds. Outside it was raining and a wind had sprung up. But inside it was all cosy and warm. They'd been listening to *Bedtime With Braden*, testing a few of the caramels while they sat there, which had cheered Dot up.

Aunty Dot tried not to worry about her charges, Lizzie in particular since she was a grown woman now and in charge of her own life, but it wasn't easy. There was always so much to worry about.

This business of her mother she was going to have to face sooner or later with this Charlie, if she was really serious about him. And there was the greater worry of Cedric Finch trying to destroy their livelihood, so unfair. The poor lass had spent years building it up into a good little business, only to have Finch demolish it just because they'd had a notion to add a few home-made sweets of their own.

Aunty Dot felt guilty about that. It had been her idea in the first place, in an attempt to save them some money and make a bit more profit, but now it had all gone wrong and backfired on her.

Dot sighed, wishing with all her heart that she felt stronger, younger, better able to help. Maybe she should see a doctor, after all, depressing though it would be to hear him tell her what she knew already, deep in her heart. She kept promising that she would but never actually got around to it. Where was the rush, after all? She was either well or she wasn't. What good would it do to learn she was off to the knacker's yard?

She resolutely set the thought aside. Eeh, but twenty years ago she'd've taken Finch on, and gladly. Given him a run for his money. But did she have the right to interfere in Lizzie's life and encourage her to do so? It would be a risky undertaking, and depended, in a way, on exactly how keen this Charlie was on her.

The sound of a coin dropping into the meter coincided with another, a noise like a scratching on wood.

'Hecky thump, have we got mice?'

'It's somebody at the door, Aunty. Shall I see who it is?'

'No, you get off to bed, lad. I'll go.' Aunty thought it might be Winnie Holmes coming to pour out her heart, not at all a suitable talk for a young boy to hear.

But it wasn't Winnie this time. It was Jack Cleaver standing there in the pouring rain, getting soaked through. 'Hello, Jack, what can I do for you at this time of night?' Aunty thought she could guess the reason for his call, and she half smiled to herself.

'Is Lizzie in, Mrs Thompson? She was supposed to meet me tonight and she hasn't turned up. I wondered if she'd happen forgotten, or maybe gone to the wrong place?'

'Nay, I wouldn't be knowing anything about that,' Aunty said. 'I can't help you, I'm sorry, but I'll be sure to tell her you called.'

Cleaver didn't appear pleased by this response, a scowl darkening his face beneath the dripping trilby hat. 'She must have said where she was going?' His voice sounded peevish.

'She's young, never tells me anything. Why would she?' Aunty smilingly remarked, and again repeated her regrets at being unable to help, wished him a polite good night and quietly closed the door. Poor soul, he'd really got it bad. Then she banked up the fire, turned off the lights and went contentedly to bed.

Pulling the blankets up to her chin, Dot chuckled to herself. 'So the lass has chosen Charlie, and Jack Cleaver has been cast off as a has-been. Watch out, Finch, it could be you next!'

Chapter Fourteen

Instinct told Dena that the authorities had acted this way because Trudy was illegitimate. Would any other abused child have been taken away from an innocent parent? Despite all her efforts to bring Trudy up in a loving, secure home, helped initially by Miss Rogers who, ironically, had been the one to find her a bedsit and agreed to her keeping the baby in the first place. Now the woman had apparently turned against her.

Dena had been aware for some time that the social worker continued to keep a close eye on her. She had been keen to see Dena respectably married, and with a stepfather for little Trudy. Splitting up with Carl obviously hadn't helped Dena's case one bit.

Barry was brought before the magistrates to be remanded into custody awaiting trial. Winnie had already instructed a solicitor, on his behalf: a thin, earnest gentleman with protruding ears. He pointed out in his measured way that since the child in question had been taken into care, his client no longer constituted any danger to her.

Dena listened bemused as he explained how Trudy came from an unstable home background, living with an immoral, unmarried mother, and had now been taken into safe keeping. Almost as if her child were a stray cat.

Barry's solicitor was also at pains to point out that the evidence against him was flimsy, little more than circumstantial. Surely the police should be asking more questions?

He suggested that the alleged abuse might not have taken place on the evening of the accident at all. He understood, for instance, that the mother's boyfriend had recently 'done a runner'. He should be found and questioned about his relationship with the little girl? 'And the child's *real* father...' Here the lawyer consulted his papers as if it were all far too complicated and unpleasant for him to come to grips with. 'He is currently serving a life sentence for murder, so no one could call the child's background a good one.'

It was these words, more than any other that brought home to Dena the seriousness of her plight.

The solicitor duly pointed out that the girl's physical state had only been discovered because she'd been taken to a doctor that night due to a near brush with death. Could she in fact have been abused on some previous occasion? Were the bruises on her body inflicted simply by the accident itself, or by earlier abuse? Excuses would have been made, children often falling down and hurting themselves. And since the child was too young to be questioned, there was absolutely no proof. Much more information, he asserted, needed to be discovered before his client should be compelled to lose his liberty.

After a week on remand Barry was relieved to be allowed home on bail. Dena wasn't sure how she felt about that. He had indeed been like a father to her, and she'd loved him dearly. He'd been good to Pete too, her lovely brother, employing him on his fruit and veg stall and often giving him extras to bring home.

As a boy himself, Barry had worked with his own father in a strong-man act touring the music halls. He was still a short, stocky man, a strange mix of tender heart and physical toughness. But was he honest? Dena hated the thought of her old friend being locked up with criminals and murderers. But neither did she wish to see his face every time she walked down Champion Street.

If he truly was guilty, why should he be allowed to continue with his life: permitted to continue working on his stall, carry on as if nothing had happened; when her lovely Trudy had been taken away and locked up as if *she* were the criminal?

How could it have gone so wrong?

Coming face to face with Barry at the door of the courtroom, Dena stared at him for a long moment, unable to find the words to express the emotions churning inside her. Then she turned on her heel and walked briskly away.

Winnie shouted after her, her voice frantic. 'Dena! Don't go like this. Dena love, we have to talk…'

But Dena wasn't ready to talk. Despite all she'd said earlier to Constable Nuttall, she couldn't even bring herself to listen.

–

Lizzie's decision to stand up to Jack Cleaver and go out with Charlie instead filled her with guilt. The shame of dumping him had niggled even as she'd run through the rain to the Dog and Duck to meet Charlie. It was heartless of her to change her mind at the last minute, when she'd promised faithfully she would go out with Cleaver. She'd been weak to agree in the first place, still not to be upfront and cancel the date properly. Utterly shameful! Yet Lizzie knew that had she attempted to tell him he would have talked her into keeping the date, and given him false hope.

'I waited for over an hour,' he complained when he came the next day to the Chocolate Cabin, a mournful look on his face, rather like a whipped puppy.

Lizzie didn't have the heart to tell him the truth: that while he was waiting for her at the Midland Hotel, she was sitting in the Odeon cinema with Charlie's arm around her.

'I'm so sorry!' She made vague remarks about something unexpected having come up, without saying precisely what that was, but she could see the knowledge that she lied in his hurt expression.

Oh, but she'd made the right decision. She wouldn't have missed that date with Charlie for the world. He'd kissed her again when he'd taken her home, and she hadn't slapped him on that occasion. The kiss had been long and lingering and

Lizzie had savoured every second of it. But it wasn't just the way that he kissed her, it was everything about him that she liked.

She loved his floppy fair hair, his cheeky smile, the twinkle in his grey eyes, and his impish perversity. Charlie had a most idiosyncratic way of looking at things. He was fun, and filled with a determination to enjoy life to the full.

And she'd agreed to see him again tonight.

–

Dena went to Miss Rogers and asked if she could see Trudy.

'I hardly think it likely they'll allow a visit at this early stage,' the older woman retorted, in a tone indicating that she was surprised Dena had even asked.

'But she's only a baby, and I'm her mother.'

'Don't get upset, Dena. Having a tantrum will do no good at all.'

Dena took a steadying breath, striving to calm herself. 'I'm not having a tantrum but am a little upset. I've every right to be.'

'It could be said that you should have thought of your child when you sent Carl Garside packing. You'll not do any better, not with your reputation.'

Dena froze. 'I don't have a reputation.'

Miss Rogers looked down her long nose at Dena. 'It would be naïve of you to think so. Having an illegitimate baby at sixteen doesn't make you Queen of the May. I'm sure arrangements will be made for you to see your daughter, eventually, when Trudy has had time to settle. You will simply have to be patient. Perhaps in six months or so.'

'*Six months!*'

'It is far too soon at this juncture. You wouldn't be allowed to bring her home, and it would only upset you both. Now concentrate on your work and be thankful Trudy is in the care of experts.'

Trudy was not settling well. The experts at Ivy Bank, if that was the correct term for the teachers and minders employed in that establishment, were at a loss to understand how to deal with the child. She still refused to speak, her soulful amber eyes watching the business of school life around her while she herself took little part in it.

Being so young, and so small, she'd become an obvious target for bullies. The older girls in the dormitory picked on her and called her names, such as 'dumb', and 'stupid' because she never said a word. They would push and shove her, laugh at her, hide her clothes or her hairbrush, put worms from the vegetable garden into her bed. They would take food from her plate, even steal her night-time cocoa and biscuit, so that more often than not the little girl went to bed hungry. All of this was intended to force her to speak up or to protest against their bullying. The less she responded and took their bullying as her due, the more they stepped up their campaign.

They liked to pretend to forget something vitally important for a class and make her run back to fetch it, and then when she returned, all hot and bothered, and shook her head because she couldn't find the book or pencil or whatever it was, they would laugh and produce it out of their own pocket.

'Oh, dear, silly me, I had it with me all the time.'

Hot water was expensive and baths had to be shared, the girls taking turns to use the same water. Trudy was always last in line, pushed to the back of the queue, and the water would be cold and filthy by the time she got to it, many of the girls having peed in it too, to make it even worse. They were merciless to her when she wet her bed, and sadly Trudy had found that happened fairly often. Every time she closed her eyes she would see that man's face, feel his fingers hurting her, and she'd wake up crying in a warm, damp patch of smelly urine.

The next morning, filled with shame, she would try to scrub at the patch with her flannel when no one was looking. But it became nasty and smelly, and she would have to wash that out before she could use it. Often the sheet was still wet when she climbed back into bed the next night.

Trudy itched constantly, and the other girls teased her about that, saying she'd brought the bugs in with her, when she knew this wasn't true. When they'd cut off all her hair it had been clean. Her mummy had seen to that. Everyone had bugs at Ivy Bank. She'd heard people say so.

After breakfast her morning was spent in the nursery class learning to recite the alphabet, do counting and read flashcards. Sometimes they would be allowed to play with bricks or the sand tray, and they would all sit down in the afternoon to *Listen With Mother* on the wireless. Trudy enjoyed the stories on the programme but took no part in nursery play.

Things would often go mysteriously wrong and she would always be the one to get the blame.

One afternoon while they were all taking their afternoon naps on their camp beds, Trudy noticed a movement out of the corner of her eye. The teacher, Miss Livesey, was nodding in her chair and nobody else seemed to be watching, but Chrissie, one of the older girls who came to help the little ones tie their shoe laces and button their coats, was crawling about on her stomach under the camp beds. Trudy watched through her eyelashes, lids half closed so that she looked as if she were asleep, and saw how the girl collected up everyone's shoes and heaped them into a pile. Everyone wore identical black lace-up shoes, so it would be impossible to tell them apart.

When the teacher woke up, she was horrified. 'Who is responsible for this? Who has mixed up everyone's shoes? Come along now, own up at once or you will all be in trouble!' Some of the little ones began to cry. Trudy watched horrified as the girl responsible whispered in Miss Livesey's ear while pointing straight at Trudy.

The teacher glowered at her. 'Trudy Dobson, come here this minute. Is it true what Chrissie says, that you did this? Well, speak up, child! Did you or didn't you?'

Trudy shook her head but was smacked anyway, right there in front of everyone. Miss Livesey pulled down her knickers and smacked her bare bottom while Chrissie, the girl who'd really done the deed, smirked behind her hand.

'You're a bad girl to take everyone's shoes,' Miss Livesey scolded her. 'That was very naughty. No supper for you tonight, madam.'

Trudy knew already that she was bad. The man had told her so. That was why her mummy had let her be taken away.

Dena was once more vomiting into the sink. There was no doubt about it, she was most definitely pregnant. Not yet two months gone but fear was growing inside her hour by hour, along with the child. What would happen when it was born? Would they take her new baby into care too?

Dena was desperate to get some advice on what to do. Not about whether or not she should keep it. There never had been any question of abortion with her first pregnancy, nor with this one. But how to protect her child and not have *them* – the authorities – take her away, that was the question. That was Dena's big worry.

Usually she'd turn to Winnie for help, but relations between the two women couldn't be called easy. The horror of what had happened to Trudy hung between them, dark and untouchable, like a threatening shadow.

Dena had expressed no opinion on the matter beyond saying that she really didn't understand any of it. Nothing she had ever had to deal with before, and she had endured many difficult times, could have prepared her for this. Winnie too had suffered when she'd lost her first husband, her beloved Donald, but was equally at a loss.

Winnie, however, had made it abundantly clear on the day of the magistrates' hearing, as well as every day since, that she believed implicitly in Barry's innocence. 'I don't care what they say, my Barry would never do such a thing. He loves that child. Absolutely adores her. And he was a father himself once, so why would he want to hurt her? I hope you believe that, Dena, because it's true.'

'I don't know what to believe,' she wearily and constantly remarked.

Winnie no longer came to make her breakfast or popped round of an evening with a plate of dinner for her. Conversation between the pair of them was awkward and stilted. Yet they were old friends, and since Dena occupied the adjoining stall to Winnie's they could hardly avoid each other.

The arrangement between them was that when Dena had finished her morning stint in the workshop, she would help out on both stalls in the afternoon. It eased some of the load on Winnie's shoulders, and Dena always used to enjoy the change of scene, a period of time when she actually got to meet her customers as she sold them the skirts and blouses. Now, she was only too thankful for the comparative privacy afforded her by the workshop. With things as they were, she only came to the stall reluctantly.

The two women worked alongside each other in almost total silence, measuring and folding, smiling at customers but exchanging only essential remarks with each other over which customer had ordered what, the price of a skirt or length of fabric, generally spoken in cool, crisp tones.

But then everything had changed. People gave Dena pitying smiles she hated, or else they made veiled comments that they'd always had their doubts about Barry Holmes. Some old women were ready to heap blame on her too, bluntly stating that a mother should never leave her child with a male babysitter, however well known he may be to the child.

And Belle Garside took every opportunity to remind her that she wouldn't be in this mess now if she hadn't dumped both of Belle's fine sons.

Cedric Finch's new stall set up in opposition to Lizzie's, appeared to be thriving, and as she had anticipated he was indeed undercutting her on price. They even ran a special offer, giving away a free lollipop to every customer who bought a pound of sweets, while she was rapidly running out of stock to sell. Lizzie did once manage to find a new supplier willing to deliver some boxes of sweets to her, but the second time they came their delivery van was stolen. It turned up in Salford a few days later, but it was clear to her that Finch was responsible. It made her feel deeply uncomfortable knowing that he was watching her so closely, aware of any deliveries she had due.

'I wouldn't object to fair competition,' she complained to Charlie, 'but your father isn't playing fair. He's using underhand methods, almost criminal, in order to beat me.'

'That's my pop,' Charlie agreed, a growl of fury in his voice.

They'd talked and talked about how Lizzie could hold her own against Finch, and no solution had as yet been found. Aunty Dot was working far too hard already to make any more sweets. In fact, Lizzie had finally persuaded her to see a doctor although, disappointingly, she'd only come away with a tonic. Lizzie wondered if Aunty had in fact told him the whole story and owned up to the mysterious pain in her side. She thought not.

Coping with the stall and helping Aunty Dot with the children was more than enough to be going on with for Lizzie too. It would take money to start up a sweet manufacturing business, money she didn't have. Charlie suggested that she borrow it from the bank but this sounded far too risky and Lizzie couldn't summon up the courage. The way they were going, rapidly downhill, there'd soon be no business left to save.

But she could still dream. Every evening as she and Charlie walked by the canal, or sat for hours over a glass of shandy in the Dog and Duck, they would talk endlessly over plans for making their own sweets, even though they knew it was hopeless and would probably never happen.

Just to be with him filled her with happiness, and Lizzie knew that he felt the same way about her. Their eyes would meet and they would both smile, knowing precisely what the other was thinking. It had been like that from the start. Nothing needed to be said between them, they just knew that this was it. They were in love. Lizzie was twenty-two years old and felt as if she was on the brink of a wonderful new adventure.

–

Dena was walking home, morose and unhappy, dreading the loneliness of the empty house that awaited her when a figure suddenly appeared at her elbow. She knew by the smell of tobacco and whisky emanating from him that it was the bookie, Billy Quinn, although she didn't pause or turn to address him, simply kept on walking.

He rested one hand on her shoulder, forcing her to slow to a reluctant halt. 'I just wanted to express my sympathy over your loss.'

Dena bit back the desire to tell him she didn't need, or want, his sympathy. But this was Billy Quinn and it wouldn't have been wise.

'Thank you.'

'You must be worried sick about the poor wee lass. All I would say is, when you get her out of that place, you should take her to live somewhere else. Barry could well get off, and he won't ever change his nasty, dirty ways. Haven't I seen with me own eyes what he's capable of?'

Dena did turn to look at him then, to gaze straight into those piercing blue eyes and ask, 'What do you mean? What have you seen?'

Quinn laid a finger along the side of his nose. 'Now wouldn't that be telling? You haven't been to his boxing club and I have, do you see, so I know what goes on down there. It's not what you would call pleasant, no indeed. I'd offer to be a witness for ye, but who would believe Billy Quinn? And I'm what you might call allergic to police stations and magistrate's courts.' He gave a nasty little laugh. 'No, you start planning a new future for yourself and the nipper, girl. Get out of here before any more harm is done, or find yourself a husband and turn respectable. She's a tempting little charmer, to be sure, and you don't want anything worse to happen to her, now do you?'

Dena watched him swagger away, her heart pounding in her chest. What had he meant by that? Had he seen Barry do something with one of the lads at the boxing club? And if so, what?

And how could she leave the market? Where on earth could she go? Champion Street was not only her home, it was her livelihood. Without that, and regular money coming in, they'd never let her have Trudy back. As for finding herself a husband she had no wish to be lectured about becoming respectable by the likes of Billy Quinn!

Besides, *she* shouldn't be the one forced to leave, or change her life, any more than Trudy should be the one incarcerated. *They'd done nothing wrong!* If Barry was guilty, he should be the one to pay.

Chapter Fifteen

One day as they walked along the towpath by the canal, Charlie asked Lizzie how she came to meet Aunty Dot. The sun was shining, and Lizzie was contentedly watching the ducks swimming along in little family groups, happy to feel her hand so warmly held in his, so she told him about the two years she'd spent in the industrial school.

'I was looked after by hard-hearted nuns until she, Aunty, rescued me. I think she'd come looking for a boy. Aunty Dot loves little boys, but then she found me. I was in something of a state at the time and she felt sorry for me, I expect. Anyway, she took me home with her there and then, and we got on so well we've never looked back since.'

Charlie was watching her carefully as she told this story, all too aware of her ability to make something bad sound trivial and of no consequence. 'What sort of a state? What were they doing to you, these nuns?'

Lizzie wiped away tears with the flat of her hands, glad to lean against him and draw comfort from his strength, relishing the knowledge that he didn't blame her, that she wasn't going to lose him, not if she was careful. Cuddled close in Charlie's arms, she told him everything. Almost everything.

'Oh, nothing they hadn't done a dozen times before. I was always hungry. Starving! There never seemed to be enough on my plate for a growing child, so I would steal anything I could get my thieving hands on. If I was on kitchen duties, I'd eat bits of raw potato when no one was looking, or apple peel. Apple peel is scrumptious! On one occasion I'd been taking out the rubbish and found an apple core and some bits of carrot that I simply couldn't resist. Sister Ignatius spotted me rummaging in the bin, feeding out of it like some sort of demented rat. I was locked up for forty-eight hours on bread and water to teach me not to be greedy. I think they forgot all about me because I was there for days, much longer than usual.'

'It had happened before then?'

'Oh, yes! I was a rebel, you see, the kind of girl who caused disruption in the ranks, as it were, stirring up the others to stand up for themselves and complain about the bitter cold in the dormitory. Or, like Oliver Twist, ask for more.'

Charlie chuckled at that, and squeezed her hand. 'There's my girl.'

'We were always so cold, and constantly hungry. And I'd nothing to lose, you see, no home to go back to, so I was prepared to fight for everything.'

Charlie opened his mouth to ask her more about why it was that she had no home, but the expression on her face and her tone of voice were so bitter and hard that he instantly changed his mind. One thing at a time, he thought. This was the first occasion she'd allowed him a glimpse into her background and he didn't want to push her too hard or she might clam up altogether.

'The Sisters of Mercy would lock me up in one of their smelly, old cells for the slightest thing. If I climbed up on to the hard bed I could catch a glimpse of the main courtyard through a tiny window, and I'd spend hours looking out of it, desperate to see a scrap of blue sky, a bird flying, a cheerful face. I was watching one day when I saw this woman walk up to the front door and decided to attract her attention. She heard me yelling and kicking up a fuss and insisted I be let out for her to examine me.

'It was Aunty Dot, who they knew well. She found me covered in sores and bruises, my hair alive with lice, and she took me home with her that very day. The nuns weren't happy, said it was against the rules. There was a furious row, but Aunty being Aunty, she told them to sue her if they dared. And that was that. I was saved.' Lizzie gave a tremulous smile.

'And you've loved her ever since.'

'I have. She's the best mam in the world. She has loved me and cared for me, seen me through some bad times and made me whole again.'

'And now I love you too, Lizzie,' Charlie said, kissing her.

–

Lizzie was happy. At least she would be if only Jack Cleaver would stop pestering her. Even this morning, although he wasn't allowed to sell her anything because of Finch's ban, he'd cornered her in Belle's café to ask if another day might suit her better for their date. Why couldn't the poor man take the hint? Lizzie had stirred her frothy coffee, smiled brightly up at him and tried to let him down lightly.

'Look, I'm really sorry, Jack, only I can't promise anything right now. Aunty isn't well, not at all herself, so I have to help with the children.' This made her feel even worse because although it wasn't exactly a lie, she was nevertheless managing to find plenty of time to see Charlie. Aunty Dot had told her how Jack had come to the house that night looking for her, the poor soul looking like a drowned rat. She'd warned Lizzie to come clean with him and tell him the truth: that she wasn't interested and had fallen in love with someone else.

Lizzie offered up an apologetic smile. 'See, the fact is, Jack—'

'It's all right, I understand,' he said, interrupting her, and Lizzie could tell by the haunted expression in his brown eyes that he understood only too well that she was simply making excuses. 'I wouldn't expect a lovely girl like you to look twice at a boring chap like me.'

'Don't be silly, you mustn't say such things! You aren't boring at all.' But even Lizzie could hear the lack of conviction in her tone.

To her dismay Jack sat down opposite her and leaned across the table, so close that the scent of camphor from his shiny suit wafted over her. The intensity of his expression was unnerving as he dropped his voice to a whisper.

'I saw you the other night, Lizzie, with the boss's son. I know Charlie is young and good-looking, much more your type. I'm not sure though that his father would necessarily agree that *you're* right for him, lovely as you are. I'd take care if I were you. Once Finch has taken against someone, that's it. Besides, he expects to marry his only son and heir to someone with pots of money, and Finch isn't a man who takes kindly to being crossed.'

Lizzie gave a half laugh, feeling slightly unsettled by these words, as well as his closeness. 'Goodness, that's jumping the gun a bit, isn't it? I do like Charlie, it's true. In fact, that's what I've been trying to say. But who's talking about marriage, for goodness' sake, not me?' And then muttering another apology, she took advantage of the ensuing silence and fled, leaving her coffee largely untouched. She really couldn't bear to witness Jack Cleaver's misery any longer.

Jack Cleaver was not at all happy. He would willingly marry Lizzie Pringle tomorrow, given a modicum of encouragement, but she stubbornly resisted his every advance, pushing him further and further away, and he did so hate to be rejected. That's what his father had done, no matter how hard he'd tried to please the man.

He stood dawdling at the corner of Champion Street, watching the children play, when really he should be getting into his old Ford and driving off to the next market, to Bolton, Preston or Blackburn to show his samples and acquire more orders for Finch's, but he stood riveted to the spot, fascinated by the children's antics.

Why had Lizzie stood him up that time? He'd done everything he could think of to please her, taking as his guide all the matinee idols he'd seen at the cinema on rainy afternoons.

He watched Joey and Alan whizzing about on their trolley-cart. A small girl – Cissie, was that her name? – was skipping and singing to herself. A pretty little thing, Jack thought. He walked a few paces along the street to take a better look.

Deep down Jack Cleaver realised that he was not good with women. He was not, like some he could name, a ladies' man. He was no Cary Grant or Burt Lancaster. Even so, he'd make Lizzie Pringle a much better husband than a young idiot like Charlie Finch.

What did that frivolous young man have to offer? Nothing. He'd never done anything to earn his place in the Finch empire, as you might call it. Even his own father had little time for him. The pair of them were constantly at each other's throats, and was it any wonder with the way the lad had thrown away all his chances?

Jack, on the other hand, had a great deal of business experience. He saw himself working to develop Pringle's sweets and chocolate business into an empire to rival Finch's, Lizzie standing loyally at his side, as a good wife should. He craved the security and respectability he'd once taken for granted, and had great plans and dreams, seeing Lizzie's sweet business as a means of an escape from his current employment, and from a situation he was beginning to find irksome.

When he'd first got in with Cedric Finch everything had been fine and dandy. They'd got on well since they had one or two shared interests. Consequently, Jack had hoped his employer would show appreciation for favours done, by offering him quick promotion. He'd even dared dream of becoming a partner. Sadly, that hadn't happened. Finch treated him with contempt, simply took advantage of him, as he did everyone else.

But Jack had decided it was time to take control of his own life. Setting up in business for himself seemed the best way to do it, and Jack believed he could make Lizzie happy. A steady, reliable husband was surely all a woman needed.

Another child came running out of number thirty-seven. Jack recognised her as Beth, young Alan's sister. Hands on hips she was clearly telling him off, apparently insisting it was her turn on the trolley, but for once Alan wasn't having it and a real ding-dong battle was taking place. He liked a child with spirit, Jack mused. Poor little so-and-sos didn't have much of a life since their parents had rejected them, just like his own had.

Beth gave the trolley a hefty shove and the front wheels came off. Alan was shouting at his sister at the top of his voice while Joey chased after the wheels, now rolling away down the street.

Jack hastened over. 'Let me help. We can fix that in no time.' He took the wheels from Joey's hands, though the boy didn't relinquish them willingly and there was a resentful glare in his eyes. Eyes that were far too knowing for such a young lad.

He would be kind to these children, Jack thought, as he struggled to latch the old pram wheels back into place. He was very fond of kids, always felt comfortable with them, anybody would tell Lizzie that was the case. Didn't he often bring children like this little gifts of sweets, take them out on treats and picnics? Although his motivation for doing so was entirely his own affair. His main priority, naturally, was to make Lizzie like him and agree to go out with him.

The wheels were fixed, and Alan had reluctantly agreed to allow his sister to have a turn, mollified by the chocolate drops Jack was handing out.

They weren't bad children, after all, a bit wayward and lacking in discipline. Particularly Joey, who'd turned his nose up at the sweets and almost shouldered Jack out of the way to prevent him from helping Beth to sit properly on the trolley-cart.

They were obviously in need of a man around the house, someone to exercise better control and discipline over them, instead of all the namby-pambying they got from Aunty Dot. Jack would enjoy bringing some order to the household.

As he walked away and left the children to their squabbling, he reminded himself that he had a great deal to offer any woman. He was, after all, a reasonable man with an equable disposition and money in his pocket. He owned his own house, so Lizzie couldn't complain that he wouldn't be bringing something to the marriage. Thanks to Aunt Doris, he had a bit put by.

Jack did worry slightly about how he would feel about having another person, and a woman at that, always around day and night: living with him, sharing his bathroom and his bed.

The latter wouldn't be strictly necessary, not every night. He'd always enjoyed being alone. Jack valued his privacy, didn't care to reveal too much about himself. He'd learned to develop a social patter, obviously essential in his job as a salesman, but he didn't like or trust people as much as he pretended to, and had no wish for them to know his personal business. He much preferred to keep his distance, be a little detached as it were, although he could put on a show of being sociable in order to achieve his object.

Once they were man and wife and it was all signed and sealed, he could stop bothering about such things, as he would expect Lizzie to be content to live an equally quiet life, confining herself to the home and not going out gallivanting in the Dog and Duck every night. She would have to cease being a silly young girl and become much more dignified and restrained. The kind of wife his own dear mother had been before her breakdown, undoubtedly caused by the criminal actions of his father.

He'd thought he was winning Lizzie round when she'd agreed to go out with him, and his hopes had soared. But it had been false. She'd forgotten all about him the minute she'd fallen for Charlie Finch.

Jack didn't care to be treated with such contempt, to be left hanging around for everyone to laugh at behind their hand. To have to go cap in hand, metaphorically speaking, to her door in the pouring rain; asking for the favour of her company that night had been humiliating. He'd felt demeaned, having to swallow his pride in such a way.

The more he thought about it, the more the resentment built up in him. He was only too aware that people thought him a bit odd because he lived alone and liked to keep himself to himself, but Lizzie making promises that she'd no intention of keeping wasn't nice, not nice at all. Did she think him so weak and feeble that he'd just take it, without complaint? If so, she was very much mistaken.

There were one or two things about Lizzie Pringle that Finch might find interesting. Much as he protected his own privacy, Jack had always made it his business to find out everything he could about other people, and he knew about her. It was amazing what you could discover if you watched carefully and listened at doors.

–

Lizzie privately conceded that Jack Cleaver may have a point. She would not in any way be the kind of girl Cedric Finch would choose for his only son, for more reasons than one. He would indeed want someone rich and respectable, not a cheap little stallholder with a shady past. But later when she casually said as much to Charlie, he told her she was talking utter nonsense.

'You're wonderful! Anyway, *I* choose who I go out with, not my father.' Then he'd kissed her some more, just to prove his point, and before Lizzie knew what she was doing, she'd agreed to have tea with his family, so that she could meet them properly. It was typical in a way, of Charlie's stubborn optimism. To be fair to herself, Lizzie did try to point out, as tactfully as she could, that although they'd been seeing each other every day for several weeks now, Sunday tea with his family might be rushing it a bit.

'Maybe we should wait a little while longer,' she urged him. 'I mean there's no hurry, is there?'

'There is if your stall is to remain solvent.'

It was true that it was proving to be a hard struggle keeping the stall going. 'Even so—'

'If I love you then they'll love you too. That's all there is to it,' Charlie said, kissing the tip of her nose, her eyebrows, her lips. 'You'll like Ma, she's a sweetie, and Father will just have to get used to the idea. I'm sure he'll admire the fact that you're a competent businesswoman, once he gets to know you.' A longer kiss this time that left her breathless. 'And once he sees we're very much a couple, he'll stop this stupid vendetta and start supplying you again.'

Lizzie's heart always lurched slightly whenever Charlie spoke with such calm assurance about their relationship, even without those heart-stopping kisses. She felt exactly the same. There'd been no other man for her from the moment she'd first set eyes on Charlie Finch. Though she might have tried to pretend otherwise, and imagine she could avoid him in the beginning, it had taken only one date to convince her that she was wasting her time protesting. They were destined to be together. They belonged. Finch would just have to be made to recognise that fact.

—

That evening was poker night, which took place as usual at Quinn's Palace, so-called because although outwardly it was nothing more than a seedy-looking warehouse at the back of the docks, the elaborate interior could have come straight from Los Vegas. Hung with velvet curtains and crystal chandeliers, it was fitted out with gaming tables: blackjack, roulette and baccarat. Other activities were made available for clients, but these took place behind closed doors, not in the gaming room.

It was here that Cedric Finch held his weekly poker sessions. A part of Jack hated himself for getting involved, while another part of his warped soul always kindled with excitement at the prospect. It wasn't poker as he knew it, but even if Jack wasn't personally involved in the other treats Quinn lined up for his clients, made for an entertaining evening.

The moment Finch walked in, his huge bulk in an expensive grey worsted overcoat and Homburg hat seeming to fill the small, dimly lit room, Jack politely enquired if he could have a quick word.

'What about, Cleaver?' Finch snapped, his gaze fixed on the pretty young girl who was relieving him of his hat and coat. 'If it's about work this isn't the time or place. I've come here to relax. You can see me in my office in't morning. Speak to me then, so long as it doesn't take too long. Time's money.'

The other men in the room were taking their places and Quinn was hovering close by, whispering in Finch's ear and making him smile. Jack knew it was now or never. No good broaching the subject later when Finch was in his cups and had other matters on his mind.

He gave his most obsequious smile, and, after carefully clearing his throat launched into his prepared speech. 'It's not about work, it's about your... well, I don't know how to begin.'

'What's your name, sunshine?' Finch asked, nipping the girl's softly rounded buttocks and making her squeal. Jack realised he wasn't even listening, but his employer's next words proved this to be false.

'Spit it out. I've better things to do with my time this evening than listen to your problems.'

'It's about that lad of yours, Charlie—'

'I'm aware of his name,' Finch impatiently interrupted. 'What about him?'

Jack gulped, already regretting his decision, although now that he'd started he couldn't stop. 'I understand he's seeing that girl, Lizzie Pringle, and you're not too happy about it.'

Thick black brows glowered in cold fury. Finch didn't care to have his workers poking their noses into his private affairs. 'And what business is that of yours?'

145

Jack cleared his throat once more. 'It's just that I know the family well, in a manner of speaking, and could fill you in on her background, should you feel the need of it.'

There was a small silence while Finch digested this interesting piece of information, then he half turned to address Quinn over his shoulder. 'I'll borrow your office for a moment, if I may?' And he stalked into it without even waiting for permission to be granted.

Jack followed and quietly closed the door after him. One day soon Lizzie Pringle might come to regret the selfish manner she had snubbed him.

Chapter Sixteen

Barry Holmes continued to come and go about the market as usual, making every attempt to continue with his routine of buying fruit and vegetables from Smithfield Market each morning, setting out his stall, and cheerfully calling out his wares to encourage customers to buy.

Sadly, word had got around about the charges and his sales plummeted. People were avoiding him and shopping elsewhere, some even crossed the street rather than walk by his stall. No matter that he hadn't yet stood trial, the people of Champion Street Market had found him guilty and were inflicting their own punishment upon him. Barry's business was dying before his very eyes.

'You've got to speak up for him, say something in his defence,' Winnie told Dena one afternoon when she returned from the workshop to do her usual stint on the stall.

'What can I say? I'm not the one who's tried and found him guilty before ever he's seen a judge.'

'You could speak on his behalf though.'

'But if Barry didn't do it, who did? Tell me that. He was the one with the opportunity. You surely aren't suggesting it was Carl on some previous occasion, or Jack Cleaver, who everyone is calling the hero of the hour? Constable Nuttall has proved him to be innocent. Anyway, what does it matter? Whoever did this terrible thing, the end result is the same. It's me they're blaming. Trudy has been taken into care because she's illegitimate.'

Her lovely, innocent child had been removed from her mother and put into that dreadful place where Dena herself had spent so many miserable years. The very thought made Dena shake with anger.

Winnie's face had turned ashen. 'I can't believe you're saying all of this. You're falling into the same trap as everyone else, listening to gossip and hearsay. I'd have thought you'd be the first to stick up for him and make a stand against tittle-tattle, having suffered from it yourself in the past.'

'If Barry's guilty he should admit it and get some help.'

'But he's *not* guilty. How can you even think he is?'

'What am I supposed to think?' Dena almost shouted, then put a hand to her mouth to calm herself.

'You're supposed to trust the people who are closest to you, that's what.'

Dena knew this to be true, in theory, but when had those close to her ever proved themselves worthy of that trust? Her own mother had abandoned her to a children's home. Her friends had turned away from her when she'd found herself pregnant at sixteen. Carl had walked away when she'd needed him most, following the trial. Who was she supposed to trust?

She felt cold, frozen almost, determined to keep herself detached and remote. Wasn't that essential if she was to remain strong? Dena hated to be quarrelling like this with her oldest and dearest friend, but she couldn't seem to help herself. True, it was Winnie, who'd been the most supportive, right from the start. The one person who had never wavered in her belief in her, and the one to give Dena a job at a time when nobody else would give her the time of day.

Barry Holmes was more of a puzzle, but she wanted to believe in him, she did really.

But Dena kept at the forefront of her mind what had happened to her lovely child and kept her voice cool. 'Barry spent all evening with Trudy. Doing what? I wonder. And he was always desperate to babysit. It was Barry who was seen chasing her out into the street. Now why would Trudy run away from him, tell me that?'

'Why don't you ask him yourself?'

But Dena couldn't bear the thought of even speaking to him. It was bad enough to see him out and about around the market when her beloved daughter was the one locked up.

She remembered what Quinn had said, and used his comments to challenge Winnie. 'This isn't the first time rumours have circulated about Barry, is it? Admit it, Winnie, a great deal has been said about the way he runs that lads' boxing club of his, how he goes into the showers with those boys.'

Winnie's face was red now, scarlet with rage. 'He only wants to make sure they're properly clean. Not many of them lads have showers in their own homes, and he needs to tend their cuts and bruises before they go home or their parents wouldn't let them come again.'

Dena stubbornly shook her head, her anguish not allowing her to concede an inch. 'There were also rumours about his friendship with Pete, my own brother, for God's sake! In fact, I've had it from the lips of an eye-witness that he's seen Barry doing things he shouldn't with the lads at the club. I'm sorry, but that's what I've heard.'

'That's a wicked lie!' Winnie spluttered. 'Who said such a thing? I'll black his eye for him. Go on, tell me, who was it?'

Dena was too far gone in her accusations to back down now and the words seemed to burst out of her mouth of their own accord. 'Billy Quinn, if you must know. Isn't he always going round to Barry's club? And I've seen the two of them arguing on more than one occasion recently, so there you are, absolute proof!'

Winnie puffed out her cheeks to stare at Dena, dumb-founded with fury. 'You dare to stand there and tell me that you'd rather take Billy Quinn's word before my Barry's? Dena Dobson, how could you? *And* he's allus loved you as if you were his own lass, and little Trudy his grandchild.'

It occurred to Dena then precisely what she'd said and she gazed at her old friend, aghast. Winnie was right, how could she possibly take Quinn's word before Barry's? Didn't she hate Billy Quinn? Didn't everyone? He was a despicable man, wicked and evil. And hadn't she always loved Barry? She looked into Winnie's shocked eyes and suddenly the ice inside her began to melt. It flooded down her face in great wet tears. 'Dear God, what's happening to me, Winnie? What am I saying? What am I doing? Help me, please. Help me get my little girl back, and save this new baby too.'

She was near to collapse as sobs wracked her slender body, and Winnie gathered Dena in her arms. She stroked her hair, wiped the tears from her cheeks, cuddled her close, all the hard feelings between the two of them forgotten. 'There pet, don't take on. We'll sort it out, don't you worry.'

Winnie's face was thoughtful. So that was the way the land lay? The poor lass was upset. She wheedled the whole sorry tale out of her. Dena had only confirmed her condition after the trial and Carl had gone, when it was too late.

'Not that I would've wanted him to stay just because I was carrying his child.'

''Course not,' Winnie said, though without much conviction. Then, patting Dena's shoulder, she offered a consoling smile. 'We'll get through this somehow. We allus do, love.'

And somehow this recognition of the new life growing within Dena seemed to cement their friendship anew.

–

Afternoon tea with the Finch family had been changed to Sunday lunch, which seemed worse in a way, and Lizzie felt as if she were about to be put on trial.

Charlie walked her to his house one bright Sunday morning in early May, apologising in advance for the fact that this wouldn't be easy for her, not helped by the fact that he and his father didn't get on. 'He'll probably say something nasty to me but you mustn't let that bother you. I'm used to it. We're constantly at odds as he's determined to see me as a failure.'

Lizzie thought this dreadful. Apparently, Cedric Finch was a rampant snob. He'd attended some minor public school in Yorkshire and had since built a large and profitable business. Charlie explained that his father saw himself as a self-made man of some importance in the community. Treasurer of the local golf club, secretary of Rotary, a generous contributor to local charities and on first name terms with the vicar. A man of affairs.

His only son, on the other hand, had been expelled from the very same school for climbing out of his dormitory window in the middle of the night, hitch-hiking to the next town and attending a friend's party, even though he'd been refused permission to attend. Charlie called it his rebellious era. He'd also been found smoking behind the bike sheds once too often, had shown no interest in studying for his exams and ended up at the local council school, crimes his father had never forgiven.

'I really didn't see the point in trying to work hard and please him, since he found fault with everything I did. Father never does anything but criticise. I'd largely given up on life by the ripe old age of twenty-three when I met you, Lizzie. You saved me from disaster. I might very well have felt obliged to join the Foreign Legion or else become a tramp sleeping rough on the streets, had you not suddenly appeared like an angel of mercy on that mucky step.'

Lizzie burst out laughing. Charlie's picturesque mode of speech and fondness for exaggeration always made her laugh. He was so funny! He was also kind and understanding. Only once had he asked about her own background and, seeing that it was difficult for her, had never broached the matter again.

Lizzie prayed that his father would adopt a similar approach. The last thing she wanted was Cedric Finch probing into her past. Some things were best left buried. Lizzie kept these dark secrets locked inside her head, which was where they would remain if she had any say in the matter, believing resolutely in looking forward, not back.

Oh, but she loved Charlie dearly. Why couldn't his father love him too? In her heart, Lizzie nursed a secret hope that she might be able to bring about reconciliation between father and son, if she could succeed in making a good impression. It was surely worth a try.

–

Lizzie knew instinctively, the moment they arrived at the house and she had clapped eyes on Finch, this was a vain hope. The angular lines of his face, with bags under his eyes and drooping jowls, seemed frozen in disapproval. White whiskers sprouted from out of his nostrils as he breathed deeply at the sight of her.

'Miss Pringle,' he frostily remarked, with not even a good morning or a handshake. If it hadn't been for Charlie's arm firmly clamped about her waist she might well have turned tail and run.

Evelyn Finch, Charlie's mother, was indeed a sweet, kind lady with eyes even paler than her son's. Her hair was pure white and very curly, her figure round and cosy, and she quickly stepped forward to welcome Lizzie with a kiss on each cheek.

'How delightful to meet you, my dear. We are so pleased you could come.'

Lizzie handed over a small bunch of violets she'd bought from Betty Hemley's stall, together with a packet of Aunty's sugar bon-bons. Evelyn appeared to be delighted.

'Oh, how very kind. Most thoughtful of you. Cedric, do look what Miss Pringle has brought. You must share them with me later.'

Finch said, 'We're not having that rubbish in this house.' Grasped the packet of sweets out of her hand and tossed them into the bin.

Evelyn gave a small gasp but made no attempt to retrieve them. Instead, she turned back to Lizzie with an even more dazzling smile, as if this act of supreme rudeness had never taken place. 'Charlie never mentioned how very lovely you are, dear. Such a beautiful face, pale as alabaster and utterly serene.'

Inwardly shaking with indignation at Aunty's carefully prepared packet of bon-bons being so summarily tossed aside, Lizzie took her cue from Evelyn and likewise ignored the incident, pretending it had never happened. But it was not a propitious start.

'I'm not at all serene. I can be something of a fire ball actually, if the need arises. And very stubborn, or so Aunty tells me.' Lizzie met Finch's glowering gaze with a slight upward tilt of her chin, hoping he would get the message. Charlie squeezed her hand.

'I'm so pleased to hear it,' Evelyn said, beaming with a kind of desperate pleasure. 'I do so wish I were, but I don't have the right spirit for rebellion, I'm afraid. Let me take your coat. Oh, what a pretty dress. It matches the colour of your eyes. Why did you not tell us, Charlie, how very lovely Miss Pringle is?'

She was wearing the plainest, most sensible shirtwaister she possessed in duck-egg blue, desperate to make a good impression. 'Do call me Lizzie, please.'

'How charming. Yes, I can see you are a Lizzie and not an Elizabeth. I do hate formality, don't you? Did your mother call you Lizzie? My own mother called me Evie. I always did prefer it. Now that's what *you* shall call me. Evie.'

Lizzie flushed. 'Oh, no, I really couldn't.'

'Disrespectful,' snapped Finch.

Evelyn caught the glowering look her husband was sending her to make her frenetic chatter worse. 'Blue suits you well, my dear, a perfect foil for those lovely auburn curls. I never aspired to anything more than mouse myself.'

'And now you're old and grey,' her husband drily commented as he ungraciously removed Lizzie's coat from his wife's grasp and flung it on to a chair in the hall, as if not wishing to contaminate any of the family's coats by hanging it next to them on the stand.

Evelyn again made no comment. Finch apparently reigned supreme in this household. 'But then I always was plain, even as

153

a girl. I really can't imagine what dear Cedric ever saw in me.' She gave a trilling little laugh.

'Neither can I,' he snorted, making the long hairs bristle in his cavernous nostrils.

This was all horribly embarrassing. Lizzie didn't know what to say next. She thought she could make a fairly accurate guess as to what had attracted him to this small, over-fussy, but likeable woman. Evelyn Finch possessed that indefinable quality that proclaimed her to be a lady. She had class, breeding, whatever you liked to call it. Lizzie thought she'd probably had money too, and would explain Cedric's motivation for marrying her. But what on earth had she seen in *him*?

Thankfully, and much to Lizzie's relief, Evelyn led everyone into the drawing room, still chattering away. 'I always longed to be tall and elegant like you, dear Lizzie. And clever. My darling Charlie is so bright, not like me. Takes after his father, I dare say. He can speak French, would you believe?'

'Mother, for goodness' sake, Lizzie has no wish to hear a litany of my supposed accomplishments.'

'Why not?' his father said. 'It won't take long. And of what use French is in the making and selling of sweets, I have yet to discover.'

Lizzie thought she had never seen such a huge room in all her life, large enough to house two substantial sofas, several easy chairs and, amazingly, a grand piano. She had never seen such a thing in someone's house before, only on the town hall stage. Evelyn caught her glance of astonishment.

'Do you play, dear? Charlie plays a little, don't you, darling?'

'Mother!'

'I was all thumbs on the pianoforte myself, don't you know, but then I'm not gifted like my darling Charlie, you see. As Cedric is fond of reminding me, I'm really not much use at anything. But one learns to make the best of what one has, doesn't one?'

Lizzie thought she probably didn't have any other choice, married to Cedric Finch. Fortunately her nervous babble ground to a halt, while already perfect cushions were plumped and chairs rearranged.

The house was a three-storey Victorian villa and Lizzie wouldn't have been surprised if a maid in a black frock, lace cap and apron were to appear carrying a silver tray, but it was Evelyn who scuttled about fetching glasses and filling them with sherry. She poured a small glass of lemonade for herself.

'You can pour yourself a small sherry, Evelyn, as I told you,' Finch regally informed her.

'Oh, but I thought it better if I simply partake of half a glass of wine with my meal. Alcohol goes to my head,' she explained to Lizzie with a giggle.

'It would be rude to our guest not to display the proper social graces.'

'If you say so dear! Silly me, why not a small sherry indeed?' In her haste to rectify this apparent mistake, Evelyn spilled some of the sherry on to the dresser and her husband clicked his tongue in irritation.

'You're making a mess, woman.'

'Oh, dear, I'm always so clumsy, aren't I? What was I thinking of? Now then, just a small one.' Evelyn finally subsided on to the sofa with a thimbleful of sherry in her glass.

Lizzie was secretly appalled by the ill-disguised contempt Finch treated his wife. She glanced at Charlie to judge his reaction, but he didn't seem to be paying any attention. He sat hunched in his chair, in apparent misery, as if he'd heard it all before and saw no point in intervening. But he was deeply embarrassed, she could tell.

'Isn't this lovely?' Evelyn said, letting out a small sigh. 'Now what shall we talk about?' as if she'd been utterly silent thus far and not desperately striving to fill the long silences left by her grumpy husband.

'I would reckon Miss Pringle has no wish to listen to any more of your silly prattling, woman. She'll have heard enough of it already. Why don't you go and find out what's happening in the kitchen? It would never do if you burned the beef, now would it?'

'Oh, dear me, no! Perhaps you're right, dear. Do excuse me, Miss, er – Lizzie.'

Lizzie leaped to her feet. 'Can I help?' Never had she heard anyone addressed in such a rude, condescending manner before. Lizzie might be no expert on the subject of relationships, not having enjoyed the benefit of being part of a normal family, but Charlie's mother surely didn't deserve this.

'Certainly not, you must sit and enjoy your sherry with Charlie. I won't be a moment.' And Evelyn hurried from the room, leaving an aching silence in her wake.

Lizzie felt the comforting touch of Charlie's hand slide over her own, a gesture she felt in dire need of right then. Even so, the afternoon seemed to stretch endlessly before her. How would she ever get through it?

–

It did indeed prove to be the most painful social occasion that Lizzie could ever remember. Finch took every opportunity to belittle, criticise and confuse her. Almost the moment the beef was brought to the table, he turned his steely gaze upon Lizzie and fired his first question, asking if she'd managed to find herself an alternative supplier yet, and briskly interrogating her on how she hoped to manage in the future. Lizzie attempted to remain outwardly calm and polite without responding properly to any of his questions.

'I have plenty of stock, thank you,' was all she would say on the subject.

Finch chewed his beef and roast potatoes in silence for a while, and Lizzie thought that might be an end of the matter, but suddenly he changed tack and began probing her about Aunty and how many 'brats' she was currently minding.

Inwardly seething at this description of the children, Lizzie remained obstinately silent, turning instead to Mrs Finch and complimenting her on the excellent beef.

'It's so tender it positively melts in the mouth, and how do you get your Yorkshire puddings so light?'

Evelyn glanced nervously at her husband and it was Finch who answered, 'I believe I asked you a question first, miss. I said it must be very crowded for you all in that miserable little house. I wonder your so-called aunt has time to play at sweet-making.'

Lizzie tilted her chin, a silent anger burning beneath her fixed smile. 'We manage very well, thank you.'

'No thanks to you,' Charlie snapped. 'Isn't it time you put a stop to this stupid vendetta, Father? Opening up in competition to Lizzie isn't going to do either of you any good. There isn't sufficient trade, and I doubt the factory can afford to lose out on the deal.'

Finch carefully cut himself an extra slice of beef and as he speared it on to his fork, carelessly let the juices drip on to the pristine white tablecloth. 'What would you know about what the factory can afford? You've never shown any interest in the financial stability of Finch's Sweets.'

'Because you won't allow me, you keep the entire thing under wraps, part of your secret domain behind the locked doors of your office. You treat me as if I were still an ignorant boy of thirteen instead of a man of twenty-three.'

'Perhaps because you act like an ignorant boy of thirteen.'

Charlie clenched his teeth, a stain of crimson creeping up his neck. Lizzie slipped a hand on to his knee in a gesture of sympathy, desperately trying to catch his eye to beg him not to quarrel with his father on her account. Evelyn remained studiously silent, even her lively chatter stilled as she kept her attention fixed firmly upon her plate, making no attempt to intervene in this escalating quarrel.

Finch again addressed Lizzie. 'I expect you imagine you've fallen on your feet nicely, catching the eye of my son? I admire your skill. It was neatly executed.'

'For God's sake, Father, lay off, will you?' Charlie shouted. 'We met by chance the day Lizzie came to see you at the office and just hit it off right away.'

'Oh, I'm sure you did. But you'd do well to remember that she *chose* to come to my office that day and she's clearly no fool. She can spot an opportunity a mile off. Latching on to my son would be no bad move on her part.'

'That's enough, Father! I won't have you speak of Lizzie like that. We fell for each other, all right? Where's the harm in that? We love each other.'

Finch's lip curled, his gaze resting inscrutably upon Lizzie, ignoring his son completely. 'I'm not so easily taken in as my gullible son, but you're wasting your time, lass, if you think you'll get your scheming, grubby little hands on my fortune. Charlie is the laziest, most useless and obstinate son ever to be inflicted upon a father. He'll never make anything of his life, and I am not going to give him a soft landing when he falls flat on his stupid face. He'll get nothing from me if he marries you, or any other fortune-hunting little madam.'

'I don't want your fortune,' Lizzie sharply retorted.

Evelyn had flushed scarlet with embarrassment but still didn't lift her eyes from her plate, making no attempt to come to her son's defence. Lizzie wondered, fleetingly, why that was.

Charlie flung down his knife and fork, hot-cheeked with indignation. 'I had hoped we could enjoy a civilised meal for once, like a proper family, but it was in vain. I thought you might recognise your mistake when you talked to Lizzie properly and saw how lovely she is, how sweet and kind, and that I love her. But you can't resist any opportunity to put me down, can you, Father? No matter what I do it's never right. Whoever I brought home wouldn't be good enough because *you* have to control everything. *You* have to be the one to make all the decisions, the one in charge. You issue your orders and expect to be obeyed like some sort of tin-pot dictator.'

Cedric Finch watched his son through narrowed eyes, smirking as he chewed a mouthful of beef, gravy dribbling from one corner of his mouth. 'I feel it incumbent upon me to show young Lizzie here the reality of the situation. She'll get nothing out of me. She must stop selling that rubbish on her stall or it'll be closed down within the month. The fact is, no matter how much she sucks up to me or lets you shag her, I still won't back down.'

Lizzie felt the colour drain from her face at his words, her mouth going dry with shock. Charlie was on his feet in a second, pushing aside his plate with such violence that it knocked over the silver cruet.

'How *dare* you! How dare you use such foul language in front of Mother and Lizzie. You're despicable!'

Finch too had risen to his feet, his belly seeming to swell beneath the napkin that flapped beneath his fleshy jowls. Evelyn put up her hands ineffectually, begging them both to please sit down and eat the food before it got cold.

Finch snatched away the greasy napkin and whipped it across his son's face. For one horrifying second Lizzie thought father and son might actually come to blows, right there over the lunch table. But as Charlie clenched his fists, holding on to his temper with difficulty, Finch turned on her yet again, shouting out his next words with such ferocity that flecks of spittle rained upon her face.

'I see no need for me to watch my language in front of Lizzie Pringle. Didn't she tell you, lad, that her mother was a whore? A prostitute. Like mother, like daughter, eh? That much is obvious.'

Chapter Seventeen

With Winnie's help Dena embarked upon a campaign to get Trudy out of care. They contacted local and national newspapers and wrote a blizzard of letters to the local authority, the welfare office, her MP, the magistrates, even the BBC. Anyone they could think of.

Customers and stallholders alike rallied round to help. They collected money and signed a petition saying what a good mother Dena was. They also sent small gifts to Trudy at Ivy Bank, and Miss Rogers, moved by their support and despite her better judgement, agreed to deliver them. There were sweets, colouring books, crayons and cuddly toys, although not the rag doll, Looby Loo, which Dena was waiting and hoping to take herself one day.

Sadly, Trudy never received these treats. They were shared out amongst all the children at the home and, although they were much appreciated, Trudy never got to touch or see any of them. She didn't even take part in the games they inspired, still doing little more than watch the other children play.

Lizzie and Charlie too tried to help, if only by encouraging Dena to join them from time to time for a drink in the Dog and Duck, anything to take her mind off her problems.

And one day, as Dena and Lizzie sat in a tucked away corner of the bar, copying out yet more letters to send to the mayor and their local MP, complaining about the fact that Dena still hadn't been allowed to see her child after nearly a month in care, she revealed her secret to her friend.

'Lizzie love, Trudy isn't the only problem I've got. I'm pregnant again.'

Lizzie looked at her, stunned. Then seeing Dena's chestnut brown eyes fill with tears, she opened her arms and gathered her friend close. 'Oh, Dena, not again.'

Even as she sniffed back her tears, Dena couldn't help chuckling at her friend's reaction, almost the same as Winnie's. 'Bit careless, I know. Carl and I resisted each other for months, all the time I was desperately trying to convince Kenny that it was over between us. Finally, we succumbed to our feelings and I must confess we've been lovers ever since. But I was so certain that we'd get together in the end, that we would be married, so it didn't seem to matter.'

'So why did you send him away?'

'I didn't. I asked for breathing space, that's all. A little more time to get over the trial. Then he told me there was to be an appeal and I'll admit I was upset about that. Thought it would open up the old wounds yet again. The sad truth is we just kept quarrelling about it. We had a final big row and Carl took off. Oh, if only I could turn back the clock, take back the horrid things I said. I never meant him to go. I love him, I really do – it's not that I'm simply needing a father for my child.'

Lizzie was silent for a long moment. 'But you do though, don't you? Need a father for your child. Correction – children. If you and Carl were married, you'd be safe then. They'd give you Trudy back and the new baby would no longer be in any danger either.'

Dena was weeping again, that familiar cold fear gnawing away inside of her, recognising the truth of Lizzie's words. 'I'm sorry, I can't seem to stop crying at the moment. I wish I knew where Carl was, but I've no idea. Belle thinks he's gone abroad, or to London, and she's probably right. I wish I could talk to him, tell him how much I love him, but he said he couldn't carry on living and working on the market if we weren't together. It's my own fault, I said all the wrong things, missed my chance, and he's gone.'

'Oh, Dena, I'm so sorry. What about Winnie, does she know?'

Dena bleakly nodded. 'Yes, and she's being a tower of strength, as always.'

'Despite...?'

Dena nodded again. 'Oh yes, despite all this other messy business. Oh God, and it is a mess, isn't it?'

'I wish there was something I could do to help, but I can't see that there is, except to keep on writing these blasted letters. No, there *is* something I can do. I can buy us both a brandy and Babycham. I think we need it after what you've just told me.'

'Nice idea, but I'd best stick to soda water, love,' Dena said, giving a rueful smile.

And as Lizzie went off to the bar, leaving Dena to mop up her tears and regain control of her emotions, neither of them saw a figure slip out of the back door of the pub.

–

Unaware she'd been overheard, and with Lizzie claiming to have told no one about her confession, Dena was astonished when within days word of her pregnancy had spread round the market like wild-fire. And then out of the blue, Jack Cleaver came to Dena, hat in hand, to make an astonishing offer.

'Begging your pardon, but I heard on the grapevine all about your bit of trouble. I know I'm not a patch on Carl Garside, but I'm steady and hard working, respectable and fond of children. If you'd consider me as a husband, I'd be happy to step into the breach.'

Dena stared at him as if he'd just grown two heads.

'Excuse me, what did you say?'

Cleaver repeated his offer, word for word, exactly as he'd rehearsed it. The idea had come to him when he'd overheard the whispered conversation between the two girls in the pub the other night.

He'd almost given up hope of ever getting Lizzie Pringle. He'd seen her and Charlie Finch billing and cooing together and realised that his chance of ever separating them was remote. The silly girl was utterly besotted. However peeved he may be about that, he recognised that his chances with Lizzie were now very slim. Dena Dobson, on the other hand, was ripe for the picking. So if he couldn't have one, why not the other instead?

Admittedly, he knew nothing about skirts and frocks, fashion not being at all the sort of business he'd had in mind. But he could find a way round that. He could employ girls, including Dena to do the actual work while he would be in overall charge; drumming up orders was what he was best at. And organising the finances, naturally. The business was surely capable of expansion, broadening its sales base by supplying other markets, and he was surely the man to tackle that job. What did a young girl like Dena know about such things?

And he really had no objection to Trudy. No objection at all. She was a proper little treasure, in fact.

Dena said, 'I'm lost for words. I can hardly believe I've heard you right.'

Cleaver smiled and smoothed one hand over his oiled locks. 'I know it's 1958 and arranged marriages are no longer in vogue, not like they were in 1758, for instance.' He chortled to himself, as if he'd made a joke. 'To be honest, you wouldn't imagine something like illegitimacy would matter so much in this day and age, would you? But it obviously does, to the powers-that-be anyway. Poor little Trudy!

'To be utterly frank, Dena, I've always had a soft spot for you,' he lied, eyes soft with assumed sympathy. 'And once I'd heard about the other expected addition to the family, my heart went out to you. So I thought, where would be the harm in offering? The marriage would be in name only, I'm sure you'd prefer. I'd not intrude upon your privacy, if you catch my drift. But I hate the thought of two children not having a father. I care about you, and that nipper of yours. I suffered in my own childhood, abandoned as a baby on a doorstep and moved from one home to another, so it breaks my heart to see another child ill-used. Think about it. You don't have to answer right away. Give it some thought.'

And with a slight inclination of his head, Jack Cleaver replaced his trilby hat and walked briskly away.

—

Silence, the minister told them when he read prayers every morning, was golden. Trudy did not agree. She hated the silence most of all. She missed the happy noises of the market: the sound of the man slapping his roll of linoleum, the one who juggled plates and sometimes accidentally dropped and smashed a few; the brightly dressed Bertalone girls squabbling at the tops of their voices, and her friend Gabby bossing her about. Always there would be music pumping away in the background; people laughing and joking. Happy sounds. Oh, and she missed the sound of her mummy's voice.

All Trudy could hear as she stood shivering in the queue for the bathroom was the raucous call of rooks cawing in the trees that overhung the yard. They frightened her so badly she hated going outside, convinced they might fly at her head and peck her.

Trudy comforted herself by thinking of the picture she'd just carefully tucked away in her locker. Knowing she couldn't read yet, Mummy sent her one every week. It might be a picture of the market, perhaps the lady on the flower stall, or funny Mr Hall with his big pink bow tie, and once she'd drawn big fat Mr Ramsay with a string of sausages draped around his neck that had made Trudy laugh.

Sometimes Trudy couldn't make out what the picture was supposed to mean. Like this one. Last night, in bed, when she'd studied it just before they switched the lights out, she'd thought the lady must be Mummy because she had Mummy's bright brown hair and was wearing that pink frock Trudy liked so much. And the little girl holding her hand must be herself, but what were they doing, and where were they going?

They had big smiles on their faces and looked so happy. But that couldn't be true because Trudy wasn't happy, and she didn't feel at all like smiling. She found very little to smile about. And how could Mummy be happy, without her little girl to kiss and cuddle, make her giggle, and wash her hair for her in the bath? Mummy loved her, Trudy knew that for a fact.

But if it were true that Mummy loved her, why had she sent her away to this dreadful place? It was all very puzzling. Trudy ached to see her mummy again, so badly that she felt all sore and bruised inside.

Trudy knew now that this was Ivy Bank, a large Victorian children's home run by Wesleyan Methodists, but secretly thought it more like the house where the wicked stepmother lived in *Snow White*. She didn't like it one little bit and cried every night to go home.

Nobody was kind. No one ever gave her a cuddle, or said anything nice to her. It smelt funny too, of stale cabbage and sick. Trudy had noticed that girls were often sick, would suddenly vomit all over the floor, and even, on one occasion, all over Trudy's black lace-up shoes. She'd got into terrible trouble for not cleaning them properly because 'cleanliness was next to Godliness' and you were expected to be clean, and on your best behaviour, at all times.

She knew why she was here: because she'd been bad. Trudy was trying so hard to be good so that she'd be allowed to go home, but it wasn't easy. She tried to be as quiet as a little mouse so that no one would notice her, and still she got into trouble for doing nothing at all.

–

Miss Rogers came to Dena with some news. 'The staff at Ivy Bank are concerned about young Trudy. She isn't settling. The child hasn't spoken a word since she arrived, nor is she eating properly. They think it might help if you went to see her and urged her to conform.'

'Conform?' Dena's heart thumped at the prospect of seeing Trudy at last, but Miss Roger's words confused her. 'I'm not sure I understand.'

'They think that if you, as her mother, tell her to eat up her dinner, urge her to join in with the lessons, and try to make friends with the other children, it might help.'

Dena looked at her askance. 'Help whom? Trudy shouldn't even be in that place, let alone being told to *conform*. She's done nothing wrong. Neither have I. We're both innocent in all of this mess and she should be home with me, her mother.'

Miss Roger's mouth thinned. 'This kind of attitude won't help your case one bit, Dena. Accept the judgement of the experts and you can help your daughter, as well as see her from time to time.'

Dena wanted to shake the woman, to scream at her that as a mother *she* was the expert, not those do-gooding wardens at Ivy Bank, but she managed to bite back the retort, even managed a little smile and a nod. It galled her to be forced to accept the unacceptable, but what choice did she have?

'I do want to see her.'

'Well then, we'll arrange it, shall we?'

—

'I love *you*. I don't care who your mother was – is.'

'It matters to your father,' Lizzie said, giving Charlie a rueful little smile.

'It's nothing to do with him. This is between you and me.'

'But it's not just your father, is it? It's everyone. I can't see your mother being too chuffed about being related to a prostitute either. And other folk on the market would take exactly the same attitude.'

'Blow them. I don't care what other folk think.' Lizzie melted with fresh love for him at these brave words. They were sitting down by the canal, watching the narrow boats with their brightly painted bows drift to and fro. It was one of their favourite spots. The awfulness of Sunday lunch; that moment when Finch had accused her of being like her mother, calling her by that filthy name, still reverberated in her head. To his credit, after his single explosion of outrage Charlie had said nothing more. He'd simply taken her by the arm and led her out of the house.

He'd taken her straight home and told Aunty to look after her. Aunty Dot had guessed at once what the problem was and had tucked her into bed, still shaking with shock; later she'd brought her up hot cocoa and home-made truffles, which Lizzie couldn't bear to eat. Charlie had promised to call to see her the next day, and he'd kept his word.

'Is she a prostitute?' he asked, his voice soft.

'Yes. Her real name is Marie Pringle, but that's not the name she uses, thank goodness. Her professional name is Maureen Moss. She chose it out of a twisted sense of mischief because she enjoys her freedom and doesn't like to gather any moss. No one knows she's my mother. I've told no one and neither has she, I'll give her that at least. I think she prefers to forget she ever had a daughter.'

'Where does she live? Near here?'

Lizzie nodded, her face bleak. 'Down by the arches, much to the displeasure of her neighbours. It's no coincidence. She followed me here when I came to live with Aunty. You might have heard of her, by reputation at least. Famous, she is, our Maureen, or infamous, on Champion Street Market, well known for her back-street abortions.' Lizzie shuddered.

'You can't be held responsible for what your mother does.'

'Easy to say when she's not your mother.'

Charlie gave a tired smile. 'Okay, I can see that.'

'Look, you don't want to shackle yourself to someone like me. Best you walk away now, before it's too late, and forget you ever met me. I wish I'd never gone to see your father that day. I wish I'd never met you.'

Charlie smiled, rubbing the back of one hand over her pale cheek in a gentle effort to bring colour back into it. 'No, you don't, and I can't walk away. It's already far too late. I love you, Lizzie.'

Lizzie glanced up at him, at the proof of that love shining in his eyes, and managed a weak smile in response. Even so she had to make sure. 'Don't say it if you don't mean it. I couldn't bear that. It's not too late to change your mind and make your escape.'

He smiled at her. 'As if I could. Tell me about her.'

Lizzie drew a shaky breath. She hated to talk about her past, preferring instead to keep it all locked away in her head, but Finch had made certain it could no longer stay there. 'I'm ashamed of her! I hate my own mother for what she does, for who she is. I *hate* her for what she let happen to me.' There was no serenity now in Lizzie's lovely face, only a contorted rage.

Charlie stared at her, stricken. 'What? What did she let happen to you?'

Lizzie's fists clenched as her mind recalled the horrifying events of her childhood. But bitterness and anger only destroyed, hadn't she learned that over the years? Once again she drew in a steadying breath; although her voice, as she began to talk, was anything but steady.

'You need to know how it all began. She blamed the war as people do. Said she couldn't bear to be alone, with Dad away in the Army, and that she needed the money. Yes, we were dirt poor. More often than not there was no food in the house, and a never-ending stream of men came calling, whom I hated. The place stank of my mother's cigarettes and booze, and something else, something unclean and nasty. I longed for us to be like other people, ordinary and normal. You know, with clean lace curtains and an aspidistra in a pot on the windowsill.'

Charlie smiled. 'Very Victorian.'

'You know what I mean. Respectable.'

He stroked her hair and pulled her close in his arms. 'I do, love. Go on, I'm listening.'

'Maureen claims that she was young and pretty then, easily flattered by the attention men gave her, absolute nonsense. They were paying to use her body. She has this idiotic notion that she's in control, and can pick and choose who her clients are, but that's rubbish. She has no full control over her life. She disgusts me! Says she never did want the same sort of life for me, and that she never did attempt to get me on the game. But I don't believe that either. It's a lie to ease her conscience. I'd never have been put at risk in the first place were it not for her lack of morals.

'When her clients, those so-called "uncles"' started taking an interest in me, a pretty young girl, she did nothing to stop them. She claims she didn't realise what was happening.'

'Maybe she didn't.' But Charlie's face had gone white to the lips at Lizzie's words. 'Are you saying she let them use you? That you too...?'

Tears shone in Lizzie's eyes and it was some long moments before she could speak. When she did, it was in the smallest, softest voice. 'It happened once. Only once! I swear I'll never forget that day as long as I live. He was a big bull of a man and I was a mere child, little more than ten or eleven. Others had tried to touch me up before, but he was the worst.'

'My God, what did he do to you?'

Lizzie's voice dropped to little more than a whisper. 'I went to Mam's room and found him in her bed. She'd gone downstairs to make them some tea. He pulled me under the bed clothes and shoved his fingers... you know. Said he was playing a game. Then he grabbed hold of my wrist and made me touch him and... well, you can guess what happened next. I was terrified. Utterly helpless. I didn't understand at first what he was doing. I thought he would smother me, that the pain would never stop. But then Mam came in carrying the tea tray, realised what was happening and it's true she did put a stop to it. She dropped the tray of hot tea all over the bed and hit him over the head with the chamber pot. He turned on her and beat the living daylights out of her. She ended up in hospital with two broken ribs and several missing teeth, and I was taken into care.'

The silence following this dreadful story seemed to stretch interminably; Charlie could see it being enacted clearly in his head…

Lizzie tried to swallow the hard lump that had wedged in her throat. She knew in her heart that no man could be expected to live with this knowledge, that it was the end for them. She'd known it even before she said the words, but Lizzie felt she'd no choice but to tell him the truth. Finch had made sure of that. Charlie would walk away now. Any moment he would get up and walk out of her life, as others had done before him.

She sat up, distancing herself from him by shuffling along the wall, slapping the unshed tears from her glittering eyes as she glared furiously at the happy families enjoying their happy Sunday on the narrow boats.

'So there you have it, I'm not a virgin. I'm unclean. Used goods. Like I say, you really don't want to have anything to do with me.' When he didn't immediately react she raised her voice. 'Are you listening to me? Do you hear what I said? Do you understand? You're free to leave. You can go now. I won't try and stop you.'

'I heard.' Charlie's voice sounded sad, so full of sympathy she could hardly bear it. 'I heard everything you said.'

She didn't believe he could have, otherwise he would have gone by now. 'I was raped! Do you hear me? *Raped!* At ten years old.' Tears were clogging her throat, making it hard for her to breathe. 'Are you satisfied now that you've made me tell you?' She was almost shouting, yelling at him, but still he didn't respond.

Lizzie jumped to her feet and might have walked away herself, or more likely run, had not Charlie grasped hold of her hand and held on to it, preventing her from moving another inch. That surprised her. She'd assumed that he would let her go. Then he surprised her even more by saying, 'It wasn't your fault.'

'What?'

'I said, this dreadful thing that happened to you wasn't your fault.'

Lizzie laughed, a harsh brittle sound that held no humour in it. '*She* said it was. *Maureen* said I must've led him on. He was one of her regulars and she'd never had any trouble with him before, apparently. No doubt she thought I'd lost her a good customer.'

Charlie pulled her back beside him and, wrapping his arms about her, gathered her tight in his arms. The tears came then, running down her cheeks and nose, the all-too-familiar band of pain constricting her chest, making Lizzie gasp and sob while he rocked her, stroked her hair, told her it didn't matter, that she was safe now and he would look after her.

'Nobody will ever hurt you again, Lizzie, I swear it, not even my father with his nasty remarks and domineering ways. I love you. Remember that always. Thank you for telling me, for being so honest. I can see it was hard for you to talk about it, but I want you to know that whatever happened to you in the past doesn't make a scrap of difference, not to me. I love you, and I mean to marry you.'

All the breath seemed to have gone out of her, and Lizzie felt light-headed, dizzy with joy. Loving her was one thing, even after learning the terrible events of her childhood, but to actually want to marry her was a surprise.

'You don't have to…' she began. And then he kissed her, softly and sweetly, and Lizzie melted in his arms. It felt as if she had come home, and she knew in that moment that she was indeed safe, that this was where she belonged, for now and always.

Chapter Eighteen

Trudy had learned to obediently follow the sound of the hand-bell, told when to make her bed, when to queue up for her bath, and when it was time to go down for breakfast or prayers. Rarely did anyone directly use her name. If anyone did call for her, they would say 'hey you', or 'you there'. But then one morning as Trudy hung up her washbag on the special hook by her locker, she actually heard her name being called.

'Trudy Dobson, where are you, child? Come here when I'm speaking to you, don't just stand there with your mouth open.'

It was the big fat woman who reminded Trudy of Daddy Bear in *Goldilocks and the Three Bears*, except that she was a woman. Trudy didn't know her name but the other girls called her Carthorse, which she thought was a silly name for a lady. She was their housemother, responsible for seeing they went to bed on time, cleaned their teeth and didn't talk at night. She had a big loud voice and Trudy was deeply afraid of her.

'Get dressed at once then downstairs quick as you can, if you please.'

Trudy did as she was told and seconds later was scampering down the stairs, the sound of the woman's heavy footsteps echoing behind her. By the time she'd reached the hall she felt all hot and bothered, her socks had slipped down and her liberty bodice was sticking to her tummy with sweat. It always did feel itchy, but nobody was allowed to take the thing off until May was out. Trudy could hardly wait.

'Wait there,' Carthorse instructed her, ushering her into a tiny, cell-like room. It had one tiny window, which gave a view of the drive and Trudy went straight to it to peep outside. The housemother was annoyed. 'I said, wait here, child. No wandering about.' She grasped Trudy firmly by the shoulders and marched her back, indicating some imaginary spot on the floor where she must stand.

Trudy obediently stood on the spot and waited, fearing the worst as her mind quickly ranged through all the things she'd done the day before. Had she been naughty again? Had she been bad?

'I can't think why you deserve one but you have a visitor,' the woman told her, giving a loud disapproving sniff. It was constantly drummed into the girls how useless and unloved they were, how they were nothing like as deserving as the good people who lived normal lives outside. 'No wonder your mother sent you here,' Carthorse would say if Trudy spilled her custard or forgot to wash behind her neck.

So when she made this announcement about a visitor Trudy was careful to show no interest or excitement. She'd learned already that most of the teachers at Ivy Bank hated to see any of the girls happy. You knelt on the hard floorboards by your bed night and morning to say your prayers, ate up your dinner without complaint, and were careful never to make a sound out of place. No laughing, no talking, no running, no joking. That was how it was. Silence was golden.

And then the door opened and suddenly there she was.

Mummy stood before her in her best pink frock, with her lovely chestnut brown hair all shiny and glowing. She looked so beautiful Trudy could hardly believe her eyes. She felt, for a moment, as if she must indeed have stepped into one of her favourite fairy stories.

The surge of happiness was gone in a second. It seemed to pop inside her like a balloon, for Trudy, even at not-quite-three, could sense her mother's fear and desperation, recognise the shock in her face when she saw what only a few weeks in this awful place had done to her child.

She had Looby Loo clutched tight in her arms and was trying not to cry, though with little success. Great fat tears were rolling down her cheeks and Trudy began to feel upset too, thinking she might start to cry herself at any minute, and that would be dreadful with the fat woman watching.

'Please sit down, *Miss* Dobson. You can have ten minutes. I'll be out in the corridor. If she starts one of her silly tantrums, just give me a shout.'

Turning on her heel, Carthorse went out. Trudy could still see her through the round window in the door so made no move towards her mother. Kissing and touching were frowned upon at Ivy Bank.

Then Mummy sat down in the chair and held out her arms. 'Hello, love,' she said. 'I am so glad to see you.' Very slowly Trudy crept into them, despite the evidence of her own eyes, and not believing that this was real. She leaned against her, felt herself gathered up on to Mummy's lap and buried her face in her mother's neck drinking in her familiar smell, her warmth, her comfort. Only then did she let the tears fall, and a few quiet sobs escaped. Hopefully the fat lady outside wouldn't be able to hear. Mummy was crying too, her whole body shaking with silent distress as she held Trudy tight in her arms.

—

They'd managed to collect themselves at last, after several long minutes of utter despair. Now Mummy was wiping Trudy's face with a handkerchief that smelled of lavender, and kissing her on each cheek.

'I can't tell you how much I've missed you, love. Are you all right? Are they looking after you properly?' She smoothed a hand over Trudy's shorn locks, framed her small face with gentle hands. 'You must eat more, Trudy, or you'll shrivel away to nothing. You're far too thin. Will you promise to eat, for my sake?'

Trudy nodded bleakly.

'Look, I've brought Looby Loo. She's missed you, too.'

Trudy's arms curled instinctively about the rag doll, nestling her close. She even managed a little smile of thanks. Dena kissed her again, hugged her tight. 'Look, Looby Loo's smiling too.' They both chuckled.

There was so much, suddenly, that Trudy wanted to say. She wanted to tell Mummy all about the big girls who pushed her about, how they spat in her food, and why she couldn't bear to eat it. She longed to ask why she'd been sent away and when she could come home, but she'd hardly got a fraction of this out when the door opened again and the big fat lady was hovering, huge and forbidding, above them.

'Time's up, *Miss* Dobson.'

'Oh, please, it's weeks since I saw my daughter, can't we have a little more time?'

'Ten minutes, I said, and you've had almost twelve. You know the rules well enough, Dena Dobson, having spent time here yourself as a girl, so don't pretend otherwise. Though I seem to remember you were good at breaking every rule in the book, even then. We don't want to upset the child, now do we? Say goodbye nicely and you might be allowed to visit again.'

Dena gave Trudy one last hug, loathing this woman who took such pleasure in reminding her of that painful time in her life. 'Be a good girl for Mummy. I'll come again soon, I promise, and I'll send you lots more pictures, every week. Did you get the presents? Everyone sends their love.'

Trudy didn't understand a word of what she was talking about, or who she meant by 'everyone', but she did recognise that the visit was over and her mummy was about to leave. The prospect of losing her for a second time, of being left alone in this dreadful place, was just too much for the little girl and she clung to Dena fiercely.

'No, no! Don't go. I don't want you to! I want to go home, Mummy. I want to go home!'

'My word, it does have a voice then, after all,' Carthorse sarcastically remarked. 'Well, that's an improvement, I must say.

Now then, no more tears. We don't want to upset your mother, do we?'

'Oh, please don't cry, Trudy, please.' Dena was struggling to unhook Trudy's fingers, which were gripping tightly to the skirt of her dress, but then gave up the struggle and hugged her instead.

Seeing mother and daughter clinging to each other was too much for Carthorse. She grabbed Trudy by the arm and began to haul the child away. Trudy dragged her feet, and when that didn't work stamped them hard, and then threw herself on the floor in an hysterical tantrum, screaming at the top of her voice. She drummed her heels on the ground, making herself go stiff so that she couldn't be lifted. Sadly, it was all to no avail. While Mummy stood sobbing with her hands to her mouth in horror, the big, fat, nasty woman gathered Trudy up under one arm like a squirming sack of potatoes and carried her away.

But Trudy kept on screaming the full length of the corridor, relishing the sound of the echo as it beat back the horrible silence. Silence might be golden, but *she* had broken it.

–

Miss Carter came to Trudy later that evening and took Looby Loo, her treasured rag doll, away. Trudy screamed and sobbed and begged, refusing to let the doll go. She clung to its raggedy legs, stretching them almost to tearing point as the toy was pulled between them like the rope in a tug-of-war. Trudy didn't have a chance of winning the contest, even before Carthorse lashed out at her with the flat of one hand and sent her flying.

The little girl lay curled on the floor, shielding her head with her hands as blows rained down upon her, thinking furiously that *this wasn't fair*. It wasn't right for the fat lady to take away her precious Looby Loo. She loved her doll. Looby Loo was her friend, like the real one who was Andy Pandy's best friend, and Mummy had brought her specially to make her happy.

'You're every bit as difficult as your mother was before you,' Carthorse coldly informed her, not making any sense at all. 'Get to bed this minute. No supper for you tonight, you bad girl.'

But Trudy wasn't for giving in easily. She'd lost everything, so Looby Loo was worth fighting for. She got to her feet and stamped loudly on the wooden floor, first with one foot, and then with the other. '*No!* I *won't!*' she shrieked. 'I want my doll back. She's *mine!*'

Carthorse glared, her eyebrows raised. 'My, my, we have found our voice, haven't we?' Then she bent over and put her face close enough for Trudy to smell onions on her rank breath. 'Well, we've heard enough. You'll shut up this minute, madam, if you know what's good for you, otherwise I'll thrash that temper out of you. Understand?'

'I want my dolly,' sobbed Trudy, beyond reason now.

'You can't have her. She'll be put in the nursery for everyone to share.'

'But someone might take her!'

'You're a selfish little girl. I think you need to say your prayers more.'

'*I want Looby Loo!*' And again Trudy made a frantic bid to snatch back her beloved doll.

Holding it out of her reach, Carthorse gave Trudy instead a copy of the *New Testament*. 'Here, you can have this. It'll do you far more good. I know you can't read yet but if you put a bit of effort into it you soon will. In the meantime you can look at the pictures. You're beyond redemption, madam, that's what you are.'

As she hectored and bullied the child the woman stripped her down to her knickers, pulled on her nightdress, then dropped her into bed. 'Starting from tomorrow we must find a way to curb this nasty temper of yours, and no more playing with bricks and sand until you do. Do you hear me? You need discipline, and I'm the one to give it to you.'

Trudy stared up at her through a blur of her tears, not understanding one half of what she was saying, but instinctively knowing in her young heart that it wasn't good. She'd been a bad girl again, so she'd have to be punished.

As she lay that night in her cold, hard bed, sobbing quietly beneath the scratchy sheets for her mummy, and for Looby Loo, her tummy empty and aching with hunger, Trudy realised she was still clutching her mother's hanky. With a choking sob she buried her small nose in its lavender fragrance.

–

Even as Trudy created a fuss in the dormitory, Dena was making a much bigger one in the office. She banged on the desk with her fist and shouted in the superintendent's face. The woman was obviously new to Ivy Bank as she hadn't been here when Dena was a resident, although she didn't seem to have brought about any improvements to the place. None that Dena could see anyway. The home was every bit as dreadful as she remembered, and Carthorse every bit as powerful.

'How dare you take my child away from me? *I've* done nothing wrong! Neither has *she*. Yet you don't even allow us a proper visit and that woman, Miss Carter, dragged Trudy away *screaming*! How can she do that to a child?'

The superintendent, a stick-thin, sour-faced individual whose one aim in life was to instil her own unyielding version of religion into young unformed minds, looked down her long nose at Dena. 'Vengeance is mine, sayeth the Lord.'

Dena was bemused. 'I'm sorry, I don't understand. What are you saying? That Trudy must be punished because of something I've done?'

'He feels she needs a sharp rap on the knuckles. God chastises us for our own good that we may share in His Holiness. No discipline seems pleasant at the time, but it is nonetheless necessary. Later on, however, we harvest a glory of peace and righteousness in return for our forbearance.'

'Religious poppycock!'

Jerked out of her own rhetoric, the superintendent scowled. 'Miss Carter has explained to me what a troublesome child you were when you too were in this establishment only a few years ago, and sadly left under a cloud of shame. How old are you now?' She consulted a sheaf of papers on her desk. 'Going on twenty and still you've learned no sense. It is our duty to protect your daughter from following the same dissolute path.'

Dena's anger rose in her throat like bile. 'And what makes *you* such an expert on child rearing? This damn place did nothing for me. Cold, hungry and unloved, that's what I remember about being locked up in here. And that woman, Miss, flipping, Carter, was the bane of my life. Went out of her way to make things as miserable as possible for me. What good does it do for any child to be treated with such heartlessness?'

'Pandering to a child who is naturally evil and immoral teaches them nothing about discipline, and only allows them to fall deeper into the mire of sin. They must be chastised and taught the difference between right and wrong, something you have clearly failed to do.'

'That's utterly ridiculous! Children are not naturally evil and immoral, nor was my Trudy falling into a mire of sin. What kind of God do you worship who looks upon innocent children in that despicable way?'

The superintendent breathed with such fury down her long nose, that Dena wouldn't have been surprised had flames emerged from her nostrils. 'Do not blaspheme in front of me, girl. It was clearly a mistake to allow you to visit today. You have upset and unsettled the child, insulted my staff, and now you dare to question not only *my* authority but God's too. In future your visits will be confined to one a year. That will be more than enough for the poor child to deal with, and it is all you deserve. *You* are the one at fault, the one resisting salvation.'

Dena was outraged, and terrified by the prospect of seeing Trudy only once a year. She made a valiant attempt to calm herself, drawing in a steadying breath. 'I'm sorry if you're offended by my reaction, but I'm upset too and strongly object to the implication that I'm some kind of prostitute.'

'You have prostituted your soul, your body too, so far as I can see.'

Dena clenched her fists in frustration, grinding her teeth together in silent fury. How could she make this woman understand? She had to convince her that Trudy would be far better off at home.

'Do you ever take a long hard look at the children in your care? Have you looked at Trudy recently? I was shocked when I saw her today. Her hair all hacked off, her small body stick-thin, and her face as pale as paper. *What have you done to her?* When she came in here she was a bright, bouncy, loving child, now she won't speak, won't eat, won't—'

'Judge not, that ye be not judged. Cast out the mote in thine own eye first. The child was already traumatised when she was admitted. Instead of blaming us, ask yourself what you were doing to protect your child properly. You could have married her father, for a start, or any honest man. Where were *you* on the night of the accident?' The woman wagged an accusing finger at Dena. 'Out with one of your gigolos, I shouldn't wonder. And who abused your child, another one of your men friends? You remain an abhorrence on society, a fallen woman incapable of accepting deliverance from your sins, sleeping around with no thought for moral rectitude. We can at least save the soul of your child before she too is tainted by her mother's depravity.'

Abhorrence on society? Fallen woman? Tainted by her mother's depravity?

Dena's rage boiled over at these words and her response was instinctive. She spoke without thinking, the blood running hot in her head, making her reckless. 'And I suppose you'll take this one too?' she said, slapping her still flat stomach.

The superintendent's eyes almost popped out of her head. After a shocked silence, in which Dena had ample time to recognise the dangerous path her temper had led her, the woman put her hands together and began to pray.

'Dear Lord, forgive this poor creature you see before you, shows no remorse for her sins and is determined to perpetuate her wicked crimes. Help us to protect her young child from the deviant waywardness passed on to her by this woman and to teach them both the error of their ways. We beg your assistance, O Lord, for the sake of her child's immortal soul.'

Dena shut off the rest of the woman's prayer with the slamming of the door.

—

Dena didn't sleep a wink that night. She lay dry-eyed, the anger still burning in her, staring up at the ceiling, going over and over how she came to be in this mess. She'd been sixteen years old when she'd had Trudy, the result of one foolish moment of rebellion. Hardly a sin, or an act likely to constitute danger to her immortal soul.

True, she hadn't married the father because she'd realised Kenny wasn't the right man for her. Where was the wrong in that? Was it better to chain yourself to a cruel, obsessive man, rather than attempt to bring a child up alone without the so-called benefit of marriage? Utter tosh, in Dena's humble opinion.

She got up and went to make herself a cup of tea, her third during the course of that endless night. But as she waited for the kettle to boil, Dena was forced to admit to herself that the rest of society did not necessarily agree with this liberal line of thinking.

She couldn't deny that Trudy had been damaged. She'd been abused by Barry for some reason only he and his sick mind could explain. But Dena knew that any other child from a normal, happy home with two parents would not have been taken away and put into care following such an incident. Not when the police had identified and charged the perpetrator, and it was satisfactorily proved not to be the parents' fault.

The fact that Trudy was illegitimate had made her vulnerable, had meant the authorities could put the blame on her supposedly feckless, immoral mother.

Rail against it as she might, that was the truth of the matter. And Dena knew that in her haste to defend herself and win back her child, she had made matters worse. Her stupid temper had caused her to reveal the fact that she'd committed the same unpardonable sin a second time, and with a different man.

Oh, God, what had she done? They'd never let her have Trudy back now. And as soon as the new baby was born, they'd no doubt take *that* away too.

Dena put her head in her hands and sank to her knees on the kitchen floor, sobbing uncontrollably. She felt as if her heart were bleeding. She'd heard that expression many times, but until now had never understood it. Yet it was as if all the strength were seeping out of her, all the life blood that kept her heart strong draining from her body. She was lost, done for. Her beloved child was gone forever.

Later, as she lay exhausted in her bed, no nearer to sleep, Dena scoured her mind for an answer, desperate to find a solution. Carl, the man she loved, was gone. Barry, whom she'd always looked up to as a father figure, had betrayed her. Where else was there for her to turn? And then the answer came, clear and unmistakable. She could see now that there was no other way.

The following morning, Dena crossed the street and knocked on Jack Cleaver's door. When he opened it, she said, 'I've come to give you my answer.'

Chapter Nineteen

Lizzie and Charlie were making chocolate truffles, under Aunty's supervision. Charlie was carefully bringing the cream to a boil in a large saucepan while Lizzie chopped the chocolate into pieces in a large heatproof bowl.

'Take it off the heat now, Charlie,' Aunty Dot instructed, neatly side-stepping Lizzie to peer into the pan. 'Give it a couple of minutes to subside then pour it gently over the chocolate.'

Charlie did exactly as he was told, and as he poured Lizzie began to stir the mixture with a wooden spoon until all the chocolate was melted and velvet smooth. It looked and smelled wonderful.

'What now?' she asked.

'We leave it to cool a little before we whisk it.'

'Oh, I want us to have chocolate truffles at our wedding, don't you, Charlie?'

'And chocolate mousse.'

'And chocolate brandy creams.'

'Oh, don't, you're making my mouth water.'

They were so content working together, talking nonsense and happily making plans for their wedding in just a few months' time. They could have rented a bedsit and got married right away, but this delay was partly at Lizzie's instigation, in the hope that Finch might come to accept her, and to make sure Charlie had no regrets if he didn't.

Charlie had no intention of changing his mind, but he too was willing to wait because, having walked out on his father, he was now unemployed.

This worried him greatly and he'd already spent hours scouring the local papers looking for jobs. The trouble was, the only thing he knew anything about was sweet-making, so here he was, helping Lizzie to make chocolate truffles for her stall, until he could find a job that would bring money into the house. He had no intention of taking a wife until he was in a position to provide for her. They'd had a bit of a quarrel about that, but in the end both of them had agreed it was sensible to wait and get some savings behind them.

In the meantime, Charlie was grateful for Aunty's generosity in letting him bunk down in Joey and Alan's room rent-free, although it wasn't ideal. He wanted something better for his lovely Lizzie. She deserved the best.

'These truffles should bring us some much-needed custom,' Lizzie said, beating briskly.

Aunty put a gentle hand on her arm. 'Not too hard, it might separate. We just want the mixture to start to hold.'

Lizzie smiled, shaking her head a little in bewilderment. 'Start to hold. What on earth does that mean?' Aunty Dot was constantly using such phrases. Either the mixture had to 'coat the spoon' or 'leave a trail' or 'whisk until thick and creamy'. It was all most confusing. 'How would I ever remember all of this without you to remind me?' she laughed.

'You will, if you practise often enough. Charlie will help, won't you, lad?'

'How come you know so much about sweet-making?'

Dot smiled. 'My father once owned a chocolate shop, the best in all of Lancashire.'

'Really, what happened to it?' Lizzie wanted to know, intrigued by this rare glimpse into Aunty's background.

'Mam sold it after he was killed in the Great War. I was nobbut a lass. But sweets and chocolate are in my soul. Now then, you have to bear in mind that good chocolate should be flawless, and the colour rich and true. When you eat it, it should feel silky and smooth, not sticky, nor melt too quickly in your fingers. And its smell should be sweetly fragrant. We don't want it burned or musty. Then we want an explosion of flavours on the tongue – buttery, creamy, and chocolaty, with a clean aftertaste that encourages you to eat more. You can't make good chocolate if you don't love it yourself. And if we use the best chocolate, with the finest ingredients, then it deserves our best care.' As Aunty talked of her greatest passion, she kept an eagle eye on Lizzie's whisking.

Later, while the mixture was setting in the refrigerator, they sat around the kitchen table drinking a refreshing cup of tea together, and Aunty put forward a plan that had been occupying her mind for some time.

'I've been giving some thought to what you said to me a while ago, Lizzie love, about the problems you're having finding a new supplier. Considering the circumstances, what with Charlie's dad still putting the screws on, if you don't mind my putting it so bluntly...'

'Not at all, it's true enough,' Charlie agreed.

'And I still haven't found a company willing to stand up to Mr Finch.'

'Right, well, I reckon we need to do some fresh thinking. You once asked, Lizzie, if we could possibly make enough sweets to stock the stall without needing to call on any other supplier. Well, I think we could, only we'd have to be much better organised than this.'

As always the tiny kitchen shone with cleanliness, the grey Formica worktops and copper pans gleaming, but with three people at the table it was somewhat overcrowded. Aunty kept them hanging on for her next words while she darted out into the backyard to check on the baby, sunning itself in the big pram, then took several mouthfuls of scalding hot tea, sighing with pleasure. 'There's nothing better than a good cuppa.'

'Oh, do go on,' Lizzie said. 'How? How can we be better organised?'

'I'm coming to that, but we mustn't forget those truffles.'

Lizzie laughed. 'Didn't I tell you she could do three things at once?'

Aunty brought the dish from the fridge and as she spooned out balls of the truffle mixture on to a baking sheet, and Charlie and Lizzie gently rolled them in cocoa powder, she outlined her idea.

'We couldn't make enough sweets and chocolates in this tiny kitchen even for one stall, and in order to make it pay you'd have to think beyond Pringle's Chocolate Cabin.'

'What are you suggesting?' Charlie asked, setting another set of truffles on to a prepared board that would go back in the fridge.

'That we rent somewhere nearby, set it up as a kitchen, and become a wholesale supplier ourselves to others who are equally sick of Finch's overbearing manner and would welcome a good alternative. There are plenty of old cotton mills around with space going begging. I doubt the rent of a room would be too expensive. You'd need some equipment. Copper boilers and pans, a stove of some sort, tables and a pouring slab, a machine to pull the toffee, thermometers, scissors, and such like. I can lend you what I have, but that wouldn't be enough, so we'd need some money up front. A bit of capital to invest in the right equipment, and the very finest ingredients to get us started.'

'I have some savings,' Lizzie said, her blue eyes shining. 'Though not very much.'

'Me too,' Charlie agreed, and they both looked at each other, smiling shyly.

This was what she'd dreamed of for so long. And it would also answer Charlie's unemployment problem since he already knew something about the business, even if Finch had kept him very much on the fringe. But without Aunty behind them, to pass on her expertise, it would have been impossible.

Aunty said, 'I've a few bits and bobs I could sell, trinkets that are just mouldering in a drawer.'

'Oh, no, you mustn't, that wouldn't be right,' Lizzie protested.

'I'll thank you to keep your nose out, madam. It's my stuff, and if I want to sell it and invest in the new Pringle's Sweet Manufacturing Company, I will.'

'Oh, goodness, that sounds so grand. A company, a sweet-making company all of our own. But Pringle is my name, so maybe you wouldn't like that, Charlie?'

'I'm not proud,' he said, grinning broadly. 'And we don't want to call it Finch's, do we? I think it's a brilliant idea. Count me in.'

Dena couldn't believe what she'd done. Had she really agreed to marry Jack Cleaver? He was such a boring little man, that a part of her shuddered at the thought. But he had promised that the marriage would be in name only, and she must keep her mind firmly fixed upon the benefits. She would get Trudy back, which was all that mattered.

And there was the new little one to consider, she thought, resting a hand on her stomach. Right now the prospect of caring for another baby filled her with despair, even horror, but once it arrived Dena knew she would fight tooth and nail to keep this child, as she had with Trudy.

She thought of the painful visit the other day, of Trudy so upset at her leaving that the poor love had been beside herself and had thrown a tantrum. And was it any wonder? Didn't Dena herself know the horrors of that place – the cold, the hunger, the bullying; the strict unfeeling regime – having been a resident in her youth? Why did religion have to be so controlling, so hard a regime? Why was the 'Jesus is Love' philosophy so often accompanied by cold porridge?

She'd chop off her own hand, if necessary, to get her child out of that place.

Dena sat sipping her morning tea in the empty house and wept a few silent tears before dashing them away in a gesture of new determination. No good feeling sorry for herself. She had to be strong.

And Jack Cleaver wasn't a bad man. Older by some years, since he was in his mid-thirties, but he'd looked delighted when she'd given him her answer. He'd even tried to spruce himself up a bit, had bought a new suit and got his hair cut in a more fashionable style, touching in a way. Although his self-improvement hadn't yet run to a diet he was clearly doing his best to impress her, and maybe he had some interesting hobbies or hidden charms.

In an effort to get to know him better, Dena had agreed to let him take her out on a date. The fact that he'd chosen afternoon tea at the Midland Hotel struck her as quaint, but what did that matter? They needed to talk. And Dena needed to know exactly what she was letting herself in for before she entirely relinquished her freedom. Most of all, she had to be sure that it would be worth her while so far as Trudy was concerned.

With that in mind, before setting off for the market she sat down and wrote a letter to Miss Rogers, telling her the news and asking if she would call round so that they could discuss Trudy's eventual release.

> *I'm only doing this to get Trudy back, so I need your assurance that it will work. Since they insist that I provide her with a father and a respectable home, so be it. It will be worth the sacrifice to have my daughter home again.*

Dena had lost count of the number of letters she'd written to various people begging for their help, making the point that children's homes were out of date, and that they shouldn't be treated like cattle herded into great freezing dormitories, fed starvation rations and condemned to hard labour for the sake of their immortal souls. Was no value placed on love and family life, however flawed?

She'd given interviews to such esteemed newspapers as The *Manchester Guardian*, the *Evening News* and the *Oldham Chronicle* about her situation, but from the NSPCC and the social workers, she'd heard nothing.

Miss Rogers was her only hope. If she could only get a promise, in writing, that Trudy would be released, then Dena would marry the devil himself, and gladly.

—

Dena dropped the letter in the postbox at the end of Champion Street. On her way back to the market she heard a familiar voice behind her.

'It's Dena, isn't it? Dena Dobson?'

Dena turned around and found herself face to face with a good-looking young man in sports jacket and flannels whom she didn't immediately recognise. 'Sorry, do I know you?'

'Don't you remember? I looked after your little girl following her accident? Doctor Salkeld.' Dena found her hand taken in a firm, warm grip.

'Oh, hello. Sorry, I didn't recognise you, Doctor.'

'Call me, Adam. I'm not your doctor after all, am I?'

'I suppose not. We generally have Doctor Mitchell.'

'While I still work all hours in emergency at the hospital,' Adam Salkeld said with a smile.

He looked different without his white coat, and with his hands stuck in the pockets of his trousers like any normal young man. He was smiling at her and she found herself smiling back. Dena couldn't remember the last time she'd done that. She liked his red-brown hair that tumbled over a wide brow instead of being swept back in a quiff as current fashion dictated. She liked his strong features with the smattering of freckles across his nose, although the way his dark hazel eyes seemed to be quietly examining her, brought a girlish flush to her cheeks.

'Can I buy you a drink?'

'At this time of the day? I don't think so.' She almost laughed.

'You look to be in need of one.'

It all poured out then, about Trudy being taken into care. Why she told him, Dena couldn't rightly have said, but she didn't seem able to stop herself. And it was such a relief to talk about it, even down to describing the campaign she was conducting to win her child back.

'That's why I was posting the letter. I've written dozens – scores in fact – to politicians, judges, magistrates, you name it. Although, so far I seem to be getting absolutely nowhere. But I'll not give up, I'll not.'

Adam didn't interrupt, he just stood there listening and when she finally ran out of words and was fighting back tears, he silently handed her his handkerchief. 'It must be hard. I can see why the powers-that-be do these things, but all too often they get it wrong. They never seem to study the people involved properly, or take into account their personal situation.'

'They just stick a label on you – illegitimate, unmarried mother, and that's it. Decision made and acted upon without pause for thought.'

'It doesn't seem fair, I agree. What about – what about your little girl's father?'

Dena had no wish to discuss Kenny with this man. But why couldn't Carl be so caring? she thought. Why wasn't he here for her now? She dismissed the thought. 'He's history.'

'I see. Well, I wish I could help.'

Clutching the sodden handkerchief, Dena was ashamed of her loss of control, and for pouring out all her troubles in this way. 'I'm sorry, I shouldn't be bothering you with all of this. It's none of your concern.'

'Don't be silly, I don't mind.'

Dena dabbed furiously at her eyes, blew her nose on the handkerchief and then handed it back to him without thinking. Smiling, he shook his head.

'Oh, sorry, I'll wash it and see you get it back.'

'It's not important. Look, I have to dash now, I'm late for duty already, but keep your chin up, all right? And keep writing those letters.'

'Oh, I intend to. I most certainly will.'

'And we'll have that drink some other time, right?'

'Yes, okay. I'll look forward to it. Bye then.' And Dena watched him stride away with a tinge of regret. He seemed nice. A drink would have been good. But what hope was there for her if not even a doctor could help?

On her way to her workroom Dena paused briefly at Pringle's Chocolate Cabin to ask Lizzie if they could have a coffee together later. 'There's something I need to talk over with you.'

—

Over a frothy coffee in Belle's café, Lizzie's eyes stretched wide when Dena told her the news.

'Jack Cleaver? You're going to marry Jack Cleaver? I don't believe it.'

'It's for Trudy's sake, so that she'll no longer be illegitimate, and I'll be a respectable married woman and they'll let her come home.'

'But… I'm sorry, Dena, but I thought he was pining for love of me. He's been dogging my footsteps for months, calling round at the house, begging me for a date every time he sees me. He's soon got over me then.' Lizzie giggled.

Dena couldn't help but laugh too. 'I should think he's got the message that Charlie is "The One", since you're rarely seen apart these days.'

Lizzie flushed. 'That's true, we can't help ourselves. It was love at first sight. We aren't planning on rushing into marriage but I can let you into a little secret…' Lizzie leaned closer over the table, blue eyes sparkling. 'You aren't the only one with marriage in mind. We're engaged. Charlie's asked me to marry him and I've accepted.'

'Oh, Lizzie, that's wonderful!' Then both girls were embracing, kissing each other's cheeks and Dena was asking about wedding gowns, bridesmaids and honeymoons.

Lizzie quickly sobered. 'I can't see any possibility of those. A quick trip to the register office and then back to work, I should imagine. But not just yet. Life's tough enough at the moment. Charlie's fallen out with his father good and proper, been told never to darken his door again, et cetera. It's so awful! Poor Charlie is sleeping on a camp bed in Joey and Alan's room.'

Dena smiled. 'That's handy.'

'Don't you start, I get enough teasing from them. Anyway, we're prepared to wait a few months in order to save up for a place of our own, and in the hope that his father will eventually come round when he sees we're serious. Maybe he'll give us his blessing, or at least stop actively putting obstacles in the way of our little business.'

'Maybe you should agree to his terms.'

'What, stop Aunty from making any more sweets, you mean? Never! Anyway, it isn't just Aunty's sweets he objects to.'

Dena frowned. 'What else could he possibly object to? You're lovely.' She was puzzled, realising that she knew very little about her friend, except that Lizzie had come to live on the market when she was about twelve or thirteen. Dena knew nothing about her parents, or where she'd lived before, beyond that she'd been in a children's home for a while. Yet more of the flotsam that washed up on to Champion Street Market, hoping to earn an honest crust.

'Who knows?' Lizzie floundered, wishing she'd kept her mouth shut. 'I'm sure we'll sort it out eventually, whatever it is. And Evelyn, Jack's mother, is a lovely lady. I hope she at least will be pleased by our news. But you and Jack Cleaver – heavens! Are you sure it's the right thing to do? It sounds very Victorian marrying in name only just for the sake of your child.'

'I didn't make the rules,' Dena said, a bitter note creeping into her voice. 'Society seems to imply it's a crime to have an illegitimate child, not me. Miss Rogers has as good as admitted that was the real reason they took Trudy into care. I deserve all the blame, apparently, for Barry's transgressions, because of the immoral life I lead. I've written to the woman asking her to confirm it would be worth my while to go through with this.'

Lizzie squeezed her friend's hand. 'What about Carl? No word yet?'

Dena shook her head, unable to speak.

'It will be a sacrifice.'

'But worth it if I get Trudy back, and save this new little one. I'd do anything to be sure of that. And if I can't have Carl, what does it matter who I marry?'

After that, Dena listened to Lizzie talk about her own and Charlie's plans for the future, too choked to say any more.

–

Tea with Jack Cleaver proved to be something of an ordeal. True, he was impeccably correct, both in his table manners and in his attitude towards Dena. He shook out her napkin, passed her the tiny sandwiches, sausage rolls and éclairs at precisely the right moment. He filled her tea cup without asking and talked the whole time about himself.

Dena heard his entire life story: how he was found abandoned on a doorstep and spent his childhood in one Dr Barnardo's home after another, apparently entirely bereft with not a living soul to visit or care about him. The story was lacking in fine detail but filled throughout with maudlin self-pity. She really couldn't be bothered to question him too closely on the subject, merely listened as politely and patiently as she could.

Children's homes were something of a painful subject for her right now.

Having exhausted that particular subject, he went on to tell her how much he loved his work, and that he was one of Finch's top salesmen.

'Although I'd be more than ready for a change of employment if I can be of any assistance in developing your own business,' he assured her with an ingratiating smile. 'Not that I know much about fashion, but I'm sure I could soon learn.'

'Thanks, but I have all the staff I need,' Dena said, the strain of the afternoon making her face feel stiff with the effort of smiling.

'Well, you have only to ask. It may be that you'll decide to spend more time with Trudy and the new little addition,' he coyly reminded her, 'and would be glad of someone reliable to take the helm.'

Dena said nothing to this, striving to keep her mind firmly fixed on the reason she was sitting here listening to this smooth-talking idiot.

He described his hobbies at great length, reading and philately being his favourites, and bird watching down by the canal. It was amazing, he said, the wildlife that turned up there.

'I saw a kestrel the other day. Imagine, right in the heart of the city.'

Dena looked at him as Lizzie used to do, at the wide nose and the small hooded eyes, which seemed to hide all his secrets, the small dry mouth sunk between puffy flushed cheeks. Could she live with that face, day in and day out? So long as I don't wake up to find it on my pillow, she thought with a shudder. And if there's no other way of getting Trudy back!

'I see she's done it again. Having destroyed my two sons, the man-eating Dena is already moving on to number three without so much as a backward glance.'

Winnie and Belle stood facing each other, hands on hips, eyes glaring, as if preparing to fight a duel at dawn. There was a long history of discord between the two women, the pair of them having almost come to blows on numerous occasions in the past over politics, religion, the war, who to vote for as market superintendent, as well as taking pot shots at respective family members. Belle had been most sarcastic about Winnie's elusive first husband, Donald, and Winnie had never found a good word to say for Kenny.

'Dena didn't destroy your sons, you managed that all by yourself.'

'Don't you take the moral high ground with me! You've no room to talk, Winnie Holmes, married to a pervert like Barry.'

'He's not a pervert, he's an innocent man.'

'That's what they all say.'

'Your Kenny can't. It's a pity they didn't hang the little bugger!'

Belle let out a screech of rage, making heads turn and bringing Clara Higginson running over from her hat stall. 'Now, ladies, we can't have this sort of behaviour in the market hall. You'll frighten all the customers away. Do try to stay calm and—'

But neither of them was listening to Clara's gentle homily, being far too occupied spitting and hissing further abuse at each other, using certain words that caused the poor lady to cover her ears with her hands in distress.

'And if your Carl had anything about him,' Winnie concluded, wagging a finger furiously in Belle's face, 'he'd not have taken umbrage just because the lass needed a bit of time to get herself together.'

'Stuff and nonsense! She was bored with him, that's why she chucked him.'

'She didn't chuck him. Dena was just naturally upset over that flamin' trial, and the daft lad made things worse by not coming near her for days after. I suppose that was your doing?'

'I needed him most.'

'You need your head looking at, and that flipping appeal will only drag it all up again. So if she's found support from a more respectable and reliable chap, then bless her cotton socks, why not, that's what I say. Our Dena deserves a bit of happiness, and to have that little lass home and safe where she belongs.'

Even for Winnie, this was quite a speech. She took a gasping breath to collect herself when it was done, though she was still shaking with rage.

Ever the peacemaker, Clara flapped one hand ineffectually, clearly hoping this would put an end to the argument. She was sadly mistaken. Belle had no intention of allowing Winnie to have the last word.

'If she'd really cared for the child, she'd've taken up our Carl's offer of marriage in the first place. She's a selfish little madam and man mad.'

'Now why does that remark make me think of pots and kettles?'

Belle jabbed a thumb into her own ample cleavage. '*I* should have been the one granted custody of that child. I told Miss Rogers so on more than one occasion.'

There was a small silence. 'So it was *you* what set this whole pantomime off, was it? I should've guessed,' Winnie said, clenching and unclenching her fists as if she was having difficulty keeping control of them. 'Well, if you're wanting to hang on to whatever teeth you've got left, love, I'd keep me gob shut in future, if I were you.'

'Is that a threat, Winnie Holmes?'

'No, chuck. It's a promise.'

'Now, ladies,' Clara interrupted again, fearing the pair might actually come to blows. 'Isn't it time to restore some calm and civility, and call a truce?'

'Never!' they both yelled and stalked away, heads high, bosoms heaving, leaving poor Clara flushed with embarrassment.

Chapter Twenty

'You know that I love you?' They were back in their favourite spot down by the canal, again watching the barges and narrow boats. One was heavily laden with timber, making its way through the old Hulme Locks of the Bridgewater Canal. Aunty had scooted them out of the house while she put the children to bed, and the young lovers were only too glad to escape and be alone at last. The sun was setting over Manchester, washing the sky with streaks of pink and gold and saffron, as they sat with their arms wrapped about each other, Lizzie's cheek in the crook of Charlie's shoulder. 'I don't care how hard I have to work,' he was saying, 'I mean us to succeed.'

Lizzie, feeling the beat of his heart, tried to make her own keep to the same rhythm. 'Is that because you want to show your father you aren't as useless as he thinks?'

'I'll admit there's an element of that,' Charlie conceded, stroking her dark curls, as brutally honest as always. 'But mainly because I want things to be right for you and me. I want us to have a good life together – a nice semi-detached house on one of the new housing estates and maybe a baby of our own one day.'

'Hey, slow down, one thing at a time.'

Chuckling, he kissed her brow. 'I know we'll have to be a bit careful until the wedding. I don't want to risk any accidents, or Aunty throwing me out into the street. I love you, Lizzie, and I'm content to wait.'

'I'm not, I want you now.' She kissed him avidly, loving the way his arms tightened about her, his breathing growing ragged with desire. Very gently, and with a grim expression on his face, he put her from him.

'Don't tempt me. Let's concentrate on making sweets, shall we? Much safer.'

'But nowhere near as much fun,' she teased, kissing him some more.

'Stop it, you vixen. I shall love working with you, Lizzie, and being with you day after day.'

She cast him a shy sideways glance from under her lashes. 'You don't think you might get bored?'

'Not in a million years!' And to prove his point he pulled her into his arms and kissed her good and proper this time, and Lizzie experienced again that swirl of magic deep inside her, like dark chocolate, rich and mysterious, and full of promise.

When she'd recovered her breath, Lizzie gave a little sigh. 'Oh, and I love you too. You're right, though, it is going to be hard, but I don't care. I'm so excited about everything, and sure we can make a go of it. Isn't Aunty marvellous? You are too. I'm so, so happy.'

He cupped her face in his hands. 'That's all I want, your happiness. I want to spend the rest of my life loving and protecting you. I just want you to be happy and for us to be together. Nothing more.'

'In this wonderful house you've planned,' she teased him. 'No doubt with a television set, G Plan furniture, built-in kitchen and—'

'A Hillman Minx in the garage. Yes, why not? Don't we deserve it? There's a bright new world out there, full of opportunity. No more wars, no more rationing, no more pain and suffering. We're the future, you and me, and we can build it together.'

'Oh, Charlie, I do love you so much.'

They might have talked further of how this bright future could be achieved but Charlie was kissing her again, his touch on her neck, on her breast, making her tremble and Lizzie could do nothing but kiss him back. There'd be plenty of time for work and planning tomorrow. Tonight was for love.

-

They found a room to rent in an old cotton mill without too much difficulty and paid for the first month in advance. It wasn't very big, but Aunty Dot thought it would serve to get the business launched, saying they could always move to larger premises if it took off as they hoped.

It had been agreed that Lizzie would spend each morning, as usual, running the Chocolate Cabin, since it was important that this continued to flourish as it was their major source of income. Eventually, if all went well, they'd need to employ staff but for now it was just the three of them. Amy George had agreed to look after it in the afternoons to allow Lizzie time to learn the craft of sweet-making too. Aunty would pop back and forth, in between caring for the children, to give advice and assistance as needed.

This plan meant a tight schedule for them all, as well as paying out a small wage to Amy, but it was worth it to get things going.

'I don't want much,' Amy assured Lizzie. 'If I can bring baby along with me, it will be wonderful just to escape my mother-in-law for a few hours.'

'There is the perk of being able to help yourself to a few free sweets,' Lizzie smilingly told her. 'However, I have to warn you that after a while you'll get sick of the sight and smell of them.'

'Oh, don't say that,' Amy moaned. 'I was looking forward to sampling those wonderful chocolate caramels.'

'Help yourself, but not too many, mind, or you'll end up as fat as…' Realising what she'd been about to say, Lizzie stopped, appalled at herself. But Amy was laughing.

'My dear old mum, Big Molly? Don't worry, I'll make sure that doesn't happen.'

Lizzie and Charlie scrubbed out the room with copious amounts of carbolic soap and household bleach. They repainted the walls with a white limewash, bought some trestle tables, then moved Aunty's sweet-making equipment across, her recipe books and precious copper boiling pan about which she was most particular. Aunty Dot's list of instructions about how to keep everything spotlessly clean seemed endless, but Charlie meticulously wrote it all down in a little black notebook he'd started carrying in his back pocket.

'We're leaving nothing to chance,' he said.

Under Dot's supervision they bought a second-hand stove, more copper pans cost a small fortune, and a metal pouring plate where the toffee could be folded and turned as it cooled. They also purchased various small machines, a bit old-fashioned since they too were second hand but still serviceable. These were for pulling toffee, for chopping and cutting and stretching it. Then there were rollers, an assortment of moulds and frames, plus a whole battery of palette knives, sugar scissors, sieves, brushes, graters, tins and bowls, sufficient to make a good start. They used up every penny of their combined savings, plus the money Aunty raised by selling her 'bits and bobs', as she called them.

But they still had to go cap in hand to the bank manager to borrow more. They took some of their sweets along to tempt him, together with their carefully thought out business plan.

He listened attentively, considered the young couple sitting before him with a shrewd eye, and finally judged them worthy of the bank's investment to the tune of a small loan and a working overdraft. Lizzie guessed it was Aunty's truffles, which swung the balance in their favour; he licked his lips so appreciatively he helped himself to a second one.

'I shall expect meticulous accounts to be presented, and regular bulletins concerning your progress,' he warned them. 'And I may pop in from time to time to view progress for myself.'

'You'd be most welcome,' Lizzie told him. She wanted to kiss him there and then she was so relieved, but managed to restrain herself, and, following Charlie's example, proudly shook his hand in a businesslike fashion as if she'd known all along that he would agree.

Once outside the old Martin's Bank building, she and Charlie whooped with delight and hugged each other tight.

'Looks like we're in business, partner. All we have to decide now is what to make first?'

'Candy Kisses,' Lizzie said. 'With a different name on each one, starting with yours and mine.'

–

The days were growing cooler, the nights drawing in, and Dena felt that her usual energy had melted away with the summer sun. Champion Street no longer hummed with so many people now that the autumn rains had started. Brisk winds rattled dustbin lids and chased chip papers along the gutters, and trade was quiet, in its usual between-seasons dip. Not that Dena cared one way or the other about the state of her business. She felt drained and exhausted much of the time, wanting only to sleep, or be sick.

Back in the summer, she'd finally plucked up the courage to visit the doctor who'd looked at her with disapproval sharp in his eyes when he'd given her the usual perfunctory examination.

'Fallen again I see, Dena,' he'd dryly remarked, as if this were something she did on a regular basis, deliberately to annoy him.

'Unfortunately, yes.' There didn't seem anything more to say.

He'd put away his stethoscope, told her she was around three months gone and said he assumed she wasn't going to do anything silly. Dena hadn't troubled to respond, but simply thanked him and left. She hadn't been back since and now surmised she must be about five and a half months gone, maybe six.

Dena had hoped that once the three-month mark had passed the morning sickness would abate, but the opposite seemed to have occurred. She'd continued to feel sick for much of the day. Following her letter to Miss Rogers, the social worker had called to hear for herself about Jack Cleaver's offer of marriage, which she described as surprisingly generous and an interesting proposition.

But despite Dena pressing her for reassurance that it would increase her chances of getting Trudy back home, nothing definite had yet materialised. Encouraging noises had been made, half promises had eventually been wrung out of Ivy Bank, but nothing in writing had as yet appeared. Dena wasn't prepared to make such an enormous sacrifice of her freedom and future happiness on a simple leap of faith. She needed absolute proof that it would work, that Trudy would indeed be restored to her.

'They'd be prepared to reconsider your case,' was all she'd been told so far, nowhere near enough assurance for Dena. This evening she let herself into an empty house, as was usual these days, dropped her bag on the table and sat down with a weary sigh, a cold shiver running down her spine. There was no fire in the grate, no food in the cupboards, not that she could be bothered to cook herself anything even when she did remember to shop.

Sometimes Winnie would bring her round a dish of hot pot, or a home-made meat pie, but the invitations to tea or Sunday lunch had dried up. And since Trudy was no longer here, the jolly breakfasts were now a thing of the past too. All because of the situation with Barry.

It hurt that there was this continued estrangement between them, yet Dena had no wish to see him.

She'd learned only yesterday that, not satisfied they had sufficient evidence to build a case against him, the police had decided to drop all charges. Dena had been devastated.

It seemed such a pointless waste, all this anguish and misery, all this waiting and hoping that once he was finally charged and locked up her innocent child would be allowed home. But apparently that wasn't going to happen. Nothing was going to be done at all. No one would be punished for hurting her child, except Trudy herself. It seemed so dreadfully unfair.

The police might have decided the case was at an end, but the folk of Champion Street continued to gossip and pass their own judgement. 'Mud sticks', was the whisper going round the market today. 'No smoke without fire', and similar clichéd remarks really didn't help anyone. Dena was weary of the whole thing.

Leaving her bag on the table she made herself a cup of tea, which she drank standing up, nibbled half a Marie biscuit, then climbed the stairs and went to bed without bothering to make herself any supper. She closed her eyes, striving to shut out the troubling thoughts, squeezed back the tears and prevented them from falling, but it was well-nigh impossible. She physically ached for Trudy, as if a limb had been severed from her own body. At least beneath the blankets she could get warm and ease the sick ache in her belly.

–

Trudy's birthday was rapidly approaching, the little girl about to turn three on the twenty-sixth of September, and Dena was anxious to visit and take her presents. When she spotted Miss Rogers standing on Aunty Dot's doorstep, sternly reprimanding her for some supposed fault or other, she hurried over to check on progress and request a visit. Aunty bade her a polite good day then took the opportunity to beat a hasty retreat, grateful for the distraction.

The social worker was predictably pessimistic. 'I'm afraid you upset them last time, creating such a fuss. I did warn you, Dena, that you must learn to accept your lot. Haven't I been saying that to you since you were fourteen years old?'

Dena bit back the sharp retort that popped into her head, not everyone was as lacking in feeling as the staff of Ivy Bank, and simply begged her at least to try. 'I haven't seen Trudy in months. It hardly seems fair, or good for her.'

'It would be better if you provided her with a proper home and two parents, as you are only too aware.'

'And if I did, would that guarantee she'd be allowed home?' Dena swiftly and tartly responded, restraining the cold shudder she always experienced when she thought about Cleaver.

Miss Rogers sighed. 'I've already explained that I am not in a position to make such a promise, but your case would be looked at more favourably.'

'So *my* innocent child has to remain in what is tantamount to a jail even though the abuser who put her there is allowed to walk free?'

The social worker drew herself up to her not inconsiderable height and breathed heavily down her sharp nose. 'This is exactly the kind of attitude which damages your case. Do try to acquire some tact and patience, Dena. I hear you are still writing letters to all and sundry. Conducting this foolish campaign against Ivy Bank isn't helping either.'

'What am I supposed to do? Just let them steal my child without a murmur?'

'I expect you to have faith in the experts.'

'On the spurious assumption that they know how to bring up my child better than I do? Utter rubbish!'

Whereupon, clearly offended by Dena's remark, Miss Rogers stuck her beak of a nose in the air and walked smartly away.

Dena ran after her to catch at her arm. 'I'm sorry! I didn't mean it. I know that you're doing your best, it's just hard. I want to see her. I *must* see her. Surely they'll let me visit my own child on her birthday?'

Again heaving a great sigh, the social worker paused to consider. After a long silence in which Dena could hear nothing but the loud erratic beating of her own heart, Miss Rogers finally agreed to speak to the superintendent of Ivy Bank. 'Very well, in view of the fact that it is Trudy's birthday.'

'Thank you,' Dena said, impulsively hugging the other woman, which brought twin spots of colour to her thin cheeks. 'Thank you so much, I'd really appreciate that.'

'Oh, Dena, what a trial you are,' Miss Rogers said, with a sad shake of her head.

-

While her mother was pleading with Miss Rogers for a second visit, Trudy was having her hands beaten. She was unaware that she had a birthday due. Most of the time the little girl didn't even know what day it was, let alone the month or date. Getting through each day without punishment was more than enough for her to cope with.

Miss Carter had accused her of stealing an extra slice of bread at supper, to which she was not entitled, and this was today's punishment. Red-hot fire was shooting through her hands and wrists. Trudy tried to pull away, but Carthorse pinned her down by clamping one hand in an iron grip over both of Trudy's stick-like wrists, while with the other she whacked the child's small hands with a ruler. Trudy had never known such pain.

A gush of warm urine ran down her legs but she managed not to cry. It hadn't taken her long to learn that crying only provoked the woman to greater cruelty. The best thing was to bite her lip and hope the beating would soon be over.

'Now, get out of my sight,' Carthorse ordered. 'No breakfast for you in the morning. That will be your punishment for being a greedy girl.'

The tears came as Trudy made her way along the cold empty corridor and up the stairs to the dormitory, her skinny arms wrapped about herself with each hand tucked under an armpit. She cried and sobbed like the baby she still was, wondering for the thousandth time why her mummy had sent her to this cruel place. She was a good girl, not bad like everyone said.

The worst of it was that she had no one to turn to for comfort. Even her mummy never came to see her, so couldn't love her any more. Trudy had lost all hope of ever getting out of this awful place. She would be here forever.

Sometimes, and this was the most frightening of all, she couldn't even remember Mummy's face. Trudy could recall the sweet lavender scent of her, her warmth and the feel of her arms holding her tight, but trying to conjure up her face was hard. It would appear suddenly in her dreams by accident, and she'd reach for her with joy, but then like a puff of smoke she would vanish before Trudy could reach her.

Her hands had gone numb now, but by the time she reached her bed wanting only to crawl under the covers and disappear, pins and needles were bringing them back to life and there was unbearable pain running right up both arms.

Would it have helped if she'd found the courage to tell the truth? That she wasn't really being greedy because the bread wasn't for her at all. Even as the thought entered her head, as young as she was, Trudy knew that it would have made no difference at all. She was trapped. Either she stole the bread and was beaten by Carthorse, or she refused and was bullied even more by the older girls.

Chrissie, the leader of the gang, was strolling over even now, an expression of pure malice on her sneering face. She gave the smaller girl a thump on the shoulder and pushed her down on to the bed. 'You messed up.'

'I – I know, I'm sorry. I didn't know she was w – watching.'

'You'll have to try harder next time.'

Trudy was the youngest in the dormitory, and consequently the most bullied. She spent her entire time running pointless, and sometimes dangerous, errands for the older girls. Whatever they wanted she had to provide. On this occasion an extra slice of bread for Chrissie. Girls were allowed only one slice for supper, extra ones only handed out as a reward for good behaviour, or if you were Miss Carter's favourite.

Chrissie pushed her sneering face up close. 'The trouble is, I didn't get my bread and I'm still hungry. So what you have to do now is go downstairs, slip into the pantry and fetch me a currant bun instead. I know there are some there because Sal helped make them. She nicked one when cook wasn't looking but ate it all herself, the cow. I didn't get the chance because I had to work in the laundry today.'

Every girl was expected to do chores, even small ones like Trudy, who had spent the day picking stones off the land so that bigger girls like Chrissie could dig it.

'The devil finds mischief for idle hands to do', and 'Idleness is a sin', were constantly chanted at them.

Trudy stared up at the older girl in horror. 'I can't! I can't go down there. It's dark, and Carthorse might see me again.'

'Stupid child, how will she see you if it's dark?'

This kind of argument was beyond Trudy, but as Chrissie dragged her from her bed and shoved her towards the stairs, she began to cry. 'I'm not going, I'm not!'

'You'll go if I tell you to go. Stop snivelling! Walk on the edges of the stairs so the boards don't creak, and be back in twenty minutes with that bun or you'll be sorry.'

–

It was the longest, most frightening twenty minutes of Trudy's life. Her knees were trembling, her knickers, still soaked with urine, flapped about and rubbed against her skinny thighs and a thin string of green mucus dripped from her nose as she silently sobbed. The sound of every step she took seemed to echo in the cavernous hall below as Trudy crept down the stairs, even though she carefully kept to the edges as instructed.

Opening the door that led to the back of the old house and its kitchens was another major obstacle. The knob was shiny with brass polish, and far too big for Trudy's tiny hands even when they weren't turning black and yellow with bruises before her very eyes. Somehow, with a great effort, she managed it, and slipped like a ghost down the stone-floored passage and into the old Victorian kitchen.

A streak of moonlight illuminated the bleached pine table and the ancient cooking range. There were two yellow-stone sinks and beyond those lay the pantry. The door was closed and Trudy could feel her lungs growing tight with fear as she struggled to catch her breath. Even the sound of her own breathing was scaring her, and she wanted to wee again.

She pushed open the pantry door with her shoulder, quickly scoured the shelves and soon spotted the tray of currant buns. Trudy realised that cook would know exactly how many there were. She would have counted them carefully so that each girl would be allowed one for Sunday tea when their family came to visit. It gave the impression that the home was caring, as if they had currant buns every day – far from the case. And if, like Trudy, your mother didn't visit, then you weren't even given a bun but expected to stay out of sight up in the dormitory or out in the garden.

Consequently, Trudy had only ever had one bun in all the time she'd been at Ivy Bank.

She could smell them now and her mouth watered. Trudy reached for one and pressed her small nose against it, closing her eyes in ecstasy. Was it flavoured with nutmeg or cloves? Mummy used to make currant buns with cloves, and butterfly buns with butter cream. Oh, and chocolate haystacks made from cocoa powder, sweetened milk and Shredded Wheat.

Trudy's tummy rumbled. Hunger was a part of life at Ivy Bank. A dish of thin porridge for breakfast, a measly dinner of lumpy mashed potato and grey meat, and one slice of bread with watery soup for supper, came nowhere near to satisfying young appetites. Unable to resist the sweet smell of the bun, Trudy took a bite.

It was then that she heard heavy footsteps approaching.

Chapter Twenty-One

Lizzie was happy, her life full of love and laughter and sweet-making. Pringle's Sweets had been in operation for some weeks now and she and Charlie had learned a great deal about the various tasks involved: the correct temperatures for each process; how much sugar, water and glucose was needed for any particular recipe; when to add cream of tartar, bicarb for the cinder toffee, liquorice or dark molasses for the treacle toffee, as well as icing sugar, cochineal and other secret ingredients and colourings.

Lizzie learned that the colour of toffee changed when it was pulled, red paling to pink could be twisted with the original to form sweets or lollies of two distinct colours which children loved.

Much of the work was done by hand; although the simple machines they'd bought performed well, once they'd got the hang of how to operate them. But it was hot and tiring work. Lizzie loved to help with the chocolate recipes every after-noon, but toffee making was a far more taxing job. Folding and turning the great chunks of toffee mixture needed strong muscles, as well as a pair of padded gloves to protect hands from the heat.

Lizzie would watch fascinated as Charlie folded blocks of sherbet into yellow toffee mixture before lengths of it were then pulled and stretched and formed into long thin ropes, marked into toffee-sized sections, and put through the cutting machine to be chopped into pieces. Last of all the completed sherbet lemons were individually wrapped and stored in jars or put in boxes covered with waxed paper, all ready to be sold.

This was a job where the children loved to help. Joey, Alan, Beth, and even little Cissie would sit around the big trestle table wrapping each sweet with dextrous skill, filling the jars and boxes, and tasting the odd one in between.

'I like this job,' Alan would say, his cheek bulging, a trickle of treacle juice running from the corner of his mouth. Beth would wipe away her handkerchief with much tut-tutting.

'Beats school,' Joey would agree with a grin.

Aunty would remonstrate with them, reminding them of the importance of education. That they must wait till Saturday to be given their sweet ration for the week, and not forget to clean their teeth every night. But they found it so hard to resist.

Each day Lizzie and Charlie would learn something new under Aunty's strict guidance. She taught them everything she knew about sweet-making and chocolate, which she in turn had learned from her mother.

'They must not only taste good, but look good,' she would tell them. 'A skilled chocolatier should be an artist who can sculpt and decorate and create a tantalising selection of delights. One day we'll happen make our own chocolate, the very best, with an iridescent gloss and a good hard snap when it breaks.'

'Why don't we do it now?' Joey wanted to know, beginning to feel a part of this exciting new venture.

'Because it's a bit ambitious for us at this stage, and demanding of more time and staff than we can afford,' Aunty said, ruffling the spiky hair that stuck out in tufts all over his head. 'So until we're a bit more experienced we'll continue to buy it in blocks – dark and rich, smooth and milky, and sweet and white.'

'I like the white best,' yelled Cissie.

'I like Five Boys Chocolate,' shouted Alan with excitement, and everyone pounced on him.

'Traitor!'

Laughing, Aunty pushed them off him, ordering them to leave him alone while Beth busied herself cleaning her little brother's grubby glasses.

'One day, Joey my lad, when you've finished this education you've just embarked upon and proudly have a wall full of certificates to show for it, we might put you in charge of chocolate-making, eh, Charlie?'

'Why not? We'll have expanded by then and he can be department manager. That's what family businesses are all about, everyone taking part.'

Joey grinned in delight, showing the gap between his two front teeth, brown eyes shining. He'd started at the grammar school in September and wasn't finding it easy to settle, the other boys seeming much more self-assured than him, coming as many of them did from middle-class homes with two parents. Aunty's encouraging remark could well be just the motivation he needed to give him a bit more confidence in himself.

'He'd need to learn the trade, though,' she warned, warming to her theme as she grated curls of chocolate, laying one on top of each chocolate peppermint she'd just made. 'Grammar school lad or not, he'd need to go for training to a proper catering college, or better still serve his time at one of the finest chocolate houses in France or Belgium. Best in the business they are. He must learn the history of chocolate, the science and nature of it, understand how to taste it and recognise its origin like a good wine. How to fold and whisk, mould and create like a top pastry chef would. It takes years if you're going to do the job properly. But he's a bright lad, our Joey, none better. He could do it right enough.'

No one could argue with that, least of all Joey himself who suddenly saw a bright future opening up before him for the very first time, and a way escaping forever from his bully of a father.

Overwhelmed by emotion, he hugged her. 'Thanks, Aunty. I love you, and I'll make the best chocolatier you ever saw, once I've got all me certificates.'

'I know you will, poppet. Nay, what a chatterbox you've become all of a sudden,' Aunty said, and was forced to leave the room to blow her nose.

They all strived to make a product of high quality from the finest ingredients, which would also be popular with children, who would naturally be their biggest customers. At the same time their aim was to be different from other sweet-makers, and from Finch's in particular. The last thing they needed was to be accused of copying, so although Charlie and Aunty were concentrating on producing fine traditional sweets, Lizzie was also keen to think of new products, to give them something special to offer.

As well as regular lines such as sarsaparilla drops, aniseed balls, barley sugar and mint humbugs, they produced Candy Kisses in the shape of lips in pink, lemon, white, green and red, in a range of flavours. Also fruity boiled sweets such as pineapple cubes and strawberry twists. The chocolates all had mouth-watering centres: marzipan, ginger, coffee cream, hazel nut crunch, Charlie's favourite brandy cream, truffles and many more. All of them absolutely delicious.

There was just one problem. Despite all their hard work and effort, nothing was selling as it should.

'Our shelves are filled to bursting with boxes and jars of sweets and chocolates. What now?' Charlie asked, his young face creased with anxiety. Difficult as it had been to make the sweets, selling them seemed to be harder still.

–

Everything at Ivy Bank was hard, and very cold. There were no carpets, no cuddly eiderdowns on the beds, no softness of any kind. And whenever Carthorse found out that Trudy had wet the bed, the little girl would be made to sleep on the hard wooden floor with only a thin blanket to cover her.

'You're just as much trouble as that mother of yours was, in her day,' she would bitterly complain.

Trudy was ashamed that she'd reverted to this sort of babyish behaviour but couldn't seem to stop it happening. She wet herself during the day as well. She would ask to go to the lavatory and be told to wait until playtime or dinner time. She'd be crossing her legs, holding her crotch, but no matter how hard she tried she simply couldn't hold on. Then the worst would happen and Trudy would feel that betraying leakage in her knickers, or a flood of warmth on her sheet. Not only that, but her wee-wee hurt. It seemed to burn and sting, and even when she'd emptied her bladder she still felt as if she wanted to go.

One afternoon Miss Carter caught Trudy scrubbing her dirty knickers in the sink and smacked her for being a big baby. She punished Trudy further not only by making her sleep on the hard wooden floor but also by putting her on 'door duty'.

This involved standing by the draughty front door for hours on end, being ready to open it the minute anyone came along the corridor, and woe betide Trudy if she fell asleep or didn't get the big heavy door open in time.

It was yet another punishment, one of many that Trudy had learned to endure. But the more she was bullied and hectored by this woman, the more she wanted to wee. It was awful! The little girl lived in constant fear, dreading making the smallest mistake that could result in more pain and suffering.

The night she'd taken the currant bun in the pantry had been the most frightening of all. When she'd first heard the footsteps Trudy had been absolutely convinced that she was about to be caught with the cake in her hand. She'd instinctively ducked behind the big earthenware flour jar. Fortunately, because of her smallness, she'd been well hidden when invisible hands had pushed open the door and a streak of light had arrowed into the pantry.

In those few seconds of blinding fear Trudy had screamed inside her head for her mother. She'd thought of her small bed at home with its pink eiderdown and a picture of a teddy bear on it that Mummy had stitched for her; of happy afternoons spent with Mummy watching *Andy Pandy* on the television. She thought of Aunty Winnie and Uncle Barry and their silly songs and stories, of the noise and laughter on Champion Street Market, and she'd wanted to weep, only she was too terrified even to breathe.

When she'd thought her chest was about to burst, Trudy had heard Carthorse grunt with annoyance, as if she'd fully expected to find her there, and then the sound of heavy feet striding away. Trudy had collapsed behind the flour bin and wept, feeling thoroughly sorry for herself. But then she'd sat on her bottom on the cold tiled floor and eaten every scrap of the currant bun.

Living on her wits was becoming a way of life.

—

Cedric Finch was all too aware of what his son and his fiancée were up to, and his anger mounted daily. If they imagined they could set themselves up in competition, take him on at his own game and win, then they were very much mistaken.

He'd taken a dislike to the girl from the start when she'd refused to remove her daft aunt's sweets from the stall, but he'd been shocked when Cleaver had told him the truth about her background, and who her mother was. Not that he had anything against prostitutes per se, they performed a valuable service.

But Finch was a man with double standards. Although he may be content to make use of a prostitute for his own gratification, he had absolutely no wish for one to marry his son, or worse still, become the mother of his grandchildren. Not only that, more than once in the past Cedric himself had been a client of the very same Maureen who had surprisingly turned out to be Lizzie Pringle's mother.

He had no qualms about interfering in his son's love life. Evelyn molly-coddled the boy; thought the sun shone out of his backside and believed he could do no wrong. While Cedric cared only for himself, and knew he'd be ruined if word ever got out about these 'social activities' of his.

No matter what he was obliged to do to protect his own interests, and he had few scruples in that direction, Cedric didn't believe that his wife would make any meaningful attempt to stand up to him.

She'd once found some dirty postcards among his possessions, but although Evelyn had been sufficiently disgusted to leave his bed and never return to it, she hadn't been brave enough to leave him. Such an act of independence would be beyond her.

Evelyn was his second wife. He'd been obliged to divorce his first when she'd failed to produce an heir. Cedric had trumped up some tale of her having an affair, totally untrue but had served so far as the law was concerned. Being barren wasn't legal grounds for divorce. She hadn't disputed the charge since she was as willing as he to end the marriage.

Consequently, Finch had been thirty-eight when he'd married Evelyn, forty-one when his son was born and had held high expectations, considering what he'd had to go through in order to acquire one.

He regretted the fact that Evelyn hadn't produced a daughter as well. Girls were far more malleable, and Cedric had come to feel nothing but contempt for the boy. They never saw eye to eye on anything, and if the lad could find any way of disobeying his father, or of making life difficult for him, then he would do so, as he was doing now.

After some careful contemplation of the problem, Cedric decided the best way to quash this new competition was to make it his business to inform all his regular customers that

Pringle's Sweets were breaking the law. He let it be known that they operated in a dirty old cotton mill with filthy kitchens, and that as a consequence he'd felt duty bound to report them to the health inspectors.

He also claimed they were financially unsound, owing money left, right and centre. Cedric made it very clear that if anyone was foolish enough to buy from Pringle's, they would live to regret it as they too would find themselves in deep trouble, financially or otherwise.

'I have many friends,' he warned. 'Both in high places and low, if we can put it that way – the kind who don't quibble about getting their hands dirty, should it become necessary to bring folk back into line.'

The more independent-minded stallholders on Manchester, Bolton, Blackburn and Burnley markets, those tired of Finch's implacable insistence that they stock his sweets exclusively, and often more than they actually needed yet were expected to pay for them on the nail, naturally protested. But all of them, without fail, backed down when it came to the crunch. There was something not only deeply unpleasant but also overtly dangerous about the man.

Cedric himself was absolutely determined that *if* there had to be a battle, he would win, no matter what. And to prove his words weren't simply a meaningless threat, he instructed the most notorious of his contacts, Billy Quinn, to make the point more forcibly. Obstinate stallholders who gave the new company a try, found their stock mysteriously ruined or stolen, or their stalls overturned. Any thought of standing up to their sole supplier faded to nothing in their own private battle for survival.

–

Lizzie, Charlie and Aunty sat around the kitchen table discussing the unexpected and unanticipated problem of how to win customers. They were well able to supply Lizzie's own stall now, but finding anyone willing to change over from the long-established firm of Finch's Sweets to being supplied by the unknown Pringle's was proving less easy to achieve.

'He's blackening our name. Finch is going around telling his customers lies about us.'

'Then we must concentrate on those stalls and shops who don't use him, and also aim to get our sweets and our name known by the general public.' Lizzie smiled. 'And I have an idea how we can do just that.'

They gave out free samples of their sweets to men standing in line outside Manchester City and Manchester United football grounds, to courting couples standing in cinema queues, to elegant ladies going to the theatre or the opera.

'Free samples,' they cried. 'Try our free samples. Pringle's Sweets are the best!'

They even visited schools and playgrounds and gave them to children, which unfortunately brought Miss Rogers to their doorstep to object.

'Don't you know there's a campaign to stop children accepting sweets from strangers?'

Lizzie was deeply contrite and apologised profusely. 'Oh, goodness, I never thought. I'm so sorry, we won't ever do that again.'

Instead, they gave away several small packets to the local paper, persuading them to present them as birthday gifts to the readers of their children's pages; working as a treat.

'Can we have more?' the editor asked. 'We're selling more newspapers as a result.'

'Come St Valentine's Day you can give out prizes of our Candy Kisses,' Lizzie told him.

They discovered that Finch too had made a line of sweets almost identical to Lizzie's own Candy Kisses, and she fumed with rage.

'He's copying us! He's beaten us again.'

Charlie hugged her. 'No, he hasn't, not yet, but we should have thought to patent them. It's too late now for these, but if you get any more good ideas, Lizzie, then we must remember to do that first. We have to watch our backs the whole time.'

And then one day the health inspector arrived. Despite Lizzie explaining that they'd only recently been inspected when they'd set up the kitchen just a few weeks ago, he took the place apart. He scoured every corner, clearly expecting to find beetles or cockroaches, cobwebs or mice. After several hours of searching he was, however, forced to admit defeat.

'I take my hat off to you two youngsters. If every kitchen was as clean as this one, I'd be out of a job.'

'Who reported us?' Charlie wanted to know. 'I know some-body must have done for you to come again so soon.'

'Sorry, I'm not allowed to say.'

'Don't worry, I think we can guess.'

But although they were grateful the inspection had turned out as well as it had, they both knew that if Charlie's father were responsible, as they rightly assumed, he wouldn't stop because he'd failed on this occasion to close them down. The battle lines had been drawn. This was but the beginning.

'We mustn't allow him to frighten us,' Lizzie said, watching the inspector drive away. 'We must keep faith in what we're trying to achieve, and stick together.'

'Don't worry, love, we will.'

She glanced shyly up at him, worrying again about whether she could rely on his love to see them through, or if he'd call it quits and walk away. 'You aren't regretting getting involved with me, are you?'

Charlie kissed her brow, then her nose, each quivering eyelid, and finally captured her mouth with his own. When the kiss ended, he said, 'Father will need much more than a health inspector, or spreading nasty rumours around his customers, to prise us apart, let alone prevent us from building a good business together. Now can you and me go somewhere quiet so that I can remind you why I love you, and how I got myself into this mess in the first place?' he teased.

'Oh, yes, please!' she said, laughing up at him, released from worry in an instant.

No matter what Finch did to them, their happiness continued to shine through.

219

Chapter Twenty-Two

Cissie was to be sent home. Aunty was upset, as always when she had to say goodbye to one of 'her' children, but the empty bed gave her an idea. So when she took the baby out on his usual morning perambulation around the market and spotted Dena hanging new skirts on her rack, she went over to put the suggestion to her.

'What if I asked Miss Rogers if I could foster Trudy? I'm not saying she'll agree mind, but it's worth a try.'

Dena looked at her with startled, shining eyes. 'Are you serious?'

Aunty jiggled the pram. 'I never joke where fostering children is concerned.'

'Oh, Aunty!' and Dena flung her arms about the older woman to hug her tight. 'That could well be the answer to my prayers.'

The foot of the big high pram was stacked with brown paper bags full of vegetables, the latest baby being particularly fascinated by the carrots. Aunty quietly took it away and gave him a rusk instead. 'He's teething. Don't forget, fostering is never permanent, as you can see from the fact little Cissie has been returned home to her mam and dad, for now. You'd still have to find a way to persuade the cruelty man to let you have Trudy home for good. But, pardon me for asking, I heard a rumour there's another on the way?'

Unable to bear even the sympathetic gaze of this generous, big-hearted woman, Dena stared at her own feet, unconsciously rubbing the back of her hand over her aching back. 'It's true, I have fallen again and I'm not proud of myself.'

'These things happen. And Carl Garside's the father I take it, only he's done a moonlight flit, so you're thinking of getting spliced to that Jack Cleaver instead? Or so I've heard.'

'Heavens, does everyone know my business? Isn't it possible to keep a secret round here?'

'On this market?'

'He has asked me, yes,' Dena said, her expression thoughtful. 'And I will, if I must, if it would get Trudy back. It's just—'

'You don't love him and he's a bit of a queer sort,' Aunty finished for her, jiggling the pram again as the baby began to grow bored and started to grizzle.

Dena gave a philosophical shrug. 'I'm way past looking for a knight on a white charger, but... there's something about him that troubles me, though I can't put my finger on what it is. I've told him that I'll marry him if it's the only way to get Trudy back, but I'd welcome an alternative solution.'

Aunty frowned. 'He seems an upfront sort of bloke to me, a respectable, well-meaning fusspot you might say. A bit lonely since his mother died, but that apart I'd say he's been trying to smarten himself up a bit lately.'

Dena looked puzzled. 'Mother? I thought he was brought up in a Dr Barnardo's home.'

'Oh, aye, that's right, he did spend some time in one of them. I forgot. And it was his Aunty what died, not his mother. She'd gone long since. He's told us his story many times but I still get it mixed up. Anyway, I must get on. Think about it. I can't help you sort out a permanent solution, that's up to you, but we can at least try to get the little lass out of that dreadful place.'

Dena went straight to the telephone box and rang Miss Rogers. The social worker was surprised by Aunty's suggestion, even slightly taken aback, and none too forthcoming with an answer. Instead she asked a few questions of her own. 'What about this Jack Cleaver? Would the wedding still be on? Mrs Thompson only fosters, you know, she doesn't adopt.'

'I've no wish for my child to be adopted, and yes, if the result is that I can have Trudy home with me permanently, then I may well be willing to marry Jack Cleaver, for all I don't love him, or even like him very much.'

'I doubt you can afford such sentiments as love, dear, not with the mess you're in.' Miss Rogers's voice sounded even more condemnatory over the phone than it did face to face. 'I'll see what I can do about putting Trudy temporarily with Mrs Thompson, on the grounds that you're going to sort out your tangled love life and become respectable.' And she rang off, leaving Dena in something of a daze.

Oh, but she was filled with a sudden shaft of hope. 'Could it work?'

The thought that Trudy might actually escape spending another week, even one more night in that place, was surely worth any sacrifice?

–

'If you fall into a tantrum today, then I'll make sure your mother is never allowed to come again. Is that clear?'

Trudy nodded. The little girl's heart was thumping with hope and excitement. Mummy was coming. At last. She was here! Trudy had no idea that the superintendent was issuing exactly the same threat to Dena at precisely the same moment, so that when the visit actually took place, neither mother nor child knew how to cope with the burden of restraint thrust upon them.

Dena sat in the same chair as before, her hands clasped tightly on a package in her lap, chestnut brown eyes glittering with unshed tears. She was striving to smile but kept biting her lip to stop herself from crying. Trudy stood by the door, too frightened to move in case she too cried or weed her pants.

'Get in with you,' Carthorse said, giving the little girl a push. She issued Dena with the usual instruction of: 'Ten minutes and no more.' The door closed, firmly.

Dena longed to jump up and snatch Trudy to her breast but didn't dare in case it upset her and triggered the kind of tears and tantrums, which would result in a more severe ban. 'I've brought you a present,' she said, holding out a large package. 'It's for your birthday. Would you like to open it?'

Trudy didn't move. 'Have you come to take me home?'

Dena bit her lip, gave her head a little shake. 'No, love. I can't do that, I'm afraid.' She didn't dare share the fragile hope of a possible means of escape with the child, in case Aunty's offer was refused. It would be too cruel to put her through such a bitter disappointment.

Dena took a trembling breath and tried to put a smile in her voice. 'Shall I open it then?'

The small girl remained by the door, but this time she nodded.

Dena was deeply disappointed. She'd dreamed of Trudy running into her arms, her small face shining with happiness at the sight of a birthday gift, but that was pure fantasy. Reality was far different and much more painful. 'Look, it's a ball. I thought you might like one for playing games in the courtyard.'

Trudy looked at the ball, large and round and red, and inside she ached to rush over into Mummy's arms and take it from her. She didn't have anything of her own. Looby Loo was now looking very battered, as she was played with by everyone and never got to sleep in Trudy's bed any more. Inside her was this great choking pain that threatened to bubble over and start her off crying again. She had no doubt she wouldn't be allowed to play with this bright red ball either.

She reached out her hands and grasped the ball, then very gently Dena drew her close.

Mummy's arms were around her, cuddling her, and she was kissing her cheek. Trudy felt overwhelmed by her nearness, by the knowledge that her mummy was actually here, at last, but she kept herself carefully stiff and rigid. Every now and then she would glance back at the round window in the door, knowing that Carthorse would be watching.

Dena was studying Trudy closely, asking if she was eating properly, and then she glanced at the hands holding the ball and her eyes grew wide with shock.

'What have you done to your hands?'

Trudy shook her head, the choking feeling turning to panic. She dropped the ball and tucked her hands under her armpits so that the bruises on them couldn't be seen, rocking slightly to comfort herself.

'They're *purple*! What happened, Trudy? Tell me. Tell Mummy what happened to your hands.'

But Trudy knew that was impossible. If she told, Mummy would be upset and make a fuss and then they'd never let her visit again, ever. Carthorse had told her so. Trudy simply gazed at her mother in silent anguish, trying to memorise every detail of her face: the way the tips of her brown hair glowed in the light from the window, the softness of her mouth, and the expression in her shining eyes. Mummy had come, after all. Perhaps she did still love her a little.

Dena spoke in a hushed whisper. 'I *am* trying to get you out of here. I *am*, Trudy, I swear it. I'm doing everything I can think of, and I may have found a way.'

Trudy didn't respond even to this, to the sound of desperate optimism in her mother's voice. All hope was lost to her. She was resigned to her lot. 'I'm all right.' This three-year-old child, well schooled now in discipline, calmly consoled her anxious mother that she was not to worry.

Dena took a deep shuddering breath, afraid that she had failed her child. What more could she say? She felt utterly helpless. The griping pain in her belly was nothing compared to the iron band of despair that encased her heart.

By the time Miss Carter unlocked the door to usher mother and daughter apart and back to their respective lives, both had come to realise the futility of the visit. Afraid of stirring uncontrollable emotions, each had kept their distance. Dena was keenly aware that such conversation as was possible with a small child had been awkward and stilted, each of them saying only what the other needed to hear. And Trudy knew that she had lied because she wasn't all right at all.

Dena pecked a kiss on the top of her daughter's head and predictably urged her to 'be a good girl'.

Trudy longed to scream and screech and shout and say that she was *always* a good girl and that she wanted to go home *now*. Instead, she picked up the shiny red ball and watched in silence as her mother walked away. Once the front door had closed behind her, the little girl dutifully handed over the ball to the Carthorse, knowing she wouldn't be allowed to keep it, and went back outside to carry on picking up stones. At least out in the back field she was able to squat down and wee anywhere.

–

Once out on the long, gravelled drive Dena leaned against the gate post and sobbed her heart out. Never had she felt so ill in all her life. Enduring the hardships of Ivy Bank herself had been nothing by comparison to seeing her own child suffer. It was more than she could bear. But if she went back to complain and make a fuss with the superintendent, as she had done before, they'd put her on their black list and never allow her to see Trudy again.

The ache in her belly was growing worse, and Dena wrapped her arms about herself. It hadn't been an easy pregnancy but the griping pains, which had troubled her for days, now suddenly became crippling. Dena realised in a flash that she was losing the baby. Hard on this thought her waters broke and she screamed out in pain and fell, grazing her knees on the gravel. Dena felt she was being devoured by the pain and screamed again, shouting for help. It seemed like a lifetime before she heard rushing feet, and later the blessed relief of an ambulance siren.

Throughout the ensuing struggle by the doctors to save the baby, all Dena could see in her mind's eye was Trudy's pinched and pale little face. She saw the agony in her daughter's eyes, the disappointment, the way her small mouth folded in upon itself in an effort not to cry. The memory of that visit was far worse than the anguish of having her body torn apart.

And then it was all over. She'd lost the baby and Dena didn't know whether to be glad or sorry. What kind of mother could lose both her children in one day?

Chapter Twenty-Three

Over the coming weeks and months trade began slowly to improve. Shops and stalls found themselves being asked not for Finch's sweets but for 'those lovely violet creams that Pringle's make', or 'don't you have any of Pringle's whirligig lollies?' As this happened more and more often, the shopkeeper or stallholder concerned found himself obliged to order some. And since these were Aunty's personal recipes, Lizzie made sure she patented them this time: a long drawn out process but worth it, she felt, to protect them.

In view of the scare they'd had with the health inspector, and from fear of the gossip that Finch was spreading about their dirty kitchens, they decided to hold an open day. They put an announcement in the paper and stuck up posters all around the local markets, inviting people to come along personally to inspect their kitchens and watch how the sweets were made. The day proved to be a great success with a steady stream of curious onlookers drifting through.

Sections of the workroom were roped off but visitors could walk around its perimeter and clearly see Charlie and Lizzie working at the tables and with the machines. They could see the toffee mixture being boiled in the big copper pan and then lifted and poured, cooled and pulled, and finally chopped into sweets. Fascinated by the process, a large crowd gathered and Joey and his boxing pal Spider had to act as marshals to move people along and make room for the next batch.

'Maybe word will spread now that all is well with Pringle's Sweets,' Charlie said at the end of a long and tiring, but utterly satisfying day.

'We just need sales to improve then we can employ more help to take some of the pressure off you,' Lizzie told him.

'I can cope,' he said, groaning with pleasure as she started to massage his aching shoulders. 'Ooh, yes, rub my back just there, no, a bit lower down.'

Lizzie and Charlie were still as besotted with each other as ever, and counting the days till they could marry.

'Maybe if we had twenty-five customers to supply, and fifty pounds in the bank, we could afford to do it,' Charlie would suggest, and then look deep into her eyes and instantly change his mind. 'Or ten quid would do. Here, I might have a fiver somewhere, let's settle for that then I can love you properly.'

Giggling, Lizzie would smack his hands away, though not very seriously. 'Oh, but it's hard. Why do we have to wait?' she would ask as they kissed and cuddled on the sofa after Aunty and the children had gone up to bed. 'I'm not interested in whether or not you have any money. I'm just happy for us to be working on this enterprise together.'

'I know, but it could still all go horribly wrong. He's unpredictable is my father, always did keep things close to his chest, full of secret plans, so who knows what he might do next? At least we're gaining a few new customers each week, but it's going to take time. You can't build a new business overnight, and I want us to have a good start, Lizzie, love. I don't want you to turn round five years from now and tell me it was all a big mistake.'

She looked at him, shocked. 'Oh, Charlie, I would never do such a thing. I don't care about being poor so long as we have each other.'

'Aye, well, you know the old saying – when money flies out the door, love goes out the window.'

The uncertainty of their situation continued to prey on Charlie's mind. Trade might be improving, but not quickly enough to please the bank manager who wasn't impressed with their figures thus far. He'd called twice recently, issuing grave warnings when Charlie had asked for more time to repay the loan.

Their savings were all used up and Aunty's house was beginning to look strangely empty as day after day items would mysteriously vanish, to reappear in the pawnbroker's window at the bottom end of Champion Street. The latest to go were the Westminster Chime clock that had once stood on the mantelpiece, the standard lamp, and the trinket box from Aunty's dressing table.

'What's the point in a trinket box if you've no trinkets left to put in it?' she'd laughed when Lizzie had remarked upon its loss.

Charlie felt entirely responsible. The person causing them all this distress was his own father, after all.

'We have to be patient just a little while longer,' he murmured gently to Lizzie now, smoothing her dark hair as he held her close. He loved her so much, Charlie wished he could wave a magic wand and put everything right. And although Lizzie was unaware of it, he had once gone back home to have it out with his father, demanding to know why he was persecuting them in this way.

'Can't you stand a bit of fair competition, even from your own son?' he'd challenged him.

'Not if you're with that whore, no.' Charlie had ended up socking him one on the chin, that hadn't helped in the least.

'Talk to him,' he'd grimly told his mother as he'd walked away, leaving her weeping. 'Make him see sense.' But Charlie knew he was wasting his breath. When had his mother ever stood up to his father?

Yet he and Lizzie were happy together, and he blessed the day she'd walked into his father's office and he'd first set eyes on her. Pringle's Sweets would grow, albeit slowly, and things would improve, given time, he was sure of it. Then they could get the bank manager off their backs and marry. There was nothing Charlie wanted more.

'In the meantime, at least we have each other,' Lizzie would say. 'Not like poor Dena who has been deserted by Carl Garside, had her precious child taken away from her and now lost the baby. She looked truly dreadful when I went to see her in hospital. She feels as if she has nothing left to live for. We are so lucky to have each other!'

And it was true, they were lucky. Charlie knew it every time he kissed her sweet mouth, every time he gazed into those gorgeous blue eyes or watched the happiness radiating from Lizzie's lovely face. Oh, but the waiting was hard. Sometimes their emotions would almost overwhelm them as they kissed and fondled and explored the delights of each other's body. Anything but 'that' they would say, but it simply wasn't enough.

Lizzie longed to belong to Charlie entirely, every bit as much as Charlie ached to make her his. And after an undignified tussle or a few embarrassed giggles, they'd smooth each other's hair, fasten buttons and creep quietly to their separate beds.

–

As Christmas approached Miss Rogers called again at number thirty-seven to ask if Aunty would have Cissie back.

'It hasn't worked out, putting the child with her family. The rest of the children seem to be reasonably well cared for, but not Cissie. They pick on her for some reason. I shouldn't tell you this, but apparently her father put her head down the lavatory pan and flushed the chain on her.'

'Fetch her back,' Aunty said. 'Today.'

'And what about young Trudy? That would mean you wouldn't have room for another, surely, if you took Cissie back.'

'There's always room for one more. We'd manage. Trudy would only be here temporarily, until her mam marries Jack Cleaver.'

'Assuming I can get the office to agree. How is Dena? Still grieving over that baby?'

'What do you think? The lass does have a heart. You might say too big a heart for her own good.'

'She should be thankful that little problem is over and done with, at least.'

Aunty's expression grew icy. 'We'd happen all be better off if we'd never been born.' The social worker had the grace to flush and look uncomfortable. Aunty didn't let her off the hook easily. 'So are we getting anywhere with this plan for me to foster Trudy? It's taking you a heck of a long time to sort it out.'

Miss Rogers fiddled with her gloves, flicked through her notebook as if needing to check details, before falling back on a few platitudes. 'These things can't be rushed, you know. There are forms to be filled in, due processes to be gone through.'

Aunty snorted. 'The processes go through fast enough when you want me to take a baby at midnight. Come on, spit it out, what's the real problem?'

The truth was that Trudy was unwell, had been for some weeks. She'd been suffering from a cold, as had half the children in the home, and then a urinary infection had been diagnosed. She didn't seem to be responding to treatment, and her cold had got worse. But Miss Rogers had no wish for this shrewd woman to suspect the home might be guilty of neglect. That would never do. They did their best, but they were under tremendous pressure, as was she.

'The superintendent at Ivy Bank is not convinced it would be the right answer for Trudy at the present time,' Miss Rogers fabricated. 'She's beginning to settle and they've no wish to disturb the child unduly. Maybe in a month or two, once Christmas is over, and if she continues to make good progress, we'll review the situation.'

'Dena will be disappointed. She's banking on my having her, and I promised I'd do my best.'

The social worker was on her feet, anxious to leave and avoid any more of this awkward conversation. 'You have indeed done your best, Mrs Thompson, as always. Dena must learn to be patient, as I have told her countless times. I'll bring Cissie round later this afternoon, if that's all right?' And then she was gone, her task satisfactorily completed in her view.

–

Lizzie had the idea of making gift packs with little leaflets attached describing how the chocolates were handmade – without revealing the secret recipes of the delicious centres. Each cellophane bag was tied with a bright red ribbon and proved to be very popular, selling so well they made some kiddie's gift packs too and sold dozens.

'Father Christmas is going to be busy delivering Pringle's sweets this year,' Lizzie said with a giggle.

They also took a selection of sweets to children's homes and hospitals. Free samples were meant to bring in new trade but these were simply charity, out of the goodness of their hearts.

'Maybe my father is right and we aren't sufficiently businesslike. I can't see us getting many customers from Ivy Bank Children's Home, can you?' Charlie laughed.

Lizzie smiled. 'No, but those poor kids deserve a bit of fun in their sad little lives, don't they? I just hope Trudy gets some.'

They were training Spider as a salesman and people warmed to him. They liked the cheery grin of this long, lanky lad and even enjoyed hearing his fanciful tales about his supposed expertise in the boxing ring at Barry Holmes's club. And, much to Jack Cleaver's surprise and irritation, the boy proved to be remarkably efficient at the job, gaining a number of orders right from under his nose. Finch's hold was beginning to slip at last.

–

Cedric Finch was not at all happy with the fall-off in trade. The health inspector had been useless, so far as he was concerned, and the open day a disaster, giving a positive image of Pringle's Sweets, rather than the negative one he'd hoped for.

Evelyn said it was his own fault that people were turning against him and urged him to accept Lizzie into the family. He ignored her comments, as he always did, and instead pushed Cleaver into spying for him. The man had been more than willing to dish the dirt, claiming young Spider was nothing more than a con artist, willing to tell folk anything to get an order from them.

Cleaver came to him one day to say that the children were being made to work. 'Surely an exploitation,' he'd sanctimoniously remarked.

Finch laughed, seeing only the funny side of this comment that Cleaver, of all people, should be concerned about exploiting children. But then he'd seen how it could be used to his own advantage, and when he passed this nugget of information on to the woman with the whiskery chin, Rogers, or whatever she was called, who was responsible for the children's care, whole-heartedly agreed.

'I shall keep my eye on the situation, and if what you say is true, something will be done, have no doubts about that. Leave it with me, Mr Finch.'

He was most happy to do so.

Chapter Twenty-Four

January came and with it snow and hail, rain and drizzle. It was dark when Lizzie got up in the morning to go to work, and dark when she came home in the evening, but she and Charlie were determined not to get depressed or be bullied into giving up. They desperately wanted to learn everything they could about sweet- and chocolate-making, just as Aunty was secretly determined to see them established before she became really sick, as she privately believed one day she might.

As January gave way to February, Aunty told herself it was the bitter cold that was making her feel bad. She never complained about the constant ache in her side, but whenever she looked tired they'd start nagging her about seeing a doctor, which was the last thing Dot wanted. She didn't need a doctor to tell her what she already knew. In her view, she'd got her call-up papers, and the only thing left for her now was to make sure that her little family, Lizzie in particular, would be taken care of after she was gone.

'What do doctors know?' she'd say. 'I'm fine, just getting a bit old with complaining joints.' They had no choice but to believe her.

Then one day, as she lifted a seven-pound block of crystallised sugar with the intention of boiling it up in water to make peppermint rock, the pain in her side seemed suddenly to burst into flames, and she fell to the floor writhing in agony. The sugar shattered, scattering everywhere, while Charlie ran in search of a telephone. Ten minutes later she was on her way to hospital, whether she liked it or not.

For Dena, the winter was long, cold, and frustrating. Not once was she permitted to visit her child. Every week, if she hadn't seen her around the market, Dena would ring Miss Rogers and ask for a report on progress, but there never was any. They seemed to have hit a brick wall.

'Can I at least go and see Trudy?' Dena would ask.

'Not at the moment.' Then the line would go dead.

When Aunty had first made her generous offer, Dena had genuinely believed it would be only a matter of days before Trudy was allowed out and into her care. She'd felt buoyant and reasonably optimistic for all she'd been grieving for her lost child, for Carl's child.

Dena's heart cried out for Carl. Where was he? Why didn't he come home? Didn't he miss her just a tiny bit? Belle still hadn't heard from him, Kenny's appeal was looming, and Dena found it distressing to think that Carl had lost a son without even knowing he'd existed.

But as the weeks and months dragged by and Trudy had still not been released, she'd come to see that Carl might never come back, that nothing had changed, and her spirits sank to a new low.

This morning when Miss Rogers came over to speak to her at the stall, the conversation followed the same predictable pattern.

'Have you persuaded the NSPCC to allow Aunty to foster Trudy?' Dena asked.

'You know very well that Mrs Thompson has been some-what below par recently. She had a funny turn and was taken to hospital. I understand that she is back home now but awaiting the result of tests. You must be patient, Dena, and wait until Mrs Thompson has properly recovered from whatever it is that ails her.'

'But that could take weeks, months. When am I going to be allowed to visit my child?'

'Are you a respectable married woman yet?' the social worker, tartly, responded.

'Have *you* got it in writing that Trudy will be allowed out of Ivy Bank if I *do* marry?' Dena fired back.

'I can't prejudge their assessment. You'll just have to trust me.'

'How can I trust you when you don't play fair?' Dena objected, causing one or two heads to turn as her voice rose in volume. '*I* wasn't the one who abused Trudy, yet she was taken away from *me*, her *mother* who loves her. Be honest, you've admitted before that she was taken into care simply because she's illegitimate.'

'She was not considered to be living in a safe home environment, and being a single mother doesn't help you to provide one.' The social worker's voice took on a sanctimonious tone, as it often did when she found herself at a disadvantage.

'You can't claim that she was open to abuse because I'm an unmarried mother, and then not promise I can have her back if I agree to marry and become respectable,' Dena snapped. 'That's not fair!'

Miss Rogers gave a growl of impatience. 'It has to be a good marriage for the right man, suitable as a father for Trudy. More than Kenny or Carl Garside have proved to be, for instance. You certainly don't have a good record where men are concerned, Dena Dobson.'

'Oh, is that what the problem is? Then hey, why don't *you* find me a husband? That would be so much quicker. Put an ad in the *Manchester Evening News*, interview a few chaps and find someone *you* consider to be suitable. I'll agree to marry anyone, even if he has six chins and no hair, *if only you'll let me have my daughter back!*'

'Calm down, Dena! Creating a scene won't help one little bit.'

'Why not, nothing else seems to be doing any good.' She began to snatch skirts off the rack and fling them on to the sawdust-covered floor of the market hall. 'Why don't I just chuck everything away, eh? Working my socks off earning a decent living to provide a good home for my child doesn't seem to count for anything?'

Twin spots of colour appeared on Miss Rogers's thin cheeks and she began to pick up the skirts, desperately trying to put them back on the rack before passers-by trod on them. 'Stop this – stop this at once! Really, there are times when you can be most trying.'

Dena bit back her tears and temper with difficulty and for a long moment neither woman was able to speak. At last, Dena drew in a trembling breath. 'Is she well? I must know. Did you see her bruised hands? What are they doing to her in that place? At least let me see her.'

'That wouldn't be wise when the child is settling at last.' The woman walked away, leaving Dena to put her face in her own hands and cry right there in the middle of the market hall so that folk walking by turned and stared at her in open curiosity.

But crying got her absolutely nowhere. Hadn't she learned that years ago when she was in Ivy Bank herself? All she could do was to bury her pain and pray for a miracle. Nothing was happening. Nothing had changed. She was still writing dozens of letters in her campaign and getting absolutely nowhere.

–

After the social worker had gone, the woman's words continued to ring in Dena's head. There seemed no alternative but to do as Miss Rogers dictated and take the risk. She must marry Jack Cleaver and trust that the authorities would do the right thing by her. Dena could see no alternative. Hadn't she decided it was time to put Trudy's needs first, before her own happiness? Why, then, did she hesitate?

Was it because the prospect of marrying anyone but Carl was unthinkable? But Carl was no longer around. He'd let her down.

What was it about Jack Cleaver that troubled her so? He was surely a kind and thoughtful man. He'd made it clear that he wouldn't intrude upon her privacy, a tactful way of saying that he would make no unpleasant demands upon her.

'If you were to ask me,' Jimmy Ramsay offered, 'which you haven't strictly speaking, but I'll give it anyway for what it's worth, I'd say go for it.' The jolly butcher had caught her half-heartedly nibbling a hot potato pie by Big Molly's stall and asked what was troubling her.

Unable to prevent herself, Dena had poured out the whole sorry saga. 'He's steady is Jack, a good and respectable man. He'd look after little Trudy right enough.'

'But where's the excitement in him?' Patsy Bowman put in. Patsy worked with the Higginson sisters on the hat stall and had been something of a troublemaker when she first came, but was now an accepted part of Champion Street Market. 'He's dull as ditch water. God, a woman needs a man with fire in his belly.'

'Like my Mark?' Marco Bertalone teased, coming over to join in the discussion, and Patsy playfully slapped his arm.

Marco, however, urged Dena to wait. 'Patsy has a point. Love, *eet* makes the world go round, *si*? How can you live without it? Your Carl, he will not be able to live without you. He will come back, and what would-*a*-you-*a*-do then if you have married this Jack?'

It was a good point, one that haunted Dena day and night. 'But Carl *did* let me down, and if he doesn't come back, and I don't provide a father for Trudy, then I lose her. Think about that, Marco.'

'Oh, Eengland, she ees so cruel. This would not-*a*-happen in Italy.'

'No,' Patsy chuckled. 'Dena would have been marched to the altar long since, like it or no.' Everyone laughed, easing the tension a little.

Alec Hall from Hall's Music shop, looking suitably eccentric eating a Cornish pasty in his pink bow tie and black velvet jacket, asked Dena her opinion of Barry.

'Do you really think him guilty? We're all aware that there have been rumours about him in the past, him being single and spending so much time with them lads.' Heads nodded all around. 'He's a bit of an oddball, admittedly, but is he capable of doing such a terrible thing?'

''Course he is,' Joyce the hairdresser insisted. 'I can't bear to speak to the man. And his apples are far too expensive.'

Sensible Clara Higginson pointed out that it was unfair to condemn a man simply because of the price of his apples, while Amy George said he'd never been anything but a gentleman towards her.

Big Molly argued that, unlike everyone else, she'd actually been there when the accident had taken place, and the child had cried to go to Barry even as Cleaver had carried her away. 'The poor man is innocent. I'm sure of it.'

There was a small silence while the knot of listeners digested all of this.

Alec shook his head. 'I don't see how you can be so sure. She was only a small child, confused and stunned, probably in shock and not properly understanding what was happening. How would you know what she was thinking or wanting to do?'

'Aye,' Jimmy Ramsay agreed. 'Barry Holmes is guilty as sin.'

'I would prefer to believe that he isn't,' Clara said. 'Barry doesn't strike me as the kind of man who would interfere with children.'

Nobody commented on this. What would a spinster know about such men, or children for that matter? Nor did they ask for her advice on whether Dena should marry Jack Cleaver. Spinsters didn't know anything about love either, but Clara, who knew more than they realised, gave her opinion anyway.

'As for Cleaver. Leave well alone, Dena. Find some other way to win Trudy back. Remember that marriage is for life. Never marry except for love. It will bring only heartache.'

But Dena had made her decision, and unless a miracle happened, couldn't see any other way out of her dilemma.

Barry was, in fact, having a very hard time of it indeed. Not only had trade on his vegetable stall fallen away badly, but folk he'd known all his life would walk past him in the street without so much as a glance. It was rare for any of those he'd once called friends even to speak to him. Some would cross the street to avoid him. They'd effectively sent him to Coventry.

When the stallholders held meetings to discuss market business, no one would ask his opinion on anything. No one wanted to sit next to him, or listen to what he had to say. On one occasion they'd been discussing late-night opening for Christmas, making the usual plans for the Salvation Army to sing carols while they put up a tree and fairy lights around the stall. Barry had spoken up, offering to build Father Christmas's Grotto in the market hall, as he usually did.

His words were met with a complete and comprehensive silence. Nobody responded. Everybody sat there as if struck dumb, or else suddenly found urgent business to whisper about to their neighbour.

'We might give that a miss this year,' Jimmy Ramsay had muttered, as if he had no wish to encourage children to come to the market in case Barry should contaminate them. It was utterly humiliating and mortifying.

One night a brick came hurtling through his front parlour window, shattering their peace and a pretty porcelain figure of a lady holding out her blue skirts that had stood on the small table before it. Barry dashed straight out into the street but hadn't been able to catch the culprit.

Another time someone tipped the entire contents of their dustbin on the back doorstep so that the minute he opened the kitchen door old potato peelings and smelly fish bones fell in and spread everywhere, stinking the place out.

As for his boxing club, that was failing too. Most parents kept their sons away, and more often than not Barry only had old-timers coming along for a bit of sparring or a practice workout.

He felt thoroughly disillusioned, and knew that he was turning into a lonely, sad man. Most of all he hated the cold distance that had grown between himself and Dena. She'd been like a daughter to him, in lieu of the child he'd lost in the war, but the pair of them hadn't spoken in months, not since the magistrates' hearing, and it near broke his heart.

Now, as he watched Winnie write yet another letter to a politician who would no doubt toss it away without even reading it, he grieved inside that he couldn't offer to help. He would have loved to get involved in the campaign to get little Trudy back home, but Dena would only be suspicious of his motives.

Barry got up, put on his mackintosh, and left the house to walk the empty, rain-slicked streets, and then sat in a corner of the Dog and Duck sipping a lonely milk stout.

It was a total injustice. The police may have decided that he was very likely innocent, but the folk of Champion Street had made up their own mind. And how poor little Trudy was suffering, he couldn't even bear to consider.

–

Dena had been refused permission to see Trudy because the superintendent at Ivy Bank was nervous of the trouble she might cause if it came out how very ill the child had been. Thankfully she was now on the mend, but it was a slow process.

Trudy was aware that she'd really been poorly and that it had taken a long time before anyone had believed her and called a doctor.

Carthorse had bullied her out of bed at first light, as usual, ignoring her complaints about aching limbs, headaches and dizziness. Trudy had still been expected to attend nursery class every morning to do her reading lessons and practise her alphabet and numbers. And to pick stones every afternoon on the back field, no matter what the weather, although she was eventually spared this task when they were frozen solid to the ground. She was then put on to washing down paintwork instead. A spring clean, Carthorse had called it, for all it was still winter.

But then one morning her legs had simply stopped working and she couldn't seem to get out of bed at all, no matter how much the woman might shout at her. She had pains in her belly, and even more alarming, could hardly breathe, and then she'd vomited all down Carthorse's clean overall.

Trudy had only a vague recollection of being rushed to hospital in an ambulance with a clanging bell; and of lying in a fever for days dreaming strange dreams about Mummy, and having nightmares about a monster with a lot of hands and no face, while the doctors and nurses gave her medicines and injections and something called antibiotics to make her better.

Oh, but the lovely nurses never stopped fussing over her now that she was finally starting to recover. They gave her nice food to eat, in particular ice cream, saying it was good for her sore throat. Trudy dreamed of that ice cream every night.

She also dreamed of Mummy, hoping she might come and see her in the hospital. In fact, nobody ever came to visit her save Miss Carter herself on a couple of occasions. Trudy asked the nurses when her mummy was coming, and one very nice Irish nurse went to ask Carthorse about this when once she called to check on Trudy's progress.

'It wouldn't be appropriate,' the housemother coldly informed her, and nothing more was said on the subject.

Trudy didn't understand what the word 'appropriate' meant, but in her heart she couldn't believe that Mummy would refuse to come, not if she knew that her little girl was ill.

The kind Irish nurse explained to Trudy that she'd had pneumonia, serious enough, but also a urinary infection, which might well have damaged her kidneys if they hadn't managed to get it under control and bring down her fever.

Trudy listened to all of this, slightly bemused.

But as her condition slowly began to improve and the lovely Irish nurse kept on grumbling about how dreadful it was that nobody was allowed to visit her during her convalescence, Trudy began to question just how much her mother did know about what went on at Ivy Bank. It began to dawn on the little girl that her mother might be bullied by Carthorse every bit as much as she was.

Chapter Twenty-Five

Aunty Dot was back home and claiming to be fully recovered from her 'funny turn'. 'I'd just been working too hard,' she told Lizzie and Charlie as she gently heated sugar and almonds in a heavy-bottomed pan, 'and have to take it easy for a bit.'

The idea of Aunty taking it easy made even the children stretch their eyes in disbelief. But they were all aware that she hadn't got off scot-free. The doctors had put her through a battery of tests and Aunty was now waiting for the results. Lizzie guessed that she feared the worst because she'd already tidied out her drawers and put her affairs in order, even told Lizzie where she kept her Providence insurance policy and the spare key for the backyard shed. But she showed few signs of slowing down, no matter how much they might nag her to do so.

Aunty didn't really have time to coddle herself, as she described it. Where was the good in that? It wouldn't change the outcome. She felt as if she was up against a stopwatch, and all she asked was sufficient time to at least get these two young people, whom she adored, on their feet. She'd go to her rest with an easy mind if she knew that Pringle's Sweets was to be a success.

'Now we increase the heat a little, and when the almonds start to pop and turn brown we keep shaking the pan to make sure they get nicely coated with the caramelised sugar.'

'Let me do it,' Lizzie said, seeing Aunty put a hand yet again to her aching side.

'You can pour it out on to the baking sheet. When it's cold we crush it with a rolling pin then mix it with the melted chocolate. I think we'll use the little round moulds, don't you? Almond praline, scrumptious!'

With Aunty's help Lizzie had started to experiment with new sweets and flavours. She'd made rose creams using raspberry essence, chocolate rum fudge, hazelnut brittle the children loved, and her now famous chocolate mint chips. For these she would chop up green mint toffee before folding the slivers into rich, dark chocolate and forming little crunchy haystacks. Pringle's was on its way up and steadily becoming more popular than Finch's.

'Now how about some chocolate mice?' Aunty said, reaching for a large slab of white chocolate. 'With a liquorice tail.'

'Rest indeed,' Lizzie scolded with a resigned sigh. 'You don't know the meaning of the word.'

-

It was later the following week that Dena called at number thirty-seven to speak to Aunty and see how she was feeling.

'Oh, much better,' Dot lied, offering Dena a chocolate mint with her cup of tea.

Dena shook her head. 'No, thanks. I was just wondering if you'd heard anything from Miss Rogers lately? She tells me nothing, only gives me lectures on how I should get married and make myself respectable. But I need to be convinced they'll let me have Trudy back if I do. Surely she can understand that?'

'I certainly can,' Aunty Dot agreed, reaching for another mint, no doubt bad for her spreading figure but took her mind off the nagging pain and worries over the outcome of the tests. 'But the authorities have their own way of going about things.'

'It all seems to be taking such a long time.'

'I reckon that's my fault, because I've been a bit below par. I'll speak to her again. After all, I still have the other children with me so she obviously doesn't consider me to be decrepit.

Maybe there's some other reason, something they're not telling us.'

Dena started. 'You don't think Trudy is ill, do you?'

Aunty shook her head very firmly. 'No, no, I'm sure they would have said if that had been the case. Stop fretting, chuck, everything will turn out fine. Come on, have a taste of this coffee cream at least. It'll perk you up no end.'

And because Aunty Dot believed the answer to every problem could be found in a well-made chocolate, Dena relented and accepted the treat. It was but a momentary distraction from her burden of worry but it did indeed give her a brief moment of pleasure.

–

Joey and the younger children loved to help with the wrapping of the sweets but then one day Miss Rogers arrived at their door and put a stop to it.

'She's a right spoil-sport,' Joey complained. 'We aren't allowed any fun.'

Alan blinked behind his National Health spectacles. 'Aw, I was saving up fer a Dinky bus wi' the money I earned, and a *Girl's Crystal Annual* fer our Beth.'

His sister began to cry with disappointment. Even Cissie looked glum.

Aunty frowningly turned on Miss Rogers. 'Are you saying that children can't help in a family business, as the Bertalones do in their ice cream parlour, for instance? That don't seem right.'

'They can help. The law has no control over the working hours of children in their own family's business, assuming they are a proper family, as you aren't.'

Aunty Dot was affronted. 'Aye, we are! So far as we're concerned we are a proper family, aren't we chucks?' she demanded of her volunteer crew, and every head nodded vigorously.

'You could be accused of exploiting them, Dorothy Thompson, then they'd be taken away from you. Is that what you want?'

'Eeh, no, 'course I don't. Who says I'm exploiting them? No, don't tell me, I can guess! They wrap a few sweets on a Saturday morning for a bit of pocket money, that's all, or after school sometimes if they've no homework and nothing better to do. And nobody is holding a gun to their heads.'

Miss Rogers remained unconvinced. She folded her arms over her flat chest and frowned sternly at Aunty. 'If I had my way the Bertalones wouldn't be allowed to exploit their children either, no matter how they might claim to be willing volunteers. Think yourself lucky I haven't brought a prosecution already without even warning you.'

A compromise was reached that Joey, as the eldest, could help on a Saturday morning, but not after school, and the younger children weren't allowed to help at all. This obviously didn't go down too well with Alan, Beth and Cissie but it couldn't be helped. Miss Rogers was adamant, and Lizzie conceded that the woman might have a point. What they saw as fun, others might very well interpret as exploitation, but it also meant that Lizzie and Charlie missed the children's busy little fingers and had to pay a girl to wrap the sweets instead.

'If only everyone else looked after their children as well as Aunty does, there wouldn't be such nasty suspicious minds like Miss flipping Rogers's,' Lizzie complained.

But Charlie only kissed her and promised the children they'd still get their weekly ration of sweets and pocket money, so long as they remembered to clean their teeth three times a day.

Cedric Finch watched events unfold with gleeful satisfaction, delighted that the social worker had called round at number thirty-seven to put a spoke in their wheel and curb their activities. But it wasn't enough, nowhere near enough. Having failed to close down Lizzie Pringle's stall, *or* to bankrupt her, *or* keep her away from his son, he realised he must use stronger tactics.

As always he turned to his old standby, Billy Quinn. The Irishman had laughed when Finch had first asked him for help in keeping customers in line.

'You expect me to waste my time in this Battle of the Sweeties, this War of the Lollipops? And will you tell me what I'm to do if they won't play ball? Do I snap their coltsfoot rock, or jump on their Pontefract cakes? To be sure, I can't see what the hell it matters if your sweet firm gets a bit more competition. Don't ye make more money with your other, more tasty, enterprises?'

Finch puffed out his bulbous cheeks as his eyes followed three giggling girls, none of them much older than fourteen or fifteen, clattering up the rickety back staircase of Billy Quinn's illegal gambling den. He licked his lips, shaking his jowls as if he were a bloodhound about to follow a trail, which in a way he was.

'And where would those 'tasty enterprises' be without the cover of my sweet factory? I need to stay in profit if we're to maintain our mutually lucrative business interests without raising too many eyebrows about how I can afford to live so well? It means that Lizzie Pringle must be put in her place.'

Evelyn continued to nag him to call an end to what she termed 'this stupid vendetta'. But then she knew nothing of the reason behind it, nothing about his connections with Maureen Moss, the girl's prossy mother. Nor, for that matter, did she know anything about these pretty young girls who'd come supposedly to have their pictures taken. This battle had been going on for months and he was getting nowhere. Lizzie Pringle was turning into a much bigger problem than he'd first anticipated.

'I'll not have that girl prying into my affairs,' he told Quinn as he watched the Irishman set up his camera equipment, position a couple of spotlights and exchange a few reassuring words with the girls who were giggling again.

Finch had no wish for his private life, his own dark secrets, to be exposed. Consorting with a known prostitute was, in fact, the least of them.

Satisfied that he had his skinny models suitably arranged on the cushions, in an innocent pose to begin with, Quinn peered down the lens of his camera. Finch calmly whispered in his ear, 'I wouldn't mind that one,' indicating a dark, doe-eyed beauty who smiled shyly at him, although she didn't seem to know what to do with her long, schoolgirl legs. 'Not now, Finch, maybe later,' Quinn snapped. 'I don't want her spoiled before I get some good shots.'

'Well, get on with it then. I haven't got all day.' He grunted his displeasure, and winked at the girl, delighted to see her startled blush.

No, indeed, he had no wish at all for too much light to be shed on these murky corners of his life, and if the allegedly innocent Lizzie ever discussed him with that prossy mother of hers, who knows what she might uncover? That would never do.

Which was, he decided, the whole crux of the matter. Was Lizzie Pringle as innocent as she appeared and claimed to be? If so, then would she stick her nose into his affairs? She could very well discover far more than she'd bargained for, and Cedric had no doubt she would not hesitate to expose him.

'We have to stop her,' he said, speaking his thoughts out loud as the camera shutter clicked and purred. Quinn moved back and forth, encouraging the girls to smile and show themselves to their best advantage, now to undo a button, now lift the hem of a skirt, push out their skinny chests or wriggle their hips. He was no expert with a camera but knew what he wanted. This was but a softening up process for the more revealing shots later, necessary in order properly to relax them.

Quinn touched a finger to one girl's chin, gently moving her into a better position. 'Just half turn and glance sideways at me, then let me see that lovely smile. Will I pull your blouse down a touch more to show off that gorgeous shoulder? There we are, now isn't that beautiful?'

The girls fell to giggling again and Cedric too had to smile. They were like putty in the Irishman's hands.

'Sure and you have the most perfect face, darlin'. Won't it break a thousand hearts? Now put yer chin in yer hands. Lean forward a little more.' He was pushing open the blouse with gentle fingers to reveal surprisingly mature breasts before returning to Finch and coldly remarking, 'Won't marriage with yer own son shut her up?'

'Never!' Finch almost spat out the word under his breath. 'My son is as straight as a die and honest as the day is long, blast his eyes! How I came to breed such a boy I cannot imagine, but we all make mistakes.'

'Indeed, or maybe his mother did and played away.' Quinn smirked, furiously clicking the shutter button in a rapid barrage of shots.

Finch didn't trouble to argue the point. He couldn't be entirely confident that Evelyn had been faithful, nor did it greatly matter since he'd undoubtedly brought her into line since. And he really didn't give a toss about Charlie. The happiness of his own son was of small account by comparison with the jeopardy he himself now faced.

'Now can you do the same as yer wee friend, darlin'? Will we just open the buttons on your shirt, loosen the school tie a fraction more so's we can see what a fine budding woman ye are.' This girl was stick-thin, with the flat chest of a child and the knowing eyes of a woman. A winning combination for the kind of shots Quinn had in mind.

He moved on to ask the dark-eyed girl to lie on her back and lift her legs in the air, whereupon her school skirt slipped down over her thighs revealing a glimpse of a sensuously rounded bottom in green, school, gym knickers. Click, click went the camera lens and she flung back her hair and pouted delightfully for him, believing she was going to be a famous model after this.

'Why don't you just slip out of that blouse? And you don't want to be seen in them dreadful school whatsits, do ye? Would ye put on these black lace panties and suspenders for me? Ye will? What a little treasure ye are.'

Cedric Finch licked his lips.

Half an hour later all three girls were in various stages of undress and Quinn had his shots. Cedric had savoured every moment, scratching his crotch furtively and aching for more, but his mind was still on Lizzie.

'The only way to make absolutely certain that woman doesn't do something stupid, like prying into my affairs and blabbing her mouth off, is to find some way to guarantee it wouldn't pay her to do so. Lizzie Pringle's innocence is a luxury we can't afford.'

Quinn grinned as he slid the last reel of film into the camera. 'I'm thinking ye might be right. We'll have to make sure she loses it. We need her to be tarred with the same brush as ourselves mebbe. Now lean back on yer elbows, darlin'? That's it, open yer knees a wee bit more.'

Moments later, indicating the dark-eyed beauty Finch had favoured, Quinn said, 'You can go and get dressed now, darlin', while I just take a couple more snaps of your friend. And tomorrow, won't these films be on their way to Hollywood and you three little charmers about to become famous? You'll like that, I fancy.'

More squeals and giggles.

Quinn watched the girl scurry into the adjoining room then turned to Finch and winked. 'Go on, she's all yours.'

–

The stay in hospital boosted not only Trudy's physical strength but also her confidence. The nurses all thought she was a good girl, so she must be, mustn't she? They worried about how thin she was, how pale, building up her strength with beef tea, rice pudding, and a constant supply of secret treats smuggled to the ward.

For the first time since she'd been snatched from her own home, the little girl began to feel cared for and secure. Trudy came to love them all, but her favourite was the young Irish nurse who had tackled Carthorse for her about the lack of visitors. It was to her that Trudy made her confession.

One day she simply spilled out everything that had happened to her at Ivy Bank. She told how the older girls made her wash their smelly socks, steal cakes and bread for them, how they spat in her food or stole it from her, and how they pinched and punched her if she didn't obey. The nurse was outraged, did her utmost to persuade Trudy to make a proper complaint to the superintendent, but the little girl began to cry, shaking her head fiercely in alarm.

'I can't tell. They'd only do it worse.'

'All right then, this is what you do.' The young nurse sat on the edge of her bed and began to give Trudy a few tips on how to deal with the problem, how to stand up for herself and fight back. Trudy listened very carefully, gratefully accepting all the help and advice she was offered.

Once she was out of danger, Trudy was taken back to Ivy Bank to convalesce. This meant that she was put in the sanatorium to be looked after by Matron, and spared from doing chores since she was still weak following her illness.

Although she was allowed to look at books or play with dominoes instead of working, she was bored and lonely, and missed the attention of the kind nurses badly. They'd given her lots of presents when she'd left, including a chocolate cake her Irish friend had made especially for her. Trudy kept them hidden in her suitcase with her clothes, hoping Matron wouldn't notice and take the gifts away from her. She was cold and unfriendly, but didn't seem as mean as Carthorse.

Trudy ached for her mother and deep down felt a growing fear that she might never see her again, but she did her best to follow the kind Irish nurse's advice. She dutifully ate every scrap of the plain fare she was offered. By doing so Trudy hoped she would soon be fit and well again, and Miss Carter might then allow Mummy to come on a visit.

About a week after her return, she was allowed out of the sanatorium and back into the dormitory. The moment the lights went out the dreadful Chrissie swanned over to Trudy's bed and demanded that she hand over any presents.

'I know you have some because I saw you hide the box in your locker. You can't keep them all for yourself.'

'It's my cake, what the nurses made me.' Trudy's protest was feeble, knowing it would be ignored.

Chrissie laughed. 'Hand it over or you'll be sorry. I'm the eldest here, and in charge of this dorm, so I deserve it more than you.'

Trudy dutifully handed over the box containing the cake and watched in silence as Chrissie's eyes lit up. 'Ooh, chocolate!' then sat on her bed and gobbled up every scrap herself, without giving a slice to anyone.

Long before morning Chrissie had her head in the chamber pot being violently sick.

Trudy's Irish friend and fellow conspirator had carefully instructed her on no account to eat so much as a crumb of the cake herself, but to make it plain that she possessed one, and hand it over when Chrissie asked for it. Trudy knew that the nurse had put something in it to cause Chrissie's upset tummy.

'Nothing too serious, but it might make her think twice before she bullies you again,' the nurse had told her with a wink.

And the trick worked beautifully. Chrissie was green around the gills all the next day, unable to keep a thing down, and kept rushing out of lessons to sit on the lavatory for hour upon hour.

'*You* did this, you little weasel, didn't you?'

Trudy looked at her, her small face a picture of innocence. 'Did what?'

'Doctored that flaming cake.'

'Was it ill?' Trudy asked, but then smiled mischievously. 'I learned a few other tricks too in that hospital. Would you like me to show you those too?'

Chrissie never spoke to her again. From that day on she largely ignored Trudy's very existence, exactly what Trudy wanted. She was four next birthday, a big girl, and had learned, at last, to stand up for herself.

Chapter Twenty-Six

The sprawl of Champion Street Market was spreading. There were more and more stalls and barrow traders clustered together in the surrounding streets, adding to the vibrancy and general commotion of the area, and its popularity continued to grow. One side of the market hall now had an extension, with the new meat and fish market hygienically enclosed beneath a glass roof; one improvement at least that Belle Garside had managed to achieve.

Manchester folk loved nothing better than a trip to the market, and had a good selection to choose from. There were small, specialist markets where you could buy books and records, coins, foreign stamps and militaria, or good-quality meat or fish. If you got up early enough you could visit Smithfield fruit and vegetable market at Shudehill. Dena's favourite when she was a girl had been the Flat Iron Market where she would buy second-hand clothes.

She not only made her own clothes, but produced a regular supply to sell to customers on her own stall, yet as she made her way to it on this cold, spring morning, Dena lacked her usual enthusiasm and energy. She was feeling sorry for herself, with no end in sight to her misery.

Life seemed so unfair. The world was changing fast. People now decorated every wall in their house a different colour, owned washing machines and spin dryers. They shopped in self-service stores, which they called supermarkets where you didn't have to queue. Two-thirds of the population owned a television set, and motorways were being built so that people could get from place to place quicker in their new cars. There was even talk of something called a hovercraft that would bounce on a cushion of air over water.

All these amazing developments in their new modern world, and yet Dena still wasn't allowed to care for her own daughter because as an unmarried mother she was considered unfit.

She paused long enough to buy herself some smoked mackerel for her tea and a cold pork pie from Molly Poulson for her dinner. She seemed to live on the things, simple food involved no cooking, but where was the point in bothering when there was only herself?

'How's that lass of yours?' Big Molly asked, as she did every day. 'It's wicked what they've done to her.'

Dena mumbled some sort of reply and hurried away. She wasn't in the mood for talking either, but then she rarely was these days. The smell of the fish stalls brought back memories of her time in the tiny bedsit opposite, where she'd lived when she'd first had Trudy. She'd been just sixteen. There'd only been room for a single bed, Trudy's cot, and the table where she'd put her Singer sewing machine. And in this tiny space she'd started out on the long haul to building a business, which would earn a good living for them both. Now it seemed as if all her efforts had been in vain.

Where was the point of a new modern Britain, of building up her own business admittedly she loved, or renting a house she'd turned into a cosy home for them both, when she wasn't considered capable of bringing up her own child? She was the one being treated like a criminal, not the pervert who had hurt her precious child. And Trudy was the one suffering most of all.

Walking back to her stall, Dena spotted Jack Cleaver who made a beeline for her the minute he saw her. She inwardly groaned, knowing this shouldn't be her reaction whenever she met the man she was ultimately going to marry, the man who would make her 'respectable' and save the day, as it were.

'Any news?' he asked, as always. He was growing impatient, she could tell.

Dena shook her head, finding it hard even to look at him. 'Not yet, I'm afraid.'

He smiled pityingly at her and patted her cheek in a fatherly fashion, telling her not to worry, that everything would be fine, as if he could control when Miss Rogers would release Trudy from her prison.

A small shiver rippled down Dena's spine at the clammy touch of his plump fingers. What was happening to her? Why wasn't she responding to him in a more friendly fashion? They'd been out together a few times, usually to tea at the Midland Hotel, or to the pictures, and he was pleasant enough company. Jack Cleaver was a kind and caring man, and she really couldn't afford to go off the idea of marriage. Wasn't he her best chance of getting Trudy back?

And he was at least doing his best to spruce himself up.

This morning he wore a green tweed jacket that strained to fasten with one link button over the bulge of his stomach. He'd teamed it with beige flannels and a pink shirt worn with a slim Jim, black, silk tie. It didn't suit him. Had he been eighteen instead of thirty-five he might have looked better. But his brown eyes were still too close together, the nostrils too wide and his cheeks too fat. And there was something else about him, something she couldn't put a name to, but it made her feel uneasy.

'And how are you, in yourself?'

What a stupid question, Dena thought, as she told him that she was just fine, thank you very much. He was regarding her with that compassionate, concerned expression she found deeply disturbing and patronising. She had no wish to be pitied, or to be saved from the results of her own folly. If only Aunty would get better; she could then find a way to resolve the problem for herself and get Trudy back without his help. She would be delighted to do so. In the meantime, like it or not, Jack Cleaver was her best hope!

One afternoon, Matron took Trudy to see the superintendent who asked the little girl if she was feeling better.

'Yes, thank you very much,' Trudy politely answered, after some prompting from Matron.

'There's always a purpose to these tribulations we have to bear, and we must never make light of whatever the Lord sets in our path to test us. I am glad you are making a good recovery, Trudy. Do let us know if there's anything you need. We must take good care of you and make sure you grow strong and well, as we do with all the precious children in our care. Isn't that right, Matron?'

'Indeed,' Matron replied in a pleasant voice, unlike her usual frosty tones.

'Quite so,' the superintendent agreed, smiling at Trudy from behind her big desk, hands lightly clasped on the Bible set before her. 'We want you to be happy here, so you must tell us if you're not. Will you do that for me?'

Trudy nodded, even more bemused. Nobody had ever asked her if she was happy before, and she wondered if this was a good thing or a bad.

-

Alan loved Aunty with a passion. He would rush home from school and fling himself into her arms for a big soppy kiss. Then he'd tear outside again to kick a tin can about, or throw a rope over the arm of the lamp post and swing from it, secure in the knowledge that she was there, that he had a loving home and she was the one who provided it.

Number thirty-seven drew other kids to it like a magnet, not simply because of the tantalising smell of sweet-making that went on there, or at least in the old days before it was moved to the old cotton mill, but also because of Aunty Dot. Everybody loved Aunty. When it was hot she would give them Dandelion and Burdock, and on cold days hot Vimto. She would mend the broken chains on their bikes, tend their cut knees, listen to their troubles and not make a fuss if they brought mud in on her carpet.

She'd put up the wooden clothes horse in the backyard and throw a blanket over it to make a den for them to play in. Or on wet Saturday afternoons when they were bored and didn't know what to do with themselves, she'd mix flour and paste, rip up newspapers and show them how to make a bird or a cat mask out of papier mâché.

Now, it seemed, all of that had changed. She didn't even look the same. She'd stopped putting that lovely colour in her hair and it had gone all grey and untidy.

Alan didn't understand how, exactly, or why, but Aunty had stopped being fun. She no longer sang as she worked. She didn't smile so much or crack silly jokes, and she no longer had the time or the patience to let them help her make jam tarts or play at bouncing horses on Alan's bed. To his great disappointment she'd started to object to the noise and the mess, like ordinary mothers did, and she was forever scrubbing and cleaning, turning out cupboards and giving things away.

'Why don't you have this swagger coat?' Aunty said to Winnie one day. 'I'll never wear it again, and blue suits you.'

'Why would you never wear it again? It's like new. Don't be daft, put it back in yer wardrobe. It'll come in handy some time, I'm sure, when yer feeling more yerself.'

Aunty gave her what could only be described as an old-fashioned look.

Another day she cleared out all her old knitting patterns. 'No point in keeping these, I won't be needing them much longer. You don't want them, do you, Lizzie love? And look at this great bundle of knitting needles cluttering up this drawer.'

'Don't throw them away,' Lizzie said, desperately trying to think of a good reason. 'Charlie needs a new sweater, don't you, Charlie? His old one is such a mess.'

'Aye, that's right, I do,' he agreed, catching the fierce glare in Lizzie's eyes ordering him to say exactly that.

'I'll buy some wool,' Lizzie brightly told Dot, putting the knitting needles and patterns back in the sideboard drawer. Knitting a sweater for Charlie would at least keep Aunty sitting down with her feet up.

'Oh, why don't those test results come through? All the doctors seem to do is call her in for more,' Lizzie groaned as she walked home from the market with Charlie the next day. 'Why don't they tell us what's wrong?'

Charlie put an arm about her shoulders so that he could pull her close and kiss her flushed cheek. 'They're doing their best, taking her through the process step by step. I'm sure they'll tell us what's wrong when they know themselves.'

'But why does it take so long? It must be five weeks or more since she collapsed, or had that "funny turn", as she calls it.'

'Come on, love, stop worrying. Let's go out for some fish and chips and the flicks tonight. They're showing *Some Like it Hot* at the Odeon. It's Jack Lemmon and Tony Curtis and supposed to be a real hoot. It'll cheer you up. Ask Aunty if she wants to come with us.'

Aunty didn't. 'Nay, you youngsters go off and enjoy yourselves, don't worry about me. Anyway, who would we get to look after the kids?'

'I would. I'd be glad to,' offered Jack Cleaver, who happened to be sitting at the kitchen table drinking tea when they'd come in. He often called in to see how the old lady was, which Lizzie thought was really sweet of him. There were times, when he was being helpful and kind, when she understood exactly why Dena had agreed to marry him.

'We don't want to be a nuisance,' Lizzie said.

'Don't be daft. Anyway, I'm going to be family soon, in a way, when young Trudy comes to stay, so I'd best get some practice in.'

'Well, then,' Lizzie said, smiling at Aunty Dot. 'I think you should come. It'll give you a good laugh and cheer you up no end. It's supposed to be dead funny. We can go to the early show so we won't be late home, and Charlie's offered to treat us all to fish and chips afterwards.'

And so it was agreed. The threesome set off to catch the bus and Jack sat down by the fire to watch the children play.

Joey sat opposite and watched him.

–

Jack Cleaver was growing impatient. He was already smarting from having been rejected by Lizzie, and now he was getting nowhere with Dena either. It was really too much for a proud man to bear. What right did women have to think they could keep a chap dangling on a string like some sort of soft fool?

He often called in at Dena's workshop to ask when she was going to name the day, always intending to be firm, but never managing it.

'I have to be sure they'll let Trudy out before I do,' Dena would wearily explain.

'You aren't going off the idea of marrying me, are you, now that you've lost the baby?'

Jack had been deeply disappointed over Dena's miscarriage, and had visited her every day in hospital, taking her flowers and grapes and chocolates, even when she'd told him not to bother, that she didn't feel like eating.

Dena had briefly summarised her recent conversation with the social worker and again assured Jack that although she'd lost the baby she would still marry him. 'Miss Rogers seems to think it would be the answer, assuming things work out okay and that you and Trudy get on.'

Jack wasn't really concerned what the social worker thought. Nevertheless the comment had troubled him even as he'd tried to laugh it off. 'What do you mean, get on? Why wouldn't we get on?'

'No reason. Trudy is a lovable child. I'm sure it will be fine. She'll be out of that place any day now.'

'You've been saying that for weeks, months maybe, so where is she? When will they let her out?'

Dena had looked glum. 'I don't know, do I? But obviously as soon as Aunty is fit enough to have her, they'll let her come. Then all we have to do is prove what a nice family we'll make. You and Trudy just need a little time to get to know each other a bit better before we tie the knot, as it were.'

Jack had felt very slightly disconcerted by this remark, not much caring for the sound of it one bit. Children were so unpredictable. Still, it was almost twelve months since the accident. The child had probably forgotten what he looked like, he consoled himself, and would be desperate to get home. In any case, he could surely control a three-year-old.

Now, sitting by Aunty's fire, his gaze riveted upon Beth's small bottom wiggling back and forth as she rubbed chalk off the blackboard she was using to teach Alan his sums, he felt the familiar stir of excitement in that secret part of himself. Everything was going to be fine. Trudy would be home soon. No one had connected him with her little 'accident'. He was going to marry Dena Dobson and would soon have complete control not only of her delicious daughter, but also that little business he intended to make his own. He just needed to be patient.

Jack glanced at his watch and saw that it was half past seven. Cissie and the baby were already tucked up fast asleep, which just left these two. 'Shall I put these tearaways to bed?'

'No,' Joey said. 'I'll do it.' And taking both children by the hand, he led them away upstairs.

That boy could prove to be a problem, Jack thought. As if I don't have enough already.

–

Aunty spent a lot of time sitting knitting Charlie a sweater, often listening to Wilfred Pickles on the wireless. He was one of her favourite people. Alan would dash in at great speed, Beth tootling along at her own pace behind him. Their usual after-school treat of a jam sandwich or buttered scone and a glass of milk would be waiting on the kitchen table. The fire would be burning behind the big, wide fireguard and the baby gurgling on the rug, but Aunty wouldn't reach out her arms and scoop Alan up like she used to. She'd smile vaguely and tell him to help himself and not make too much noise about it. Then she'd send them all outside to play, saying she needed a lie down.

'Are you going to get better soon?' Alan asked one afternoon, a bit fed up with the way things were.

Aunty took off his grubby spectacles and rubbed them clean on her pinny. 'You're a big boy now, Alan love, so I'm going to answer your question truthfully. I'm hopeful that it will all be sorted soon, but if it isn't, and Jesus needs me to go to heaven, then you're going to have to be a brave boy. Can you do that for me?'

Alan blinked, his small face looking oddly naked and vulnerable without his National Health spectacles. It wasn't the answer he'd hoped for but he let Aunty curl the wire arms of his glasses back around his ears then went off into the kitchen, dragging his feet. He obediently ate the scone and drank his milk, his manners carefully supervised by his sister, but somehow it didn't taste as good as it should.

And then one afternoon when he came home he found Aunty sitting in her chair doing absolutely nothing at all. There was no fire lit, the wireless wasn't switched on, her knitting lay idle in her lap and Aunty Dot herself was sitting staring at a long brown envelope in her hand. Even more alarming, there was no after-school treat waiting on the kitchen table.

'Aunty?' Alan said, seriously alarmed by this further change in his routine as well as by her strange immobility.

Beth gripped his arm. 'She's got the letter. It's from the hospital. Quick, go and fetch our Lizzie. Run!'

Alan ran. He ran as if the hounds of hell were at his heels, as if he were Superman, Roy of the Rovers, or Dan Dare in his space ship. He found Lizzie chatting to Lynda Hemley who'd been looking after the Chocolate Cabin for the afternoon. He managed to gasp out their anxiety over Aunty between snatching in great gulps of air. Then Lizzie was running too, back home to number thirty-seven as fast as her legs could take her. Alan was most impressed. He hadn't realised girls could run so fast, let alone women as old as Lizzie.

Lizzie flung herself on her knees beside Aunty's chair and gently squeezed her hand. 'Has it come at last?'

Aunty Dot raised bleak eyes to meet hers. 'Aye.'

'Would you like me to open it?'

Aunty handed the envelope to her without a word. Beth silently put an arm about Alan, hugging Cissie close to her other side. The baby on the rug put his thumb in his mouth as they all waited for Lizzie to read the letter from the doctor. The silence in the room was palpable with not even the sound of a clock ticking since Aunty had pawned it.

And then Lizzie put down the paper and gave a little breathy sigh. 'It's all right. It's not what we thought. You haven't got cancer. They've decided that you've got a hernia and they can operate next week. You're going to be fine, Aunty. You're going to be just fine!'

Tears were rolling down Lizzie's cheeks by this time and the children were looking at each other bemused, not understanding the big frightening words but sensing that this might be good news.

Aunty put a hand to her mouth and then in a choked voice, said, 'Eeh, I don't believe it. You mean, they can put me right?'

Lizzie was hugging her, stroking Aunty Dot's plump cheek and crying into her shoulder. 'Yes, Aunty, yes. They can put you right.'

'Does that mean Jesus doesn't need you in heaven, after all?' Alan asked.

'Not yet, chuck. Not for a long while,' Aunty agreed. 'Jesus will just have to wait a bit longer.'

'I'm reet glad,' the small boy said. 'Cos we need you more'n He does.' And overcome with emotion, Alan flung himself at Aunty in floods of tears, which proved to be the signal for them all to start. Beth and Cissie scrambled up on to her knee as well, and the baby looked on astounded as the whole bunch of them sobbed with happiness.

Chapter Twenty-Seven

Miss Rogers came to see Dena on a cold blustery day in early March with some surprising news. She calmly informed her that there were changes in the air, that childcare policies were being modernised, and even Ivy Bank would not be immune. It was, in fact, being forced to reconsider its philosophy.

'Where once the moral and spiritual well-being of a child was considered all-important, far more than its family life or physical needs, now the reverse is true.'

'And what difference will that make?' Dena wanted to know.

'Let's go and have a coffee and I'll try to explain it all to you as best I can. I'm not promising anything, Dena, but there could well be hope for you in all of this change, in your efforts to win back Trudy.'

Over a cup of frothy coffee in Belle's café, Miss Rogers explained how, since the 1948 Children Act, the welfare of children had fallen under the remit of the local authority. 'And in 1952 they also gained powers to investigate neglect and abuse. However, it was usually left to the churches and voluntary organisations to provide the services such as accommodation and welfare – the Sisters of Mercy, or the Wesleyan Methodists at Ivy Bank, and similar religious bodies.'

Dena had her own opinion on this but chose not to inter-rupt, waiting for the social worker to come to her point.

'However, research has shown that children deprived of a normal home life can become seriously disturbed.'

Now she almost laughed out loud. 'Have they only just realised that?'

Miss Rogers frowned. 'I'm trying to explain, Dena.'

'Sorry. Go on, I'm listening.'

'As I said, things are changing. For instance, Dr Barnardo's now make it a part of their responsibility to assist parents with insufficient income to provide properly for their children. They do their best to help them find employment or find living accommodation for the family, instead of simply taking a child away.'

'Well, this all sounds wonderful, that at last the authorities are showing some common sense, but I don't need employment or accommodation so in what way have attitudes changed towards unmarried mothers?'

Miss Rogers who, to be fair, had been the only one to support Dena when she'd found herself pregnant with Trudy, had the grace to look uncomfortable. She stirred her coffee, sipped it, and took her time answering.

'Attitudes won't change overnight, Dena. There is still prejudice, I will admit. But research has shown that herding children together in big institutions isn't such a good idea. That is, in fact, rather backward looking and—'

'Victorian?' Dena tartly put in.

Miss Rogers flushed. 'I don't make the rules, Dena, I only carry them out.'

'Sorry, go on. I do appreciate your efforts on my behalf, really I do.'

'The aim in the future will be to house children in smaller units, or to put them with foster parents.'

Hope blazed in Dena's chestnut eyes. 'Are you saying that they've changed their mind, that Trudy can come to Aunty after all? Then why didn't you just come right out and say so? I'd almost given up hope.'

'I realise the procedure has been painfully slow but we all have demanding workloads.' The social worker still deemed it wise not to mention the child's recent illness. If Dena started making a fuss again, the authorities could well turn awkward.

'I'm saying there's new hope, although I still have to convince my boss that you can ultimately offer a stable home. And the prospect of Kenny Garside's appeal looming doesn't help either, so anything you can do to prove you're making a real effort to achieve stability and respectability in your life would be of great benefit.'

This sobered Dena instantly. 'Yes, I see. So I should still seriously consider this marriage offer?'

Miss Rogers quietly sipped her coffee. 'It would undoubtedly help, assuming you've chosen the right man. But this is *good* news, Dena. Your case has been reconsidered, and with due regard to these changes in the air we're at last making real progress. I'm off to see Mrs Thompson this very morning to make the necessary arrangements. I believe she's just had an operation for a hernia but that there's nothing more seriously wrong. So I see no reason why Trudy shouldn't be brought to number thirty-seven, just as soon as Mrs Thompson is sufficiently recovered to cope. At least you will see more of the child then. The rest is up to you.'

'Oh, thank you, Miss Rogers, thank you, thank you, thank you!' And in a burst of exuberance, Dena kissed her.

As always at any sign of emotion, the older woman flushed crimson and brushed Dena away with a stern reprimand. 'This is but the start, remember. What happens after this is entirely up to you. If Trudy gets along well with your intended husband, then I see no reason why you shouldn't have her back home with you in no time.' She gathered up her large bag, preparatory to leaving, but then as if by way of an afterthought asked, 'I assume you are still not in contact with Barry Holmes?'

'No, I'm not. Nor will I be.'

'Even though he was deemed to be innocent?'

'It hasn't been proved either way. Not enough evidence. Don't worry, I won't be taking any chances with Trudy.'

'I'm sure you won't. I'll be in touch.'

Dena sat for some long moments after the social worker had gone, waiting for her heartbeat to return to normal and the reality of what she'd said to sink in. Trudy was coming home. At last! She dare think no further than that.

—

Aunty was sitting with her feet up, feeling sore and uncomfortable but otherwise positively perky when she heard the social worker's familiar rat-a-tat-tat on the door knocker. She was instantly filled with anxiety, fearful she might be coming to take the children away, convinced she couldn't cope until she'd fully recovered from the operation.

Miss Rogers did have some good news to impart about Trudy, finally being allowed to come at last. The social worker also informed Dot that Cissie's grandmother had won custody of the child so she'd come to collect her.

Dot pressed her lips together and said nothing, just got up and silently started to pack Cissie's bits and pieces, not taking more than a few minutes. She saw them come and go. It was part of the job, much as she might hate it. 'You'll fetch her right back if there's any sign of trouble, like before?'

'I will indeed, Mrs Thompson, but I have high hopes that it will work out this time. It's much the best for Cissie, don't you think, to be with her own grandmother?'

Dot grunted, then hoisted the four-year-old up in her arms and gave her a smacking kiss. 'Be a good girl for yer grandma, and don't forget yer old aunty, will you?' Cissie shook her head and clung to Aunty, seeming to understand exactly what was going on. 'Right then, off you go, chuck. Here, take a whirligig lolly with you.'

Aunty Dot stood at the window wiping her eyes long after Miss Rogers's car had driven away. She'd miss little Cissie, such a sweet child. But Trudy would be coming soon. Things were looking up for Dena at least.

—

Dena couldn't believe her good fortune. She sat on the doorstep of Aunty's house watching Beth skipping with her skirt tucked up her knicker legs, and thought how Trudy might be here doing the very same thing in a week or two. One end of the rope had been tied to the lamp post, and Alan was turning it while Beth skipped.

'Faster,' she was yelling. 'Salt, vinegar, mustard, pepper...' Alan whizzed the rope round as fast as he could, the energy he was using making his glasses slip down his nose, until finally the rope tangled around Beth's ankles and she came to a laughing, gasping halt. Just normal kids having fun. Why couldn't life always be this way?

Dena was laughing along with them, so when a voice said, 'You look a lot happier than the last time I saw you.' She kept the smile on her face as she shaded her eyes against the spring sunshine and looked up.

'Doctor Salkeld!'

'I thought we'd agreed on Adam.'

To her complete surprise he came and sat on the step beside her, as if it was the most natural place in the world for a doctor to be sitting. She moved a little to make room for him and smiled into his eyes, paler than she remembered. A lovely hazel green!

'I suppose I am,' she agreed. 'Trudy, my daughter, is coming home, would you believe? At least, she's coming to this house, to be fostered by Dot Thompson, like Beth and Alan here. She'll be out of that horrible place at last and I'll be able to see her every day.'

'So you aren't able to have her home with you yet then?'

Dena screwed up her nose and shook her head. 'I'm still on probation, apparently.'

'But *you* didn't do it, that terrible thing that happened to her. You weren't the guilty party so why all the procedural checks on you?'

Dena dropped her gaze and stared at the toes of her shoes, which looked a bit scuffed and in need of a good polish. She didn't want his professional sympathy, and his nearness on the step was having a strange effect upon her. 'They need to be sure that as an unmarried mother I can provide a secure and stable home.'

There was a small silence as they both watched the children play. Beth was turning the rope now but Alan was nowhere near as proficient at skipping as his older sister. Beth was telling him off, busily ordering him to pick up his feet, to jump with both together and not one at a time.

Adam Salkeld chuckled. 'I used to love playing in the street, didn't you? Although I was as hopeless at skipping as young Alan here, and my sister every bit as bossy as his. But then girls are good at so many things. I should think, Dena, that you are an excellent mother.'

'I thought I was too.'

Again a silence fell. It wasn't awkward just comfortable in fact, and Dena warmed to the compliment. Adam was again wearing sports jacket and flannels, and she could feel the rough texture of the tweed rubbing against her bare arm. And she couldn't help but notice the power of his thighs under the light fabric of his slacks. It was intoxicating.

He stood up abruptly, and she thought he was about to say goodbye and go on his way. Instead, he said, 'I don't suppose you've time for that drink?'

Something stirred deep inside her as she looked up at the halo of red-brown hair glinting in the sun. 'Why not?'

—

About a month after her operation, Trudy was brought to Aunty Dot's house and Dena was almost overwhelmed by emotion. The reunion of mother and daughter was ecstatic, the little girl looking bewildered by the suddenness of events but the pair of them were soon hugging and kissing and weeping with joy.

'She'll need time to settle,' Miss Rogers warned. 'Don't rush her into anything, Dena. Call and see her every day and just try to be normal, but leave her care to Mrs Thompson. She is the one responsible for Trudy. There might be tantrums, sulks, who knows how the child will react to this sudden change. If there are problems, let Mrs Thompson deal with them. Don't interfere.'

Dena sat with her precious child on her lap, tears rolling down her cheeks, and nodded. The last thing she wanted was to upset Trudy.

'The fact that she's at last out of that dreadful place is enough for me, right now. Thank you so much, Miss Rogers, I really do appreciate what you've done. She looks so pale, so thin. We need to feed her up, Aunty.'

'We do indeed,' Dot agreed. 'And I'm sure Trudy will let me know what she fancies for her tea, won't you, chuck?'

Trudy looked up at the big, smiling woman and happily nodded.

'And what about Looby Loo here, has she not had any tea yet either?' Aunty picked up the rag doll. 'Eeh, hecky thump, she looks in need of a good wash, and a stitch or two here and there. I'd say she's been in the wars, if I'm any judge. What do you say you and me go and give her a nice warm bath? How would that suit?'

Trudy instantly scrambled down from her mother's lap. 'Yes, please. Can she clean her teeth as well?'

'I should hope so, we don't stand for no slacking in this household, you know, not with all these sweets around.' And beaming happily, the two of them went off upstairs, hand in hand to the bathroom, Looby Loo held fast in Trudy's arms.

Dena looked up at Miss Rogers, and for the first time in all the years they had known each other, the two women actually smiled at each other.

'Mrs Thompson ought to be made available on the National Health. Just being in her presence makes a child feel better.'

A week later Lizzie and the children were planning a party to welcome Trudy into their midst, and were spending a noisy and messy afternoon making strawberry jelly, jam tarts and chocolate haystacks, Trudy's favourite, by way of preparation. 'Why don't we turn them into nests and fill them with miniature Easter eggs?' Lizzie suggested.

This proved to be most popular and Dena laughed with delight at their industriousness. Every day she would call in to spend time with her child, getting to know her all over again. She played with Trudy, read her stories, bathed her under Aunty's supervision, and sometimes joined Aunty Dot on one of her regular perambulations. Dena felt as if she'd been reborn, as if she'd been idling in a rusty old vehicle for months, now someone had cranked the starting handle and she was zooming away down sun-dappled lanes. She felt utterly carefree and happy! But this was the first step.

'When am I going to meet her?' Jack Cleaver would ask. 'I'm making big changes in my life, planning for our future together, so I'm naturally keen for you to name the day.'

'Not yet, but soon, maybe,' Dena would tell him, wanting to keep her child to herself for a while. 'When Aunty thinks she's ready – we can't throw too many changes at her too quickly.'

What puzzled Dena most about Cleaver was that he never made any attempt to kiss her. Apart from the odd fatherly pat on the cheek, or sympathetic squeeze of the hand, he never touched her. He was a most odd little man, very restrained and in control of his emotions. Yet she supposed she should be grateful for that. If she did eventually have to go through with this farce of a marriage, at least she could be fairly confident that he would keep his word about respecting her privacy.

Lizzie wiped a smudge of chocolate from Trudy's nose, smiling at Dena as her friend happily crumbled Shredded Wheat for the nests into a large bowl. 'It seems astonishing that it will be Easter again in a couple of weeks, a whole twelve months since I first met Charlie.'

'You look so happy together,' Dena said, with just a trace of envy. As pleased as she was for her friend, Dena couldn't help wishing she too could be lucky in love.

She'd enjoyed a pleasant evening with Adam Salkeld, the young doctor, in the Dog and Duck. He'd told her all about his family who lived in Fife, Scotland; how long it had taken for him to qualify and how much he loved his work. They'd seemed to be getting on really well. Yet at the end of the evening he'd seen her to her own front door, then simply walked away. He hadn't asked if he could see her again, and Dena hadn't set eyes on him since, obviously he didn't find her nearly as attractive as she'd found him. Perhaps he'd just felt sorry for her.

When she mentioned this to Lizzie, her friend laughed at her fears. 'It's been how long since you saw him, a week, ten days? He's a doctor, he's busy.'

'More likely he's no wish to involve himself with an unmarried mother with a young child, and who can blame him?'

Lizzie reached over and kissed her cheek, leaving a smear of chocolate in its place. 'Stop being so pessimistic. Who knows what tomorrow might bring.'

Dena smiled and nodded. 'And we have today.' She looked with loving delight at her precious child, swathed in an apron and standing on a stool beside Beth, stirring the crumbled Shredded Wheat into the chocolate mixture.

Dena resolutely put all such negative thoughts out of her head. You couldn't have everything in life, and right now she felt like the luckiest woman in the world.

Everyone had great fun at the party, particularly Trudy, playing silly games like Pin-The-Tail-On-The-Donkey, Hide and Seek, and Ride-a-Cock-Horse by riding on Joey's back as he galloped around. They let her win most of the prizes and she laughed and joined in all the giddy, teasing nonsense, behaving like any normal child with no sign of sulks, tears or tantrums.

Dena was content.

–

With her day's work done, Dena pulled the shutters down on her stall and stepped out of the market hall to find Adam Salkeld waiting for her, a cheerful grin on his face.

'I hoped I might catch you. I was wondering if you fancied another drink?'

Dena's heart skipped a beat, and she instantly wished she could dash home and change into something smart and sexy, but that would be ridiculous. 'If it comes with food attached then, yes, you're on. I'm starving.'

She'd meant a sandwich but he took her to a quiet little restaurant on Piccadilly. The décor was all pink and gold, the lights dim and the walls hung with photographs of Hollywood movie stars: Grace Kelly, Marilyn Monroe, Audrey Hepburn and Cary Grant. Adam ordered prawn cocktail and steak for them both, grilled to perfection, followed by Black Forest gateau, a real treat.

Dena, more used to Belle's café or a toasted teacake at the Kardomah, couldn't remember ever having been anywhere so stylish, or enjoying such a wonderful meal.

'We could go to the theatre later, if you like?' Adam suggested. 'The Palace, or the Opera House. I think they're showing *My Fair Lady*. Or maybe do that another night, if you prefer. I would like to see you again, if that's all right by you?'

It was more than all right. Dena was entranced. He was so attentive and thoughtful, funny, and easy to talk to, and very good-looking.

In the week following Adam Salkeld took her out three more times, including a trip to the Palace Theatre. Dena wore one of the dresses she'd designed and made herself. It was an ice-blue taffeta, her favourite colour, with a scoop neck, slightly gathered waistline and self-tie bow at the front. The crinoline underslip swished against her silk-stockinged legs as she walked beside him in high-stiletto heels.

It was a long time since she'd had the opportunity to dress up and feel glamorous. It wasn't necessary whenever Jack Cleaver took her out, for all it was always to Manchester's finest hotel. But then when she was with Adam she preferred not to think about Jack. They weren't, after all, officially engaged or anything. It had only ever been a loose agreement between them. Becoming looser by the minute, she reminded herself, and unless she could rid herself of these odd reservations about him nothing would come of it at all, no matter what Miss Rogers might say. So when Adam asked if she was free and unattached, she agreed that she was.

'Good, because I like you, Dena, rather a lot.'

Dena found herself blushing and couldn't think of a thing to say.

He proved these words to be true on their second date by kissing her goodnight, and it was all Dena had dreamed of. The kiss reminded her that she was still young, only just twenty and with all her life before her. She wrapped her arms about Adam's neck and gave herself up to his kisses.

—

Easter was long over, Trudy's party a distant memory, when one day Aunty suggested Dena might bring Jack Cleaver round. 'He could come for his tea. We won't make a fuss. We'll just have him come and join us, as part of the family. Don't try and rush her, Dena, by talking about your future plans. Trudy needs time to adjust and get used to having him around first before you thrust any more changes upon her. All right?'

Dena agreed. 'I'm in no hurry.'

Jack Cleaver looked strangely agitated when she told him, as if suddenly struck by an attack of nerves. 'Are you sure she's ready? Will we be on our own, Trudy and I?'

Dena firmly shook her head. 'Don't be daft. Aunty is very much in charge and we do as she says. You're coming to Sunday tea, as part of the family. You'll be like a stranger to her, remember, so Trudy needs to be in a safe and normal environment that is familiar to her.'

Cleaver nodded, then puffed out his pigeon chest. 'I'm sure we'll get along. It'll be fine.'

When Sunday arrived Trudy was dressed in a new red and green tartan dress that Dena had made for her. Her brown hair, still painfully short, had been brushed to a healthy shine and there was far less pallor in her small face, the cheeks plumping out and with a hint of rose to them now.

She was playing Old Maid with Alan on the rug when the knock came. Aunty was in the kitchen making tea and called out for someone to answer it. Dena ran and flung the door open, a bright and happy smile on her face.

'Hello, Jack, do come in.'

He walked into the room and at that precise moment Alan gleefully shouted that Trudy had been left with the old maid. Unconcerned that she'd lost, Trudy laughingly looked up to wave the card at her mother and saw Cleaver step over the threshold.

Her terrified scream filled the small house. It made Aunty drop the teapot where it smashed on the linoleum covered floor, Alan fell over backwards in shock, Beth squealed in unison and even the baby started to howl. Cleaver turned and fled.

Chapter Twenty-Eight

'I can't believe you're saying this. Just because a three-year-old child, who's been locked up in an institution for nearly twelve months, reacts badly to a stranger, that makes Jack Cleaver into one of these perverts, does it?' Lizzie sounded shocked.

It was the day following the fateful tea party and the memory of her daughter's scream still haunted Dena. 'She was clearly terrified of him.'

'Trudy was happily playing a game of cards with Alan. Then she looks up and suddenly sees a strange man coming towards her. She was startled, naturally. She probably hasn't set eyes on a chap since she moved into that place. They're all women at Ivy Bank, aren't they?'

'That's true, but Lizzie, it was awful. Admit it, we were all shocked by her reaction. You too. It must mean something.'

'It means the authorities have screwed up your child, as you thought they might. Oh, Dena, I'm so sorry.' Lizzie put her arms about her friend and hugged her close. 'Don't expect little Trudy to get better overnight and suddenly turn into the same normal, happy-go-lucky child she used to be. It's going to take time, as your social worker said. And don't fret about a few setbacks like this. You aren't in a desperate hurry to marry the guy, are you?'

Dena shuddered. 'I've no wish to marry him at all. I don't love him. I'm only doing it so that I can have Trudy home for good. Miss Rogers puts such pressure on me to *be respectable*, whatever that might mean.'

'Jack Cleaver is very generous with it. What did he say when you went to see him?'

'Exactly the same as you, that she must have been startled by the sight of a strange man in the house,' Dena glumly admitted.

'And he's willing to try again?'

'Yes.'

'You have to admit his heart is in the right place. He's still willing to be Trudy's dad, and to try and win her round gradually, despite her taking fright at first sight of him. You've got to hand it to him. Many men wouldn't come near a child with problems.'

'Trudy doesn't have problems.'

'Yes, she does, love,' Lizzie gently repeated. 'She's bound to, isn't she, having spent time in that place? You must accept that. But Jack Cleaver is all right. I think he's a bit lonely, but he's a good man. Steady and reliable.'

'Oh, Lizzie, I wish I could believe that. What am I to do? If only I could be sure.' Dena sat on the doorstep hugging her knees, her face still etched with doubt.

'You worry about things too much, love.'

'It's all right for you, you have Charlie and a nice future planned. I have no one. Carl has gone, let me down badly. My relationship with Winnie and Barry is obviously not what it used to be, so I'm on my own. Jack Cleaver's a bit of an odd sort but I was willing to go through with the marriage if it meant getting Trudy back, but how can I take the risk if she is afraid of him? What do I do then? And what if it really was him who did that terrible thing to her?'

'Stop it, Dena. This is stupid. Put such nasty thoughts right out of your head. We all know who did it. Sadly the police didn't manage to prosecute Barry but, hard as it might be, let that be an end to the matter. Let it rest.'

–

Barry was feeling very low. Few people were talking to him, and not only the fruit and veg business but also the boxing club were dying on their feet. He decided to hold another exhibition match, one last bid to breathe new life into the place and encourage his lads to come back and give it another try.

He'd managed to get Harry Hughes, a Liverpool-born, hard-hitting fighter who'd trailed around the fairs of Manchester and Salford throughout the thirties and forties, living largely in a caravan, often enduring torrential rain and fields reduced to a quagmire. He was no stranger to misfortune. His family had been killed in the blitz, and a mistimed punch had once felled a young opponent and duly ended his career. Harry had lost the stomach for the contest after that. But he was happy to put on a bit of a show now and then, to fuel his drink habit and buy food for his dog.

Unfortunately, it was a wet, windy night and, despite all the posters Barry had put up around the market, and the handbills he'd stuck through letterboxes, hardly a soul turned up. He guessed it was more than the bad weather that had put them off.

The only takers were a few old-timers with nothing better to do with their evenings, and only too willing to risk a round or two for the chance of winning a few bob. The eager young bloods who'd once been keen to learn from the old legends were notable by their absence, kept away by over-anxious parents. But Billy Quinn was there, as usual, together with some of his cronies.

During a break in the proceedings, the Irishman ambled over to Barry. Wasting no time in pleasantries, he cut straight to the point. 'I think I once asked you to get something for me, did I not?'

Barry did not reply.

'Now when was that, I wonder? Ah, yes, isn't it all coming back to me? It was when you were doing the naughties with young Joey.'

Barry's face burned beetroot red. 'I never touched Joey and you know it. It's your own twisted imagination that paints these nasty pictures in your filthy mind. I did nothing to the lad.'

Quinn made a clicking sound with his tongue as he sadly shook his head. 'The trouble is, Barry me old fruit, it'd be my word against yours and nobody would believe you were innocent, now would they? We know people's opinion of you at the present time, do we not? So I'd look sharp, if I were you, and find some kid, of either sex, pretty damned quick for this special client of mine. We have a nice little business going, him and me, but we're allus on the lookout for new material. It's not too late. He's still waiting, though he's not normally such a patient man.'

Something ignited within Barry, something hot and angry and dangerous. He'd had enough. He was tired of the snide remarks, of being castigated, blamed and punished for something he didn't do. He was innocent, dammit!

Barry flew at Quinn, grabbing the larger man by the collar, attempting to shake him like a dog might go for a rat.

'I'll not do your filthy work for you. Get it into your thick Irish noddle that I'm innocent, right? I didn't touch Joey. Nor did I lay a finger on our Trudy. We were just playing silly games and the child ran out in the road before I could stop her. I'd never do a thing to hurt her. Never! I've had enough of being blamed for something I didn't do. Say what you like. Do yer flaming worst. *I'm not guilty!*'

Finding himself finally released from Barry's frenzied grip Quinn shook himself off, dusting the fingermarks from the velvet lapels of his jacket, but he was more puzzled than angry. It wasn't the physical assault that had startled him as much as the naked candour in the other man's eyes. Quinn had done a lot of things in his fifty-plus years, mainly illegal, although so far, touch wood, he had never spent more than a night or two in clink. But he was no fool, and if there was one thing being a bookie had taught him, it was how to sum a person up. Quinn was nothing if not a shrewd judge of character, and he could recognise an honest man when he saw one.

In that moment of startling revelation it came to Quinn like a flash who the guilty party really was, who had used that child for his own purpose. It was a piece of information, which must be taken into serious account when making his future plans.

–

Unlike Lizzie, Dena couldn't let the matter rest. When she spotted Miss Rogers on her rounds the following day, she hurried over to speak to the woman.

'I can't marry Cleaver. I *won't* marry him. I think he might be the one.'

The social worker was startled at being so accosted. 'I beg your pardon?'

'Jack Cleaver, I think he could be the one who molested our Trudy. When he came to tea at Aunty's on Sunday, she screamed the place down the minute she clapped eyes on him. He fled for his life.'

Miss Rogers looked concerned. 'Oh, dear, that's most unfortunate. Not a good beginning. I had great hopes of him being a suitable and respectable husband for you, Dena, and a good father for Trudy. But what's this you're saying about him being the one responsible? What on earth makes you say such a thing?'

Tears filled Dena's eyes. 'I don't know. I've no proof, it's just a feeling I have.'

'Then you'd best keep it to yourself. You can't go around accusing every man Trudy takes a dislike to of having been the one to interfere with her.'

'Why else would she react like that?'

'Any number of reasons, not least her mental state after all she's been through. Didn't I warn you, Dena, not to rush things? Now do try to be more mature and sensible about this, act like a responsible mother for a change.' And the woman walked away, nose in the air, leaving Dena feeling very much like a naughty child.

—

She went next to see Constable Nuttall. Maybe he would take notice of these suspicions that were haunting her day and night. Who was it who'd hurt her child? Was it indeed the much maligned Barry, or smarmy Jack? If only she could know for sure.

Unfortunately Constable Nuttall, when Dena explained to him about Trudy's reaction to Cleaver, showed no more interest than had Lizzie or Miss Rogers.

'Nay, Dena love, I don't think we can condemn a man on the evidence of a child's tantrum. We've no proof that Cleaver's guilty. He was the man of the hour, the local Good Samaritan who came to Trudy's aid.'

'But what if he wasn't? What if he took the opportunity while everyone was distracted looking after Barry, of trying it on with her?'

Constable Nuttall frowned. 'Now you're letting your imagination run away with you, girl. Why would he do such a thing? He'd be hard pushed in the time he had available.'

But Dena persisted. She talked, she argued, she pleaded, begging the constable at least to speak to Cleaver again, or to check the evidence he gave at his interview. 'I want to be sure. You must see that it's important to me. Vitally important! I've agreed to marry him, after all, not because I'm in love with him, you understand, or even fancy him. But according to my social worker I apparently need a father for my child if I'm ever going to bring her home. I've told her I won't marry him unless I'm sure he's innocent.'

Constable Nuttall was embarrassed by this confession, which Dena had poured out in obvious distress. He made a point of strictly avoiding becoming embroiled in domestic issues. 'Aye, well, it's a conundrum is that one, I can see it is,' he muttered, hastily backing away.

'Can't you look into the case again?' Dena had a sudden thought. 'Maybe you could check out Cleaver's past. We're none of us too sure of the details, which seem to change from time to time. He's mentioned Dr Barnardo's, but also an Aunt Doris. And if he's a Barnardo's kid, how can he afford to own his own house? I do need to know as much about him as you can find out.'

'Aye, right, I'll look into it, Dena love.' The policeman was already some paces along the street, anxious to be on his way and concern himself with the more usual sort of problems he encountered on his beat, such as disputes between neighbours, a bit of shoplifting, and keeping an eye on young tearaways like Jake Hemley.

Dena sighed and continued on her way to the workshop, not hopeful that the policeman would do anything at all. The question she had to decide was, should she trust a child's tantrum, or the word of the law?

–

Dena was still seeing Adam, and knew she was falling for him hard. Surely a dangerous thing to do. He was a lovely man, this doctor, and there was no doubt that she could get to like him rather a lot but where would be the point in that? She'd only end up hurt. Adam Salkeld wasn't going to get serious about an unmarried mother with a young child, one whom the authorities considered might possibly be a feckless, abusive mother who lived in Champion Street and ran a tatty little market stall. Not least one with a court appeal pending over the murder of her brother, unthinkable! They were worlds apart.

Thinking these depressing thoughts as he walked her home one night, Dena was unusually quiet and thoughtful.

'Penny for them?'

She tried to laugh but the sound had a bitter edge to it. 'They aren't even worth that. Halfpenny, more like.'

He seemed to guess that she was thinking about Trudy and asked if the little girl had settled into her new foster home. 'I'm sure everything will work out fine and the authorities will allow you to have her home with you soon, Dena.'

'I hope you're right. I really don't fancy my social worker's solution to find myself a husband.'

'*Husband?*'

The moment Dena said the words she could have bitten off her tongue. It suddenly occurred to her how it must sound, as if she were asking him to apply for the role. She flushed bright crimson. 'It's her idea, not mine. I wasn't suggesting otherwise.'

'I'm sure you weren't.' He laughed, although in Dena's mood of heightened sensitivity his tone was even more brittle and forced than her own.

She rushed to explain. 'Her theory is that since they took Trudy into care because she was illegitimate, then if I were respectably married and she had a father the authorities would allow her to come home.'

'That's a bit draconian, isn't it? I mean, fine if you're in love with someone, but otherwise... You aren't in love with someone, are you?'

His voice had taken on a more serious note, and he'd stopped walking to gaze keenly into her face as he waited for her answer.

Dena could do no more than smile and say no, she wasn't in love with anyone. It crossed her mind to mention Jack Cleaver but she decided against it. Just the thought of that man made her shiver. Why wouldn't anyone take her worries about him seriously? Nothing on God's earth would persuade her to marry him now, and she had every intention of telling him so at the first opportunity.

As if reading her thoughts, Adam asked, 'Did they catch him, the perpetrator? Did they successfully prosecute?'

Dena shook her head. 'The police seem to have dropped the case.' She briefly explained about Barry being let off for lack of evidence. To think she'd believed poor Barry to be guilty. Now she was increasingly convinced that the perpetrator of this vile act could well be Cleaver, judging by Trudy's reaction to him. A shiver ran down her spine at the thought, and Adam put his arms about her to draw her close.

'They aren't optimistic about finding the person responsible then?'

'No,' Dena mumbled into the comforting expanse of his chest.

'That's dreadful!' He was stroking her hair, sending shivers of a different sort down her spine. 'That must be so hard for you. Where's the justice in that? I remember you saying that this man they arrested had been like a father to you, and a grandfather to Trudy.'

'Not any more, we've lost touch.'

'That's a great shame. Do you truly believe he's guilty?'

There was a slight pause then Dena stepped away from him to wipe her eyes. 'No, I don't, as a matter of fact. Something happened recently, which has made me look at the matter in a completely new light. I have my suspicions about who's really responsible but I can't prove it and nobody will believe me. I can't even persuade the police to investigate. It's all rather unpleasant.'

'I see, and what about Trudy's real father? Do you mind telling me who he is?'

There was a longer pause this time. The last thing she wanted to do right now was go into all the details of her brother's death, Kenny's heartless usage of her, his trial and the coming appeal. 'I'd rather not, if you don't mind. Not just now. It's all in the past and I'll leave it there.'

'If that's what you want, Dena, but remember I'm here. Should you ever need a friendly ear.'

Adam gathered her face between his big, square hands, and kissed her softly on the mouth. It was a gentle kiss: a friendly, cautious, brotherly sort of kiss, not at all that of a lover. One that clearly stated he wasn't available for consideration as possible husband material, thank you very much. Dena realised that she'd scared him off. She'd opened her mouth far too soon and put her stupid foot in it.

Chapter Twenty-Nine

Quinn came for Cleaver at the end of a particularly long and tiring day on the road, and bluntly informed him that Finch wanted to see him right away.

'What, now? Can't it wait? I'll see him in the morning when I drop off the orders as usual.'

'He was most adamant that he wants to speak to you now. Immediately.'

Jack was not pleased, as he'd just prepared himself a meal of poached halibut and a couple of slices of brown bread and butter, after which he planned to write up the day's orders, as was his custom, and listen to *The Navy Lark*. He liked to be in bed by ten so that he could be up bright and early the next morning. Jack Cleaver was a meticulous man who disliked his routine being interfered with.

Ignoring Quinn, he stubbornly sat at his dining table, tucked his napkin into his shirt collar and continued with his meal. 'You'll just have to hang on a minute. I'm not wasting good food.'

'Then I'll do it for you.' Reaching over, Quinn took the plate and upended it on to the table top. The butter from the halibut spread across the clean white table cloth, one of Aunt Doris's best. Jack was incensed.

'There was really no need for that. I said I would come in a minute.'

'When Mr Finch says he wants to see you right away, that's because *he wants to see you right away*. Move.'

If Jack felt a nudge of concern over this maverick disposal of his supper, the sensation worsened when he came face to face with his irate employer. Cedric Finch's down-turned mouth never did lend him an air of contentment, but today the baggy folds beneath his eyes positively quivered with restrained temper. Jack couldn't imagine what had put him into such a rage.

'So, Jack, lad, I've been hearing bad things about you. What have you got to say for yourself, eh?'

'I beg your pardon?'

'Don't act the innocent with me. You were instructed from the outset that if you play with the big boys you keep to big boy's rules. Instead, you've obviously taken it into your daft noddle to set up in business on your own account, isn't that the way of it?' Finch asked, his tone falsely pleasant.

Jack Cleaver felt as if all the blood were draining from his face. Had Finch got wind of his efforts to marry Lizzie and set himself up in direct competition? Or his switch of plan to marry Dena instead, so that he could be his own boss at last? He swallowed. 'I don't know what you mean, Mr Finch – sir.'

Finch rocked slowly back and forth on his heels, thumbs hooked into the pockets of his waistcoat while he considered the man before him; watching with undisguised contempt as Cleaver seemed to shrink into himself. He'd stationed Quinn by the door, just in case he should take it into his head to do a runner, although Finch thought it unlikely. Cleaver didn't have it in him, nor was he capable of thinking far enough ahead to make any snap decision, even to ensure his own survival.

Jack was thinking very much along the same lines, although with a strong element of self-pity attached. They were not at the sweet factory but in the bookies own office on the top floor of Quinn's Palace, not an easy place to make an escape from. He could hear the eerie echo of ships' hooters as they came into the docks, the clink and chink of chains being run out, the creaking of cranes. But within the building itself, all was silent and would remain so until it opened for business at nine, prompt.

'You're a grubby little man, Cleaver, do you know that? Mucky. Nasty. Obnoxious. A loathsome creature! Can't say I've ever liked you, but I thought that at least I could trust you.'

Jack was beginning to sweat. All too aware of Quinn's presence just out of sight behind him, it made the back of his neck prickle with foreboding. He felt exposed and dangerously vulnerable, didn't trust the Irishman one little bit, nor was he taking much comfort from his boss's glowering sarcasm. He cleared his throat, but his voice came out in a high-pitched squeak. He tried again. ''C-course you can trust me. Why wouldn't you be able to t-trust me? You pay me wages, after all.' He gave a little laugh in an attempt to lighten the atmosphere, but since no one else laughed it only made him feel worse.

'I'm glad you've remembered that, at least,' Finch dryly remarked. 'So how come you took it into your head to go freelance?'

'Freelance? I'm sorry, I don't know what you rightly mean by that.'

'Don't play games with me, lad. It was you who touched up that little lass, not Barry flaming Holmes, wasn't it? You couldn't even choose a willing kid, you had to put your mucky paws on a nipper, a toddler. Your sort make me sick, d'you know that? You make a beautiful act into something unclean.'

Jack was shocked to the core that his secret had been discovered, and yet at the same time felt oddly affronted that this man who spent his every spare moment ogling pictures of underage girls and using them for his own sadistic pleasure, dared to criticise *him*.

'I don't think you're in any position to criticise,' he bravely responded, recklessly considering the circumstances.

Jack sensed Quinn edge a step or two closer. 'Would ye be wanting me to deal with this?' The Irishman politely enquired.

Cedric Finch, strangely enough, put his head to one side and smiled. 'Not just yet, Billy, not just yet. Why don't you sit down, Cleaver, so's we can talk this through, man to man.'

Since he didn't seem to have any choice in the matter, Jack sat. He was aware of Quinn, arms folded, standing behind his chair, while Finch stood at the end of the desk where he was setting out pen, paper and ink.

'You've given me a bit of a problem, d'you see, by taking such a stupid risk with young Trudy,' he began, in deceptively pleasant tones. 'You've brought the eyes of the local constabulary upon Champion Street we could have done without. We've already had Constable Nuttall sniffing round here, asking a lot of damn fool questions. I like to run a tight ship, smooth and efficient, as you well know. We have an extremely lucrative operation going for us here, and your petty pandering to the baser side of your nature could well bring down the whole pack of cards. It would be unfortunate for all concerned, particularly yourself, do you understand? Are the possible consequences of your actions finally sinking into that empty skull of yours?'

They were indeed. Although Finch's manner remained benign, Jack was in no doubt about the danger his own folly had led him into. His employer sat at the desk and began to fill the fountain pen with bright purple ink. Jack watched, mesmerised, unwilling to consider where this might all be leading. 'I didn't think. It was a spur-of-the-moment thing. But the police don't suspect me. I've been dismissed from their enquiries.'

Finch smiled, revealing his yellow teeth, rather as a shark might before it chews its prey. 'Correct me if I'm wrong but your task, I seem to recall, was to procure models for Billy here to photograph. Models of all ages and both sexes, no questions asked about how you managed it. Not too onerous a task for someone with your weasel-like skills, was it? And you were suitably well remunerated for the work?'

Jack bleakly nodded. 'Indeed, I have no complaints,' Jack hastily agreed.

'Unfortunately, you now seem to have landed us all in the mire. You've apparently taken it into your head, on a spur-of-the-moment impulse, to act independently, of your own volition, without thought for the consequences. You didn't care that you might jeopardise the entire project, ruin a profitable enterprise, and possibly put other people's reputations in danger. You were far too obsessed with your own selfish need for a bit of grubby gratification.'

'I'm sorry.' Jack was shaking now. He could feel the heat of Quinn's rancid breath on the back of his neck and was beginning to wonder if he'd ever get out of this room alive.

Cedric Finch stroked his several chins, rubbed one ear lobe between finger and thumb as though considering how best to dispatch this recalcitrant employee. Then he clicked his tongue, a sound that seemed to vibrate right to the core of Jack's terror.

'So what I've decided is this. You'll write a confession, here and now, on this piece of paper, so that should we have any problems with the police – say if you were ever stupid enough to repeat this sort of carelessness in the future – we possess the means to protect ourselves. Does that sound fair to you?'

Jack thought that a bullet clean through the head might make for a speedier and far less painful outcome in the long run, but somehow managed to nod his agreement.

Finch gave his wintry smile. 'I thought you might see it my way in the end. I do need to know where I stand with the people I gather around me. Trust – Jack, me old mate – is everything. I provide the capital for this operation, after all. I take the greatest risk as a well setup businessman in this town, and Quinn here provides the know-how, the expertise as it were. You must confess he's skilled, both with the models and his camera.' His gaze darkened as he placed the pen and paper in front of Jack, lining them up precisely. 'And you get your turn, where appropriate, to taste the merchandise, do you not? You've no complaints in that respect, I trust?'

Jack quickly shook his head and gulped. 'No, none whatsoever.'

'Well then, our little cartel seems, to my mind, to be working well. So long as we all remember to stick to our prescribed roles and not step out of line. We'd have mayhem and anarchy if everyone were to do exactly as they pleased, now wouldn't we?' he asked, most delicately. 'You can see my point of view, I'm sure?'

'Perfectly reasonable.'

'Good, I'm glad we see eye to eye on the matter. Now, allow me to advise you on what best to write. I, Jack Cleaver, do hereby confess to having molested...'

Finch dictated and Jack scribbled, painstakingly setting down, word for word, exactly what he was instructed so that there could be no possible comeback later for his employer. Jack meekly obeyed in order that he could walk out of this office with all his limbs and important bits in place.

When he was done, Quinn carefully blotted the paper and handed it over to Finch. Now his boss's smile was warmer as he read it through. 'A most useful document. Splendid!' Folding it carefully, he slid it into an envelope. Annotating this with a description of the envelope's contents, he sealed it and handed it back to Quinn who locked it away carefully in the safe.

'There we are then, all friends again, eh?'

'I hope so, sir.'

'You know I'm not one to bear a grudge.' Finch slapped him on the shoulder in a display of joviality that sent a fresh shiver rippling down Jack's spine. 'Should you be tempted to transgress in the future, you'd do well to think on this day, and the contents of that safe. I'm glad we were able to resolve this issue without any undue unpleasantness. Billy here might be a bit disappointed, as he does so enjoy a bit of blood sport, but then he has a stronger stomach than me.'

'Will that be all?' The sweat from Jack's backside was sticking his trousers to the seat of the chair and he was anxious to be out of this room before he disgraced himself.

'I dare say you still have your orders to write up.'

Jack gratefully peeled himself from the seat and headed for the door. Billy Quinn, who had remained largely silent throughout, leaned forward and whispered something in Finch's ear. Finch listened carefully, one hand raised, indicating that Jack should remain where he was for a moment. Finally he nodded.

'I was forgetting, there is one other small matter in need of attention. You're very friendly with Lizzie Pringle, I understand, so I'd be obliged, if you wouldn't mind, to sit down again, Cleaver. Now that we're all back working on the same team I have one more little favour to ask you.'

—

Lizzie was working on a big order for a new outlet, for which she was grateful, but she was rushed off her feet. Charlie too was busy, more often than not out on the road alongside Spider, attempting to win new customers. They rarely seemed to spend any time alone together. Money remained tight so they were compelled to do most of the work themselves. Lizzie didn't resent this, she accepted it as part and parcel of a growing business, but she was increasingly concerned about their financial situation. She knew that Charlie too was worried. He felt responsible because it was his father who was creating most of their problems.

This evening, for instance, he wouldn't be home at all. He was in Liverpool, attempting to drum up more business. It had been a quiet day, as usual, on the market, Finch's stall biting deeply into their profits, and Lizzie was tired and anxious, ready to put her feet up.

She'd just reached the door of number thirty-seven when Jack Cleaver, who hadn't been near Pringle's Chocolate Cabin since Finch had cut off supplies, suddenly appeared at her elbow out of the blue. His unexpected emergence out of the shadows made her jump.

'Good heavens, Jack, I didn't see you standing there.'

'I saw you coming and thought I'd just stop by and have a word. How are you, Lizzie? How's trade?'

'Much as you might expect,' Lizzie said, not wanting to give too much away. 'I hope you're keeping well, Jack.' She opened the door, her mind already on the supper that Aunty would have waiting for her. Jack put his hand tentatively on her arm.

'I won't take more'n a minute of your time, but I would like a quick word. Can we walk a bit, happen?'

Lizzie hesitated. The last thing she wanted was to go walking with Jack Cleaver, particularly at this time of the evening. The days were lengthening now that spring was here, but she'd gone over to the kitchen after closing up the stall, packing up an order ready for dispatch tomorrow, and it was gone seven o'clock, already growing dark.

'I've got a problem with Finch,' he persisted, 'and would welcome your advice. I thought we could do each other a bit of good, like.'

It was enough to persuade her. 'Just to the end of the street and back then,' Lizzie agreed, and opening the door further she called in to Aunty to tell her she'd be back in five minutes.

Jack offered her his arm, in a gentlemanly way. He told Lizzie how grateful he was that she could spare him the time, how he hoped little Trudy was settling.

'She's doing well, I believe. What is it you were wanting to say to me, Jack?'

He cleared his throat in that irritating way he had. 'The fact of the matter is, Lizzie, you've done considerable damage to Finch's Sweets. Finch himself might not care to admit the fact, but it's true.'

'I'm delighted to hear it, but he's damaging us too with that stall he's set up in competition.'

'I'm aware of that, but I wanted to say that I'm on your side. I'd be willing to help in any way I could.'

Lizzie stopped walking to stare at him. She could barely see his face, half in shadow as they stood beneath the light from the lamp. 'Why would you do such a thing? Finch is your employer.'

'Because he's making my life an absolute misery, blaming me for your defection and for the fact you're attempting to put him out of business. Orders are dropping like stones as more and more of his old customers swap over to Pringle's.' He knew this to be an exaggeration, but Finch's instructions had been clear. Jack was to say whatever he deemed necessary to win her confidence. 'Finch is constantly nagging me to buck up my ideas and bring in more orders. You know how he is, blames everyone but himself,' Jack plaintively remarked. 'Seems to think I can save the day, that I can put a spoke in your wheel, as he describes it, and ruin your new business.'

'And could you?'

Jack gave a good imitation of an embarrassed smile. 'I doubt it. You have a good product. An excellent product, in fact.'

Lizzie was tired, far more interested in her supper than in listening to Jack Cleaver's complaints. She struggled to stay focused as he droned on for a while about his employer's perceived faults.

At the end of her patience, she interrupted him. 'So what have your problems with your boss got to do with me?'

'You and me are friends, Lizzie, at least I've always believed that to be the case,' he smoothly remarked in his most unctuous tones. 'Frankly, I'd rather do something to help than be used as a means to obstruct you. I'm trying to explain that I don't enjoy working for Finch. He's not a pleasant man, you and me both are agreed on that. I'm a bit disenchanted, if you catch my drift. And I need to think of my own future, of where I'm going.'

'I see.' Lizzie stopped walking, her expression troubled. 'But why has *your* future anything to do with me? I'm spoken for. Charlie and me are—'

'Oh, yes, I understand that I've no chance of winning your heart, not any more. I gave up on that notion, as you know, ages ago. I reckon Dena and me will do well enough together, once little Trudy is settled.'

Lizzie wondered if she should say something more about that, ask him what his true motives were in offering to marry her friend, but decided it was none of her business. It really was up to Dena, who must make up her own mind whether she liked and trusted the man sufficiently to accept his offer.

Clearing his throat, Cleaver continued, 'Pardon me for being nosy, but how are things? Financially, I mean. I wondered if you might be on the lookout for a new investor.'

There was a brief silence, while Lizzie brought her attention back to Jack's droning tones. What was that he'd said about an investor? Jack Cleaver, it seemed, was making them a serious offer. Her heart leaped. If he truly was disenchanted with Finch, surely it would be immensely useful for them to be able to call upon his expertise?

Jack was saying, 'I could make you a loan at a very reasonable rate of interest. Money is always tight in a new business, I know, and it'd save you bothering the bank, I dare say.' He named a figure, which made Lizzie's eyes open wide.

She tried to be cautious, to ask the right questions, wanting to know why he would choose to invest in Pringle's Sweets and not Dena's fashion business. 'Since you and she are to marry.'

Jack had thought about this one and had his answer ready. 'I did offer to help develop her business but she declined. She's very independent, is Dena, and not as ambitious as you, Lizzie. I think she's happy just to run a small stall on Champion Street Market, something safe.'

'We want to be safe too. And you might have to wait a while before you received much in the way of a return on your investment,' Lizzie pointed out, anxious to dampen any high expectations. 'And I'd need to speak to Charlie first.'

'But you can't say that he gets on well with his father, can you? I'm sure he'd have no qualms about poaching staff from him.'

He grinned, as if saying he was worth poaching, and Lizzie thought that maybe he was right. Jack Cleaver must possess an order book full of useful contacts. 'I'd like to think about it,' she said, still hesitating but sorely tempted.

'I'd need to know soon, I can't go on like this, Lizzie, I really can't.'

Lizzie hurried home for her supper, but said nothing about Jack Cleaver's offer, either to Aunty or to Charlie. She needed to think about it herself for a bit first.

Chapter Thirty

It was May Day and Aunty had made the children a maypole. Using a long broom handle with two interlocking hoops attached, they'd spent a happy hour or two winding strips of bright green and yellow crêpe paper around the whole thing, and attached brightly coloured ribbons for the children to hold.

Now the neighbourhood children were dancing around it with Beth as self-elected May Queen, or at least the first to sit on the stool in the centre and hold up the maypole. Trudy was to be next but everyone would have their turn, one by one, even Alan. Joey had declined to take part in the dancing but was happily banging a tambourine, which was decked out with coloured ribbons, and the children sang too. Aunty sat on a chair and clapped her hands in time to the beat.

The sun was shining, with puffy white clouds prancing across a bright blue sky. The scent of spring was in the air, and half the folk of Champion Street came out to watch as the maypole began to progress slowly along the street, the children stopping every now and then for a change of May Queen and more tripping and skipping around it.

Barry Holmes stood by his market stall and watched Trudy skip by. She looked so carefree and happy. He longed to wave at the little girl who'd once been the apple of his eye, but was afraid even to smile at her in case someone should notice. She'd seen him, giving him a shy smile as she danced past, and caused herself to miss a step. Beth scolded her.

Lizzie emerged from Pringle's Chocolate Cabin to watch, and to hand a packet of sweets to each performer. As they skipped on, she instinctively put a hand to her stomach, wondering if one day a child of her own would dance around the maypole, and when that might be. She was twenty-three years old, a grown woman who had found the love of her life. What were they waiting for? Yet Charlie seemed determined there would be no wedding until Pringle's Sweets was established and the bank loan settled, which could take years. She hadn't yet mentioned Jack Cleaver's offer, but maybe she should. Maybe she was being too cautious and it was exactly the kind of help they needed. If they carried on as they were, she might never get the chance of motherhood. Lizzie sighed and went back to serving a customer.

The maypole finally completed its journey in the heart of the market among all the hustle and bustle, with the old men by the horse trough stopping their chatter to applaud and cheer. People threw pennies to the dancers and joined in the singing and the laughter. Some of the women lifted up their skirts, kicked up their legs, and enjoyed a little jig around it too.

'What a performance,' Aunty said, who had followed the little procession. 'They'll be wanting to go on the stage next.'

When the children staggered back home, puffed for breath and worn out by their exertions, Aunty Dot provided hot Vimto for them all.

'Look what Lizzie gave us. Candy Kisses,' Beth said, showing Aunty the little packets of sweets made in the shape of lips.

'If you close your eyes and wish while you eat them, you might see your sweetheart.' Aunty said. 'May Day was always the day to meet your true love, so keep a lookout.'

'How can you keep a lookout if you have your eyes closed?' Alan asked.

'You and your sharp tongue,' Dot teased the little boy, pretending to box his ears. 'Have you been in the knife drawer this morning? Yer that sharp you'll cut yerself. I'd've thought you'd be happy to meet your true love? How about you, Joey? Who you do fancy?'

Lizzie had joined them by this time, Amy George having taken over the Chocolate Cabin for a while, and she couldn't help but chuckle at the shock on Joey's face at the very idea of *fancying a girl*, while Alan pretended to vomit. Beth blushed prettily and kept glancing over at one of the Bertalone boys. My goodness, but girls grew up so much quicker than lads.

Then Dena arrived, swooping Trudy up into her arms and telling her how pretty she looked in her new May Day frock, and how well she'd danced.

'Did you see me, Mummy?'

'I didn't miss a step.'

Lizzie was distracted for a moment by Gabby Bertalone begging her for another packet of sweets for one of her sisters who had missed out, but then noticed Beth had started to skip away along the street. She called out to her. 'Hey, where are you off to, madam?'

'Just to show Mr Cleaver my new frock.'

Dena yelled at the little girl at the top of her voice. '*No*, Beth, you mustn't bother him. Come here at once!'

Lizzie frowned. Dena had been strangely insistent that none of the children should go anywhere near Jack's house. They'd had a row about it, one of many on the subject. Lizzie didn't understand her at all. One minute she was about to marry the man, the next was suspecting him of being a child molester.

'She's only wanting to show him her dress,' Lizzie hissed.

'Come here *now*, Beth. This *minute*,' Dena repeated, in the sternest voice she could muster.

Beth looked at Dena, then at Lizzie, who jerked her head as if saying she should do as she was told, and the little girl reluctantly trailed back home. Lizzie sighed, feeling sorry for her friend and her problems, even if some of them were self-inflicted.

–

It was the following morning and Dena was happily sewing on her machine. Aunty had left Trudy with her for an hour while she did her bit of shopping, all part of the plan to prove to Miss Rogers that Dena was capable of properly looking after her own child. Trudy sat on the rug playing with the bag of buttons, although not in the contented fashion that she used to once, before the terrible thing had happened to her. She was growing too big for baby games already at three and a half, and was shooting up fast now that she was being fed on Aunty's good home cooking.

Trudy glanced up. 'Why can't I go and see Uncle Barry?'

Dena was startled, this being the last thing on her mind. As she'd happily treadled and stitched, she'd been thinking that her little girl could start nursery school in September. Trudy had once been very keen to go, and Dena hoped she still was. Her old friendship with Gabby and the other Bertalone girls seemed to have fallen by the wayside and she was in dire need of some new friends of her own age. 'What makes you ask?'

Trudy looked at her mother, struggling to explain the muddle of thoughts in her head. She'd been cross with Uncle Barry at first because he'd looked after Rosemary, her best doll, but not stopped that nasty man from hurting her. Then she'd been annoyed because he never came to see her at Ivy Bank, not even when she was in hospital. But yesterday, when they were dancing around the maypole and she'd seen him on the market, she'd felt this great surge of love for him. Trudy had wanted to run to him and jump into his arms and have him swing her round and tickle her and give her a big hug, as he used to do.

'I just want to see him,' she said, unable to explain any of this.

Dena was thoughtful for a long moment, then quietly nodded. 'Let me see what I can do.'

—

Charlie was equally tempted by Cleaver's offer when Lizzie told him about it later that day, but even more cautious.

'He asked me a few days ago but I didn't say anything at first because I was equally reluctant. I needed to think about it, but he's a man of good standing in the trade so he'd be a definite asset.' She also reminded Charlie that Jack Cleaver could be marrying her best friend. She must surely speak in his favour, let alone the fact that he was seeking a way to escape Finch's dominance, as they all were.

'Even so, he's an unknown quantity. And we already owe money to the bank. Why would we risk borrowing more?'

Lizzie reminded him of the sum mentioned. 'Surely it would be enough to pay off the bank, get that off our backs completely, and we'd still have some left over as working capital.'

Charlie did some quick mental sums while asking all the questions Lizzie herself had asked, and more besides. Why Jack should do this, what he would get out of it, how much interest he would charge. Did he expect a quick return on his investment? Lizzie answered every one to the best of her ability, and finished by suggesting that he speak to Cleaver direct on the ones she couldn't answer.

'He does seem genuine. Oh, and wouldn't it be marvellous to be free of money worries, as well as have access to Jack's order book?'

Charlie frowned. 'That sounds a bit like cheating to me. I want to beat my father fair and square, not by stealing his customers.'

'He's stealing ours.'

'He must live with his conscience, and we must live with ours.'

'All right, so we'll be cautious about using Jack's order book, but he still possesses a great deal of expertise in the trade, and the money would be *so* useful. You will think about it? Please?'

Charlie kissed her lightly on the lips. 'I'll give it very careful thought.'

'And discuss the offer with him?'

'Yes, maybe I'll have a quiet word.'

'Promise?'

He put his arms about her. 'I promise. Now, no more talk of business. I want to look at you, to kiss you, to do all manner of wonderful things to you...'

Lizzie and Charlie were finding it hard to live so close and yet not be a proper couple. Sometimes it needed the merest touch, a look even, and Lizzie would feel as if her nerves were on fire. They did their best to keep busy in the kitchens or at the Chocolate Cabin, but the evenings were the most difficult time when Aunty and the children had gone to bed and they were alone, as they were now.

Moments later they drew apart, breathing hard, all unbuttoned and unpinned. 'Are we being too harsh on ourselves?' Lizzie asked. 'What are we waiting for? Maybe we should just go to the register office and hang the consequences.'

'I want us to start off right,' Charlie stubbornly insisted, and this in spite of the yearning inside him to rush her to the register office there and then, for all it must be closed at this time of night. Every time he thought about what his own father had done to them he was filled with anger. 'I don't want us weighed down by debt and worry.'

'But there isn't going to be a quick solution to our problems, not unless we accept Jack's offer,' Lizzie warned.

'I've told you I'll think about it, but we have to be patient. It takes a long time to develop a new business.'

'I know, but I don't understand why we can't at least get married. Are you changing your mind, and don't want to marry me at all?'

'Dammit, you've found out I'm only after your money,' Charlie joked.

Lizzie giggled hysterically, then for no reason she could explain, began to cry. 'Oh, I hate this waiting, this wanting you so much and not being able to have you.'

Charlie gathered her close in his arms. 'So do I, love, so do I. But what else can we do? I want us to start off right.'

'But how can we "start off right" with all this pressure on us? Oh, it's all my fault we have these money worries, and that things aren't going right for us. I should have agreed to your father's demands in the first place, and stopped Aunty from making her sweets.'

'Don't talk daft. She loves making them, and so do I. It'll all work out fine in the end. Just you wait and see.'

'But how *long* must we wait – till we're old and grey?' And as he kissed her, several times in fact, to prove how sincerely he loved her, Lizzie went on crying. 'I can't seem to stop.'

'You're tired, that's all, I expect your back is aching from all the work you did in the kitchens this morning. Isn't that right?'

Lizzie bleakly nodded, lifting her face to meet his kisses, her heart melting with love for him.

'Take off your blouse then, and I'll rub some lavender oil into your shoulders. Works a treat.'

'Take off my blouse?'

Charlie grinned. 'Go on, I promise not to look. And I know Aunty has some oil in the dresser because she's lent it to me more than once for the very same purpose.' He was on his feet rummaging in a drawer.

When he came back to her, Lizzie began to slide open the tiny pearl buttons of her blouse while Charlie poured a small amount of the rubbing oil on to the palms of his hands, except that his eyes were riveted on Lizzie's. He couldn't seem to tear them away. She glanced up at him through her lashes, then half turned her back and, very gently, he began to massage her shoulders.

'Ooh, that's lovely. A little higher. Oh, there's a sore bit just below my shoulder blades. Yes, there.' His touch was utter bliss and Lizzie could barely think straight as her conscious-ness centred completely on the effects those strong hands were having upon her senses. He kissed her bare shoulder, and the sensitive little hollow just below her ear. Lizzie half turned, lifting her face to his, sliding smoothly into his arms.

She moved against him, shyly encouraging him when he slid his hand around to fondle her breast. She even helped him to unhook her bra. Perhaps it was the raw state of their emotions that evening, their worries over the future coupled with a need to prove to each other the depth of their love, or simply the evocative scent of the lavender, but somehow they simply weren't able to stop.

A desperation seemed to come over them as they fumbled with buttons and hooks and peeled off each other's clothes. Lizzie had never seen a man naked before and yet his body seemed as familiar to her as if she'd always known it: strong and beautiful, lithe and firm; as if it were meant to be a part of her own.

He stroked and caressed her and when he entered her she was more than ready for him, giving herself with love and joy, moving with him in the time-honoured rhythm as together they discovered the enchantment of loving. It may have been a hasty coupling, and a little furtive, the fear that Aunty might get up to see to one of the children, an ever-present threat in their minds, but it was also beautiful. The most sensual, most natural thing in the world to make love to Charlie.

Afterwards, as they guiltily scrambled back into their clothing, Lizzie's cheeks blooming with love and her limbs all shaky and weak, they clung to each other for a moment, stunned by what had just happened.

'I think I should move out,' Charlie said. 'We can't risk this happening again. Not till we're wed.'

'And when will that be?' Lizzie gently asked, smoothing his tousled hair.

'Soon – God, I hope so, I really do. I'll get another job, part-time, to bring more money in. It's the only way. And I will think about Jack Cleaver's offer, I promise.'

Quinn was once more waiting for Cleaver when he got home from his round of calls. Jack didn't argue this time, or risk losing his tea, but meekly accompanied the Irishman to Quinn's Palace to report on progress. Standing before Cedric Finch he admitted, with some degree of discomfiture, that his instructions had not yet been carried out in full, but that he'd put the idea to her, and was gaining Lizzie Pringle's confidence. 'She's putting it to Charlie, and considering my offer of a loan would put me in a strong position to pop in and out of Pringle's kitchens whenever I wished.'

'Just remember that we haven't time to pussyfoot about. The girl has to be compromised, and look sharp about it. I want you to make absolutely certain she won't go prying into my affairs, that we have the means to shut her up should she be stupid enough to try. I want her out of my son's life for good.'

Jack assured him that he would very soon have Charlie doubting her innocence. It was merely a matter of choosing the right moment.

'Aye, well, we don't have many of them to waste,' Finch briskly reminded him. 'And while you're waiting for the lass to take a fancy to your manly charms, you can get hold of that young lad for me.'

'What young lad?'

'That boy, the one who lives with Dot Thompson and trains at Barry's club. Joey something-or-other. Nice looking lad, not aggressive and very amenable, or so Billy here assures me. I have a client with a liking for such boys. Fetch him over to see me, will you?'

'For a photograph, you mean?' Jack burbled, panic clouding his brain.

Finch snapped: 'No, not for a bleeding photograph, for a client who likes good-looking young lads. Are you deaf? Get him over here, soon as maybe, and don't let me down this time, Cleaver, or I might start regretting giving you a second chance.'

'Oh, I won't, I won't, Mr Finch. I'll see to it, I promise. I won't let you down.'

'I'm sure you won't, not if you know what's good for you. Should the possibility ever again cross your addled brain of sampling the merchandise, just remember the document you wrote and signed with your own fair hand, safely tucked in Quinn's safe.'

Jack thought he might never forget it for as long as he lived.

Tricking Lizzie into an indiscretion was bad enough, but how on earth was he to wheedle his way into young Joey's good books? The boy watched him like a hawk.

—

Dena at last went to see Barry. Keeping a close watch, she chose the moment Winnie popped over to the Dog and Duck for a glass of stout with her friends, and knocked briskly on his door. It was opened almost at once by Barry himself. 'What have you forgotten now?' he asked, obviously thinking it was Winnie back again.

'Can I come in?' Dena walked past him, into the house, before he had time to say no.

'Looks like you already have.'

He followed her along the lobby into the living room where they sat facing each other, Barry in his armchair by the fire, Dena on the old sofa.

She'd rarely seen him in recent months. Now, when she considered him, Dena thought that he looked like a pale imitation of the Barry she'd once known and loved: that familiar, dapper figure with the bowler hat and carnation in his button-hole.

This Barry was thinner, scrawny almost, as if he was less of a man. He'd even lost some of his hair, and had aged considerably since last she'd sat in this chair. But then, they all had.

'I thought it was time we had a talk,' Dena said. 'And before you say anything, I know you asked me to do this months ago, but I wasn't up to it then. I am now. At least, I think I am. I hope I am.' She stopped, struggling to catch her breath and organise her thoughts.

There was a short silence. 'Would you like a cuppa? I was just going to put the kettle on.'

'Thanks, that'd be grand.'

Nothing was said while Barry clattered about in the small kitchen, and Dena gazed at the familiar pictures of Blackpool on the cream flock wallpaper. How she'd loved to hear the stories of the exciting life he'd once led working on the North Pier at Blackpool. She remembered him telling her he'd tried his hand at all manner of activities from running a flea circus to being a caller for bingo, or housey-housey as they called it in those days, as well as performing with a Punch and Judy show. She'd always enjoyed Barry's tales, his caustic wit and droll sense of humour.

No one could call Barry Holmes mundane, even if, in his own opinion, he'd come down in the world by working on a market stall in Champion Street.

Dena mentally re-lived all the times she'd sat in this very chair: when her brother had drowned, when her mother had been fading away through grief, when she'd given birth to her own precious child and needed help to care for her, and when she'd dumped Kenny but he'd continued to pester her. She'd come asking for help and Barry had given it unstintingly, together with much sound advice.

He brought the tea and Dena sipped the refreshing brew for a moment, welcoming the comfort it brought, not lifting her eyes to meet the condemning gaze she fully expected to find fixed on her.

Cradling the mug in her hand, at length she found her voice. 'At the time it happened, I was in shock. What Adam – what the doctor, told me, threw me completely off balance. It was bad enough that there'd been an accident at all, but that – that some pervert should have touched my child was too much to take in. And then it just got worse and worse. Miss Rogers taking Trudy into care, getting over the trial, the gossip and suspicion and Carl not around to stand by me. It was as if I'd lost all my family, my child, the man I loved, even some of my friends, in one go. I felt utterly alone, bereft and deserted.'

'Same here. I felt that way too,' Barry said, his voice little more than a whisper.

She looked up then and met his gaze, finding it not condemning at all but very sad.

'You didn't do it, did you? You never touched her.'

'No, love, I'd never do such a thing with any kid, let alone our Trudy. I couldn't love her more if she were me own.'

Dena swallowed. There was a great lump in her throat, which she couldn't seem to shift. 'I realise that now. I'm sorry I didn't before.'

'That's all right, love. You weren't the only one.'

'But I should've been the one to stand by you, to believe in you.'

Barry shook his head. 'Easy said, but like you've just explained, you were in shock and there was a lot going on. I knew it was just a matter of time before you came round. But why now? What made you come to see me today?'

A short silence while Dena steadied her breath. 'Something happened the other day and I think I know now who was responsible, but I can't persuade anyone to believe me.'

'Why don't you tell me then, and see if I do? 'Cause I'm the one who's known all along.'

Chapter Thirty-One

Dena hadn't seen anything of Adam Salkeld in recent weeks. Having thought she'd blown it and lost him, she'd been delighted when today, being Saturday, he surprised her by calling to ask if she'd care to go Ten Pin Bowling. Dena had never been bowling in her life before and found it great fun, though she proved to be a rotten shot and didn't knock down many pins.

Best of all, he'd invited Trudy to go along with them. The little girl was far too small to handle the large heavy bowls but the club had a children's play area and she happily played on the climbing frame, and with the skittles and giant building blocks, where Dena could keep an eye on her.

'You're a good mother, and scarcely let her out of your sight. Why can't the powers-that-be understand that?'

'Don't ask, you'll only hear answers which will raise my blood pressure.'

He grinned, telling her Trudy was a lovely child and would soon forget all about her trauma in Ivy Bank. 'Children are very resilient.'

'And also vulnerable! Those busybodies damaged her far more than I ever did, even if I am an *unmarried mother*. Whoops, there I go again, let's change the subject.'

Adam laughed. 'Okay, how about a Coca-Cola, and would Trudy like an ice lolly?' They all sat laughing together on a bench, telling jokes and having fun.

It was the best afternoon of Dena's life, she glanced at her watch and pulled a face. 'Five o'clock! I must take Trudy back to Aunty's now.'

'Are you on a curfew?'

'Sort of.'

'Come on then, I'll walk both you lovely ladies home.'

'You don't have to.'

'I want to. Is that allowed?'

Dena smiled at him, feeling her cheeks grow pink with pleasure. And with each of them holding Trudy's hand, they set off in the direction of Champion Street, almost as if they were a proper family.

–

Jack Cleaver had been stalking Joey for days and was getting absolutely nowhere. The lad was as slippery as an eel, never still for a minute, seeming to spend every waking moment either helping to mind the children or else working in Pringle's kitchens. He'd even stopped attending Barry Holmes's boxing club. But then, most young lads had.

Jack watched and waited, hoping for an opportunity. The trouble was, this was a big lad, not some nipper you could just pick up and run off with. Going on twelve years old and with a quiet maturity about him for all he was still in short trousers. Finch knew how to present him with a problem. Jack believed his boss had done it deliberately to reinforce the control he held over him.

This evening, on his way home after a long day on the road, Jack had spotted the younger boy with the National Health spectacles. Alan, that was his name. He was playing hop-scotch with his sister when Jack sidled over for a chat. 'Having fun?'

'Aye,' Alan said, wobbling slightly as he hopped on each chalked square. He picked up the stone they were using as a marker, and managed to reach base without stepping on any lines or falling over.

Beth took the stone from him and slid it expertly. It landed on the eight, exactly as she'd planned. If she did this one right, she'd have won again. Alan could rarely beat her at this game. He didn't have her sense of balance.

'Do you like model aeroplanes?' Jack asked.

'Aye, 'course I do,' scoffed Alan, clearly thinking this a stupid question.

'Would you like to see one? I make them myself, you know. I could show them to you.'

'Yes, please,' Alan said, eager to go with him that very minute.

Beth had picked up the marker and was hopping back to base, pleased that she had won again. She'd heard the conversation and answered for Alan in her sing-song, I-know-best tone of voice. 'Sorry, Mr Cleaver, our Alan can't come right now. Us tea'll be ready in a minute.'

'Oh, another time then, eh, Alan?' Drat it, nothing seemed to be going his way at the moment. He couldn't even catch Lizzie alone, Pringle's kitchens being largely shut up at the moment. What was going on there? he'd very much like to know.

'Aw, why can't I go *now*?' Alan moaned, deeply disappointed. 'You're a right spoil-sport, our Beth. It wouldn't take a minute, would it, mister?'

Beth put her hands on her skinny hips, looking cross. 'You can't go, and that's that. Go and wash your hands or Aunty'll have your guts for garters.'

Alan knew when he was beaten and made his way slowly to their front door, scraping the toes of his boots as he did so. 'What are guts? Are they in yer head like brains or summat? And have *I* got any?'

'No,' Beth said. 'You haven't many brains either, but we live in hope.' Then she turned and waved at Jack. 'Bye, Mr Cleaver. We'll happen see you after us tea.'

An hour later he was still there, waiting, but disappointingly it was only Beth who came out to play this time, skipping with her rope all by herself. Jack quietly approached. 'Where's your brother?'

'It were fish for us tea and our Alan doesn't much care for fish so he wouldn't eat it. He wanted beans on toast but Aunty said no, he had to eat the fish. So he started to sulk and then got into a scrap with our Joey. They were both sent to bed for misbehaving at the dinner table. I'm only allowed ten minutes skipping while Aunty washes up, then it's my bedtime too.'

'That's a pity,' Jack said. 'I have a collection of dolls I thought you might be interested in. One of them is Japanese, another is a Spanish flamenco dancer, and there's a lovely ballerina. They're very beautiful and once belonged to an old aunt of mine. Would you like to see them? I live just a few yards further along, across the road from Barry and Winnie Holmes. It would only take five minutes and we're good friends now, you and me, after all the babysitting I've done for you, aren't we? You'd be back before Aunty had finished the washing-up.'

Eyes shining, Beth quickly agreed, happy to have got one over on Alan. Slipping her hand into his, she skipped happily along by his side as he led her to his house. They'd nearly reached the door when a voice boomed out: 'Beth Grimshaw, where have you got to now?'

Then Lizzie's voice. 'I'll look for her, Aunty. She can't have gone far.'

Aunty Dot was standing in the doorway of her house, light from the warm living room spilling out on to the cobbles. Her face was in shadow but it was clear from her tone of voice that she was anxious. Lizzie was walking away in the opposite direction down the street, calling her name.

'Oops!' said Beth, smiling up at Jack and hunching her shoulders in a conspiratorial sort of way. 'That's Aunty. She wants me home. Sorry, I'll have to go.'

Cleaver had an instant desire to shove the little girl into his house, but thought better of it. Far too risky with both Aunty Dot and Lizzie so close by. Instead he said, 'Hold on a minute, love,' and, keeping a firm hold of her hand, stepped forward into the street and called out to Lizzie.

'She's here, with me. Quite safe.'

Lizzie spun about at the sound of his voice, and smiled with relief. 'Oh, there you are, Beth. We were looking for you. It's nearly your bedtime.'

'I was just going to show her my collection of foreign dolls. Is that all right? I'll not keep her a minute.' He told himself that he wouldn't actually do anything, not right now, but showing Beth the dolls would at least spark her interest, hoping that she'd come again if he asked her.

It was then that Dena appeared, and she wasn't alone. There seemed to be a young man with her. The pair of them went over to Lizzie and stood there, in the middle of the street, having a conversation. Oddly enough, it sounded like they were having some sort of argument, although he managed to catch only snatches of it.

'Didn't I tell you...' he heard Dena say.

'For goodness' sake, where's the harm in...'

At one point Dena started up the street towards him but Lizzie dragged her back. Jack was puzzled by this performance but felt obliged to wait for a decision, his hand still firmly gripping Beth's. All he wanted was a little more time to win the child's confidence but she was growing impatient.

'I'm sorry, Mr Cleaver, but I'd best go. Happen you can show me tomorrow, eh?' And slipping her hand free from his, Beth skipped happily away, twirling the rope in time to her steps.

'There you are, missus,' Aunty said. 'Get in here this minute afore I tan your backside. What is this, some sort of rebellion?'

Giggling, knowing Aunty would never lift so much as a finger to hurt a child, Beth happily obeyed.

Still watching from his doorstep, Jack saw Lizzie and Dena, together with the young man, follow the little girl into the house and the door slam shut.

Jack Cleaver frowned. He'd be luckier next time, he told himself. He'd get the child then, no problem. Or, better still,

Joey. But what had that argument been about, and who was the young stranger with Dena? Now that *did* trouble him.

--

Adam was doing his best to intercede and calm both girls down since no real harm had been done, but Dena was hugely embarrassed that he had witnessed this unpleasant little scene. Just her luck that it should happen when Adam was around. Dena felt as if she was jinxed.

She kissed Trudy goodnight and dutifully handed her over to Aunty, wishing she could just take her child home and put her to sleep in her own bed, where she'd be safely away from the creepy Jack Cleaver. Dena glanced back up the street to his closed front door. The man was a real problem. Why did no one else share her distrust of him?

Adam insisted on walking her home.

'You're a glutton for punishment. I should've thought you'd be glad to escape from this mad street.'

'Why would I, if it's where you live?'

Something warmed inside her at the compliment, but when they reached her door he made no effort to kiss her. He could see that she was still upset, and quietly asked if she was all right.

'Why wouldn't I be?' Dena snapped, her mind elsewhere.

'You think he's the perpetrator of the crime, don't you? You believe Jack Cleaver was the one who hurt Trudy.'

Dena looked up at him out of blank eyes, then nodded.

'But you can't prove it, that's what you said.' There was a silence as he waited in vain for her answer. 'Is there anything I can do or say to make it better?'

'No, there's nothing anyone can do.' Dena could hardly recognise her own voice, all cold and flat.

'Well, if you should change your mind, you've only to ask.'

'Thank you.'

Another long silence, an awkwardness wedging itself between them as Dena thought of the ruined afternoon. Would this nightmare never end? Would it ruin their entire lives?

'I'm glad we get on so well, you and I. Remember, you can always talk to me, Dena. Friendship is important, don't you think?'

Dena quietly agreed that it was. In her head she was thinking that talk did no good at all and friendship could be fickle. She'd always believed she had friends but none of them was much good to her now. Who would listen if not even Aunty and Lizzie believed her, if not even the police would do anything? Barry was the only one who understood, but he wasn't in any position to help either. Who would take his word? Somehow she had to get Trudy away from that house. It was far too near to Cleaver. A chill wind brushed the hairs at the back of her neck and, realising she must have been ignoring him, she brought her straying attention back to Adam.

'Sorry, I'm a bit distracted this evening but it's been a wonderful afternoon. Thank you for taking us. Would you like to come in for a cup of tea or coffee? I've nothing stronger, I'm afraid.' She knew that she would very much like him to come in, to have him hold her in his arms and kiss her, for him to come to her bed and make love to her. And not simply to take her mind off her troubles either.

'Sorry, best not, I've got to be up early and at the hospital first thing. Sorry,' Adam said again, shuffling his feet as if anxious to be off this very minute. 'Most girls hate my hours. It doesn't leave much time for a social life.'

Dena tried to smile. 'I'd noticed.' She could have kicked herself. What kind of remark was that? It sounded petty and sarcastic, she really hadn't meant it to be that at all. She just kept saying the wrong thing.

'I don't suppose you're on the phone?'

Dena shook her head. 'But you know where to find me.'

'I do.'

317

There followed another of those awkward moments: a vague smile, a slight movement as if he might be going to kiss her after all, and then a step back as he obviously changed his mind. He gave another mumbled apology and then Dena watched him stride away, his tousled red-brown hair a glowing halo in the lamplight. At the corner of the street he turned and waved to her, and she waved back. She let herself into her empty house and sat on the stairs in lonely silence, grieving for her child, and for a man she couldn't get to know because of this enduring pain.

—

After a largely sleepless night, Dena awoke feeling anything but refreshed. She was deeply disappointed over the on-off nature of her relationship with Adam. He might simply be shy, or over-cautious. But there were so many complications standing between them, besides the long hours he worked as a young doctor: chiefly the fact that she was more concerned with getting her daughter safely back in her own home than with finding a new boyfriend; no matter how much Miss Rogers might emphasise the need for a stepfather for Trudy.

It felt as if Cleaver had not only damaged her precious child but taken Dena's life too into his mean little hands, and crushed it. Something had to be done about him. He should be run out of town like they did with the baddies in those cowboy pictures Alan and Joey went to see on a Saturday morning at the Odeon.

Once Trudy was settled back in her own home, she and Adam could find time to get to know each other properly. Maybe then she would feel more relaxed, stop blurting out stupid remarks, and learn to flirt and smile a little. And Adam didn't seem entirely immune to her daughter's charms; they'd spent such a lovely afternoon together, until Cleaver had ruined it.

As she boiled the kettle for her morning tea and ate her cornflakes while watching the early morning mist settle over the distant canal, Dena reminded herself that at least she'd made her peace with Barry. She'd left him promising that she'd be back to see him again soon, and that next time she'd bring Trudy with her.

Inevitably he'd asked her about the appeal and Dena had spoken of her fears that Kenny would have his sentence reduced to a mere fifteen years, which wouldn't seem like justice, but of her relief that she wouldn't need to attend. 'The solicitor told me that the judges will make their decision at the appeal court in London, on the evidence already presented. So at least I'm spared having to go through all of that again,' she'd told him.

'And what about Carl, will he go?' Barry had wanted to know.

Dena had shrugged. 'I've no idea. Carl has made no contact with me in over a year. I don't even know where he's living now.'

'And if you were to see him again, how would you feel about him?'

Dena had remained silent for some moments as she'd wondered very much the same herself. Had she got over Carl or not? In the end, she'd simply shaken her head. 'I don't know, is the honest answer. Maybe. I'll never find out.'

—

Aunty Dot had been given strict instructions over what she was and was not allowed to do during the course of her recovery. There was still some soreness around the wound so lifting anything heavy was out of the question. Walking, however, was encouraged, and she could climb stairs with assistance, which was a relief since she had no wish to sleep downstairs on the sofa for all Lizzie's fussing that she should do so. She was even allowed to take a bath.

'I should think so too,' Aunty Dot had sternly told the doctor, challenging him to suggest otherwise.

She was permitted to eat whatever she liked, had been provided with medication for the pain, plus a laxative, for obvious reasons, with strict instructions to call the doctor if she had any problems in that direction. Aunty Dot had no intention of discussing her bowel movements with anyone, least of all a male doctor. She would much rather have curled up and died than do any such thing.

She'd lived with her rupture for years and although she was deeply thankful to be free from the pain and the constant ache, the nausea and the constipation, she thought it all a big fuss about nothing. She couldn't spend all her time walking the pram around the market, listening to *Housewives' Choice*, or reading her *Woman's Weekly*. She'd had her operation and Dot considered she should be getting on with life, going out and about, not living like an invalid.

The trouble was that Lizzie absolutely refused to consent to her doing the least little bit of housework. Dot mustn't so much as lift a finger: no dusting and polishing, no sweeping or washing-up, no running the Ewebank over the carpet, no climbing up ladders to clean windows, and no sweet-making.

Dot was bored out of her mind.

She wasn't permitted to do any washing as it involved bending and scrubbing, or operating the heavy rollers on the old boiler. And Lizzie had firmly banned her from changing the beds. But this morning she rebelled.

Dot decided she was fit enough now to get back to work. It must be seven weeks or more since her op. Where was the harm in stripping off the beds as she normally did every Monday, and shoving the sheets in the wash tub? Lizzie had missed doing it this week because she'd been run off her feet with the childer, as well as dashing to and from the kitchens and minding the Chocolate Cabin. The poor lass was getting well behind with the chores, not surprising as she had more than enough on her plate and was looking a bit below par herself these days. Dot hated to see the children's rooms neglected, and the washing was crying out to be done.

She filled the wash boiler with hot water then dragged herself slowly up the stairs and went to the boys' room first, carrying the dirty linen down a little at a time so there was no danger of her tripping and falling over it. She made up her mind to give the sheets a good scrub first, as she usually did before putting them to soak. So what if the possing with the dolly-stick and scrubbing on the washboard was a bit hard on her unused muscles? Do her good, Dot thought. It was long past time she started using them again and got back to normal. And she managed perfectly well on her own, feeding the heavy wet sheets through the mangle.

Lizzie was always going on at her to buy one of those new-fangled Hoover twin-tubs with a spin drier.

'And have everything come out all wrinkled? No chance,' Dot had objected. 'This boiler and mangle have worked perfectly well for years. I see no reason to change.'

It was when she was reaching up to peg the sheets out on the line that it happened. One minute she was coping nicely, anticipating the nice cup of tea and ginger biscuit she would enjoy in a minute when she'd pegged everything out; the next she was lying on the flagstones in absolute agony. Dot shouted for somebody to help her but Trudy was upstairs playing in her bedroom, and all she could hear was the baby gurgling in her pram.

–

'I think I must've done meself a mischief,' Aunty said to Lizzie when she came to visit her later in hospital. Ever one for understatement she was all trussed up and unable even to get out of bed.

'I think you have,' Lizzie agreed with a sigh. 'What am I going to do with you?'

'Hang me out on the line with them sheets?'

'They must be dry by now.'

'Well, that's something then. Save you a job.' They both chuckled.

'You realise you've set your recovery back weeks.'

'Eeh, I hope not.'

'How am I supposed to manage without you, and not even Charlie around to help?'

'Why, where's he gone?'

'Oh, everything's getting to him. He doesn't think it would be proper for him to stay at ours any more.'

Lizzie rarely saw Charlie these days. He'd called a halt to any more toffee production for the present, and gone out on the road to try and sell the stock they already had. He stubbornly refused to accept Jack Cleaver's offer of a loan, claiming he still needed time to think about it. Instead, he'd taken an evening job at the Dog and Duck, pulling pints behind the bar to earn a bit extra. Lizzie missed the happy mornings they'd spent working together in the hot kitchen, but most of all those private moments of lovemaking after the children went to bed, were a thing of the past. There were no more romantic strolls by the canal, no kisses and cuddles, or sweet dreams of a future together.

Charlie had packed his bags and moved out.

She was struggling to come to terms with the rapid changes in her life. She had a new business to cope with, owed a considerable sum of money to the bank, and Cedric Finch was still hell-bent on destroying her. Now Aunty was laid up again, and they were both terrified Miss Rogers might find out and take the children away. It seemed like the last straw.

'I'll be back home in no time,' Aunty assured her, with more optimism than genuine hope.

'Is that a threat or a promise?'

Lizzie made her way home on the bus along Piccadilly, not really taking in the familiar city scenes: people rushing around, the newly extended bus station, and the rows of parked cars lined up where large warehouses had once stood during the war, soon to be ousted from their spot by re-development. A brave new world was dawning and she and Charlie were supposed to be a part of it.

Lizzie told herself that she would have coped with her usual robust good sense had things stayed the same. Molly Poulson had offered to mind Aunty's baby now and then, but for much of the time she had to manage on her own.

Since the day Charlie had left, Lizzie felt as if she were falling through the air without even a parachute or anyone to catch her.

He claimed that their living so close in the same house was too risky, too difficult, particularly after what had happened the other week. He could no longer trust himself, he said. And he really couldn't make big decisions about their future until they were in a much stronger financial position.

'So there will be no June wedding?'

'I'm afraid not.'

To Lizzie it felt very like rejection.

The moment he'd walked out was like a kick in the stomach. All he seemed to care about these days was money. She understood that it was all tied in with guilt over his father's vicious campaign but she had no wish for Finch to rule their lives. He could have married her, instead he chose to leave. He'd deserted her, and Lizzie wasn't sure if that meant he didn't even love her any more.

Chapter Thirty-Two

A week later Aunty was still in hospital, the doctors keeping a stern eye on her this time, and Lizzie was desperately trying to find solutions to her many problems as well as coping with the practicalities of life. She'd asked all around the market and, apart from Amy George who was willing to do the odd extra hour on the stall, she was largely dependent upon her own resources.

Surely there must be someone to help her, if only by minding the children for an hour or two each day? They must be got ready for school every morning and provided with breakfast, met at the school gates on the dot of four o'clock and taken straight home for tea. And throughout the day she must keep the baby and Trudy with her, as they didn't yet go to school.

Later Lizzie would make their supper, supervise their bathtime, feed and change the baby, put them all to bed and read them a story. Even then there were still all the household chores, once the children were settled for the night.

Gone were the fun times spent chocolate-making. She hardly had the energy to blink, let alone make sweets.

Nevertheless, the stall must remain open for business, orders needed to be checked and work done at the kitchens because not for a moment dare she contemplate taking time off, as she still needed to earn her living.

Lizzie supposed she should be grateful that Charlie was still prepared to go out on the road and try to get orders. He dealt with all the correspondence, paid the bills and such like, and would leave a note for her at the kitchens telling her what needed packing up ready for dispatch the next day. Sometimes she could tell that he'd been in and made more toffee, often in the middle of the night. He said it was the only free time he had available but Lizzie became convinced he did the work so he could avoid seeing her.

Dena too was a worry. She was in and out of number thirty-seven all the time, always willing to mind Trudy, but fretting about her own unresolved future. Neither young woman dare mention Aunty's accident to Miss Rogers, in case the social worker should take Trudy or the other children away. Were the children to be re-homed, they might not be allowed to come back. Apart from any other consideration, Aunty would never forgive them if they allowed that to happen.

'She'll be home soon,' Lizzie kept saying, trying to convince herself as much as anyone.

She welcomed Dena's support, but she too had a business to run and problems of her own to deal with. Even so, Lizzie dare not risk allowing Dena to break Miss Roger's very strict rules, much as she might long to let Trudy go straight home, as that would be one less child to worry about. Nor did Lizzie dare tell Dena that Jack Cleaver had several times collected the children from school and nursery, since Aunty's fall. He'd stay for a while and make them their after-school treat, although she made sure Trudy was never alone with him. It was understandable that Dena trusted no one with her child after what happened, but how would she have managed without his help?

One evening Lizzie was in Aunty's kitchen preparing meals for the next day, as she did every evening, despite the heat of a soft June evening. All the children were in bed, save for Joey who was allowed a further half hour to play in the street with his mates.

Lizzie was trying not to think that if things had gone right for them she'd have been Charlie's wife by now, that she could have been a June bride, this being the month they'd intended to marry. She heard a rat-a-tat on the door knocker. As always her heart gave a hopeful lurch at the sound, even though she knew it wouldn't be Charlie. He never called to see her of an evening, not any more. Lizzie wiped her hands on a cloth and went to answer it, only to stare in disbelief at her visitor, utterly lost for words.

'Evelyn?'

Charlie's mother smiled. 'I thought we agreed you were to call me Evie? But never mind about that. I know it's taken me a long time to call on you, Lizzie, but I've only just heard about your aunt's accident. At least I'm here now. I'm so sorry she's ill again. I think my son is a fool and my husband is mad. I want to help. I do hope you'll let me?'

It was a day or two later on her afternoon off that Dena told Lizzie about her visit to Barry. Her friend seemed somewhat startled by the news. 'Goodness, I thought you'd sworn never to speak to him again, let alone cross his threshold.'

'Haven't you been listening to a word I've been saying lately? Barry is innocent, as maligned as I was myself in this whole messy business. He isn't the guilty party.'

'Then who is?' Lizzie frowned at the expression of impatience on Dena's face, and then gave a small grunt of disbelief. 'Don't tell me you're still nursing a grudge over that silly reaction Trudy had to Jack? Honestly, that's ridiculous. I thought we'd agreed that she was just reacting to a strange man in the house, and having a bit of a temper tantrum? That was perfectly clear to me.'

Lizzie trusted Jack Cleaver completely, and she believed Charlie did too in his own cautious way, for all he still hadn't yet agreed to accept his offer of a loan. Lizzie knew that he held back only out of a sense of pride and a strong streak of independence. Every day Jack called at the Chocolate Cabin and offered to deposit that much-needed money into their business account. He was already successfully steering more customers in their direction. Lizzie lived in hope that soon their efforts would be successful and Pringle's Sweets would take off, which might well be thanks to Jack Cleaver's assistance. She had no reason not to believe in him.

Dena said, 'Well, it wasn't clear from where I was standing.'

'Jack is a quiet, respectable man. A bit of a loner, likes to keep himself to himself, but to be perfectly honest I'd never have got through this last week without him, not with Aunty back in hospital. Thank goodness Charlie's mother has turned up trumps, taking the baby off my hands, at least. Which reminds me we ought to get going or we'll be late for afternoon visiting and Sister will do her nut.' She reached for her coat, urging Dena to do the same.

Dena tied on her headscarf and patiently waited for Trudy to fasten the buttons on her coat by herself, as she always insisted on doing. 'Don't you remember how eager Cleaver was to get Beth inside his house that time?'

Lizzie collected her bag and house keys and began to walk away. She really didn't have time for all of this right now. Amy George was minding the cabin, and the other children wouldn't be back from school until four. This was her best chance in a busy day to visit Aunty. 'I'm not listening to any more of this. Are you coming or not?'

'Yes, I'm coming,' Dena agreed, gathering a protesting Trudy by the hand and running after her friend. 'But promise me that you won't take any chances? You won't allow the children to go anywhere near Jack Cleaver.'

Lizzie stopped dead in the street, looking shocked. 'I won't promise any such thing. Anyway, what is all this nonsense about? You were going to marry the bloke, last I heard.'

'Well, I'm having second thoughts about that. Wouldn't you if you suspected he'd damaged a child of yours?'

'You've absolutely no proof. This is all some fiction you've made up in your head. Why? That's what I want to know.' And then Lizzie's face cleared.

'Ah, you've fallen for this doctor, and you haven't told Jack that you're two-timing him.'

'I'm not two-timing him. How can I be when I don't even care for Cleaver, never wanted to go through with this crazy marriage idea.'

'Well, if you've changed your mind, Dena, don't you think you should at least have the courtesy to inform him? Jack was telling me only yesterday that he was thinking of taking you to Bournemouth for your honeymoon.'

Dena looked momentarily stunned. 'You're absolutely right, I should tell him. And why not now? No time like the present. Let's see if he's in.' Paying no heed to Lizzie's cry of protest, she thrust Trudy into her friend's arms and marched up the street. Lizzie scurried after her.

'You can't mean this... think what you're doing. This could be Trudy's future you're throwing away. Think, Dena, think!'

'I *am* thinking. I'm thinking that I'll never put my child at risk ever again.'

Dena marched up to Jack Cleaver's door and hammered on the knocker. It was opened almost immediately and he beamed down at her, a smile of delight on his rotund face. 'Dena, how nice to see you. Oh, and Trudy too, a family visit. Lovely! Come in, I was just writing up my orders, but I'll put the kettle on, and I'm sure I can find some sweeties for Trudy.'

They both knew that Dena had never so much as set foot in his house before. Nor had she any intention of doing so today.

'I don't think so. What I have to say won't take long. I'm sorry, Jack, but it's all off between us, this crazy idea of yours that we marry. I've decided I can't go through with it. I'm sorry, but you aren't my type. I don't marry child molesters or offer them free access to my daughter any time they choose.'

She was half aware of the colour draining from his face at these words, and of Lizzie's gasp. Her friend stood only a few paces behind, holding Trudy in her arms, her daughter's face buried in her neck while Lizzie desperately tried to cover the little girl's ears. Dena didn't pause, even to draw breath, her voice filled with an icy fury.

'Oh, I know I'm the only one who's rumbled you, so far, and I can't prove it, much as I would like to. But you and me are finished. If you come within half a mile of our Trudy, or any of the other children for that matter, you'll be mincemeat. Understand? Is that clear enough for you?'

It was Lizzie who answered as she rushed up to Dena, white-faced, and shook her by the arm. 'Stop it, Dena, that was unforgivable. I can't think what's come over you. You have absolutely no right to make decisions about who the children will or will not see. That's for Aunty to decide, or myself in her absence. I'll thank you to mind your own business. I'm so sorry, Jack, she's in a bit of a turmoil over this coming appeal and…'

Dena turned to look at her friend, a mixture of anger and deep sadness in her face. 'That's enough, Lizzie. All I can say is – on your head be it.' And taking Trudy into her own arms, she marched off down the street. 'Come on,' she called back over her shoulder. 'Let's go and see how Aunty is, shall we? There's nothing more to be said on this matter.' Only then did she realise she was shaking, and that Jack Cleaver hadn't spoken a word, not even to deny the accusation.

-

Dena had arranged to meet Miss Rogers at her home. The Bush television set sat silent on a table in the corner, the fire brasses had been cleaned till they shone, and as always the second-hand gate-legged table was polished to a fine gloss. Dena intended to give a good impression. The social worker sat with her feet on Dena's homemade clippy rug, sipping tea from her best cup and saucer, patiently waiting to hear whatever she had to say.

Dena didn't keep her waiting long. 'I thought it was time you and me had a little chat – a civilised conversation – woman to woman.'

Miss Rogers cast her a sharp look, oddly defensive. 'About what exactly?'

'I'm told Ivy Bank has closed down, thank goodness. Trudy has been with Aunty Dot almost two months. I've been a regular visitor, listened and learned from her. I always felt I was a good mother anyway, but Aunty is a good teacher.'

The social worker put down her cup and saucer as if about to interrupt but Dena silenced her with the flick of a hand.

'No, let me finish. We both know why Trudy was taken into care. They blamed me for what happened to her because I'm an unmarried mother. The fact I consider that to be unfair and unjust I'm willing to set to one side. I've made my feelings on the matter perfectly plain, so I don't need to repeat them. Now, however, I feel it's time you too put the past aside, and let Trudy come home.'

'But you still aren't married, Dena. You still aren't respectable.'

Dena put her hands to her head and gave it a little shake of despair. 'You see, what I don't understand is how getting married will make me respectable, any more than I am already. I have a nice little home here, as you can see. I earn a fair living on my dressmaking stall, humble though it might be. I have good friends, including Barry Holmes who has been as ill-used by the system as Trudy and myself. He is innocent, I'm convinced of it. Trudy still loves him and is desperate to see him again.'

Miss Rogers frowned, then stuffily remarked. 'Since the man was acquitted, I dare say there's no reason why she shouldn't.'

Dena went on. 'I don't drink or smoke, gamble or fritter my money away on daft rubbish. I don't bring men home or sleep around.'

'Goodness, I never suggested that you did.'

'That's exactly what you're accusing me of. I made a foolish mistake when I was unhappy, a rebellious sixteen-year-old, then fell in love with the wrong man, apparently. But you *did* suggest that I should marry a perfect stranger, a man I don't even like, let alone love, so that my child can no longer be called by that word. People like you have attached yourself to her illegitimacy.

330

I know there are worse words but I won't have them spoken out loud, not in my house. Yet being illegitimate isn't a crime. My daughter is the innocent one in all of this. I accept that if there is guilt, it is mine. But I don't – won't – *ever* regret having her. She's my lovely girl and I want her home with me as I'm her mum. I love Trudy more than anything in the whole world, and she needs to be with *me*, not some foster mother. Aunty Dot would be the first to say so.'

Miss Rogers looked as if she was struggling to find the right words, a way out of a tricky situation. 'Well, I never *personally* considered being illegitimate a crime, or you to be wanton. I said *society* took a dim view of—'

'Oh, and one more thing,' Dena put in, having little patience with the social worker's excuses and no wish to become embroiled in yet another argument. 'I've told that pervert Jack Cleaver there'll be no wedding bells for us. I'm not giving him free access to my child, to any child if I had my way.

'It's true that I do have a boyfriend, sort of. He's a highly respected young man, and who knows, maybe it will turn out to be serious, maybe it won't. But I'm not, in fact, ready to marry anyone right now. Being a mother is a very important job and I intend to give it my full attention and do it right. I don't intend to rush headlong into a loveless marriage just for the sake of *society*. So how about it, Miss Rogers? Can Trudy come home where she rightly belongs? Do you trust me to care for my own child properly?'

The social worker, cheeks flushed and breathing hard, agreed that she probably did, that Dena had fulfilled all the *essential* requirements to prove herself a fit mother. The necessary forms would be filled in to allow Trudy to come home.

'When, tomorrow?'

'By the end of the week at the latest.'

'That's a promise I shall hold you to.'

'It will be kept.'

Whereupon, Dena embarrassed the other woman by kissing her flushed cheek yet again.

It was Winnie who brought her the news. 'Belle Garside would like you to pop over to the café when you've got five minutes.'

'What is it this time?' Dena wearily asked.

'They've heard the result of the appeal. Carl attended, apparently, and they want to tell you in person.'

Dena felt as if her insides had turned to water. Kenny had been charged with murder, but the death sentence commuted to life imprisonment. Reducing that still further to a charge of manslaughter with little more than fifteen years spent behind bars would not seem like justice at all, not in Dena's eyes. But whatever the verdict, she must somehow learn to face it. And face Carl too, it seemed, at last.

'Thanks, I'd best go right away, eh?'

Winnie squeezed her arm. 'I'll keep an eye on the stall, and be here for you when you get back.'

Dena hugged her. 'My dearest friend, as always.'

-

Carl was indeed there, sitting with his arm about his mother on the sofa in the small living room behind the café that smelled of stale perfume and bacon fry-ups. He got up when Dena came in and stepped towards her. Ignoring him completely, Dena saw at once that Belle had been weeping as streaks of mascara ran down her face. Her lips were pale, washed clean of the brash scarlet lipstick she usually wore.

'It's come then, the verdict?'

Belle looked up at her out of eyes filled with hatred. A sense of huge relief washed over Dena as she realised she didn't need to be told the result, it was written plainly on the other woman's haggard face.

'I hope you're satisfied,' Belle hissed. 'My boy, my lovely boy, is condemned to spend his entire life behind bars because of that poxy brother of yours!'

Dena bit her lip. A part of her still felt sorry for Belle as they'd always rubbed along fairly well. Belle had never been one to make quick judgements about people, and there had been a time when they'd been friendly. Apparently not any longer!

'I'm sorry, but Kenny is only getting what he deserves. He bullied and killed our Pete, and there's an end to it. I expect he won't actually serve life. They'll give him parole in – what – twenty years, twenty-five? Whatever they do to Kenny won't bring my Pete back, will it? He's the real victim here, don't forget.'

Carl at last spoke up. 'You may be right, Dena, but Ma was hoping for the best. You can't blame her for that.'

'It's too late for blame,' Dena said. 'It's long past time we put this tragedy behind us. Kenny must serve his time and we have to get on with our own lives.'

'It's all right for you to talk,' screamed Belle. 'You haven't just lost a son.'

'No, I lost a brother, before ever he had a chance to start his life.'

Carl lifted both hands, as if afraid the two women might fly at each other. His mother was capable of it, even if fisticuffs weren't Dena's style. 'Dena has a point, Ma. It's time to put an end to this matter. We aren't going to agree so let's leave it, shall we?'

Belle flung herself out of the room muttering a string of furious curses.

As silence returned, Carl gave a half-hearted smile. 'She'll come round. She'll put on a brave face with her brightest lipstick and visit Kenny every month for the rest of her life.'

Dena looked at him, not answering. She'd forgotten how good-looking he was in a rugged sort of way, disturbingly so. A real man with a strong square face, heavy eyebrows and a broad jaw, olive skin and black, curly hair. She'd loved to run her fingers through it once, to kiss the curve of that insolent mouth. And the merest glance from those dark blue eyes used to send a shiver of desire to the core of her being.

Not any more. Dena found that she could look upon Carl dispassionately. She felt no urge to fling herself into his arms, to be touched or caressed by him as she'd so ached for in the long months after he'd gone. Something had changed in her. The love she'd felt for him had died from neglect, or because she was more interested in a red-headed young doctor.

Life was all about change, and Dena knew that she'd grown up a good deal in the last twelve months following the terrible thing that had happened to her daughter. And she would never be the same again, as a result. She always had been fiercely stubborn and independent, had refined those skills as a young girl, but now she had gained maturity too. She'd forever been troubled by a sense of insecurity. Not any longer. Dena knew she could cope, on her own if necessary, and would do so because her daughter depended upon her.

Carl was studying her every bit as keenly, a slight pucker marking his brow. Then, as if reading her thoughts he asked, 'What about you? I must say you look lovely, Dena. You've grown your hair longer. It suits you. What have you been up to since I last saw you?'

Dena unconsciously lifted her chin. 'I'm very well, thank you. I've had a few problems, as I expect you've heard, but everything is sorted now. I'm good at looking after myself, as you know.'

He gave a half smile. 'You missed me though, right? And I expect you're glad to see me back. I've missed you. Maybe we could get together later, talk some more?'

Dena stiffened. 'Have we anything to talk about?'

Carl raised his dark eyebrows in surprise. 'Well, I've had a pretty tough time of it too, in a way. You might want to hear about that. I gave you the space you asked for, but I'm glad to be home. I always planned to return, after the appeal. We agreed about that, didn't we?'

'I don't remember us agreeing anything. We quarrelled all the time, and I seem to recall that when I asked for time to

334

think and recover after the trial, you weren't keen to give it and went off in some sort of a huff. You left without even saying goodbye.'

'Aye, well, maybe I was a bit hasty, but surely you've had plenty of time to think by now.'

'Oh, yes, indeed, more than enough time! And do you know what I've decided? That I really don't need anyone in my life right now. I'm only twenty years old, with all my life before me. Maybe I'll find Mr Right. Maybe I've found him already. Maybe I never will find him. Who knows? But one thing is certain, he's not you.'

Carl's smile of confidence was quickly fading, replaced by a frown of concern. 'What are you saying?'

'I'm saying that you're someone from my past, a person I was once fond of but who let me down. You weren't there when I needed you. You went away, never told me why, or where you were. Never wrote. Nothing!' She walked to the door. 'So let's leave it at that, shall we? No recriminations, no hard feelings. It just didn't work out, right?'

'You aren't leaving me again?'

'*You* left *me*, Carl, if you remember. Now I'm telling you that I don't want you back.'

Chapter Thirty-Three

When Jack Cleaver called in at Pringle's rented kitchen Lizzie and Charlie were making lemon drops. Seven pounds of crushed sugar had been dissolved in a quart of water and allowed to boil, the glucose had been added and the boil continued until the temperature had reached 320 degrees. Now Charlie had it on the oiled slab where he'd already cut it into two portions. The smell of lemon and boiled sugar was almost overpowering in the small room, deliciously sharp and sweet.

'Most impressive that you do all this by yourself,' Jack said. 'I tell all my customers that yours is a very different sort of operation from Finch's.'

'Small and amateur, you mean?' said Lizzie.

'Not at all! There's nothing wrong with handmade sweets and chocolates. Much the best, in my opinion, but hopefully you'll be able to afford some staff to help you soon.'

'Huh, I'm not sure when that will be,' Charlie muttered, as he added yellow colouring to one half of the mixture, and to the other a touch of blue. Then he began to pull this latter portion over the twin hooks on the machine.

Watching him with feigned interest, Jack said, 'Thanks for your support the other day, Lizzie, when Dena was sounding off.'

'You mustn't take what she said to heart,' Lizzie assured him. 'She isn't thinking clearly right now.'

'Oh, I understand she's in something of a state over the appeal. Must have put a strain on her. I shan't give it another thought.' In reality Jack had been deeply unsettled by the attack, and alarmed by her accusations. It had made him feel that time was running out for him. He had to finish the job in hand, and get out of this street while he still could. 'Actually, I've popped in today to give you a warning.'

Charlie hadn't been paying much attention to their conversation. Now he glanced up from the pulling machine where the blue toffee was turning pure white, and frowned. 'What sort of warning?'

'Your father plans to open more stalls, exactly the same as the one he's started here on Champion Street, but on other markets. Namely, Blackburn, Bolton, Burnley and Liverpool to begin with, but ultimately the whole of the northwest, which will exclusively sell Finch's sweets. His intention is not only to do you out of business here on Champion Street, but to buy up or ruin all your likely wholesale customers too.'

There was a silence as Lizzie and Charlie attempted to absorb this new blow.

'He can't do that,' Lizzie said, once she could find her voice.

'Even my father doesn't have sufficient funds for such an undertaking,' Charlie scoffed. 'I don't believe a word of it.'

'He can and he does. He has the backing of the bank.' Cleaver made every effort to pitch just the right amount of confidence into his voice to disguise the lie. Finch had instructed him to say all of this on the grounds that even if he didn't entirely succeed, it might worry them sufficiently to make the young couple reckless and over-reach themselves. 'So if you're to beat him, you'll have to take him on at his own game. You'll have to expand quickly and open more stalls of your own before he gets there.'

'How can we?' Lizzie lifted her hands and let them fall in a gesture of despair. 'He's the one with the financial clout, not us.'

'In any case, expanding too quickly is dangerous,' Charlie put in. 'We'd be stretched too thin and then he could easily move in and wipe us off the face of the earth.'

Jack's expression became thoughtful. 'I was thinking about that loan I've offered to make you, and I've had an idea. It doesn't have to be a loan at all. It could be a straight investment in your company – if I were a partner too, that is. Then you wouldn't ever have to pay me back. A partnership would cost a bit more, I realise that, but I'm a man with money to invest, as well as experience in the confectionery business. We could make a good team.'

Charlie was looking thoughtful while Lizzie just stared at him, startled by this suggestion and more than a little wary of it. Did she want Jack Cleaver as a partner? Wouldn't it be better if it was just herself and Charlie? But then she thought of the bank overdraft weighing them down. She considered the dire lack of trade as Finch played every trick in the book to damage them; some so underhand he really ought to be reported. And she would have reported him, to the market committee at least, were it not for the fact that he was not only Charlie's father, but any complaint might only serve to make him even more vicious.

Finch was maligning their good name and undercutting them on price, doing everything he could to put people off buying from them, even down to sabotaging their deliveries.

'Maybe it's the answer,' she half whispered to Charlie. 'Remember the other day when an entire order went missing? One minute it was sitting on the table waiting for Spider to pick up and deliver to a market in Stockport, the next it had gone. Vanished off the face of the earth. I'm sure that your father employs some of his men to snoop around and watch for any opportunity to damage our trade, on this occasion by stealing boxes of sweets from right under our noses. Maybe we'll never be free from the fear of his ruining us if we *don't* do as Jack suggests.'

Charlie turned on her, his face tight with temper. 'You think I like it that it's my father who is doing all this to us? You imagine that I want to keep borrowing money and getting deeper into a mire of debt?'

Lizzie was startled by his sudden spurt of anger, clearly borne out of frustration. 'Neither of us imagined it would get this bad or that he'd use such underhand tactics. That's why I think Jack's offer is worth considering.'

'You believe that I'm hopeless and can't control my own parent?'

'No, because Cedric Finch is uncontrollable and we need to be as big as he is to beat him.'

Jack Cleaver gave a polite little cough. 'Have you spoken to your father about this vendetta he's conducting?'

'I have not.'

'I wonder if you should,' Jack suggested artlessly, as if the idea had only just occurred to him. 'Why not go and have it out with him? Tackle him on the subject, man to man.'

Charlie stared at him for a second, then began to pull off his protective gloves and went to the sink to wash his hands. 'You're right, I'll go this very minute and ask him to his face what the hell he thinks he's playing at.'

'No, don't rise to his bait,' Lizzie cried, running to stop him. 'Anyway, what about the toffee? You can't leave it like this, it'll go all hard and unworkable.'

Charlie glared at the heap of toffee mixture as if he'd forgotten its very existence. 'I'll finish that first, but I *am* going to see him. I refuse to be bullied any more. I've had enough.' He looked across at Cleaver. 'And once I've spoken to him, tried one last time to bring my father to reason, then I'll consider your offer.'

Jack nodded. 'Fine. I'd best be off. I've work of my own to do.' Lizzie had been afraid even to speak to him, as he looked as if his temper might erupt at any moment.

After he'd gone, Charlie continued working in tight-lipped silence. He added a touch more lemon flavouring, then pounded one half of the toffee on top of the other with more than his usual force, before pulling the whole thing into one long, twisted, yellow and white rope. He expertly cut it into toffee-sized pieces by passing it through the large rollers. Then Charlie took off his apron, tossed it aside, and reached for his coat. 'Right, that's it. I'm going to settle this matter once and for all.'

'Please don't! You'll only end up rowing with him. Please don't go.' Lizzie went to put her arms around Charlie. 'Why don't we stop worrying about Cedric Finch and just concentrate on our own lives? It doesn't matter about the business, not in the slightest. We could nip to the register office, get married and...'

'...live happily ever after? With all these debts hanging around our necks and the business dying on its feet? You must be joking! You can put that idea right out of your mind. My father has a stranglehold on us, and it's going to get worse if I don't put a stop to it, here and now.' And he stormed out of the room leaving Lizzie in tears. It was their first real quarrel.

–

Lizzie was deeply upset. It hurt her badly that Charlie should suddenly become so obsessed with money. Although she realised he did still love her, this so-called vendetta of his father's was spoiling everything between them, could kill the relationship in the end, if it wasn't stopped. It was all Cedric Finch's fault for making him feel inadequate throughout his young life.

No, it was *her* fault. She had been the one who'd stubbornly wanted Aunty to help them make *more* sweets, not stop altogether as Finch had insisted. Now look what had happened: Aunty was back in hospital because she didn't dare take the proper time off to rest, and Charlie was about to fall into a fight with his own father. All *her* fault! Oh, what on earth had possessed her to set herself up in competition to the man? She must have been mad.

Lizzie put her head in her hands and wept.

Jack was at Lizzie's side in seconds, barely making a sound.

Startled by his sudden presence, Lizzie quickly dashed away her tears. 'My goodness, Jack, you do have a knack of making me jump.'

'Has he gone?' Cleaver knew very well that Charlie had left, because he'd hung around outside long enough to check. Now he looked at her more keenly. 'Hey, have you been crying? He didn't hurt you, did he?'

Lizzie looked up at him, all swimmy-eyed. 'No, I just can't cope. I'll never get through this lot on my own. And I'm due back on the stall by two.'

'Let me help,' Jack offered with a simpering smile, privately delighted by this unexpected show of weakness on Lizzie's part. He was thanking his lucky stars that the scheme was progressing even better than he'd hoped. He'd riled young Charlie good and proper and persuaded him to go and see his father, as instructed. Now he could turn his attention to Lizzie for the final task, not too difficult to accomplish as he'd gradually been winning over her trust these last weeks.

This particular mission was fortunately progressing well, but Finch was growing increasingly impatient with Jack's lack of progress in other directions. He still hadn't got his hands on any of them kiddies, never mind the wily Joey. But they weren't his main priority today, and this particular plan to compromise Lizzie seemed to be on track. It all depended upon timing, which would ultimately scupper the young love-birds' dreams for good.

'Oh, thank you, Jack, I'd be most grateful for your help,' Lizzie was saying as she went to wash her hands and face in the sink. 'We have a part-time girl but she isn't in today. We do appreciate the warning about what Finch is up to, even if your news did upset us.' She dabbed herself dry with a clean towel, then managed a brave smile. 'I'm sure Charlie will consider your offer more seriously once he's spoken to his father one last time. He just longs to make things right between them.'

'I know, don't worry, I'm only too happy to help.'

He was so wonderfully sympathetic, so understanding that as they steadily wrapped sweets together they began to talk. Jack asked her questions about her childhood, the years she'd spent with the Sisters of Mercy. They'd talked a little about this before, but today Lizzie's misery was such that she was unable to prevent herself from letting it all pour out.

She confessed the truth about her mother, not realising that he already knew it, that she'd let fall sufficient information in the past for him to make a few enquiries and come up with the full story. Nor did she realise that it had been Cleaver himself who had passed this information on to Finch. Lizzie explained, shame-faced, how Charlie's father had sworn he would never allow any son of his to marry the daughter of a prostitute.

'She's always been a blight on my life, and now more than ever.' Lizzie was sniffing into her handkerchief, then having to wash her hands all over again. She sat down on a stool, suddenly bone-weary, and found herself weeping again. 'Oh, it's so awful! No wonder Charlie's family is against me, though at least Evelyn is more friendly now. She's secretly minding the baby while Aunty's in hospital, just while I'm at work.'

Jack went over to pat her awkwardly on the shoulder. 'Don't rely upon her too much. Evelyn is very much under her husband's thumb. Absolutely hopeless.' He loved the softness of this girl, her vulnerability. Lizzie wasn't usually a needy person so it excited him all the more when she succumbed to her emotions. His mind raced, anxiously wondering if the moment to take advantage of that weakness had finally come. 'Why do you need Finch's approval anyway? If Charlie really loved you, he'd marry you tomorrow, no matter what his family thinks of you.'

'He *does* love me. I know he does. It's just that there's been no time to think about our personal happiness, not when his father's been hell-bent on destroying us, as you said yourself. It's not Charlie's fault that all this nastiness has come between us and spoiled our happiness. It's just circumstance. And he's so worried about these debts we have. You can understand that.'

Jack nodded, his eyes soft with manufactured sympathy even as his mind calculated how best to bring her down. He felt no regret over doing this, as Finch wasn't a man to cross. Either he destroyed Lizzie or he himself was done for. Besides, she'd let him down, hadn't she, in the past? Led him to think something might be growing between them and all the time she was falling for Charlie Finch. She'd betrayed him, just as Dena had. Jack Cleaver had no time for women, none at all. He was finished with all of that nonsense, forever.

'Oh, Jack, the truth is, if I'd realised half the problems Cedric Finch would cause, that my fight for independence would come between Charlie and me and spoil our plans to marry, then I never would have embarked upon this business in the first place. What good will it do me if I lose Charlie's love? And what good will it do for Charlie to fall out with his father?'

Jack cleared his throat, as he always did to soften unpleasant words. 'Have you thought,' he cautiously remarked, 'that you might be looking in the wrong direction for a solution? Instead of battling with Finch, it's happen your mother you should be talking to. From what you've just told me this conflict seems to have precious little to do with business and everything to do with her chosen profession. Why don't you go and see her, explain the problem, and see if you can talk her into leaving the area?'

Lizzie was looking at him with new hope in her eyes. 'Oh, do you think she might?'

'If you ask her personally, she might very well. You're still her daughter, after all. Wouldn't she want you to be happy?'

Jack was feeling remarkably pleased with himself. The difficult part, as Finch had conceded, would be to entice Lizzie into the vicinity of her notorious mother and her house of ill repute. The rest would be relatively easy. Nothing need actually happen to her there, Jack told himself, salving his conscience slightly. He must simply ensure that Charlie *believed* something unsavoury had taken place, and was made aware of Lizzie's visit.

Timing was everything though, a real worry. He may well have to improvise and do something further to push things along, and he wasn't good at making snap decisions.

Lizzie was thinking that if she could only persuade Maureen to leave the Castlefield area altogether and ply her nasty trade elsewhere, then there would be no risk of her bringing shame upon them all. Finch could then raise no further objections to their marriage and this campaign he was waging against them would no longer be necessary. Jack was right, speaking to her mother was indeed a possible solution to the whole problem.

While Charlie tried to reason with his father, she would talk to Maureen. It was long past time that she did.

Chapter Thirty-Four

'Larkspur, I'd say, will suit you nicely, Lizzie love, seeing as how you're so tall and slender. They're blue to match your eyes, and meant for lightness and levity. Whenever I see you serving those delicious chocolates from your cabin, you always look so happy and full of life. A real ray of sunshine.'

Betty Hemley, who ran the flower stall, was forever trying to match her flowers to a person's character or mood, generally with remarkable accuracy. Today, however, she was way off course. Lizzie had never felt less happy in all her life.

On impulse as she'd walked through the market she'd taken it into her head to buy Maureen some flowers, to soften what could be a difficult meeting. Wasn't that what daughters did, take flowers to their mother? But was it the right thing to do for a mother she hated?

Not for the world did Lizzie intend to reveal the purpose of her purchase to Betty Hemley, inquisitive though the woman undoubtedly was. She was already bitterly regretting the moment of weakness that had led to her confession to Jack Cleaver, though surely she could trust him since he was so keen to come into the business with them?

Lizzie managed to answer Betty by saying that she loved making sweets and chocolates, so why shouldn't she be happy? She did, however, let slip a small hint about the current problems in her life. 'I have to say, Betty, appearances are not always what they seem.'

'Don't tell me you're another suffering from problems of the heart? I've enough of those with our Lynda. Are you married, chuck?'

Lizzie shook her head. 'Nope, single but not entirely fancy-free, I live in hope.'

Betty began to sort through her flowers to choose exactly the right ones to go with the larkspur. Something for grace and beauty she claimed Lizzie had in plenty. 'Or red roses for love?'

Lizzie picked up the bunch of flowers and escaped, her own nervous laughter echoing eerily around the market as she walked away, thinking she might come to regret this visit.

—

The meeting with his father was not going well. Finch laughed at Charlie and mocked him, or refused to listen to a word he said. Evelyn, as usual, kept well out of it.

She was pleased enough to see her son, who hadn't been near the house in weeks. She hugged him and brought tea and biscuits, then vanished to some distant corner of the house to play with the baby, who was utterly delightful. Evelyn was beginning to think there might be some real advantages to Charlie and Lizzie getting married, if it resulted in one or two grandchildren as pretty as this little one. She picked the other children up from school at four but apparently she wasn't needed today, according to Jack Cleaver. She was disappointed about that.

Evelyn took the baby out into the garden. Meanwhile the two men in her life continued to argue, very nearly coming to blows.

Charlie was saying, 'My entire life has been blighted by your constant carping and criticism. What is the problem now, exactly? Have you got some rich heiress tucked away that you planned for me to marry or something?'

'Don't talk daft.'

'You're the one who's talking daft and making so much fuss. It's not as if there's anything wrong with Lizzie, she's lovely, as you know she is. What does it matter who her mother is? Lizzie isn't responsible for whatever life she chose. Anyway, *I love her*. If you were a proper father that would be enough for you.'

'This isn't just about your stupid notion to marry the girl, it's a question of business,' Finch roared. 'If it ever got out who her blasted mother was, I'd be ruined.'

'Rubbish, Lizzie is a thorn in your side, a woman with a mind of her own. She's independent and won't do as you tell her, any more than I will. You always have to be in control, don't you? You're angry because you can't control me, never have been able to. But this can't simply be about profit, surely? You don't need the money, don't need to take any more risks with your business. Finch's Sweets is well established and you and Ma are nicely placed, so why not leave room for someone else to have a turn?'

'You don't know everything,' his father growled.

'So tell me. Explain!'

Cedric had no intention of explaining anything, although the row continued for the better part of an hour. Several times Charlie nearly walked out but his father always prevented him from leaving, blocking the door or snatching at the sleeve of his jacket, even pinning him against the wall on one occasion.

At length, Finch completely lost control and bellowed at his son: 'She's a *tart*, a *whore*, that's what she is! Once a prossy, always a prossy, just like her flaming mother.'

Charlie shouted right back. '*She never was a prossy!* Lizzie is innocent.'

'Don't make me laugh! That lass doesn't know the meaning of the word. She's canny and clever and does exactly as she pleases. Don't for one minute imagine she's honest and faithful, because she damn well isn't! She's over twenty-one, past her prime and desperate for a fella. She was ready and eager to marry that Jack Cleaver before you came along, ugly though he may be, and the pair of them still have a lingering fondness for each other.'

'Don't talk daft!'

'I don't, I talk sense. Cleaver is never out of number thirty-seven. Haven't you noticed? You aren't always there, so how would you know?'

'Jack comes to babysit, to help out if Aunty Dot is ill and to get to know little Trudy.' But Charlie was remembering how Lizzie always took Jack's side in any dispute, both with him and with Dena the other day. The two women had hardly exchanged a civil word since. Lizzie had actually fallen out with her best friend over the man. He also recalled how *she'd* been the one who was keen to accept the loan, and make Jack a partner.

His father was sounding dismissive. 'Believe me, that's a cover-up. It's Lizzie he's interested in, not some unmarried mother with a poxy kid. I'd watch that Lizzie Pringle, if I were you. She's a whore like her mother and playing you false.'

And this time Charlie did leave. He stormed out of the house, leaving the door swinging open in the cold breeze, and his mother crying in the garden as she rocked the pram and saw all her hopes for a family reconciliation finally dashed.

–

The moment the door was opened a foul odour of urine and stale sweat, badly disguised by a sickly, sweet perfume, washed over Lizzie. She almost gagged as the smell struck her.

The woman who stood staring at her looked younger than she'd expected, with a good figure, fashionably dressed in a knee-length black pencil skirt and a shocking pink blouse that clashed with her Titian red hair. One or two buttons were missing and the blouse strained over breasts hoisted high in a black bra that showed through the thin fabric. Yet as Lizzie considered her more closely she saw deeply etched lines at the corners of the blue-grey eyes and discontented mouth; a well-worn look about the once-pretty face that failed to be disguised by the make-up she'd plastered on.

'By heck, would you look at what the wind has blown in. Are them for me?' Maureen was staring at the flowers in derision. 'I'm touched.'

Lizzie wondered what on earth had possessed her to buy them. 'I'd like to talk, if that's all right?'

'Is there anything left worth saying? I mean, I'd ask you in only it's the maid's day off and me best lace tablecloth is at the cleaners.'

'Stop it!' Lizzie said. 'I'm not enjoying this any more than you, but I need to talk to you about something important. I have a problem you might be able to solve.'

The older woman gave a cackle of laughter. 'Don't tell me you're up the duff?'

'No! It's nothing of that sort,' Lizzie retorted, furious with herself for having bothered to come. 'Obviously this was a dreadful mistake. Forget it!' She turned to go but Maureen stepped out into the street and caught at her arm.

'Don't rush off. I'm curious to know what's fetched you to my door after all this time of ignoring your old mam's existence.' She glanced around at the twitching curtains. 'You'd best come in afore half the street gets an earful of our business.'

-

Charlie was feeling deeply guilty about his quarrel with Lizzie. He really shouldn't have lost his temper like that. It wasn't Lizzie's fault that his father was creating these problems for them. Taking it out on her was unfair. His efforts at reconciliation had been a complete waste of time, his arrogant parent as foul-mouthed and unfeeling as ever. The stupid man didn't care about anyone but himself. Charlie no longer considered that he had a father. If the man was determined to be so vile to the girl he loved and wished to marry, then there was no possibility of any agreement between them, either now or in the future.

But Charlie saw that he was in dire danger of losing Lizzie too. He'd upset her badly and must put that right at once. He set off at a run back to the kitchen, anxious to say that he was sorry, to tell her how much he loved her. He needed to tell her that he was ready to call it quits with his father. Let him do his worst. Charlie intended to beg Lizzie to marry him, on bended knee, just as soon as he could get hold of a licence.

The kitchen was locked up and empty. There was no sign of Lizzie anywhere. Nor was she at the Chocolate Cabin, Amy explaining that Jack Cleaver had asked her to do an extra hour or two since Lizzie wasn't feeling well.

Charlie was appalled. He must have made her ill by shouting at her. What had he been thinking of? Not wishing to waste another moment, he turned and dashed off down Champion Street in the direction of number thirty-seven. Perhaps she'd gone home with a bad headache, or to cry her eyes out, all because of him. Oh, Lord, what a heartless beast he was! Maybe she wouldn't ever want to see him again, would call the wedding off entirely, just because he'd behaved like an idiot.

Cursing himself for being all kinds of a fool, Charlie hammered on the door. 'Lizzie? Lizzie, if you're in there, please let me in. I'm so sorry, please forgive me.' What was he thinking of now, talking to a closed door? He knocked again, and then someone stepped out of the alley just across the street.

'She isn't there. You won't find her in.'

Charlie swung round. 'Jack, thank God, where is she? What's happened? Amy says she's been taken ill.'

'She was a bit upset, to tell the truth.' Truth and Jack Cleaver were largely strangers, but he wanted to sound convincing. 'She said you'd had words, that you'd refused to marry her. With Aunty still in hospital, she asked me to pick up the children from school and to be perfectly frank, Lizzie has gone.'

'Gone where?'

'Back to her mother, isn't that where women always go?'

Charlie stared at him, dumbfounded. 'What are you saying? Why would she do such a thing? She and her mother don't speak, or get along very well.'

Jack gave a little shrug, exhibiting an expression of deep concern upon his face. 'I'm sure I wouldn't know anything about that, but she was determined to go. I tried to talk her out of it but she wouldn't listen. She believed it was all over between the two of you, the wedding called off, she said. Surely that can't be right, can it?' he finished, as if the whole thing saddened him deeply.

Charlie gave a low groan. 'I swear I never meant it. I just got all hot under the collar thinking of what my father has done to her, to all our hopes and dreams.'

Jack clicked his tongue sympathetically. 'It must have been difficult, your father being at odds with your girlfriend, I can see that.'

Charlie was thinking hard, struggling to understand. 'Tell me exactly what she said, word for word.'

Jack stretched his eyes wide, as if genuinely puzzled. 'She just told me there was nothing else for it but to go back to her mother. That it was the only way she could think of to pay off the debt. I repeated my offer of a partnership, and swore I'd wipe the slate clean but she wasn't having any of it. Said you'd never agree. Kept on sobbing that nothing mattered if she'd lost you. Where was the point in going on?' This was near enough to the truth, Jack thought, pleased with his performance.

'Oh, my God, I don't believe it!'

Jack frowned. 'Are you suggesting that I'm lying?' He knew full well that was exactly what he was doing, but it was vitally important that Charlie believed him.

Charlie shook his head. 'I'm saying, I can't believe she'd even consider going back to her mother.' He looked about him, as if at a loss to know what he should do next, then he asked, 'When did she go? How long was it since she told you this?'

'Quite a while,' Jack confirmed, sadly shaking his head. Knowing the moment had come at last, he asked with carefully contrived innocence, 'Do you by any chance know where her mother lives? You might be able to catch up with her there?'

'Oh, yes,' Charlie agreed, already striding off down the street at a brisk pace. 'I know where she lives all right.'

Chapter Thirty-Five

With the door shut fast against prying eyes, not to mention wagging ears, mother and daughter sat facing each other. Maureen was in an armchair by the empty hearth, her face bathed in the rosy glow from a lamp bearing a crinoline lady that stood on a small table beside her, and Lizzie on a scratchy, old settee. The flowers lay in her lap, the sweet scent of the blooms unable to compete with the sourness of the fetid air in the room.

Tatty lace curtains hung at the grimy windows. A milk bottle and several dirty mugs cluttered the table, but Maureen made no attempt to offer her tea. Lizzie was truly grateful, having glimpsed the unwashed dishes in the sink in the back kitchen. Even the four plush velvet chairs that stood about the table looked in need of a good scrub.

'So now you've got an eyeful, why don't you spit it out? Say what you've come to say, then go.'

Lizzie had known it wasn't going to be easy but this woman, her own mother, seemed intent on making the visit as difficult as possible. Lizzie placed the cellophane-wrapped flowers on the table beside the milk bottle. As one, mother and daughter stared at them, as if this simple, traditional gift represented a world lost to them both, a bridge too wide to cross. Lizzie took a breath and launched into her story.

'I don't know whether you've heard but I'm seeing Charlie Finch. We were hoping to be married very soon.'

'So what's that got to do with me? Not wanting my blessing, surely?'

Lizzie ignored the taunt. 'Someone has spilled the beans about you and me being related, and his family are none too pleased at the prospect of Charlie walking out with the daughter of a prostitute. Who can blame them? Cedric Finch, Charlie's father, is a respectable businessman with a reputation to consider. He seems to think he's in danger of losing it if his son ever marries *me*.'

Maureen put back her head and began to laugh. The muscles and tendons of her scrawny throat gave her the appearance of a chicken in its final throes. Or maybe an old hen would be more appropriate, Lizzie thought, as she sat and patiently waited for the hilarity to subside.

'I didn't realise I'd said anything amusing.'

Maureen wiped the tears of laughter from her eyes. 'Nay, don't go all hoity-toity on me, not when we were getting on so well with the flowers an' all,' she said, clearly wishing to provoke. 'It were that word you used – *respectable*. Now what fool gave you that idea? Any hope Cedric Finch had of being respectable was lost long since when he were first weaned. Right selfish brat, he is, and I should imagine the son is a chip off the old block.'

Lizzie abruptly got to her feet. 'I can see that it was a mistake to come here. I was simply going to politely request if you would consider conducting your notorious business elsewhere, so that your daughter, that is me, who you used and abused...'

'I never abused you, nor put you on the game. Never!'

'...whom you treated abominably and abandoned to the harsh charity of the Sisters of Mercy might have a chance of a decent life. I can see that was too much to ask.' Lizzie walked quickly to the door, aware that her knees were shaking. She was almost through it by the time Maureen caught up with her.

'It would be a bigger mistake if you got yourself mixed up with Cedric Finch. I know what you think of me, that you see me as the scum of the earth, the worst mother any girl could have, but I'm pure as the driven by comparison with Finch. Mark my words, he's the lowest of the low.'

354

'I foolishly imagined you might put my happiness first, for once. You ruined my childhood, but I thought you might at least agree not to ruin the rest of my life. You might be decent enough to get out of it altogether. Leave Castlefield. Leave Manchester. Leave me in peace! How stupid of me even to hope for such compassion on your part!'

'I *will* keep out of your life. I said I would, and I have. It weren't me what told Finch. I haven't told a soul, I swear it, girl. Nor will I. But Cedric Finch is a nasty piece of work.'

Lizzie was no longer listening. She was far too upset, her nerves in shreds. 'Insulting and maligning others doesn't turn you into some sort of plaster saint,' she snapped. 'Finch might be unpleasant, bombastic and domineering but he doesn't sell his body for sexual favours, does he? And his son, Charlie, *isn't* a chip off the old block. He's wonderful and I love him. I just wish with all my heart that *you* weren't my mother.'

And on these bitter words Lizzie turned and walked away beneath the railway arches, back to Champion Street just as fast as her wobbly legs could carry her without losing her dignity. She didn't hear Maureen's parting words about how Finch sold much worse than she ever had. Nor did she see a figure dodge quickly out of sight into the shadows of a nearby alley as she passed by.

—

Jack Cleaver was standing at her door when she arrived home and Lizzie felt such a wave of relief at the sight of him that it didn't occur to her to wonder why he was waiting there. At least Jack was reliable, a friend in need. She hurried over to him smiling sweetly, ready to thank him for his support even though the visit to her mother had gone badly wrong. Instead, the words seemed somehow to be lodged in her throat, refusing to come, and Lizzie burst into tears.

He put his arms about her, murmuring soothing words and patting her awkwardly on the shoulder. 'Did you see her?'

'Yes,' Lizzie mumbled into the scratchy tweed of his jacket. He smelt of pipe tobacco, smoked mackerel and mothballs. Not entirely pleasant.

'That good, eh?' he said.

'It was *awful*. You wouldn't *believe*!'

'I'd believe you right enough. My mother abandoned me too, remember? You and me understand each other, right?'

Lizzie bleakly nodded.

'Did you see, Charlie?' Had Charlie seen her; that was the question? If so, then his mission was almost complete and he could expect the lad back any minute.

'No. Have you?' Lizzie looked up, rubbing the tears from her cheeks, and with such pleading in her blue eyes his heart was almost stirred by her plight. Almost, but then he remembered Finch and the confession he'd been forced to sign, and stiffened his resolve.

'What you need is a cup of hot, strong tea to soothe your nerves. You look all in. Then while you go and visit Aunty, I'll pick up the kiddies from school. You don't have to worry about them, at least.'

'Didn't Evelyn say she'd pick them up?'

'She can't make it today. Don't worry, I'll see to them.' He'd lied to Mrs Finch, told her she wouldn't be needed. He still hadn't risked taking Beth or Alan over to have their picture taken, let alone tried to get Joey on his own, but if his luck held, then today might well be the day. The boy was growing used to seeing him around and becoming bored with the whole childminding routine. If all went well, Jack thought he might take a chance on persuading one or both of them kiddies to step down to the waterfront with him.

That would get Finch off his back nicely and he'd be a free agent again. Happen he might consider moving on after that. He'd been fortunate but his good luck couldn't last, not with Dena hot on his trail. There was a whole world outside Champion Street, and he hadn't actually paid over any money to Lizzie yet, so could just as easily find some other way to invest his money. He'd worked for it after all, doing Finch's dirty business.

'Chin up,' Jack said, patting her arm.

-

Less than ten minutes later Lizzie was lying on the sofa sobbing into her handkerchief. Jack had insisted she needed to lie down, to recover from the shock. He'd brewed tea which so far she hadn't touched, wiped her tears and daringly kissed her cheek. He'd removed his jacket and tie, opening the top two buttons of his shirt. Now he was stroking her head while she lay with her eyes closed, near exhausted with emotion.

Lizzie was almost asleep and didn't hear Charlie come in, but having caught a glimpse of his imminent arrival through the window, Cleaver almost threw himself upon her, murmuring whispers of comfort as he pressed a kiss to her brow. From behind the sofa it wouldn't be apparent what he was doing to her, exactly. At least that was his hope.

Charlie stood stock still, taking in the touching little scene. It was perfectly obvious to him what was going on. The pair were wrapped in each other's arms, entirely engrossed in each other.

He took a step closer and they both glanced up at the same moment, looking oddly surprised and flustered to find him standing there, as if they hadn't expected him back so soon. Jack Cleaver actually jumped to his feet and moved guiltily away from Lizzie, knocking over a small table and a mug of tea in his rush to do so, and making a great fuss of picking them up again.

Charlie probably wouldn't have thought anything of this behaviour had it not been for the poison his father had dropped in his ear, as well as having personally witnessed Lizzie coming out of that notorious house.

Lizzie pushed her hair off her face and sat up, looking flushed and flustered herself, her eyes over-bright. 'Oh, there you are. How did it go? Did you have a big row?'

'You could say that.'

She rushed to put her arms about him. 'Forget him, Charlie. Let's just accept Jack's offer and have done with it.' She strived to sound cheerful and happy while inside she ached with regret at her failure to deal properly with her mother.

All she'd achieved by the visit was yet more humiliation. She wanted to tell Charlie all about it, but something about the tightness of his jaw held her back. He was clearly still hurting from the argument with his own parent, and her first concern was to try and soothe him. 'Jack is ready and willing to be a partner in the business and share his expertise.'

Charlie looked at her in silence, then across at Cleaver who was mopping up spilt tea as if his very life depended upon it. Was it simply the venom of his father's remarks or did he feel that she was once more taking Cleaver's side rather than his? Could there possibly be an innocent explanation for Lizzie to be lying on a sofa with this man, let alone visiting the mother she claimed to hate? She wasn't meeting his eyes and the pair of them were giving the impression of guilt. Charlie did his best to fight the sinking feeling in his stomach, but he was deeply suspicious that he was being made fool of, and jealousy was hot in him.

'Is that what your mother suggested when you spoke to her about this problem earlier? Did she advise you how to earn a few quid while you were there? Or was dumping me for Jack all part of the plan, if I couldn't come up with the cash you need?'

Lizzie's eyes went round with shock. 'You *saw* me?'

'I saw you come out of her house, yes. Would you like to explain how it was you happened to be there, when you fervently insisted not so very long ago that you never wanted to set eyes on your mother as long as you lived?'

There was the smallest pause while Lizzie absorbed the shock of this remark. 'I wasn't talking about dumping you for a bit of cash. Whatever makes you say such a horrible thing?'

Jack was edging towards the door, in case either of them should accuse him of being the person responsible for this volatile situation, which might be difficult to refute since in fact he was. Finch would be proud of him.

Charlie's tone, and the expression on his face were rich with disbelief. 'So what were you discussing, the weather?'

Lizzie shook her head, ignoring his sarcasm as her eyes once more filled with tears. 'It was all a complete waste of time as it happens, but I thought it was worth a try. Jack thought so too, didn't you, Jack?'

Jack evaded the question. 'I'd best go and pick up the kiddies, Lizzie. I'll keep them at mine till you can collect them later on your way back from seeing Aunty, all right?'

'Right, thanks,' she responded, hardly taking in what he was saying as she kept her gaze fixed on Charlie. 'You went to see your father and I went to talk to my mother, so what? It's no different.'

Jack snatched up his jacket and tie and escaped.

–

Charlie slammed the door shut after Jack's departure and turned on Lizzie. His response, coldly issued, was that if she couldn't see the difference, there was little point in him trying to explain it.

'Would you at least care to explain why *you* were hanging around outside watching me?' Lizzie persisted, unsettled by the whole argument.

'I wasn't *hanging around*. Jack himself told me that you'd gone to see your mother, and he told me why.'

'Then you'll understand.'

'Oh, *yes*, I understand perfectly. Jack Cleaver is clearly the man of the moment, our local hero striding in at the eleventh hour, cash in hand, ready to save the day.'

Lizzie almost chuckled. Charlie's voice held a dangerous calm, which should have alerted her but she wasn't thinking straight. Too much had happened, too quickly, and she was blithely unaware of how they'd both been manipulated. 'You surely aren't jealous?'

'*Me* jealous of Cleaver? Don't make me laugh!'

'Then why can't we discuss his offer, properly and sensibly?'

'There's nothing to say. It's not important right now. Anyway, *you're* clearly very much in favour of accepting.'

'Can you think of a better solution to our problems?'

Charlie seemed irritated by this remark, as if Lizzie were in some way criticising, or accusing him of failing. 'I've done my best, for heaven's sake. This morning I made a vain attempt to reason with my father – although I do wonder if he might have a point, after all, since the minute my back is turned you're cavorting with Cleaver.'

'You *are* jealous!' Lizzie teased, tweaking his nose, determined not to take his glum mood too seriously. 'Anyway, we weren't cavorting, don't be ridiculous.'

'Ridiculous, am I?' Charlie looked hurt. 'Maybe I've just had my eyes opened. Why were you cuddling up with him on that sofa, if it was all perfectly innocent? Was he kissing you?'

Lizzie gasped. 'Certainly not! And we weren't cuddling up,' Lizzie protested. 'I was crying and he wiped my eyes, that's all.'

'Then why did he look so guilty?'

'If he did, he had no reason to, it was because you'd come sneaking in and stood there watching us as if we were doing something wrong. No wonder you unnerved him. For goodness' sake, Charlie, what has brought all this on? What *is* your problem?'

'I'd simply like to know what's going on between you and Jack Cleaver.'

'*Nothing's going on!* I was upset because I'd been to see Maureen. I went to see her to talk about *us*, you and me, not Cleaver.'

'Really.'

'Yes, I foolishly believed that if I explained the situation, the fact that your parents disapproved of our getting married because of what she was, then my notorious mother might actually do the decent thing for once in her sad, shameful life and go away. She thought the whole thing was highly amusing and made some nasty remarks about your father.'

'More likely she suggested another way for you to settle your debt! To draw you back into the fold, as it were. Is that why you were with Cleaver on the sofa? Making a deal were you, or whatever you call it? And him half dressed by the look of it.'

The silence following this remark was appalling. Lizzie stared at him, unable to believe her ears. Had Charlie really said what she thought he'd said?

A tide of crimson washed up Charlie's neck, as if he too couldn't believe it, but the words were out, echoing in the empty room, sounding like a death knell in her heart.

He no longer believed her to be innocent.

It made Lizzie sick to her stomach to contemplate he could even think such a thing of her. It hurt so badly that it should come to this. They'd fallen in love at first sight, had known from the start that they were meant for each other, and now, incredibly, she was losing him.

But *why* didn't he trust her? What on earth had his father said? Why had things gone so badly wrong between them? And what bad luck that he should walk into the house just when Jack Cleaver was mopping up her tears and trying to comfort her. Lizzie conceded that might have looked bad, particularly following his father's acid remarks. She'd meant well but seemed to have made matters ten times worse by going to see Maureen.

Lizzie struggled to remain calm, her voice barely above a whisper. 'You think I've been on the game myself, don't you?

You believe I wanted to go back on it to earn a bit of brass, is that it?'

Charlie's face seemed to drain of colour right before her eyes. Without another word he turned on his heel and left. This time, Lizzie realised, it would be for good.

Chapter Thirty-Six

It was five o'clock and the children still weren't home. At first Lizzie hadn't noticed the time, too upset over the row she'd had with Charlie, too absorbed in the consequences of facing life without him. She'd gone from laughing at his jealousy to feeling like hitting him. Now she doubted if they ever would get married. Charlie had deserted her, and she couldn't understand why he was so stubbornly determined to believe the worst.

Whatever they'd had together was clearly over. Finch's poison had won and Charlie had left her, for good this time.

Then she'd remembered that she was supposed to collect the children from Jack's house. Guiltily she realised that she'd forgotten all about them in her misery. She'd even forgotten to visit Aunty. Lizzie pulled on her coat and went straight round.

Nobody answered her knock, even though she hammered as loud as she could on the door. The house was clearly empty, so where were they all? Where could they be? He'd maybe taken them for a walk to the park or somewhere, to give her and Charlie time to get over their row. Not knowing what else to do, Lizzie went back home. She paced up and down, continually looking at the clock where the minute hand dragged ever more slowly. Five minutes past five; ten past, quarter past. Where were they? Even if Jack had taken them to the park or the rec, he should have had them home in time for their tea.

She heard running footsteps outside, then the front door banged open. Joey stood gasping for breath. 'He's got them!'

'What?'

'Cleaver, he's got them – both of them – down at that place.' He was holding a stitch in his side, clearly having been running hard. 'Mrs Finch was supposed to pick them up but I've just seen her and apparently Cleaver told her not to, said that he would collect them from school himself if you couldn't. I tried to get there first… I told them to wait for me, not to go off with anyone but me or Mrs Finch, not even Mr bleeding Cleaver… but I was kept in for not finishing my homework on time.'

'Oh, Joey, what are you saying?'

They were interrupted by Evelyn herself, equally out of breath and deathly pale, the baby clutched in her arms. 'Oh, Lizzie, thank goodness you're here. Has Joey told you? We've been searching everywhere for those children. Jack Cleaver told me that you didn't need me today, that you would pick them up or else he would. Then Joey called to ask if I'd got them. I'm beginning to have a horrible suspicion about where they might be.'

'Me too,' Joey said. 'He's been after them for weeks.'

'Where? What place do you mean? Never mind, you can explain it to me as we go.'

–

Evelyn had trouble keeping up with Lizzie, as she had already been rushing up and down these streets for the better part of an hour. 'I should have called the police right away. Oh, I do wish I had. I knew in my bones that something wasn't right. Oh, why didn't I ring Constable Nuttall?'

'I didn't do anything either,' Lizzie mourned. 'I kept thinking they'd walk through the door any minute.'

'Better still, why didn't I go and pick them up at school anyway, just to be safe? I'll never forgive myself if something has happened to those children.'

'I'm sure there must be a perfectly logical explanation for them being late.'

Joey was well ahead of them both, already approaching the edge of the market where the stallholders were busy putting away their trestles at the end of a long, tiring day. Barry Holmes was sweeping up cabbage leaves and stacking boxes in the back of his van. Winnie was covering the racks of Dena's skirts and wheeling them away. Amy George had already shut up the Chocolate Cabin and Jimmy Ramsay was swabbing down his empty butcher's counter, the soapy water running over the cobbles and down the drain.

It was then that Lizzie spotted him, walking towards them leading a child by each hand.

'Oh, my goodness,' Evelyn cried. 'There they are!'

Lizzie rushed over to them sweat breaking out all over. 'Where have you two been? I've been worried sick.' Beth stuck her chin up high, a suspicious pink sticky substance around her pursed mouth but her eyes were wide and dark and the little girl didn't say a word. Alan blinked up at Lizzie owlishly.

Jack Cleaver looked a bit disconcerted by such overt concern, but silkily remarked, 'We took a bit of a stroll down by the canal, didn't we, children? I'm sorry if you were anxious. I thought you might need a bit of time on your own, you and Charlie.' He winked at her, but Lizzie wasn't so easily mollified.

'I'm not sure why you took it upon yourself to pick them up at all, since Evelyn has taken on that duty.'

'Indeed I have, and gladly,' said that good lady, coming up beside her, puffing for breath as she jiggled the baby who had started to grizzle with hunger. 'I believe you lied to me, Jack Cleaver, when you told me I wasn't needed today. Or did my husband ask you to do that?'

Lizzie frowned. 'Why, would Mr Finch ask you to lie?' She turned back to the two children, standing so quiet and biddable, and suddenly she couldn't seem to get Dena's warning out of her head. *Don't let them go anywhere near Jack Cleaver.* And what was this place Evelyn and Joey had mentioned?

'Where exactly by the canal did you go? To the rec?' Lizzie asked Alan. Something about the children's manner was troubling her. The little boy was surely her best bet for wrinkling the truth out of them, as Beth was always the secretive one. Her judgement proved sound.

'We had us pictures took,' Alan mumbled, his small mouth set in a sulky pout. 'But I didn't like that chap with the camera. Beth didn't like him neither, did you, Beth?' Then he reached up and whispered confidentially in Lizzie's ear, '*He told her to take her knickers off, but our Beth kicked up a right fuss and wouldn't do it. He lost patience with her in the end and sent us home.*'

Beth slapped him hard before bursting into tears. 'You weren't supposed to *tell*! Didn't Mr Cleaver say it was *our secret*?'

'I believe,' Evelyn said slowly, 'that Alan is not speaking of holiday snaps.' Lizzie stared at her in dawning horror.

'I found some pictures once, in my husband's study. To my eternal shame I ignored them, pretending, even to myself, that I'd never set eyes on them.'

'Your *husband*? Charlie's *father*? Oh, dear God!'

And then a surprising thing happened. Lizzie was still in shock, even as she tried to comfort the distraught little girl. But before even she'd had time to fully appreciate what Beth's obstinacy had saved her from, let alone decide what to do about this dreadful revelation, Joey clenched his fist, took a great swing exactly as he'd been taught, and punched Jack Cleaver on the nose. Blood spurted everywhere and Jack fell to his knees before the boy, squealing like a stuck pig.

'*Theer*,' said Joey, with great satisfaction. 'That'll learn ya.' Oh, but it felt good! He'd been trying to pluck up the courage all his life to thump some bully that hard. It should have been his own *da*, but Jack Cleaver would do just as well.

Evelyn clapped her hands. 'Well done, Joey!'

Then everything seemed to happen at once. Jimmy Ramsay came running, hatchet in hand, although thank goodness he never got the opportunity to use it as the street was suddenly filled with the sound of Constable Nuttall's police whistle.

'I think,' Evelyn dryly remarked, 'this is what they mean when they say, the game is up.'

'Man cannot live by chocolate alone, but woman will have a jolly good crack at trying,' said Aunty as she gently stirred melted butter, cocoa, corn syrup and brown sugar in a large bowl resting over a pan of hot water. 'It's an aphrodisiac, Lizzie love. Did you know that?'

'I don't think we'll need any of that,' Charlie said, nibbling her ear.

'Nor do I,' Lizzie agreed, lifting her face for more kisses.

'What's an affro dizzy hack?' asked Alan.

'Never you mind. You ask too many questions, you.'

Undeterred, he asked another. 'Do you know how to stop chocolate melting too fast?'

'No, how do you stop chocolate from melting too fast?'

'Eat it quicker.'

Aunty laughed. 'Hold your noise. We've had enough sauce from you already for one day.'

Alan grinned happily up at her while she wiped a smudge of cream off the lens of his glasses. 'Are you whipping that cream or painting this table top with it? Beth love, how are you getting on with crushing them nuts? We'll need them in a minute.'

'Right, Aunty. I'm nearly done.'

'Good lass.'

They were making chocolate nut fudge, and everyone's mouths were watering as the smell of chocolate and vanilla overwhelmed their senses. Dena and Adam were also there, joining in the fun, together with Trudy and the rest of the children. Even the baby had a rim of chocolate around her mouth. They'd already made and tasted chocolate raisins, brandied chocolate dates, chocolate cherries, and chocolate cream truffles. But the children adored fudge best of all.

The unpleasant incident down by the canal was far from their minds here in the security of Aunty's warm kitchen, and Dot intended to keep it that way. They'd been fortunate to get off so lightly. Beth's intransigence and moral rectitude had apparently saved the day. And when they'd turned on her precious brother instead, she'd shouted the place down, apparently kicking their shins and slapping everyone in sight.

Jack Cleaver had promptly panicked and hustled them off home. Good for her, Dot thought. I expect Cedric Finch was glad to be shot of the two little blighters, God rot him.

'You aren't feeling too tired, are you?' Dena asked her, frowning slightly.

'Don't you start – I've enough with our Lizzie here bossing me about like a good 'un the whole time. She should get a job in the armed forces if she ever finds herself unemployed.'

'I hope that won't ever happen,' Charlie said.

'I'm sure it won't,' Lizzie agreed, 'not now we've talked things over with the bank manager and Evelyn has agreed to invest in the business. We are truly grateful.'

Evelyn was sitting with the baby on her knee, unsuccessfully attempting to clean her up, while in her small clenched fists were clasped some chocolate raisins which she kept popping in her mouth every time Evelyn wiped a sticky hand. She laughed at her own doomed efforts and gave up, letting the baby give her a chocolate kiss instead.

'It seemed the least I could do after all the trouble your father caused, Charlie. I wish I'd stood up to him years ago, I do really. I always knew he was a bully, but I'd no idea what a monster he'd turned into.'

Charlie dropped a kiss on his mother's head. 'You stood up to him in the end, and that's what counts. I would've loved to have seen his face when the police raided that place.'

Constable Nuttall, having been apprised of the true circumstances behind the little fracas in the market, had wasted no time in calling on his colleagues for back up. Quinn's Palace had been raided and hundreds of pornographic pictures retrieved, many of them of young children. Finch, Quinn and Cleaver had been taken into custody and were not expected to be let out again any time soon.

'Quinn's Palace indeed,' Dena scoffed. 'Quinn's Den of Iniquity more like. They got what was coming to them, all of them. I for one won't miss seeing Billy Quinn around the market, I'll tell you that for nothing. It's long past time he got his just desserts. I hope he rots in jail along with your father. Begging your pardon, Charlie boy.'

'Don't apologise,' Charlie said, his tone grim. 'Justice has been served, and at least he can't hurt any other children.'

'Nor can Jack Cleaver,' put in Joey.

Charlie grinned at the boy. 'You saw to that, eh? Good lad. One of those occasions when a bit of healthy aggression is no bad thing, eh?'

Aunty was giving Lizzie instructions not to let the mixture boil until the sugar had dissolved or the fudge would crystallise. 'That's grand. Now we can add the condensed milk and bring it nicely to the boil. Keep it bubbling for five to ten minutes till we get a soft ball forming when we drop a bit in a cup of cold water.'

Later, with the task done, she was putting the kettle on while the mixture cooled when there came a knock on the door. 'Answer that Trudy, love, will you? My hands are full.'

Trudy looked from one face to the other, but since nobody moved she went to answer the door, more out of curiosity than anything. She gasped out loud when she saw who it was.

'Aunty Win, oh, and Uncle Barry!' The little girl launched herself into his arms on a squeal of joy and Barry caught her in a big, enveloping hug.

'Come in and join us, won't you?' Aunty said. 'We're having a chocolate party to celebrate our Lizzie's coming nuptials. It is going to take place before the month is out or she's off to join the Foreign Legion.'

'Foreign Legion indeed,' Charlie protested. 'I'm not letting her out of my sight ever again. And the only way to make absolutely sure of that seems to be to marry the woman.'

'Do you think you can bear it?' Lizzie asked, kissing him some more while Alan groaned that they were being all soppy again.

Charlie gave a dramatic sigh. 'Well, I'll just have to try, won't I? Don't worry, I only intend doing it for one lifetime.'

'That's all right, then.'

Alan was puzzled. 'Do we sometimes have more than one lifetime, Aunty?'

'No, love, it just feels that way sometimes. Right, we only need Beth to add those nuts she's crushed up so beautifully with my big rolling pin, and the job's a good 'un. I hope you like chocolate nut fudge, Barry, because we've made a lot of it.'

'I'll have my share later,' Barry said. 'I'm going to eat this little sweetie first.' And Trudy fell into delighted giggles as he pretended to gobble her all up.

Dena felt Adam squeeze her hand as he whispered in her ear: 'Didn't I tell you it would all work out right in the end?'

Aunty's Recipes

Aunty's Chocolate Fudge

Ingredients:

- 395g (14oz) can sweetened condensed milk
- 1 cup firmly packed brown sugar
- 100g (3½oz) unsalted butter, chopped
- 200g (7oz) dark chocolate, chopped
- 1 teaspoon vanilla essence

Method:

Grease a 11 x 7 inch baking pan.

In a large saucepan place the condensed milk, brown sugar and butter.

Stir over a low heat for 3–4 minutes until butter has melted, sugar has dissolved and it is well combined.

Add the chopped dark chocolate and vanilla or peppermint essence.

Cook and stir for a further 3–4 minutes until all the chocolate has melted and the mixture is smooth.

Pour fudge into pan.

When partly cool, mark into squares with a sharp knife.

Chill in fridge until fully set (about four hours).

Easy Chocolate Nut Fudge

Ingredients:

- 400g (14oz) dark or milk chocolate, chopped
- 397g can condensed milk
- 25g (1oz) butter
- 100g (3½oz) icing sugar
- 55g (2oz) roasted chopped nuts

Method:

Place the small chunks of chocolate with the condensed milk and butter into a non-stick saucepan and melt the ingredients gently over a low heat, stirring until smooth and silky.

Sieve in the icing sugar and mix well.

Press the fudge into a 20cm/8in square tin, smooth over the top with the back of a spoon. Press the nuts into the surface.

Chill in the fridge for four hours until set, cut into squares.

Aunty's Caramel Fudge

Ingredients:

- 400g (14oz) tin condensed milk
- 450g (16oz) brown sugar
- 150ml milk
- 115g (4oz) butter

Method:

Grease a 20cm/8 inch square baking tin.

Combine the condensed milk, butter and sugar over a low heat in a non-stick saucepan for 10–15 minutes, stirring occasionally, until the mixture forms a soft ball when dropped into a cup of cold water.

Remove from the heat and beat for ten minutes until the mixture thickens.

Add nuts, raisins, rum, cherries, (whatever you fancy).

Pour into the baking tin.

Mark into small squares when partly cooled.

Chill in the fridge for four hours until set.

Aunty's Toffee Apples

(For six dessert apples)

Ingredients:

- 115g (4oz) butter
- 100g (3½oz) golden syrup
- 200g (7oz) light brown soft sugar
- 200g (7oz) condensed milk

Method:

Place all the ingredients into a large pan and melt over a low heat.

Bring to the boil to crack temperature, (300 degrees F/150 degrees C), about 15–20 minutes, stirring frequently.

Remove from heat.

Insert a lolly stick into the apples near the core, and carefully dip into the toffee mixture to coat.

Leave to cool on a rack.

Aunty's Coconut Ice

Ingredients:

- 100g (3½oz) condensed milk

- 115g (4oz) icing sugar, sieved
- 85g (3oz) desiccated coconut
- 1 tiny drop red food colouring

Method:

Mix together condensed milk and icing sugar.

Stir in coconut (mixture should be very stiff) and divide in half.

Colour one half of the mixture pale pink.

Double line a small plastic box or loaf tin. Place the white coconut ice on the base and press into a rectangular shape. Form the pink coconut ice into a similar shape and press firmly together.

Leave 2–3 hours until firm.

Cut into squares.

Aunty's Chocolate Truffles

Ingredients:

- 225g (8oz) good-quality dark chocolate (70% cocoa solids), chopped into small pieces
- 175ml double or whipping cream
- Unsweetened dark cocoa powder/icing sugar/or crushed nuts(for rolling)

Method:

Chop the chocolate and place into a large heatproof bowl.

Put the cream into a saucepan and heat gently to simmering point.

Remove from heat and allow the bubbles to subside for 1–2 minutes.

Pour over the chocolate.

Stir the chocolate and cream together with a wooden spoon or spatula until all the chocolate is melted and you have a smooth mixture.

Add any flavourings to the truffle mix at this stage. You can divide into different bowls and add various flavouring: vanilla, Grand Marnier, coconut rum, or simple orange juice (50–75 ml for alcohol).

Chill in fridge for an hour or so.

Making the truffles:

Remove from fridge and allow the mixture to come to just below room temperature.

Using a teaspoon or melon ball shaper, scoop out portions of the mixture and roll into small balls in cocoa powder on a board. Or you can roll them in the palm of your hands dusted with icing sugar. Or you can coat in crushed pistachio nuts, desiccated coconut, or grated chocolate.

Place on greaseproof paper.

Store in the fridge in an airtight container.

Aunty's Peanut Brittle

Ingredients:

- 1 cup white sugar
- ½ cup corn syrup
- ¼ teaspoon salt
- ¼ cup water
- 1 cup peanuts
- 2 tablespoons butter, softened
- 1 level teaspoon baking soda

Method:

Butter a large baking tin approx 7 x 11 inches.

Bring to the boil the sugar, corn syrup, salt, and water in a large saucepan, over low/medium heat until sugar is dissolved.

Stir in peanuts.

Continue cooking, stirring frequently, until temperature reaches crack temperature (300 degrees F/150 degrees C), using a thermometer, or until a small amount of mixture dropped into very cold water separates into hard and brittle threads.

Remove from heat and immediately stir in butter and baking soda.

Pour into baking tin.

Use a fork to pull peanut mixture out.

Leave to cool then snap into pieces.